DEVIL MAY CARE

Chani Lynn Feener

ALSO BY CHANI LYNN FEENER

*For a list of YA books by this author, please check her website. All of the books listed below are Adult.

Bad Things Play Here

Gods of Mist and Mayhem

A Bright Celestial Sea

A Sea of Endless Light

A Whisper in the Dark Trilogy
You Will Never Know
Don't Breathe a Word
Don't Let Me Go

Abandoned Things

Between the Devil and the Sea

Echo

These Silent Stars

Call of the Sea

His Dark Paradox
Under the penname Avery Tu with Kota Quinn

DEVIL MAY CARE

Chani Lynn Feener

CHANI LYNN FEENER

This is a work of fiction. Names, characters, places, and incidents are the product of the author's imagination, and any resemblance to actual events or persons, living or dead, is entirely coincidental.

Devil May Care

Copyright @ 2024 by Chani Lynn Feener.

All rights reserved. No part of this book may be reproduced, distributed, or transmitted in any form without written permission from the author.

Front Cover design by Creative Paramita.

Printed in the United States of America.

First edition—2024

AUTHOR'S NOTE

Dear Reader,

Even if you've read one of my books before please do not skip this note. As some of the triggers couldn't be included on the books main listing, I wanted to take the time to include them here.

This book is a Dark MM Romance, and as such it contains certain situations and themes not suitable for all readers. Kazimir Ambrose is a selfish, arrogant mafia member who has some major issues. He isn't kind, or caring, and isn't above using manipulation tactics on the people around him, including the love interest. If you're looking for a knight or a redemption story, this is not it. Nate Narek is depressed and has a severe case of people-pleasing. He sometimes disassociates when he feels he's become a burden to those around him. While I don't go too deeply into these episodes, they do happen on page, and want to be upfront about that in case it's triggering to some of you.

I want to be clear that I don't condone anything that takes place in this book in real life. This book is purely fiction. These characters are not real and this takes place on a made-up planet in a made-up galaxy. None of my characters are human, though I sometimes use the word humanoid, and this galaxy is nowhere near ours. If you or someone you know is ever in a toxic relationship, please seek help. You deserve better. And if you ever find yourself seduced by someone like Kazimir, leave immediately.

Kaz takes advantage of Nate throughout the entire book, in more ways than one. This relationship is toxic, and not a dynamic I suggest exploring in the real world. He's also a character that more often than not, makes no sense. He doesn't operate on logic, and is instead ruled by his mercurial emotions. If you're looking for a character that's cut and dry, he isn't going to satisfy you. If you're bothered by characters using coercion and sex as weapons, he really isn't going to satisfy you.

Now onto the triggers. **If you aren't easily triggered or you want to avoid potential spoilers, feel free to skip the rest of this note.**

I tried to note down all of the ones I can think of, but please keep in mind I may have missed one or two. Your mental health is important, if any of these do not sound appealing or may put you at risk, please skip this book. I have other MM books that don't fall under the Dark category that may be better suited for you.

Most, but possibly not all, notable triggers

include: Noncon, dubcon, bondage, intoxication, sexual assault while drunk, manipulation—both physical and psychological, conditioning of a main character, mild Stockholm syndrome, disassociation, depression, burdenism (feeling like you're a burden to everyone around you), stalking, mention of deceased parents, slight exhibitionism (but not really), violence, murder, and graphic sex scenes. While Kaz does have sex with someone else (off page), there is NO cheating in this book. And finally, lube is only sometimes and sort of used. Spit and other bodily fluids are sometimes used. I know this is a dealbreaker for some. Please keep in mind these are not humans, and only practice safe sex in your real lives.

Again, **this book does have a HEA**. Still, this relationship is incredibly messed up, and starts off that way from the jump. I in no way, shape, or form condone anything mentioned above in real life. This is purely fiction.

This book is intended for a mature adult audience only.

Remember, your mental health and well-being is more important than reading this book. Always put yourself first, and be responsible for your own triggers. You're worth it and you matter.

CHANI LYNN FEENER

BLURB:

A Devil of Vitality always rises to a challenge.

Nate Narek is barely keeping his head above water.

But no one would guess that by looking at him. He's got camouflaging himself down to an art form. Feelings? As far as anyone else is concerned, he's happy and satisfied all the time. Only he isn't. Nate's always been the glue that holds all the shit around him together, and he's afraid that if he shows weakness, those people will be disappointed in him. It's better to keep it all in than to be a burden, right? Then suddenly there's a Devil of Vitality at his door, demanding he open up and let him into his twisted thoughts. A Devil who takes sexual deviancy and pigheadedness to a whole new level. For the first time in his life, Nate's no longer sure he can handle things on his own. Too bad Kaz won't let him run off to anyone else for help.

Kazimir Ambrose has a few...issues.

He wouldn't say they stem from his mother abandoning him at a young age, or the fact that his father remarried his work and was never around. But his cousin Baikal Void probably would. And does. Repeatedly. Especially when he wants to get under Kaz's skin. Typically, Kazimir can pretend like it doesn't affect him, but after one particularly frustrating night, he decides it's time he does something to prove the rest of the mafia wrong about him. If the other Devil's can manage being in relationships, he can as well. How hard could it be to make someone irrevocably and undeniably fall for him?

When Kaz sets his sights on an uninterested Nate, the two are thrust into uncharted territory. What starts out as a means to prove himself quickly turns into an obsession that Kazimir can't seem to shake. There's something about Nate's sadness that calls to the monster in Kaz, and if he's learned anything from the Brumal mafia, it's that taking what you want, no matter the consequence, is always the right move. Nate tries to resist, but with Kazimir showing up anywhere and everywhere, it soon becomes apparent he's only got two options. Give in to the Devil.

Or be taken by him anyway.

PROLOGUE:

"What the actual fuck kind of driving is that?!" Kazimir chucked the glass bottle in his hand, already storming away before it hit the brick wall and shattered.

No one else seemed to notice or care, too busy either cheering or cursing up a storm same as him. The crowd was pretty thick for an impromptu race, and Kaz had mistakenly taken that to mean the racers themselves were worth the attention.

Bull.

Fucking.

Shit.

It wasn't often that he bothered coming down to these events at the Docks. Hoverbike racing was one of the very few illegal things he didn't dabble in personally, but most of his friends and well-known associates raved about the place, so every now and again he'd cave, show up, and throw some money at it.

Money he typically won back.

He kicked at one of the metal poles that held up the fencing surrounding the makeshift track.

For an under-the-table event, it was always nicely put together. No one would be able to tell that it wasn't legally sanctioned—not only because of the professional look and feel of it either. A quick glance around and one could easily pick out more than a few familiar faces.

Like the Chief of Valeo Police.

Or Professor Wilks.

Or Redwood, the Heir Imperial's personal bodyguard.

Kaz swore again after seeing that guy and spun on his heels, pushing his way through the throngs of people. The last thing he needed was to make this day worse by running into that asshole. Given his current mood, he'd most likely end up punching Red in the face.

Again.

Several streets surrounding the docks had been cordoned off for the races, the large parking lot at the main location filled with all kinds of makes and model of hovercars, from expensive luxury vehicles to junkers that were honestly a miracle to see working. His XF-57 was parked in a private lot close to the boathouse though, because like hell was he risking his baby amongst the idiotic masses. People were stupid by nature, and Kazimir was under strict watch at the moment, which made impromptu murder a bit riskier than it typically would be.

In a very short period of time, Kaz had been promoted to

underboss of the Brumal mafia. Up until recently, he and the next in line for the throne, his cousin Baikal Void, had merely been in training for the positions. They were seniors at Vail University, too young to be taking on the massive responsibilities their new titles required of them, even though they'd always known they were destined for them.

Their previous Dominus, Baikal's father, had succumbed to an incurable illness. He'd held on for as long as he could but, in the end, had lost the battle. One day he'd been there and the next, he was simply gone. Sickness was fucked up like that.

The deadliest killers were the ones you couldn't see coming.

Understandably, his impending doom had put the entire Brumal on edge, and the Satellite—those who specifically followed under Baikal's leadership—weren't immune. Hell, they probably had it worse even.

That was why Kazimir had come here in the first place, to blow off a little steam and distract himself. Betting had always taken the edge off, playing the odds. Tempting fate. He'd placed a bet on some hot racer he'd never seen before because he'd been told the opponent was good. If not for that pesky fact he was under close watch by Whim, the previous underboss, he'd be off right now to find the lying bastard who'd given him that bullshit piece of information to wring the man's damn neck. As it were, he was just going to have to settle for breaking one of his legs.

Because Kazimir could exercise self-control, no matter what his cousin thought.

Which was why he only *lightly* slammed open the wooden door of the boat house on his way in. Technically, there were three boathouses: the main one used to actually house boats during the winter months, another that was utilized by the Academy and Vail crew teams, and then this one, which was owned by Royal Madden Odell, or as Kaz liked to call him—

"Royal Asshole," he didn't pause as he entered and spotted his target standing in the center of the building, "Care to explain what the actual fuck —" Kaz did however stop when he realized Madden wasn't alone.

The boathouse was mostly used as an office space for Madden, the top racer, and the person responsible for starting the whole event. It had two levels, the main which was open space, and the loft above where the Royal kept a bedroom. The walls were decorated with posters, and glass cases held trophies and medals from his past wins, both professionally and unprofessionally, since the illegal dock races weren't the only ones he participated in.

A large area had been sectioned off with bookshelves and turned into a hangout pad of sorts, and one of those shelves had been blocking Kazimir's view when he'd entered, so he hadn't noticed the other man talking with Madden until he'd cleared it.

The guy had his helmet off and his arms down

at his sides, but it didn't appear as though he'd been in the midst of getting torn a new one by Madden —like he damn well should have been. Kaz may not have gotten a look at his face before the start of the race, but the outfit was the same, the tight black pants tucked into a pair of workman's boots and the gold and black racer jacket giving him away.

"You." He snapped his fingers and started heading for them again, his anger now directed at the racer instead of the Royal who'd suggested where Kaz placed his bets for the evening. "You owe me five thousand coin. You call that driving?"

Madden blew out a breath and rested his hands on his hips, sending the man an apologetic glance that only served to set Kaz off even more.

"You're not innocent in this either, Royal Asshole," Kaz snapped.

"You take a bet, you take a risk. That's how it works," Madden said, moving forward to block Kazimir's path so he was standing between him and the racer. "Plus, didn't you hear the announcement beforehand? The racer who was meant to be here couldn't make it. Nate stood in for him so there'd still be a show. We were upfront with the whole audience. It's not our fault you were too busy doing…?"

He'd been on the phone with Zane, listening to his excuses as to why he couldn't meet up with Kaz tonight like they'd planned. Not that he could tell Madden that, considering Zane and he worked for the same annoyingly pretentious Imperial Prince.

The Satellite, who followed Baikal Void, and the Retinue, who orbited Kelevra Diar, were tentative...friends? Of a sort? They got along mainly because they had to, though some were closer than others. It wasn't a secret that sometimes Kazimir and Zane fooled around, but the details behind their strange on-again, off-again relationship were strictly confidential. Not even Baikal knew about them, and Kaz planned on keeping it that way.

"Whatever," he snapped, shoving Madden away from him. "Still doesn't change anything. How could you let someone with no skills participate in a race like this?"

There were tiers to the races: Elite, League, Mid, and Rookie. Kazimir had been betting on a League race, meaning he'd expected better than he'd gotten. The race itself was meant to be between two well-known racers, Flash and Pandaveer. Only, now he was being told the latter had apparently never shown.

"Guy doesn't even deserve to race Rookie," Kazimir added, even though that was hardly the truth. He could probably lead in Mid races, in fact, had carried his own pretty well against Flash up until the final stretch even. But Kaz was pissed off and when he got this way, facts weren't important, only striking the hardest blow was.

"You think it's so easy?" the racer snapped back. "You do it next time then, hotshot."

"Excuse you?" Kazimir took a step forward but Madden blocked him again with a strong hand at the center of his chest.

"Back off, Kaz. And Nate," he shot over his shoulder at the racer, "really not helping, man."

"Why should I help soothe some loser's ego?" Nate glared down his nose at Kaz.

At first glance, the racer didn't look out of place here, but then, they were currently standing in a boathouse, made of wood with low lighting, no matter how decked out it happened to be. Nothing too fancy. Upon closer inspection, the worn boots and the goldenrod and black plaid button-up he wore under his expensive jacket gave away that he wasn't from the same kind of money as his present company.

He had nice hair, though; whoever his barber was, they deserved a raise. The dark chocolate locks were windswept and appeared messy in that way that was always done on purpose. It was cut short in the back, practically buzzed. Two diamond studs were set in each of his ears, but there didn't appear to be any other piercings. He'd be hot if he weren't such a prick.

Strike that. He was totally hot despite that fact. If Kaz had been feeling any other sort of way at the moment, he'd most likely switch gears and seduce him instead. He'd never caved for dick before, though, and he wasn't about to start now.

"He's just upset about losing," Madden said to the racer then. "Nate isn't exactly pleased about the outcome either, by the way. He did his best."

"Doesn't look like he needs money," Nate

countered. "He placed a bet and lost. Shit happens. Get over it."

Murder was off the table, he reminded himself.

He couldn't afford to draw attention right now.

Whim would be pissed.

"I'm going to snap that pretty neck of yours and shove your head up your ass," Kazimir growled. Screw the underboss. *He'd* get over it.

"Nate, let's finish this conversation later," Madden said, holding his ground when Kaz tried to get past him a second time. "Seriously, stop."

"Not until his blood has coated my hands." No one spoke to Kazimir like that and got away with it. Not even pretty racers who looked like they worked out. The two of them were probably around the same build, but Kaz had a couple of inches on him and Brumal training under his belt, which was something he doubted the other guy could claim.

"He's not joking," Madden warned Nate. "He's crazy enough he really will hit you."

"I was ten seconds behind!" Nate stated, clearly frustrated. "It's not like I lost by a landslide."

"You still lost," Kaz growled.

"Hey, what are you doing?" a new voice had Kaz stilling and Madden sighing in relief. Flix, another member of the Satellite, entered from the back of the building, taking in the three of them with a quirked brow. "Wow, a party, and not a single one of you invited me? Some friends." He walked right up to Nate and tossed an arm around the guy's shoulders. "Tough luck out there, my dude. You'll get him next time."

My dude?

"You know him?" Kazimir took in the racer a second time. He didn't look like Flix's usual type, and even though they were standing close and the racer allowed the continued contact, he was still stiff and glaring daggers Kaz's way. Didn't seem like anything romantic was going on between the two of them.

Which was good, because murder was one thing, but killing his friend's lover was a total no-no. Even a person like him had lines they refused to cross, and that was one of them.

"Do you know how much he just cost me?" Kaz stated.

"Someone's in a mood," Madden filled him in.

"Yeah, probably the grief talking," Flix said. "We all know how well Kazy copes with being abandoned."

"Sullivan Void didn't *abandon* us," Kaz snapped. It's not like the man had chosen to die.

"Exactly," Flix held his gaze pointedly. "So stop acting like he did. I swear, you're such a prick. This is why no one can tolerate you as soon as you've charmed your way into their pants and drop the act."

"I'm about to shove my blaster into yours and pull the trigger."

Flix whistled. "Scary. Anyway." He shook Nate a little. "Ready to go? Berga's already waiting after the afterparty."

"He knows Berga, too?" Damn it.

The future Butcher of the Brumal was scary, even by Kaz's standards. And not in that in-your-face tough guy kind of way either; that's half of what made him so creepy. On the outside, Berga looked like your run-of-the-mill nerd. He sort of was, considering he was dedicated to his experiments and the obtainment of knowledge.

"Told you it was a bad idea," Madden mumbled out of the corner of his mouth.

"I'm not really in a partying mood," Nate said, his tone lowering some.

At least the guy felt bad about his loss. Good. He deserved it after the crappy driving he'd done tonight. Kazimir hoped he felt terrible about it for weeks. It wasn't too often that he lost his cool, but Kaz had really needed a fun night out, and this? Losing?

Not. Fun.

Kaz didn't lose. Ever. No matter what the stakes.

"Sounds like that's exactly what you need, actually." Flix tugged Nate back and started for the exit. "We'll catch you all later then!"

"Don't let me catch you first, Pretty Boy," Kazimir warned, unwilling to give it up entirely despite knowing he couldn't lash out right now.

Nate made a sound of frustration and stopped, jostling Flix in the process. He shoved Flix's arm off his shoulders and spun back on his heels to face Kaz, that insufferable, arrogant look still in his eyes.

"You go to Vail, right? I'm older than you," Nate said tightly. "Didn't anyone teach you how to treat your seniors?"

Madden and Flix both made a choking sound that they smartly covered with fake coughs.

Kazimir's eyes narrowed, but before he could respond, Nate swiveled and headed for the exit, leaving Flix to follow or not as he stepped out into the inky night and the forest that surrounded the back of the boathouse.

Flix shook his head and then took off after him, possibly a little afraid if he didn't move quickly Kaz would go after him instead.

He wasn't entirely wrong. The idea was there circling his brain, but fortunately—for Nate—Madden cut through his thoughts before he could come to a decision.

"Take a breather, it's not that big of a deal." Madden clapped him on the back and then moved over to drop into one of the three maroon leather loveseats. He tore the black t-shirt he'd been wearing over his head and dropped it to the cement ground with a sigh.

"Sort of like how keeping your clothes on isn't that hard of a thing to do?" Kaz drawled, but just like that, the anger he'd been feeling drained out of him and was replaced instead with curiosity. He plopped down on the arm of another of the couches and asked, "How do they know each other?"

"Not really sure," Madden said. "All I know is they've got a mutual friend. To be honest, I didn't think they were that close up until now. Maybe Flix was passing by and overheard you threaten him or something." He shrugged.

"You think he just played me?" To protect someone? Flix wasn't the type to go out of his way like that for someone he didn't at least have a slight fondness for.

"Nah," Madden seemed to agree. "Clearly they're close enough for him not to want to see the guy's face rearranged. Which, for the record, neither do I. Nate is a good guy. Super helpful around here."

"Why haven't I heard of him before then?"

"This isn't exactly your scene, Kaz."

He hummed because there was no arguing with facts. "Define good?"

"What?"

"You said he was a good guy." He strummed his fingers on his thigh and peered out through the opening in the back where Nate and Flix had disappeared a few minutes ago. "What's that mean?"

"I don't know. He's always on time, hardworking, polite—when people deserve it," he cut Kaz off before he could interrupt. "Loyal. That mutual friend they share? Nate covered for him today because he was a no-show, and if you think you're the first dick to stroll in here tearing him apart for losing tonight, think again. He'll probably take crap for this loss for weeks, if not months."

"He sounds like a drag."

"He doesn't start random fires or blow things up on a daily basis like the crowd you're used to hanging with, no," Madden drawled. "Look, just forget about him. We both know you're not actually this pissed off about the race anyway."

He was trying to avoid bringing up what Flix had mentioned, but they both knew it'd been true.

Kazimir had been in a bad mood for days, ever since the funeral when things had become entirely too real for his liking. He'd lost people to death before, of course, but Sullivan Void had been a paternal figure to him, and now he'd up and left just like every other adult in Kaz's life had. Logically, he understood it made no sense. But he rarely operated on logic when it came to emotional responses.

"I'm not the letting go type." He flashed Madden a wicked grin and winked before he got up and headed toward the attached lot where he'd stashed his car earlier.

"Yeah," Madden groaned behind him but didn't get up to follow, "that's what I was afraid you were going to say."

An idea started to formulate and the corner of Kazimir's mouth turned up. "Where's this afterparty at?"

"Kaz. Seriously. Contrary to what it looked like tonight, Nate's not bad on a bike. I need him. He helps keep operations running smoothly and he's basically the only person who isn't a complete asshole around here."

"I won't actually kill him," he reassured. He'd

just mess him up a little, that was all. He'd come out for a good time? He'd fucking get one, damn it. "Just tell me where the party is or I'll find out from someone else."

Madden sighed and lifted his multi-slate to tap out a message, and a second later, Kaz's device dinged. "I really wish you'd stop messing around with people I know."

"Yeah, sure." Kaz was only half listening, already adding the address Madden had just sent to his GPS.

Besides, it wasn't his fault that he was smart enough to manipulate people into doing things he wanted and falling for him. When he got what he wanted from them and kicked them to the curb, their negative reactions were their own issue to deal with. All Kazimir cared about were his own feelings.

Given his piss poor mood right now, everyone should beware. The only way he could see himself letting these frustrated emotions go would be to get a proper apology from the man who'd instilled them in him.

The pretty racer might understand how the hierarchy at Vail worked, but it was obvious no one had ever taught him the most important lesson of all.

Never taunt a devil, especially not a Devil of Vitality.

CHAPTER 1:

It was too loud in here and his head was starting to hurt, but the raucous sounds of beat music and the screaming crowd in the bar helped drown out the memory of how awful he'd been on the track tonight, so Nate didn't even consider leaving.

Flix had brought him to the main downtown area, a place Nate rarely hung out at on his own. Even during college, he'd never had the time for partying, and drinking wasn't a pastime he typically enjoyed. It'd been too important for him to show off his grades to his brother whenever Nuri found the time to call, to prove that Nate could be trusted to be on his own and take care of himself and their younger sister, Neve.

He snorted into his glass and then downed the amber contents, coughing a bit at the bittersweet drink. It burned on the way down, but he sort of liked that about it, kept tapping the rim so the bartender would refill it and he could feel it again. Chasing after that lingering discomfort and the way it sat like molasses in his stomach.

There was no one around to tell him to stop, even though he swayed a bit on the stool, his drunken mind chuckling slightly at that. He was meant to be home right now, tucked into bed, getting his eight hours so he wouldn't be exhausted tomorrow at work. The only reason plans had changed was that he'd had the unfortunate luck of losing the race and coming into contact with that pissed-off gambler.

Contrary to what the guy currently believed after his poor racing, Nate wasn't stupid. He'd recognized Kazimir Ambrose immediately, and if he'd been more in the right state of mind, he most likely would have walked without stoking the flames and talking back. He'd been too upset with himself, however, to think clearly and had been two minutes away from locking himself in the bathroom so he could disassociate for a minute. Or ten. Flix had merely been passing by at the right time and taken pity on him.

Flix hadn't said as much as they'd walked out to his car and headed here, but he hadn't needed to. While the two of them were on friendly terms, Nate wouldn't really consider them friends. They got on and talked, sure, but that was mostly because they both knew Bay Delmar. Bay was close to Berga, which meant he was close to Flix. Nate was close to Bay, therefore, Flix tolerated him enough not to want his fellow Brumal member to beat him to a pulp.

There was little doubt in Nate's mind that was

the exact direction the night had been about to take, too. Kazimir didn't seem like the type of guy to make idle threats or misspeak. No, he probably only ever said exactly what he meant. Only did the things he meant to do.

Unlike Nate.

He swallowed more of that burning liquor and motioned for another. When the bartender, some girl he'd had one or two classes with in the past, hesitated, he tapped his glass with a bit more force until she caved.

When his hand shook a moment later as he was lifting it to his lips, he realized she'd probably been right in her hesitation. He should quit now, but a quick glance around reminded him he was currently seated alone with no way home since he hadn't driven himself. It was impossible for him to recall exactly when he'd been abandoned by Flix and Berga, but it must have been some time ago and there was still no sign of their return.

Flix had spotted someone in the crowd and excused himself. A few minutes later, Berga had gotten a call on his multi-slate and left as well. Actually, neither of them had given any clear indications they even *would* be back.

Someone bumped into him from behind, and Nate's drink sloshed over the rim and onto the counter.

"I'm so sorry!" Nate rushed to stand, reaching for a pile of napkins nearby, even as the bartender—Sally?—started to clean the mess herself with a rag.

"It's no problem," she told him, but the smile she gave didn't quite reach her eyes and his stomach clenched tightly. "That guy walked right into you."

"Still. Let me—"

"It's totally fine," she insisted. "It's my job to clean it up anyway."

Nate deflated. It was stupid, but it was similar to a heavy weight settling onto his shoulders, forcing him down lower and lower until he wished the floor would open up and swallow him whole.

"Are you all right?" she asked, noticing his change.

Usually, he was better at masking his moods, hiding the signs that he was about to slip.

Usually he was sober though so, yeah.

"Fine." He forced a smile he knew she didn't believe and then motioned over his shoulder, wobbling some more from the effort. "I'm just going to head to the bathroom."

She didn't need to know that.

Idiot.

He was only bothering her with details that she didn't need.

After giving her a mess that she hadn't needed to waste time cleaning up either.

She'd probably been watching him down those drinks, wondering how long it would take before he became sloppy enough that she'd need to call over one of the bouncers.

Nate pushed his way through the masses of people, keeping his eyes glued to the neon orange sign hanging high over the archway that led to the bathrooms. He'd tuck himself away in one of the stalls and give himself a minute to sober up before calling for a cab. There'd be no risk of him getting into anyone else's way so long as he did that.

He'd already ruined the race, made Flix feel bad enough to invite him out, and made that bartender's job five times harder than it'd needed to be. What next? Whose life was he going to trample all over?

Shouldering the bathroom door open, he gave a deep sigh of relief when he saw that it was empty. He was in the process of using the wall to help guide him toward one of the stalls when that relief died a swift death at the sound of the door reopening behind him.

"I came here to mess you up for costing me tonight," a familiar voice drawled, "but it looks like you've already beat yourself up plenty."

Nate leaned back against the white tile and turned his head toward the new arrival, grimacing when the image of Kazimir before him spun and seemed to double. He squeezed his eyes closed and then tried again.

Kaz quirked a brow at him. "It's only been an hour since you left the boat house. How much did you drink at that time? Don't tell me you're a lightweight?"

"Don't know." He didn't. If he had to guess how many he'd had...He shook his head. "I don't drink often."

"Often and not at all are two different things," the hotshot pointed out. He shifted on his feet and crossed his arms, giving Nate a lengthy once over. "Breaking a couple of your fingers won't be any fun now. In your current state, you'll hardly even feel it."

"Sorry," the apology slipped past his lips naturally, before he could even consider why it didn't make sense for him to say it in this context. The guy was threatening to hurt him, and yet here he was, feeling bad for ruining his good time.

Kazimir gave him a funny look. "I'm being serious."

"Yeah." Nate nodded. "I got that."

"...About breaking your fingers. And possibly your nose, although," Kaz cocked his head, "now that I'm looking at it again, you've got such a nice face. Maybe I'll leave the nose alone."

Nate grunted. "Thanks. You too."

That dark brow lifted a second time.

"I meant you also have an attractive visage," Nate reiterated, waving a hand in front of his own and almost falling in the process. He caught himself at the last second, propping his shoulders back against the tile before exhaling. "Close one."

Kazimir merely watched him silently, his expression suddenly enigmatic.

Or maybe Nate was just too drunk to process things like that anymore.

"If that's all," he said, breaking the quiet, "you should probably go now. If you don't, I might end up ruining your life."

"Is that a threat?"

"No." Nate wasn't too far gone to understand threatening a Brumal member would be the same as courting death. "I might hate myself, but I don't actually want to die."

"That's a very interesting and personal thing to tell a stranger."

Nate winced. "Sorry. You didn't need to know that. I'm bothering you. That's why I said you should leave. If you stick around for too long, I'll inevitably do something burdensome and—"

"Stop talking," the order was delivered in an authoritative tone.

Nate instantly shut his mouth.

"Anyone ever tell you you're the worst kind of drunk?" Kazimir asked, taking a step closer.

Nate risked shaking his head once. "I've only ever been drunk in front of a couple of people before." Mostly other Vitality students who'd been too wasted to notice if he was acting out or being moody. Kazimir had most likely come in here to take a piss, and yet now he was forced to deal with a blabbing Nate. "Sorry."

He was in the process of dropping his gaze when suddenly Kazimir captured his chin and forced his head back up. The breath caught in Nate's chest, and a flash of annoyance at being handled like a kid shot through him before it was snuffed out by the reminder that he was the one causing the problems here, not the Brumal member.

That was actually almost funny. That he could

be worse than the mafia. Cause more trouble for others. Be a public menace.

"Why are you smiling like that?" Kazimir questioned with a frown. "No. Don't stop. It's better than the weird, timid act you've been putting on since I came in. I don't recall you being the type to cower, Nate Narek. Why start now? Is it the alcohol? Does it make you weak?"

"No," he admitted, another pain shooting through his chest at the admission. "This is who I really am. I'm weak."

Kaz released him with a scowl. "Pathetic."

"Yeah," he agreed. "I know."

"This isn't any fun."

"Sorry."

"Stop saying that." Kaz eyed him and seemed to come to some grand realization. "How much of this will you remember in the morning?"

Nate thought it over. "I'm not sure."

"Do you usually remember the day after you've been drinking?"

"I've never had this much to drink." Because that would have meant giving up control to something else, a substance no less, and then how would Nate be able to try his best? What if Nuri called him, or Bay, or literally anyone else that he knew, needing something? "I can't be useful if I'm drunk. If I can't handle my own shit."

Kazimir clicked his tongue. "Hate to break it to you, Pretty Boy, but you're failing at both of those things at the moment. You're drunk off your ass," he dug his pointer finger into Nate's shoulder, pushing him against the wall, grunting when Nate almost fell over again from the movement, "and you for sure can't handle anything right now."

"That's not true." It was. It totally was, but that didn't mean it didn't suck hearing it coming from someone else. Especially someone like Kazimir Ambrose. "I suck. But you suck too."

"That so?" Kaz drawled, and Nate was too far gone to take note of the warning bells.

"You're mafia. Of course, you suck. People are afraid of you."

"Not everyone," he said. "Even when they should be."

Nate blinked at him, his mind taking too long to catch up, but he got there eventually. "Oh. You mean me. That was a dig."

Kazimir grew quiet again.

"Aren't you going to leave?" Nate asked. "Or like...use the bathroom?" Hadn't he come in here to lock himself in a stall? Right.

He went to move past the Brumal member, only to be yanked back by the sleeve of his jacket. Nate yelped, glaring when his back hit the wall again, though his annoyance only lasted so long since, not a second later, Kazimir had his arm propped at the side of his head, crowding him in.

"I'm still deciding," Kaz told him.

"...On whether or not you have to use the bathroom?" Seemed like a weird thing to be uncertain over, but what did Nate know. Tomorrow, he'd probably look back on this moment and wonder what the hell he'd been thinking, allowing someone like Kazimir to get this close to him without arguing, but for now...He sniffed not so subtly at the air. "You smell good."

Forget about the drinking, when was the last time Nate was this close to a person? He had friends, but none of them were the touchy-feely type. Growing up with Neve, he'd had to be the parental figure, so while they'd hugged every now and again, they certainly weren't the kind of siblings that were comfortable with loads of skinship.

"July," he blurted, the answer coming to him.

"What?" Kazimir asked.

"Three years ago." It'd been the start of his senior year, and he'd foolishly believed he could handle being in a romantic relationship and keep up with his studies and part-time jobs. In the end, he'd lasted less than two months before the realization he wasn't anywhere near as skilled as he'd believed himself to be became apparent. "I ended things with her. She cried."

"What are you going on about, Pretty Boy?"

"The last time I was with someone." He pursed his lips. "And why are you calling me that?"

"Define 'with someone'," Kaz ignored his question. "Like, the last time you dated another person or the last time you fucked?"

"Both." Maybe if he wasn't drunk this conversation would embarrass him. Then again, Kazimir had been there earlier, at the race. He'd seen how Nate had lost. Sure, it'd been close, and he'd been racing against someone with more skills than him, but that didn't change the fact that Nate felt useless.

"I like hoverbikes. They're simple. I don't care what tier I'm in, I only want the rush. I like that all you have to do is climb on and feel the vibrations. I like riding because you don't have to think about it."

"Focus," Kazimir said. "This is why drunk people aren't fun. We were talking about the last time you had sex, Pretty Boy, not how much you like racing."

"Riding," he corrected. "Racing just gives me an excuse to do it."

"Riding?" Kaz repeated silkily.

Nate nodded his head. "Yeah. But," he lifted an arm and tried to squeeze it between the two of them, only managing to plant his palm against the younger man's side, "when did you get so close?"

"You're stupid drunk."

"You keep saying that."

"I'm reminding you."

"Why?" Nate didn't need any reminders.

"Because I want you to feel embarrassed."

"About drinking?" He might.

"No," Kazimir grinned. "About this."

"What—" Nate was silenced by plush lips. The words died in his throat the second he felt Kaz's warm tongue dart out and flick against his own. For a moment, he wasn't sure what to do or what was happening, but then the Brumal member gently forced his knee between Nate's thighs.

Nate gasped, and that tongue went in deeper as Kazimir pressed up against the spot between Nate's legs.

"You're getting hard," Kaz pulled back long enough to inform before his mouth reclaimed his a second time, the kiss more forceful than the last as he nipped at Nate's bottom lip and sucked lightly on his tongue. "Have you ever slept with a man before?"

Between the kisses and the questions, Nate's mind was struggling to keep up. "I—No."

Kaz made a disappointed sound. "Don't lie and say you're not into men, Pretty Boy." He pressed that knee against Nate's swollen cock even harder. "This says otherwise."

"I'm into men, too." It was just he'd never gone all the way with one before.

The most sexually active he'd been had been when he'd attended high school, and at the time, he'd only ever been interested in other female students enough to sleep with them. His feelings toward other men had come later, and while he'd messed around with other guys in an exploratory fashion, no one had ever stuck around long enough for him to attempt going all the way.

"How quickly do you think you'll sober up?" Kazimir surprised him by pivoting yet again.

Nate propped his head against the wall and tried to breathe through the pangs of lust now zipping through him. His dick felt achy, and without really noticing, he began rubbing himself against

Kazimir's knee, chasing any sort of friction he could get. When his eyes drifted shut, and he let out a soft moan, Kaz shook him.

"Answer me, Pretty Boy."

"Not sure," he said. "Drank a lot. Probably not till morning? Why?"

"And you've never had sex with a man before? Never felt one take you up the ass? Pin you down and fuck into you like you're nothing but meat?"

Part of him was certain he should be afraid, that there was something seriously off here, but Nate couldn't grasp the feeling, no matter how hard he tried. Instead, he found himself replying, as though he didn't have control over his own voice anymore. "I've never done any of that before, and I'm not sure I'd like it."

"Always pictured yourself on top, that it?" Kaz chuckled when Nate nodded. "Even better. How much do you know about me, Nate Narek?"

The constant switching of topics was starting to give him a headache, and Nate decided, boner or not, he wanted this to end so he could go home and wallow in peace. "Just that you're an important Brumal member. Oh. And a dick. I learned that last part for sure earlier."

"That so?"

"Yeah. You were a total jerk to me."

"You cost me money and tried to convince me it wasn't your fault. Tell me, if it wasn't your fault, whose was it?"

Nate dropped his gaze again.

"That's what I thought." Kazimir yanked him off the wall so quickly he got whiplash, tossing Nate across the room carelessly.

Nate hit the sinks, the breath whooshing out of him as the hard porcelain dug into his ribcage. Before he could right himself, however, Kaz was there at his back, gripping his neck to shove his face down so it was hovering over the basin of one of the sinks. He struggled to right himself, but it was like fighting against a vice grip.

"I didn't know much about you tonight either," Kazimir said then, his tone far too casual for their current situation. The sound of a zipper coming down a second later may as well have been a gunshot in the otherwise quiet room. "But the two of us are about to become well acquainted."

"What the hell are you talking about? Stop."

Kazimir's grip on his neck shifted so he could grab onto a handful of Nate's hair before he tugged his head up just enough for Nate to see their reflections in the wall-length mirrors hanging over the sinks.

Nate's cheeks were impossibly flushed, his eyes wide, pupils blown. His shoulders shook from the strain of the position, and maybe even with a bit of fear, as that particular emotion finally found its way past his drunken haze.

Behind him, Kazimir stood impossibly close, his garnet-colored eyes seemingly piercing straight through Nate's soul. There was so much threat and dark promise swirling in that wicked gaze that Nate felt his chest seize up as the full realization of what he'd gotten himself into finally hit him.

Maintaining eye contact all the while, Kaz reached around and made quick work of Nate's pants and boxers, shoving them down until they bunched at his knees. Then he stuck two fingers into his mouth, lewdly swirling his tongue around them as Nate continued to watch in shock.

"In the old days," Kazimir's voice made Nate jerk in his hold, "people would pay off their debts by giving away their virginity."

"I'm not a virgin," he stated dumbly.

"You are where it counts," he disagreed. "For me, anyway."

"I'm not having sex with you. I'm drunk, but I'm not—"

"Yes. You are. And, Pretty Boy?" Kazimir leaned in so he could press his face against the side of Nate's. "I don't recall asking. You owe me a debt. Time to pay up."

Nate opened his mouth to argue, but the press of one of those fingers at his tight entrance had him instantly stilling. All of his muscles locked into place, his eyes conveying his shock and confusion as they kept contact with Kazimir's unwavering reflection in the mirror.

He wanted to stop him, had no clue how they'd gone from talking to *this* but knew he didn't want it.

"Please, I—" Before he could get more than two words out, that finger slipped past the tight ring of muscle, forcing its way into his entrance. It stung a little, but the pain eased quickly, leaving nothing but pleasure in its wake.

Nate meant to curse and order the man to stop.

Instead, he moaned.

CHAPTER 2:

This wasn't what Kazimir had had in mind when he'd come here tonight.

But then, plans tended to change, and only those who could go with the flow could survive the cruelties of this universe. Being adaptable was a skill set, one that Kazimir happened to have in aces.

Originally, he'd thought beating the older man before him would help appease some of the irritation swirling in his gut. Things had been more difficult with the Brumal as of late, and Kaz needed an outlet away from his friends and family, something personal he could use to alleviate the stress without letting the others know just how twisted his mood was actually getting.

Versatility came with many factors. Kaz needed to be aware of those around him, adjust to their wants and needs, and always be prepared to tell them what they wanted to hear—or what they didn't, depending on his end goal. His cousin and a few of the other Satellite members knew what he was, knew how to guard themselves against him, but the rest of the planet?

He had the rest of them fooled.

On campus, they swooned over him and called him a Devil of Vitality. He hadn't gained a Prince title like some of the others—like the Prince of Music, Rabbit Trace, for example—but that had more to do with the fact he didn't study anything that sounded poetic enough for it. The way they all looked at him was proof enough that they revered him the same way they would actual royalty, and that was more than enough for Kazimir to get off on.

He liked the rush he got whenever he was given someone's full, undivided attention.

Which was probably why his brain had taken this sudden turn and opted to bend Nate Narek over the bathroom sink.

Kazimir hadn't liked the way the pretty guy's mind had wandered. It felt too much like he wasn't giving Kaz the undivided attention he deserved. Like he wasn't taking Kaz, or the threat he posed, seriously. That wouldn't do.

There were many ways to rule over people; admiration and respect were just one of them.

Fear was another.

Since one could catch more flies with honey than vinegar, more often than not, Kazimir chose the first way over the latter. Tonight, however, wasn't a good night. He'd already stormed into the boathouse and set him and Nate off on the wrong foot, so what was the point in backtracking now? First impressions were important, and Kaz had already made his. A pity, since luring Nate into his bed instead would have been more satisfying.

Not because Kazimir had a problem with taking Nate Narek outright, but because Nate would hate himself more in the morning if he'd agreed to it himself.

"Want to know a secret?" Kazimir asked as he twisted his finger deeper into the warm, tight heat that was Nate's hole. The squeeze around his digit was tighter than anything he'd ever felt, and since he was enjoying it, he decided at that moment to give the poor guy an explanation. "I'm insanely good at reading people. All those little tells they try to hide? Those inner thoughts they keep so close to their hearts? I can see them. I'm reading you right now, Pretty Boy. Want to know what your pages say?"

Nate's breath stuttered, and he gripped the edge of the sink with white knuckles. His eyes were filled with anger and fear, but when he opened his mouth, another moan slipped past those full baby-pink lips of his.

"You hate losing as much as I do," Kazimir said, even though Nate hadn't given him an actual answer. He wiggled his finger once more and then slowly eased it out to the tip, pausing for a moment just to see how Nate would react.

The racer tried to stand and Kaz clicked his tongue, shoving his finger back in with less tact than he had before. Feeling a little rush of adrenaline when Nate cried out. There was no pain in the sound, just a mixture of disbelief and bliss.

"There's a difference though, isn't there?" Kaz pulled out a second time, and then he brought two fingers together and carefully pushed them inside. The goal here wasn't to hurt him—that would only make Nate blame Kaz, which would be a waste of his efforts. "I don't like losing because I know I'm above that. You, however..." He felt around until he found Nate's prostate and pressed, laughing when that had the older guy bowing off the sink. "Losing makes you feel like a loser, doesn't it?"

"Please," Nate adorably shook his head, as though trying to knock some sense into himself. "Stop."

"Stop finger fucking you?" He scissored them and grinned when that had Nate mewling like a cat in heat. "Or stop pointing out your inadequacies?"

"I don't care about losing!" Nate stated.

"No?"

"No!"

Kazimir removed his fingers and then grabbed hold of Nate's balls, giving them a tug before he started rolling them in his palm. A quick glance down showed the racer was at full mast and dripping for him, thick drops of milky precome rolling down to plop onto the disgusting green tiles of the bathroom floor.

"This is hardly the place for one to *lose* their virginity," he taunted, knowing it would tick Nate off, even in his frazzled state. There was little doubt in Kaz's mind that he wouldn't have been able to take things this far if the other man hadn't been wasted off his ass.

Kazimir had at least three inches on him height-wise, but Nate was fit, with broad shoulders, and looked like he could hold his own. Of course, a fight between them would result in Kaz winning, since he'd had extensive combat training, something he doubted the racer had much experience with, but now that he remembered Nate from school, he recalled his mouth as well.

Nate Narek was a senior when Kazimir started at Vail University. He'd been the resident golden boy, in fact, gaining everyone's attention wherever he went. Both girls and guys alike wanted to bed him, but he'd rarely, if ever, paid them more mind than flirting here and there. There'd been one girlfriend at the beginning of the first semester, but that hadn't lasted. Kaz didn't know why because, aside from finding him hot, he'd had no use for Nate.

Still, Nate's reputation had proceeded him, and it'd been impossible not to hear about the things he'd said to others throughout the single year they'd occupied the same campus.

Apparently, the cool-as-cucumber senior could flip a switch the second he felt like there was injustice happening.

"Where's your hero complex now?" he teased, releasing his balls to return his fingers to his entrance. This time, he slid three in at once, stretching and opening the older man up, anticipation for what was to come growing with each passing second and hitch of Nate's breath as he wiggled and writhed against him. "Does it not apply when you're the one being abused?"

Nate was known for defending the weak and bullied. If anyone stepped out of line and was mean to another student, word would spread about the scathing things Nate had said to them in retaliation. His verbal barbs were supposedly succinct and incredibly on the nose.

Looked like Kazimir wasn't the only one good at reading people, something he should remember during this little game of his.

"Stop," Nate managed to say, voice shaky. His eyes slipped closed and his pinched expression gave him away.

"Does it hurt?" Kaz asked anyway, just to make the pretty racer admit otherwise. Sure enough, Nate refused to answer, and he chuckled triumphantly. "It feels good, doesn't it? This is nothing compared to what my cock will be making you feel in a moment."

His eyes shot open and Nate tried to straighten again, gasping when Kazimir shoved his face all the way down until his forehead was pressed against the bottom of the cold porcelain basin.

Kaz had wanted to make him watch the whole thing, but if he wasn't going to cooperate...This could work, too.

"Shouldn't have let your guard down," he said. "Someone like you, someone who tries so hard at doing the right thing, should know better than anyone how this world works. This is Vitality. You said you hate yourself? Because you lost a single race?" Kazimir ignored the fact he'd also been pissed at Nate for losing. "Here, let me give you a real reason. You've tried so hard to project this perfect image, even I've noticed."

Nate struggled, trying to lift his head, but he didn't say anything despite his obvious frustrations.

"Campus hero, valedictorian, golden boy," Kazimir ticked them off as he pumped his fingers with more vigor than before, really preparing him now. "But that's not all you are, is it. You like hiding just like the rest of us. Who's the real you? Who's the one you hate?"

"I don't!" Nate insisted, and he was starting to sound more together than he had before.

Was he sobering up already? That wouldn't do.

"Should I tell you who you really are, Nate Narek?" Unfortunately, it looked like he was going to have to speed this up. "Illegal street racer, drunk," he bent and nipped at the back of Nate's left shoulder, "and now, Kazimir Ambrose's little bitch."

Kaz didn't give him time to react to that, yanking his fingers free so he could grab his weeping cock and line it up to that fluttering hole. He'd worked him open nice and good, so the initial press of his thick shaft against that entrance was met with little resistance. He groaned as he watched himself disappear into that hot, narrow passage, his other hand around Nate's neck tightening to keep him in place when he was finally met with resistance a few inches in.

He rolled his hips and forced himself in deeper, getting off on both the feel and the sharp sounds Nate was now making. It no doubt hurt despite Kaz's best efforts to prevent that from happening, but he was too far gone himself to bother being careful as he drove himself in all the way to the hilt.

Lights exploded behind his eyes, and for a moment, he simply stood there, cock buried in all that tight, wet heat. Nate's muscles contracted around his length, and he actually had to bite down on his bottom lip to keep himself from coming then and there.

That was practically unheard of. Kazimir didn't have any issues with premature ejaculation. His eyes narrowed down on the back of Nate's head.

"Was that on purpose?" he asked. "Trying to make this end quickly?"

"I," Nate gasped, "don't know what you're talking about."

Kazimir slapped his right ass cheek hard, watching the pale flesh there turn red with the outline of his fingers.

Nate swore and pulled his hips forward, dislodging a few centimeters of Kaz's cock from him in the process.

He grabbed onto him and thrust, the urge to spank him again, even harder this time, scratching at the edge of Kaz's psyche. The only thing that held him back was his plan. This wasn't about hurting Nate physically.

He wanted to wreck the man mentally.

"Moan for me," he ordered as he started fucking him with deep, steady motions, keeping his hands around Nate's waist to force him on and off his cock. "I want you to remember how good this felt in the morning when you wake up and realize what you did. That you slept with a Devil and enjoyed every second of it. That you took my cock and my come up this sweet ass of yours and that I was your first."

You never forgot your first, wasn't that the saying? Good. Kazimir's punishment would last a lifetime then. No matter how many weeks or months or years passed after this night, Nate would never forget how he was taken in a dirty bar bathroom against his will.

And how much he liked it.

"You're going to remember what it felt like being stretched by my cock," Kazimir continued, picking up the pace in the process as desire took hold. Nate was sobbing now, the sounds echoing in the basin, music to Kaz's ears as he drilled into him. "From now on, every time you lose a race, you'll be brought back to this moment."

He reached around and found Nate's dick, stroking it in time with his thrusts, vaguely noting how impressive the pretty racer's girth was in his hold. If this had been meant as anything other than a punishment for the way he'd spoken to Kaz at the boathouse, maybe he would have slowed down and flipped Nate around, as it were...

Being fucked like this, powerless to stop it yet loving it all the same, that's what was going to really drive Nate crazy. What was going to make him feel debased and small. Drunk Nate had given away that he had low self-esteem, and Kazimir was going to feed that particular monster of his as recompense.

"Should have been nicer to me," he whispered to Nate before he gave into his own monsters completely and went wild on him.

The sink shook, and the mirror rattled against the wall as he fucked Nate like the devil he was known to be, no longer caring that with each inward thrust, he was grinding Nate's hips against the hard porcelain edge or that it would result in serious bruising tomorrow. He'd taken as much pain out of the experience as he could, felt confident his point had been made, and frankly, now Kaz wanted to focus on himself and his physical needs.

Sealing his front over Nate's back, he pinned him down more firmly as he took him, groaning as the new angle helped his cock slide in deeper than he'd imagined. It didn't take long after that for both of them to find their release, Kazimir's cock spurting inside of Nate's hole a second before he felt the pretty racer paint his hand in thick globs of white.

He continued to fuck him until they'd both spent their last drop, then and only then did Kazimir pull away. His cock drooped, slick and shiny in the overhead bathroom lighting, and he smirked at it as he tucked it away and resituated his pants.

Nate remained bent over the sink, his abused

ass high in the air, his hole still stretched and open.

Kaz lifted his multi-slate and snapped a photo, his cock already twitching with renewed interest at the sight of his come seeping from that entrance. There was no time for another round, however. Almost as soon as he'd taken the pic, his device rang with a call from his cousin, the one person not even Kazimir could ignore.

He grabbed a fistful of Nate's jacket and pulled him off the sink, tossing him to the ground at his feet. It gave him his first look at the pretty racer's face in a while, and despite knowing Baikal hated to be kept waiting, Kaz momentarily stalled to take it all in.

Nate's cheeks were red and streaked with tears, his pants still caught around his knees to display the way his limp dick rested between his thighs. His hair was in disarray from when Kaz had grabbed it, and he looked like the mess Kaz had wanted him to be. The only thing he hadn't anticipated was the defiance.

Those lips of his trembled as he glowered, those chocolate eyes clear and intense as they locked onto Kaz's.

Had Kazimir fucked the alcohol out of his system? Any other time he'd find that concept funny, but right now…

The phone stopped and then abruptly started ringing again, the jarring sound enough to pull him out of it.

"Consider us even, Pretty Boy." Kazimir gave

him a wink and then turned on his heels, shoving the door open and exiting into the hall with a spring to his step that hadn't been there an hour ago.

In fact, he felt better than he had in weeks.

All that coin he'd lost tonight?

Money well spent.

CHAPTER 3:

"You've got to do better than that to keep up in this industry, Narek."

Nate nodded his head absently as he emptied his bladder at the stall next to Donaver, the coworker who thought he wrote the damn textbook on automotive-craft mechanics. He bet if they checked, Nate had better grades than the vapid prick—who was tiny in *all* the ways it counted—standing next to him.

They were around the same age, though Donaver considered himself a million times wiser since he'd started working at Quartet Air a full three months before Nate had been hired.

Idiot.

It was true that Donaver got more clients than the rest of the mechanics there, but they all knew why. His daddy owned a popular grocery chain and was constantly sending clients his son's way. Typically, Nate wouldn't begrudge a little nepotism —who could afford to get by on their own in this day and age—but he drew the line when it was used as a means to look down on others.

Donaver wasn't particularly clever or more skilled than the rest of them. He simply had connections, and while that was dandy for him and all, it didn't mean he had a right to stand here pissing next to Nate, talking to him in that condescending tone of his.

The interaction reminded him of the one thing he'd spent the past two weeks desperately trying to purge from his recollection. At the docks, that damn Devil had sneered down his nose at Nate like he shit out the moon and controlled the tides and therefore deserved to be revered. Then later, when he'd found Nate drunk...

Kazimir Ambrose had fucked him.

No, he'd sexually assaulted him—Nate couldn't bring himself to use the other word, even knowing that's what it'd actually been. He hadn't been able to consent, had in fact, told him to stop. Did it matter that he'd been hard for Kaz and that he'd come in the end as well?

No.

No, because it couldn't. Because that would mean that Nate had liked it, just like Kazimir had claimed, and...

He had issues, sure, but he couldn't be that messed up in the head, right? He hadn't *liked* the fact that a basic stranger had taken advantage of him. But the act itself had been... eye-opening? Maybe that wasn't the right term for it. All Nate knew was he'd enjoyed the sex on its own, even if he'd loathed the person who'd been forcing him to do it.

Nate could still remember with perfect clarity exactly how it'd felt to be held down. The way his body had internally protested the intrusion, first of those deft fingers and later of Kazimir's wide cock. The stretch, the burn, the intense waves of heat, all of that could be brought back to the forefront of his mind easily. But other details were harder to grasp.

Whenever he thought back on the things Kazimir had said to him, it was a bit hazy. He knew there'd been words during the act itself, that Kaz had whispered them into his ear and breathed them hotly against the back of his neck, but try as he might, Nate could only pick one or two of them out here and there. The rest were a mystery.

Except for his parting ones, of course. The way the Brumal member had looked down his nose at Nate and left him there sitting on the dirty floor in a mixture of their fluids was seared in his brain. He might have even been able to forgive Kaz for the rape itself—there, he'd acknowledged it—but whenever he thought back on how he'd just walked away after...

His hands clenched into tight fists.

Nate had felt the sting of rejection stronger than anything else that night, even his own sense of being a burden.

And then, once he'd gotten home, cleaned himself off, and tucked himself into bed he'd felt something entirely different.

Relief.

Kazimir had used him and been satisfied, and

in his own twisted, fucked up way, wasn't that Nate's one true goal in life? It'd been his first time ever, but he hadn't been burdensome with Kaz. He'd been discarded in the end, sure, but so what?

Kazimir Ambrose wasn't someone that Nate wanted to keep, either.

It was the relief that angered Nate the most, though that was aimed at himself more than at the Brumal member who deserved it. Maybe he should talk to Bay. Bay Delmar was a professor at Vail University and had a pretty solid grasp on the psyche and how it typically worked. He'd be able to help Nate sort through these contradictory feelings in no time.

Only, Bay had his own shit to deal with...
Nate couldn't bother him with his own crap.
Fuck.

It didn't even matter that Bay bailing on the race was what had kick-started this whole mess in the first place. Logically, Nate understood he had a right to be annoyed and to confront his friend, but that tiny voice in his head told him not to be a burden and make it worse. To stay silent. To tolerate it.

To compress those feelings down until they were so minuscule, he'd hardly remember them at all.

Just like he did with every other problem he'd met in his life.

Contain. Compartmentalize. Compress.

Nate shook his head at himself and realized

with a start that Donaver had continued babbling this whole time, completely clueless to the fact he'd been ignored for the past five minutes.

"Mr. Mit is a big ticket." Donaver tucked himself away, zipped up his fly, and then propped a shoulder against the wall so he could continue the conversation while Nate finished up.

Like a complete and total creep.

Nate wasn't a particularly violent person, had been raised to keep a level head and fight with words, not fists. He very rarely ever pictured what it might be like to punch someone in the throat and yet...Watching his annoying coworker's Adam's apple bob up and down as he spoke really made the whole throat-punch thing sound appealing.

He blamed Kazimir. All of his patience and concentration were dedicated to that night and how Nate could properly sort through those feelings. He didn't have any energy left to deal with the likes of Donaver or the man of topic, Mit Parker.

"You should be a little nicer to him is all I'm saying. Kindness goes a long way." Donaver clapped him on the back, jostling Nate, but then finally headed out the door of the small restaurant bathroom.

Bastard didn't even wash his hands.

Nate scowled. He hated these damn work dinners. They never went well and were always more of an attempt to show off in front of the shop's bigger clients than any team building or whatever other bullshit the boss used to explain why it was mandatory. For the past three, Mit Parker had been showing as well, and that guy gave Nate worse heebie-jeebies than Donaver did.

Maybe even more than Kazimir Ambrose. No, that wasn't fair. Nate had known to give any Devils of Vitality a wide birth, but he'd trusted himself enough not to get in their way, so had never had the foresight to consider Kaz a personal threat of any kind. Even that night in the boathouse when he'd been pissed off and raging, Nate's own anger had gotten the better of him and he'd snapped back.

If only he'd kept his mouth shut, stuck to character and bowed his head and walked off quietly, none of the events afterward would have taken place. Hell, he wouldn't have even been at the bar for Kaz to find. Really, it was his fault that had happened.

"Shut up," he cursed himself. "It's not your fault."

Entirely.

But maybe a little bit?

No, that wasn't right either. Blaming himself was stupid. Yet he couldn't seem to help it. A part of him had secretly hoped this dinner would help with that, but so far even being this close to a creep like Mit wasn't enough to wipe thoughts of Kazimir —and the way his cock had felt inside of him—off Nate's mind. Thoughts of the Devil were still there, lingering next to the disgust he felt whenever Mit not so subtly propositioned him.

It wasn't that big of a secret that Mit's money

wasn't exactly clean, or that he spent many a coin on skin service—aka renting people out for the evening or long weekend. While Nate would never begrudge anyone that type of work, it pissed him off that Mit walked around assuming he could buy anyone he pleased.

Sex work wasn't Nate's thing. Full stop.

No matter how much money the fifty-year-old man waved in his face.

Could what have happened between him and Kaz be considered sex work? Hadn't Kazimir mentioned clearing the "debt"?

"You didn't owe that asshole anything," he reminded himself bitterly. Gambling was gambling. Nate hadn't made him place that bet.

He pumped way too much soap in his palm at the sink and glared at his reflection in the polished mirror hanging over it. The restaurant was expensive and was paid for by Mit as a "treat for the hardworking people who always came through for him." Pretty much the only good thing about the millionaire was his collection of hoverbikes and the fact he allowed Nate to touch them.

How a garage like Quartet Air had managed to snag a high roller like him was beyond Nate, but Mit was pretty much the only reason the shop hadn't completely gone under, so the boss was always willing to drop to her knees and lap at the man's boots at the snap of a finger.

"Good Light," Nate squeezed his eyes closed and inhaled slowly, seeking patience, "I fucking hate this job."

Not even working on those prized bikes was enough to keep him happy anymore. Mit had started to get handsy with him whenever he came around, supposedly to check on the work being done. Yet every time Nate finished work on one, the guy would show up with another that supposedly needed modifications or repairs. It was getting to the point where it was so obvious what was actually happening that even Nate's coworkers were starting to gossip amongst themselves.

The funny thing was, it wasn't like Nate was above being bought—everyone and thing had a price and he was no different—but there was no way in hell he'd ever give in to a guy like Mit Parker. Sure, he was in great physical shape for someone in their mid-fifties, and he had more money than either of them would be able to spend in a lifetime, but he was also a sleaze.

On more than one occasion at these mandatory dinners, Nate had seen the man treat waitstaff like his own personal slaves. He'd snap and yell and belittle them as if they didn't have feelings. It was disgusting. Having grown up needing to take care of himself and his younger sister, Nate understood the struggle of working a shitty 9-5, and how one bad customer could ruin an entire week just by making a single shitty comment.

People who looked down on those who had less than them were the worst kind.

His multi-slate rang and he actually felt a

wave of relief since it meant he had an excuse not to head back to the table just yet. His brother's name flashed over the screen, and the corner of his mouth tipped up before he pulled the attached earbud from the side of the rectangular device at his wrist and popped it into his right ear. As soon as he hit accept, the soft hum of an engine came through the line.

"Finally headed home from the office?" Nate asked, checking the time. It was late, well past regular working hours. But then, his older brother, or more aptly, his older brother's boss, had never understood the concept of time.

"Yes, we were busy preparing for the upcoming Midnight Gala," Nuri's voice, light and comforting in that familiar way, helped ease some of the tension Nate had been feeling as he spoke. "That's actually why I'm calling. I reserved tickets for you and Neve. I know you're always saying you're too busy, but it would be great if the two of you could find the time to come this year."

Nate started crunching numbers, trying to figure out if a trip like that was even possible for him.

Though the three Narek siblings had been born on the planet Ignite, after the death of their parents, the oldest, Nuri, had sent the two younger to attend schools on the neighboring planet Vitality. The distance wasn't too great via spaceship, but it would still take at least a full day for them to make it from one to the other. Then another day in order to make the return trip…

"I don't know," he admitted. He wanted to go, mostly because he wanted to see Nuri, but this was reality, where wishes didn't mean shit. "I have to double-check, but I'm pretty sure there's no way Sier will approve my time off for that."

His boss definitely wouldn't, not when it was Nate who kept their best client coming back for more.

"Well," Nuri's disappointment was impossible to miss, "let me know. There's no need to worry about the cost of the ship tickets. I can purchase those for you if you decide you can make it after all."

"It's not about the money." Nate rubbed at his temple, that stress from earlier slowly creeping its way back in now that the topic had shifted to this. "I have money, brother."

He wasn't rolling in it by any means, but Nate had made enough racing on the side for the past four years that he could get by so long as he kept his regular working hours. Of course, most of that money had gone towards his sister's needs while she'd still been in university and to help pay for any of the side bills neither of them had wanted to tell Nuri about. He didn't exactly live paycheck to paycheck, but there wasn't very much in the bank as far as savings went. Still. He could afford a single ship ticket.

"Yes," Nuri sighed. "I forget sometimes that you're an adult now."

"What's that supposed to mean?" Nate bristled at the sarcastic remark. "Look, can we not have a fight right now? I'm at this dumb work thing, and I'm mentally exhausted already."

There was a moment of silence, and then, "You should reconsider—"

"I don't want your boyfriend's handouts," Nate growled. He could take care of himself. Hell, he'd been doing it for years now already. The last thing he wanted was to rely on the Emperor. One of the major reasons he'd refused to return to Ignite was to avoid that very thing.

Nuri was pushy on the best of days, but his husband/boss was on a whole different level of controlling and overbearing. No, thank you.

"It's not a handout," Nuri argued. "We're family."

"Not my family." As far as Nate was concerned, there was Nuri and Neve and him and that was all. The three of them against the worlds. That was how it'd always been and that was how he wanted it to stay.

Even if both of his siblings had left the proverbial nest and settled down with life partners.

This was the one thing he allowed himself to remain firm on, even at the risk of burdening Nuri. He didn't hate Silver, per se, but he definitely wasn't ready to welcome with open arms the guy who'd all but stolen and hogged his brother all these years.

Nate also didn't fully trust him, despite the fact Silver and Nuri had been together for over a year now. Silver Rien was capricious and selfish. Nothing he ever did for others, aside from maybe Nuri, came without strings, and more entanglements of any kind were the last thing Nate needed.

That wink Kaz had sent him at the end before he'd left Nate on the ground flashed through his mind and he scowled all over again. Even if he'd wanted to press charges against the Brumal member, it wouldn't work in his favor. People like Kazimir Ambrose got away with murder, let alone taking advantage of a drunk. He'd spin things so it sounded like Nate had wanted it, and then the entire planet would hear. It'd get to Neve and, eventually, find its way to Nuri.

Nate would never embarrass either of them like that. So he'd opted to keep quiet, try and forget, and pretend like the whole ordeal hadn't happened.

It was going really well for him so far.

Not.

"Fine, a favor then. He won't get you the job outright, I would never allow that. But he can get you a foot in the door, so to speak. The rest will still depend on you," Nuri said.

"I don't want to be in debt to anyone," he stood firm, grateful for the distraction from his thoughts, even if it was a mild argument. "Besides, you were against this initially as well. What happened to believing I could do this on my own?" That wasn't fair, and he knew it, knew he was being a brat, but sometimes, when he spoke to his older brother, it just came out in him.

When the three of them had separated, it'd been Nate as the second oldest who'd had to take the reins and help raise their sister. They'd been on a foreign planet for the first time, not knowing a single person, and Nate had felt just as lost and confused as she had, yet he'd had to step up. He'd never regretted it, had always acknowledged that Nuri had been forced to do the same after the sudden death of their parents, but taking on that role at such a young age had definitely had an effect on him and his overall personality.

It wasn't so much that Nate had an overabundance of pride. No, what he had was guilt. If Nuri could do so much on his own, surely Nate could as well. That was the mantra he'd told himself all throughout his teen years, and even now that they were all technically adults, it still stuck with him.

Nate refused to be a burden on anyone, especially his brother. Nuri thought Nate was clueless when it came to his relationship with the Emperor of Ignite, but he wasn't. It was a little bit fucked up, with abuses of authority and power all throughout. But Nuri also saw it for what it was and still chose to remain in the relationship, so who was Nate to tell him to end things?

If his brother was happy, that was all that mattered, and he wasn't about to judge someone for the things they were into.

But that didn't mean he'd also aid in exacerbating the situation.

If he took Emperor Silver Rien up on his offer to get him an interview at a new job, there was absolutely no doubt in Nate's mind that something would be required of Nuri in return. Be it some weird twisted sex thing or something as simple as working even more overtime, Nate didn't want to be a part of it. His brother had done enough for him already.

"Of course I still believe that," Nuri reassured. "There's nothing wrong with accepting—"

"Gotta go," Nate really didn't want to have this conversation again. "At a work thing."

Nuri sighed. "All right. Call me later?"

"Sure." He wouldn't. He'd make an excuse the next time that he'd forgotten or gotten too busy when they both knew the reality was, he was avoiding things.

Avoiding the fact that their sister's newfound happiness meant there was less of a need for him hovering about.

And less of a reason for him to call to update Nuri.

Avoiding that he actually didn't like living alone half as much as he'd teased them both he was going to when Neve had sat them down and explained she was planning on moving in with her boyfriend.

Avoid.

Avoid.

Avoid.

Except for his responsibilities. Those he couldn't afford to overlook or sweep under the rug. That was most likely why, even though Nuri knew exactly what he was doing, his brother didn't press the issue and instead made a humming sound in the back of his throat and said goodbye as though everything was fine.

In a sense, everything was.

And yet...

Nate shoved the earbud back into the device and then swung open the bathroom door, squaring his shoulders on his way down the narrow hall back toward his current hell.

Dinner.

"What took you?" Port, one of the few coworkers Nate didn't find annoying for one reason or another, asked as soon as Nate slid back down onto the end of the packed booth their boss had chosen for this outing.

That was another thing. Sier always squeezed them into the tightest of spaces whenever she insisted on taking them out for a company meal. He'd yet to decide if it was because she wanted to save money on having to pay for a second table, or if she secretly got off on being squished.

"My brother called," Nate said as he took a sip of the beer he'd left half-finished before he'd gone to the bathroom. It was lukewarm and tasted like it belonged in the urinal he'd just used, but whatever.

"You have a brother?" Mit Parker, who was slightly drunk by this point, called from the other side of the table, lifting his glass when Nate glanced over at him. "Is he half as good-looking as you are? I'd like to meet him."

"His husband wouldn't approve," Nate stated

tightly, noticing the way Donaver smirked triumphantly at his tone, as though the guy was waiting for Nate to step in it. Fuck. He needed to get the hell out of here before he really did say something he couldn't take back. "Actually, there's been a family emergency so I—"

"Doesn't your brother live off planet?" Sier asked. Her calling him out like that was only made worse by the fact she was a total clueless ditz and didn't actually mean any harm. Her uncle had left the shop to her a year ago and things had only gone from bad to worse since the changing of hands.

For one, no one had ever actually taught her how to run a business properly.

He had no clue what she'd been doing with her life prior to taking over, but Sier's way of doing things was mostly bringing in flashy clientele from the clubs she used to frequent. The type who didn't actually care about the work being done on their vehicles and instead were more interested in... different types of bodywork.

Pretty much all of the older staff had already jumped ship—or been fired if their looks weren't up to snuff in her opinion—but Nate had stayed on since no one had ever pushed him for anything he wasn't comfortable with, despite the new underlying type of business they apparently ran.

Until now.

"It's my other sibling," Nate said, not wanting to name Neve and bring his sister into this filth. It was his job to protect her, not drag her into this fucked up world he had no clue how he'd even entered in the first place. He stood and gathered his thin coat, tossing it on as quickly as possible without looking too desperate to leave, hackles rising when suddenly Mit was following suit.

"Allow me to walk you out," Mit offered and Nate shook his head.

"That won't be necessary."

"He'd love that, Mr. Parker," Sier interrupted. "Could you help him hail a cab? Nate is always too nice to bother them and ends up walking."

"In this weather?" Mit made a big show of looking toward the window and shivering. Outside, snow was coming down, but it was light, the type that didn't even stick to the ground for longer than a minute or two.

This type of weather was nothing to him. Nate's home planet was way colder than this, but he didn't bother saying as much. The less the other guy knew about him the better.

"I should be going as well, before it gets much worse," Mit announced.

Everyone there chose to pretend they didn't catch the innuendo in his words.

Which was how Nate found himself forcing a smile as he followed Mit Parker out of the crowded restaurant downtown, trying not to give into the images in his mind of punching the guy whenever his gaze lingered a bit too long.

One day Nate would get his shit together and not have to worry about pleasing those with more

power, he comforted himself.
>One day.
>But not today.

CHAPTER 4:

Kazimir wouldn't say he had trust issues, more that he was cautious about the company he kept. He'd grown up in the Brumal mafia on the planet Vitality, groomed for a high-standing position from a young age, and the cousin to the current leader. Very few ever dared try and get close enough to cause him harm, but that didn't mean it was unheard of.

And there was something about the man seated across from him that gave him the actual ick.

As the newly appointed underboss, it was Kazimir's job to handle all the extra important work that Baikal Void, the Dominus and said cousin, didn't want to or wasn't able to find time for. In this particular case, Kaz's money was on the first scenario.

"We're here to broker a deal," the creepy guy with the eerie orange eyes replied in a cool tone. He was leaning back in the leather seat, relaxed in a way no one else in the room was currently able to be.

A bit too relaxed for Kaz's comfort, in fact. Typically, when requesting a meeting with the

Brumal, a person came a bit more prepared and on their toes. But this guy had come alone, not a single bodyguard in sight, and had been lightly sipping from the glass held loosely in his left hand since Kazimir's arrival fifteen minutes ago.

The dark blue liquor was strong enough to put a grown Vital man on his ass with only half a glass, and yet an almost empty bottle was perched on the end table at the man's side.

Kazimir wondered if Nate would even be able to handle a couple of sips. He'd gotten wasted off a single bottle of hard liquor at the bar that day, but that was nothing compared to the drink their guest was downing like water.

And there he was doing it again. Thinking about the pretty racer when he should have been done and over it already.

"You're refusing to tell us exactly what it is you're looking for," Flix, the official Runner/Fixer of the Satellite, stated from where he stood at the end of the long couch Kaz was seated on. "You're basically asking for permission to let you loose on our planet, and for what?" He clicked his tongue. "Very little return, that's what."

"I understand Baikal is new to playing the part of a king," the man drawled, "but surely he should have known to send better than a snarky platinum blond and his brooding sidekick."

Kazimir's brow quirked, and he chuckled. "You talking about me?"

"You've been sitting there in relative silence

since your arrival."

"I'm not brooding." He took the man in from head to toe pointedly, then glanced around at all the empty space in the room. "And I don't think you should be talking shit about how Baikal does things. What kind of king enters into enemy territory alone?"

"The kind that can take care of themselves," the guy smirked, the vicious expression cutting through his relaxed demeanor to show a glimpse at the monster beneath the mask.

"There you are." Kaz returned it with a grin of his own. "I've been waiting for you to show your true colors."

Pious Prince, better known as the Emperor of Old—whatever the fuck that meant—was dressed to the nines in fancy charcoal duds and polished shoes. His dark hair was slicked back, and his face was clean-shaven. The glittering rings adorning each of his fingers and the expensive half-empty bottle at his elbow only added to the picture of wealth. From a passerby's perspective, he probably looked like a celebrity, or a man who'd come from generational money, but according to their research, Pious was neither.

The Ancient were a mafia group that typically kept to their galaxy, which was located a good way away from Kazimir's. They'd only had minor interactions over the past couple of decades, all of them kept private by Sullivan Void, Baikal's deceased dad and their ex-Dominus. All the secrets made Kaz itchy for answers, but Whim, his predecessor, had warned him beforehand not to overstep here. While he liked to tease Whim that he made decisions like his namesake, that was only a joke. He knew the previous underboss never did anything without a lengthy risk assessment first.

Apparently, Pious was a big bad who needed to be handled with care.

Ironically, Kazimir happened to be a big bad who liked breaking things, so they'd see how this meeting would end once they crossed that proverbial bridge. As it were, he wasn't really feeling it, since Pious had been putting on that princely act this whole time.

"I don't like to be bullshitted," Kaz said, dropping his own glass down onto the coffee table before him with a loud clatter. Screw Whim's advice. "You want access to our resources? Gotta give me something worthy in return."

"You've already insulted me," Pious stated, "and now you're threatening me? Sullivan had much more decorum."

"Yeah, well, now you're stuck with me. Tough."

"And if I demanded to see Baikal Void in person?"

"You could," Kaz shrugged. "Might be waiting a while though, and from the little you have shared, I get the impression you're in a bit of a rush, Prince."

"I'm an emperor, *boy*." Pious leaned forward, more of that calm mask slipping away.

Exactly what Kaz wanted. He hadn't been lying—this time. He didn't like dealing with people he couldn't get a clear read on. It was too obvious that something was off about Pious; Kaz needed a better grasp on his personality in order to ensure things went his way.

That's why Baikal gave him this position in the first place. Kaz had a way of worming his way through another person's psyche, learning what made them tick, what made them passionate and excited, and using those things against them without them even realizing.

Manipulation was an art form, and he was a master craftsman.

Just ask Nate Narek.

"We look close to the same age." Kazimir was good with gauging that type of thing, too, considering Vitality was a planet that operated on filial piety. Knowing your stance with another person was important, especially if that other person was a Devil.

"I assure you, I am much, much older." Pious licked his lips and then strummed his fingers on his knee. "All right. We've been handling your phkin shipments for eight years now with a cut of thirty-seventy. I'll drop it to twenty if you give me access to your imprinting system."

That wasn't a bad deal. The only problem was that the Brumal didn't have control of the main system; only the Imperial family, those who ruled the planet's government, did. They were in league with the Brumal, of course, but that didn't mean getting them to hand Pious a keycard was easy. Kelevra Diar, the Imperial Prince, third in line for the throne, was a royal pain in the ass on a good day who loved making things difficult. If Kaz went to him for this favor, there was no telling how much he'd try to milk him for it in return.

Good thing Kazimir had another option. He'd skip straight to Zane and ask him to help instead.

"Some ground rules before I agree," Kaz said. "You're obviously looking for a person. If this individual turns out to be Brumal, or part of the Imperial Retinue, you'll report it to us before making any further moves."

"Starting a war is very low on my to-do list, I assure you," Pious replied. "I'm confident it won't come to that anyway. The person I'm after prefers sticking to the shadows and staying out of the limelight. Getting involved with either of your parties would make it more difficult for him to remain hidden."

"It would give him a support system against you on the day you come knocking," Kazimir pointed out, but Pious merely shook his head.

"He doesn't need protection. The man I'm after is more than capable of defending himself."

"So he's dangerous then?" Flix frowned. "And he's been hiding out on Vitality for how long?"

"Unclear," Pious told them. "If I'd known about his presence sooner, I would have been here sooner."

"He's that important to you?" Kaz asked.

Pious's expression darkened. "He's everything."

Flix shifted on his feet, and Kazimir let out a low whistle.

"Are you authorized to give me what I want or not?" More of Pious's calm façade cracked.

Kaz got to his feet. "You have a deal. I'll draw up the paperwork and get it to you before the night is through. Any action on your part before then will be taken as a sign of aggression, so try to keep that leaking impatience of yours under control in the meantime, yeah?"

"You're a very abrasive individual, has anyone told you that before, Mr. Ambrose?"

"Yeah," he chuckled and then turned for the door. "I get that a lot."

Club Visros was bumping, the sounds of beat music coming up through the floors as Kazimir made his way down the velvet strip of black carpet that led from the private meeting room in the back of the second floor. None of the Satellite typically hung out there, but the crowd was packed with other lower-level Brumal members. Located smack dab in the center of Valeo, the capital city, it made for the best meeting place with outsiders.

"You were meant to play the part of charming intermediary, a role you excel at. If he complains to Baikal that you went a different direction and were a jerk, you'll regret it," Flix said, coming up on his right as they reached the end of the long hallway and began the descent down the winding metal stairs. It emptied out on the side of the main dance floor, the raucous sounds of the patrons making it harder to be heard even with them standing so closely together.

"I got the job done, didn't I?" Kaz yelled back. "Besides, if he does get pissed, we can just point out how he was meant to be here with us."

"Interesting how this suddenly turned into a 'we' scenario."

"He's probably too busy fucking—"

"Show some respect," Flix cut him off. "That's the Possessio you're referring to."

"Yeah, yeah." That was why Kazimir wasn't saying this in front of Rabbit, was it not? He'd never insult the guy to his face. In actuality, he was sort of even fond of the musician. He had drive and had proven himself loyal to Baikal and the Brumal. That didn't mean he couldn't complain now and again about how he now sucked up all of Baikal's time and attention. "Kal is the Dominus, not me. That's all I'm saying."

"Thank Light for that." Flix clapped him on the back and then stepped ahead to shove open the metal double doors with more flourish than necessary. The brisk air from outside slapped them in the faces, and they both took a moment as they stepped out to breathe it in. "It's always way too stuffy in there."

"Smells like ass," Kaz agreed. The top floor where they'd been meeting with Pious may be decked out in velvet and gold, but the bottom main level, which was open to the public, was a hot mess of spilled booze and drunken hookups. Before anything else could be said, his multi-slate, the body-borne computer they all wore strapped to their forearms, rang. "Speak of the hooky playing Devil."

"Kal?"

"Yeah," Kazimir answered the call with a grunt. "What?"

"That the tone you used with Pious just now?" Baikal's deep voice came through the other line, the annoyance ringing loud and clear.

"Don't tell me he ran off and tattled already?" What a little bitch. Kazimir spat onto the sidewalk and rolled his eyes.

"He didn't," he replied. "I just know you, that's all."

"Sure you haven't forgotten all about me now that your 'little bunny' is in the picture?" he taunted. It was petulant, even he knew that, but he couldn't help it. The two of them had been thick as thieves —both literally and figuratively—since they'd been children, but now that his cousin had someone special, they mostly talked about Brumal business and nothing else.

Kazimir was feeling neglected. Sue him.

"Watch how you talk about him," Baikal warned.

Flix must have overheard despite the fact Kaz had put the earpiece in, because he chuckled at Kaz's side and pretended to find interest in the stars twinkling above them when that earned him a glare.

"Whatever," Kazimir conceded, knowing from experience there was no arguing with the Dominus anyway.

"Stop pouting," Baikal said. "You're the underboss of the largest criminal organization in the galaxy, and the son of global tycoon Ersa Ambrose. What if the press takes pictures of you throwing a hissy fit like a twelve-year-old?"

The Devils had been photographed by tabloids in the past, but they both knew those were controlled situations. The Voids owned all of the most prominent news outlets on planet, after all. Anything they didn't want out in the world, they could easily wipe from all records. Baikal was only saying all this now to rub salt in the wound.

Dick.

"Forgive me for actually enjoying your company," he stated, though he was questioning why he did at this point. "How quickly you forget how I was the only one who could even tolerate your presence for longer than an hour before you met Trace."

"Sure you're not referring to yourself?" Baikal countered. "You've got the personality of a boar. Hot-headed and brash."

"People love me."

"People love the idea of you and the carefully curated false images you project," he corrected, and though the words were cruel, his tone had lightened in a poor attempt to make it seem like he was only teasing in good fun.

He was not.

Baikal Void could cut a person down with nothing more than his tongue, and when he was in the mood to do it, no one was safe from his wrath, not even family.

"The reason you're so bent out of shape about Rabbit and I is because you've never had a relationship more meaningful than a one-night stand. Your dark empathy can only—"

"And this is where we put this ever so thrilling chat to an end." Kazimir didn't like talking about the things that had gone on in his childhood, or how they'd helped form him into the person he was today. Which his cousin very well knew. "Throwing that diagnosis in my face? Low blow, even for you."

"Shouldn't talk shit about my Possessio."

"I didn't—" Kaz blew out a breath. "Fine. Whatever."

"You're sulking again."

"Fuck you."

"Find someone else to stick your dick in," Baikal said. "Want to know why I'm so satisfied with my *little bunny*, cousin? Try to get over yourself long enough to give finding the one a try. My bet's you can't."

He bristled. "If you can do it, of course I can too. How hard could it be?"

Baikal grunted through the line. "For you? Nearly impossible. There's a reason I'm the Dominus and you're just the underboss, cousin. You'll never be as good as me."

"That's—"

Someone called Kal's name, and though it was muffled, it was obvious it was Rabbit a second later when without so much as a goodbye, the Dominus hung up.

"Fucker!" Kazimir ripped the earbud out of his right ear and almost chucked it into the street before he got a hold of himself.

"Temper," Flix clicked his tongue. "He's right, you know? Your tendencies make you good for the underboss job, but make it impossible for you to properly connect with the people around you enough to lead."

"You couldn't even hear everything he said." Kazimir barely resisted the urge to break the other guy's nose. The two of them had been friends for a while, but that didn't mean he'd be opposed to causing him bodily harm. "I don't have a problem connecting with people either, for your information."

Flix shrugged. "Don't need to have. You only act this way when he pushes your buttons. Brought up your diagnosis again, didn't he?"

"Stop throwing that word around like it's something I picked up off the street one day and carried home." Kazimir had not and would not have chosen this life if he'd been given the chance. As it were, it turns out that when your mom skips out on you before you turn one and your dad is too busy working for a criminal ring and running a conglomerate, you develop certain...problems.

It didn't help that he'd been trained in deception and combat, taught how to bend those around him to his will without batting an eyelash while doing so. Kaz had quickly thrown everything he'd had into things, excelling immediately. Though they'd trained alongside one another, things for Baikal had gone a bit differently.

In the beginning, when they were ordered to hurt, maim, or kill someone, Baikal asked for details. He wanted explanations, wanted to understand why the person was being punished and decide if the punishment fit the crime.

Kaz had wanted that too, but for very different reasons.

Baikal Void could connect with those around him on an emotional level. Even if he chose not to give in to those feelings, he could still relate and understand.

Kazimir Ambrose, however, struggled with forming those types of bonds. He grasped basic emotional responses—could tell when someone was sad, and knew what sadness felt like—but he couldn't apply those emotions to himself. A sad person was a sad person. Didn't mean Kazimir had to feel sad seeing it.

Lack of a deeper sense of empathy. That's what the doctor had told them when Kazimir's father had ordered the tests done on him during one of the few instances he'd bothered paying his one and only offspring any attention. Kaz had cognitive empathy, took in the cues of those around him and understood what they were feeling, it was just he didn't allow their emotions to affect *his* emotions.

So what if Kaz didn't feel bad when he saw a little old lady slip and split her head open on the pavement? If the need called for it, he could fake it convincingly enough. It only really became an issue after time had passed to become noticeable, and even then, it was only those who paid attention that caught on. He'd never cost the Brumal anything because of what he was.

"Relax," Flix clapped him on the back and left his hand resting there for a moment longer than Kaz was comfortable with. "Your cousin was a major prick before he met Trace too, remember? Not to mention the Imperial Prince. That guy's temper has seriously leveled since he hooked up with that Academy Cadet. You'll find your thing eventually."

"My thing?"

"Yeah. You know. That thing that helps make you feel centered and all that other crap. The thing."

Kazimir's eyes narrowed. "I can't help but notice you're implying I need to find an outlet that's an object, and not a person."

"Person?" Flix laughed and then seemed to realize Kaz didn't find it funny. "No offense, man, but you and people? Don't really get along long term. You've got like three friends and that's because we sort of have to be."

"Wow."

"Am I wrong?"

Kazimir wanted to disagree and be pissed but...no. He ran a hand through his hair, frustrated by the night's turn of events.

"Truth hurts," Flix said. "But hey, it's not like you're the only single one here. I have commitment issues, too."

"I don't have commitment issues." What he had was an inability to properly connect, or even the urge to *want* to do so. Relationships, at least in the traditional sense, require emotional stability and being able to express and receive things like affection.

Kazimir had never seen the appeal of affection. It wasn't a necessary component of anything important. If he was horny, he fucked, and then afterward, he left. Affection didn't get someone into his bed, charm did. And affection wouldn't get him to stay the next morning. It only made him bail faster.

There was no set name for what he was. According to the doc, he'd tested positive for narcissism, psychopathy, Machiavellianism, and dark empathy. It was the last that stuck the most as the medical field in their galaxy continued to learn more and understand what dark empathy entailed. No one had outright labeled him a psychopath, but the words Machiavellianism and dark empath were thrown around *a lot*.

Or, at least they had been before Kazimir's dad had thanked the doctor and then promptly slit his throat so the news wouldn't spread past the main

Brumal's front door.

And Ersa Ambrose thought *Kaz* had problems.

Insert eye roll here.

He'd picked up a new therapist, one that he'd been seeing ever since, but even then, the details of his situation had been carefully contained and minimized. His father ordered him to get help, yet didn't want him sharing all the details he'd need to in order to properly receive it.

"Screw you guys for putting this bullshit in my head." He needed to fight someone. Preferably someone with skills that would allow him to break skin and potentially even bone. Checking the time on his multi-slate, he wondered if it was too late for anyone to be at Friction, the private fight club they co-owned with the Retinue. There was one member of that group he needed to contact anyway…

"Maybe you should give what Baikal did a go," Flix absently suggested. "Worked for his cranky ass."

Kazimir quirked a brow. "What did Kal do?"

"You know," he waved his hand in the air between them. "Hunted Rabbit down like an animal and didn't leave him alone until the feelings were mutual. Forced proximity with a dash of Stockholm syndrome. Find a good guy and corrupt the shit out of him. That sort of thing."

Sounded like it'd take time and effort and energy, three things Kaz wasn't really in the mood to part with. How his cousin had managed to bother was beyond him, even if the final results had gained him a Possessio.

Actually, Rabbit had come along at just the right time. Baikal had lost his father shortly after, and having another family member in the form of his boyfriend seemed to be helping with the grief. He hadn't gone out to the docks to blow money on shitty races the way Kazimir had, anyway.

Rabbit had been a good guy and now he belonged to one of the wicked Devils of Vitality.

Claiming someone like that…That…didn't sound half bad actually.

At his extended silence, Flix turned to look at him, blinking when he noted the expression on Kaz's face. "Wait. I was totally joking. Don't do that. I wasn't serious!"

Kazimir wasn't listening. Baikal had all but challenged him just now, and though Kaz hadn't taken it to heart initially…It really irked him that his cousin truly thought he was better. Sure, he was the leader and, rightfully so, but that didn't mean he had the right to look down on Kazimir. Maybe he didn't have Shout blood coursing through his veins, but he was every bit as Brumal as Void was.

"For real though," Flix tried again. "Don't do anything stupid. I don't want to get in trouble for putting crap in that thick skull of yours. I really didn't mean it. I—" Something caught his attention across the street and he stopped abruptly, brow furrowing. "What's he doing with that asshole?"

"Who?" Kazimir followed his gaze, pausing when his eyes landed on a familiar form.

Nate Narek.

The pretty racer was currently dressed in a tight navy blue t-shirt that hugged him in all the right places. He'd tossed a brown leather jacket over it, but it was far too thin for the cold winter night they were standing in the midst of. His dark brown hair blew wildly in the wind but he didn't so much as flinch from the chill, as though he hadn't felt it at all.

Or maybe he was simply too distracted from helping the old man in his hold into the shiny limousine that had pulled up to the restaurant they were standing in front of.

Kaz scowled at the sight, instantly pegging Mit Parker. He did business throughout the planet, but nothing that involved the Brumal. Still, his reputation proceeded him, and it was well known that the man in his late fifties had a proclivity for buying younger men to warm his bed and keep him company. Typically, sex work wasn't something that bothered Kaz, but seeing this...

"Nate knows Mit Parker?" his voice sounded gravely and low even to him, but Kazimir didn't tear his gaze off the two across the street to bother checking to see if Flix had noticed as well.

"I didn't think so—Wait." Flix turned to him. "You're not still holding a grudge, right?"

He shrugged. He'd kept what'd happened between them at the bar to himself, and from the sounds of things, so had Nate. Not that Kaz was surprised by that fact. He'd anticipated as much.

There'd been two Nareks in attendance when Kazimir and Flix had started school as Freshmen.

Nate was the oldest and was already a junior. His younger sister had been a sophomore. She'd graduated last year, and Nate had attended the ceremony, a fact Kaz knew only because he'd also been there to support a couple of Brumal members who were walking as well.

Kazimir had found him attractive then, but hadn't made any sort of move. If he had, the two of them might have undergone a very different kind of sexual experience with one another. Eventually, Nate would have ended things or Kaz would have gotten bored, but their time at the bar would never have come to pass.

Despite Flix's suggestion, Kazimir was known to only take things by force when it was absolutely necessary. He got off on twisting people around his fingers, on knowing he was above them like that and could play them for a fool and turn them to putty in his hands. It was in his nature to manipulate, to coax and convince. Playing people kept the boredom at bay, so if things had been different and he'd been able to get Nate to sleep with him willingly…

"I don't like that look," Flix stated, but he wasn't referring to Kaz. "At least we know nothing is happening between the two of them."

Across the street, Nate finally managed to get a very drunk Mit into the car with the help of the driver. He rested his hands on his hips and watched the limo pull away from the curb, not taking his eyes off of it until it'd turned the corner down the street and vanished from sight. Then he sighed, long and hard, and ran a hand through his dark hair.

"You know," Flix said. "Mit notoriously only goes for virgins. Gets a sick kick out of busting their cherries. Nate's no virgin."

Something ugly unfurled in Kaz's gut and he carefully settled his expression so his friend didn't notice. "How do you know that?"

"Saw him wander off with some guy once last year," he explained. "Later Nate told me they'd gone drinking and when I asked if they'd fucked he laughed in that telling way and changed the subject. Guy like him doesn't kiss and tell."

Had Pretty Boy been lying to him when he'd claimed to have never slept with a man before? Kazimir found he didn't like that prospect. At all.

"Actually," Flix frowned. "Now that I'm thinking about it, that guy I saw him with was in a pricy three-piece suit. Maybe Nate has a type. Could be he isn't as good as he wants us all to believe." When Kaz stared at him, Flix snorted. "I'm joking, man. What's it matter anyway? You can't seriously still be that pissed about a handful of lost coin. You make that type of money in your sleep thanks to your shares in Daddy's company."

"So this is what he's been doing with his life since graduation?" Kazimir wasn't willing to drop the subject like his friend seemed to want. "Selling himself to the highest bidder?"

"Shut up," Flix said. "I was really just kidding. What's wrong with you tonight? Your sarcasm sensor is busted. Look, Nate has a job. He's a mechanic and he races on the side. He doesn't need to sell himself for money, so whatever you're thinking—"

"Who says I'm thinking anything?" Kazimir was tempted to tell him he'd already taken Nate's payment, but smartly closed his mouth. Something told him that Flix liked the pretty racer more than he was letting on, and that bothered Kaz, but not enough to irritate Flix on purpose.

"Oh, that's right. You'd need a brain for that and you don't have one."

"Ouch." Kaz pressed a palm to his chest. "You wound me."

"Whatever, man. Let's get out of here." Flix bumped his shoulder into his arm and then turned to head down the street away from the club and the restaurant.

Kazimir's mind inadvertently wandered back to the conversation he'd been broaching with Flix before they'd gotten distracted. Since Baikal was so busy these days with his musician, maybe it was far past time for Kaz to find something else to occupy his time as well.

Nate may have paid off his debts, but now there might be a new score to settle between the two of them. If he'd lied about being a virgin and tricked Kaz, he owed him.

And if he hadn't lied, and this was all just some big misunderstanding, well...He still owed him. Why? Because Kazimir said so.

Madden had called Nate a good guy the

other night...Wasn't Flix's suggestion that Kaz find someone who fit that bill?

If Baikal Void could corrupt someone like Rabbit Trace, surely Kazimir could do the same. He'd prove to his cousin and to Flix that there was nothing inherently wrong with him, that he was capable of being a part of a relationship. He'd make Nate Narek turn to putty in his hands.

And then, once his point had been made, he'd toss the older guy aside and return to the life he preferred.

One on his own.

CHAPTER 5:

"Hey, have you seen Port?" Annya leaned over the body of the hoverbike Nate was working on, nibbling nervously on her bottom lip. She was around the same age as him and had joined Quartet Air the same week, so they'd gotten to know one another fairly well during working hours.

"He called out sick," Nate reminded, getting up off the floor so she wouldn't have to bend in order to talk to him. Grabbing at a rag, he started wiping the grease off his hands as she continued to chew on her lip like it was a New Year's feast instead of her own flesh and blood. "Stop doing that."

She let go of her lip with a popping sound and huffed. "He called out last week. Shouldn't he be back by now? You two are close. You haven't spoken to him?"

"Not recently." He'd actually sent Port a couple of messages that had gone unanswered over the weekend and had been planning on stopping by his apartment after work, but he didn't want to worry her further so kept that to himself. Instead, he shrugged like it was no big deal—because really, it most likely was. "Maybe he just got tired of this place and finally found something better."

"He was looking…" she agreed, though she didn't sound convinced.

"We're all looking." Nate had been trying to get out of this place for almost a year now, but nowhere else was hiring. He'd actually been close to caving and accepting his brother-in-law's offer to get him an interview somewhere better after the last company dinner with Mit Parker, but then he'd woken to a "gift" from Silver that had thrown a wrench into that plan.

How Silver had found out he was racing, something Nate explicitly kept a secret from Nuri, was beyond him, but he shouldn't be surprised the guy had found out. And how had he chosen to deliver that news? By purchasing the latest model hoverbike and having it dropped off at Nate's doorstep with a big shiny red bow and everything. There'd even been a card.

It'd been creepy and amazing.

And Nate had immediately slipped into a depression great enough to keep him inside for the rest of the day. He'd felt worthless and burdensome despite not having asked for the expensive gift. Had been torn over whether or not he could accept it, and then if he wasn't going to, how he would convey that to Silver without making things worse for either him or his brother.

He wasn't stupid. He understood that Silver Rein, even as his brother-in-law, wasn't a man to mess with. The gift had been sent and was already there and...In the end Nate had kept it.

He still couldn't figure out if it was meant as a threat or a peace offering, though. With Silver, it could be either or both. Eventually, he was going to have to make a call and find out, but he'd put it off.

"I might swing by his place later," Annya said.

"I'll come with."

"I think you're going to have your hands full, actually," she winced apologetically. "The boss wanted me to tell you you're wanted out front. There's a new client who's requested you. Upside? He's younger than Mit Parker. Downside?"

"Don't tell me," Nate tossed the rag onto the workbench and headed around the bike, "He looks like a rich asshole?"

"More like a rich devil," she corrected.

"Fantastic." If his sister hadn't decided she loved Vitality so much, there was a really good chance Nate would have returned home to Ignite after graduation. The only things keeping him from doing so were Neve and, now, Silver. Being around his brother-in-law made him antsy and overprotective, and no one wanted or needed that.

But if was seriously becoming tempted to find some way off this planet.

The front of the shop was a lot quieter than the back where most of the work was being done, and Nate easily located Sier standing by the open garage doors.

Next to Kazimir Ambrose.

Nate slowed before he could help it, his chest tightening as alarm bells went off in his head. For some reason, he hadn't put two and two together when Annya had mentioned devils, and now felt foolish for not making the connection. There were a lot of Devils on the planet, though, some of them even sort of his friends, so it was just his luck that he'd get saddled with Kaz.

Who'd apparently asked for him.

Fuck.

"Nate, there you are!" Sier waved him over, giving him an annoyed look when she turned her face away from Kazimir. The smile was back in place by the time Nate approached, fake, just like everything else about her. "I didn't realize you were friends with an Ambrose!"

Friends?

He sent a questioning look Kaz's way but the Devil merely shrugged.

Nate didn't correct Sier.

The Ambrose family was well known on the planet for the work they did with Void Corporation. If the Voids had their hands in a proverbial cookie jar, it was a good bet that the Ambroses did as well. Hell, the company Nate really wanted to work for, Flircorp, was actually a subsidiary of Void Aero Dynamics.

"Mr. Ambrose needs someone to check on his bike," Sier motioned to a cherry red hover bike parked nearby. "I told him you were the best!" She leaned in and clapped Nate on the shoulder, whispering, "Don't let me down, kid."

"Should we just leave it here?" Kazimir asked.

"Yes, of course, much easier than you trying to make your way into the back where all the grime and grease is." Sier gave them both a thumbs up. "I'll leave you to it, Nate, and I'll just be in my office if you need anything, Mr. Ambrose."

Nate watched Sier walked away and then sighed. There were a couple of ways he could approach this, but avoidance of the elephant in the room seemed to be the smartest. He didn't want to discuss what had happened between them. It wouldn't make a difference in the long run and would only serve to embarrass him further. "What seems to be the problem with it?"

"Straight to business," Kaz clicked his tongue. "That's kind of boring."

"This is my job," he pointed out. "And yeah, it's kind of boring, but it pays the bills so…"

"Does it?"

Nate didn't like the way the other guy was looking at him. "What's that supposed to mean?"

"Come on, we both know you've got other types of work to help keep the heat on at night."

What the fuck?

"Like racing?" It was the only thing Nate could think of. "I don't make that much, actually. If you recall, I'm only Mid tier. There's not that much coin in those types of races. I don't do it for the money."

"I wasn't talking about that," Kazimir said. "But now I'm curious, if not for the money, why do you do it?"

"Because it's fun." He set his hands on his hips. "Can we please get to the reason you're here?"

"That's what I'm doing."

Nate glanced at the bike, noticing the smears of dirt over the body and the way one of the wheels looked like it'd been stabbed with something sharp and pointy. "This isn't your bike, is it."

It wasn't a question, but Kaz answered anyway. "It is now. I bought it, fair and square."

"Right." Because that made sense. Not.

"Kind of like how I'm about to buy you."

"Ri—" His brain took longer than it should have to catch up, and he stopped himself just in time. "Hold up, what?"

"You don't really think I came all this way to get a piece of junk looked at, do you?" Kazimir took a step closer, closing the distance between the two of them and making Nate realize just how near the Devil had been all this time. "At an unknown shop like this? Please. If one of my vehicles really did have a problem, I've got a personal mechanic back home who would take a look at it within seconds of my call."

Instincts told him to retreat, which was why Nate stubbornly held his ground even when Kazimir took another step closer. He could feel the warm gusts from the man's breath fanning his cheeks, the sensation only adding to his confusion. Flashbacks of that night in the bar threatened to return, but he refused to give in to them.

"Madden tells me you're a good guy, Pretty Boy," Kazimir said silkily. "A *nice* guy. That true?"

"What the hell?" He snapped out of his momentary confusion and shoved Kaz away, hard enough to make him stumble.

Kazimir's eyes narrowed, but he kept his distance and didn't try to corner Nate again. "Not so nice after all, huh. That's okay." His expression changed again, morphing back to that almost maniacal grin that had Nate's hackles rising. "I prefer that."

"I'm not drunk this time," he regrated being the first one to bring it up almost instantly, but kept going. "Whatever you think you're going to get here, think again."

"Confident what I want is another go inside of you, aren't you?"

"If you didn't come to get that bike fixed, I'm going to have to ask you to leave," Nate said, trying not to give away just how unnerved he was by all of this.

He'd handled assholes before, hell, that was practically his life's story, and if anyone had asked prior to now, he would have even claimed he was an expert at it. But...Devils were on a whole different level than the dicks he was used to putting up with, even the rich ones like Mit Parker. Nate had already learned that the hard way, and he had no interest in going through that lesson a second time.

Being involved with someone like Kazimir was dangerous, not just to him, but to his siblings and their reputation. He needed to make himself clear, here and now, so that Kaz left and never bothered him again.

"Going to tell your boss you chased me off?" Kaz lifted a mocking brow. "Something tells me she won't like that, and according to you, you need this job so…Why risk it?"

"What do you want?" For the life of him, he couldn't figure it out. "You said the other night we were square."

"Admitting you owed me after all?"

"No." Nate clenched his hands into tight fists but stood his ground. "I didn't owe you then, but I absolutely don't owe you shit now after what you did."

"What did I do, Pretty Boy?" Kazimir took another step, the corner of his mouth lifting. "Tell me. Spell it out for me. I want to hear everything you remember. You do remember, don't you?" He brought his mouth to Nate's ear. "What it felt like to have me inside of you?"

"Enough." Nate pushed him away. "You could be arrested for what you did to me."

"*I* could never," he arrogantly corrected, brushing down the part of his shirt that Nate had just touched when he'd shoved him. "Laws aren't meant for people like me."

"You're friends with Madden," he pivoted in the hopes of finding a solution and quick. "Take this up with him."

"You want me telling him that we've fucked?"

He felt his cheeks heat and glared. "You both have enough coin he can pay you out of pocket for whatever you still feel you're owed. This has nothing to do with me. He runs the races, I just happened to be a part of that one."

"Someone sounds bitter," he said, then corrected, "Or is envious a better word choice? We do have money, more than you could ever dream of. But that's not what this is about anymore. I like getting what I'm owed, is that so wrong?"

"It is when what you lost was placed on a bet," Nate snapped back, cursing under his breath and risking a glance over his shoulder toward his boss's office. When the blinds didn't shake or anything else to indicate he'd been overheard, he turned back and forced himself to lower his voice. "I don't owe you anything. As far as I'm concerned, there's literally nothing between us and no reason for you to be here other than you're bored. If that's the case, go find someone else to bother because I'm too busy for this shit."

"Make time then."

Nate blew out a breath and pinched the bridge of his nose. "Seriously? There are loads of people who'd love to throw themselves at a Devil of Vitality. Go find one of them."

"Nah, I'm good here."

"I—"

"You aren't catching on quick enough, Pretty Boy." Kazimir crossed his arms. "You owe me not because you lost that race, but because I say so. I'm coming to collect," he shrugged a single shoulder, "This is merely advanced notice, brought on by my generous heart. Keep ignoring my generosity, and I might have to rearrange your face a bit before we proceed. I don't really want to do that. I actually kind of like your face. It's hot."

Nate scowled. "Do you hear yourself when you speak?" He held up a hand before the other guy could respond. "Never mind. Look, can we just get this over with so I can get back to work?"

"You're not nearly as concerned about all of this as you should be."

"Trust me, I am." He was just too poor to allow that type of thing to get in the way of his job. "I just know better than to show fear in front of a predator. I get it, okay? You're terrifying and intimidating and all the other words ending in 'ing' that mean badass. You're also three years my junior and currently standing in my place of work interfering with my livelihood. Maybe it's because you're rich, or maybe it's because you've yet to join the adult workforce, but there are a lot scarier things in this world than a spoiled trust fund baby waving his mafia connections around."

There kind of weren't, but Nate was admittedly afraid of being broke so…It wasn't a total lie. Of course, Kazimir didn't need to know that Nate's brother had recently married into wealth and there was no way Nuri would allow Nate to become destitute. Not that Nate would ever be able to live with himself if things ever came to that.

Good Light. How would he be able to look Nuri in the eyes if it got that bad?

If he became that big of a burden on the one person who'd always put him and their sister first? No, Nuri had finally found happiness. Nate couldn't—

Kazimir snapped his fingers in front of his face, forcing him out of the spiral his thoughts had been taking him down. "What the fuck was that?"

He cleared his throat. "Nothing."

"Do you have some kind of psychological damage, Pretty Boy?"

"Again, I'm older than you."

"We're not on campus, and no one is around to hear me be disrespectful."

"Stop calling me that."

"Don't like it?"

"I don't like anything about you or whatever this is."

"Even better. Apparently that's how things started for them as well."

"Started for...who?" Nate frowned.

"My cousin and his Possessio."

"Your...What?" He waved a hand in the air. "I'm sorry, you're making even less sense than you were a moment ago. What does you being here bothering me at work have to do with your cousin?"

"It's simple really," Kazimir replied, and it was obvious from his cavalier tone he truly believed that. "All our lives, we've always had the same things. Sure, he was raised to be the leader, but that's different. I don't mind taking a step back when it comes to business, but our regular lives? Hell no. If Kal has something, I want it too."

Nate blinked at him, certain he was misunderstanding, but when Kaz didn't elaborate it became apparent he was not. "You're not seriously telling me this is all because some weird complex you have with your cousin, right? Like, you feel competitive toward him or some other such nonsense and somehow that's why you're here right now?"

"You can call it whatever you want to," he said. "All I know is seeing Baikal happy made me want to give it a try."

"Okay…So go," Nate made a shooing motion toward the door, "do that. You certainly aren't going to find happiness here, with me."

"I'm guessing that's what Rabbit said in the beginning, too." Kazimir smirked. "I knew you were the perfect candidate."

"For what?" Did he even want to know? Nate was pretty sure the answer was he did not.

"I told you. I'm here to buy you, Pretty Boy." He snorted when Nate made a face of disgust. "Don't act so high and mighty. I saw you with Mit Parker the other night. It's obvious the types of things you get into when you aren't here getting covered in grease."

"I was too wasted the other night to properly covey this, so let me try now." Nate straightened to his full height. "I think you're disgusting and I want nothing to do with you."

"Sure you're not just mad at yourself?" Kaz suggested. "Mad that, ultimately, you're the reason that happened to you in the first place. You made yourself vulnerable to predators the second you started drinking to access."

"You raped me!" Nate hissed, lowering his voice at the last second. "And now you're trying to say it's my fault?"

"You gave in eventually," he shrugged.

"That's..." Nate was at a loss for words. "You're insane."

"You keep saying. Luckily for you, I don't bruise easily, and I won't take the name-calling out on your ass the next time I bend you over. There's some more generosity for you. Make sure you're taking notes."

"I'm never having sex with you again."

"You didn't think you'd have it with me the first time either."

Nate stilled. "Are you actually telling me right now that you intend to force me—"

"To take my cock?" Kazimir cut him off. "Yeah. Yeah, that's exactly what I'm saying. So, be good for me and give in, just like you did that night. Didn't it feel better once you had? Once you were moaning and riding me—"

Nate swung before he could help it, his fist connecting with the side of Kazimir's face with a loud sound. His hand instantly exploded in pain, but aside from the slight hiss of breath, he kept that to himself and immediately retreated a couple of steps.

His electricity bill was two weeks late and if he didn't get his paycheck Friday he was going to be royally screwed, but suddenly that fear was a distant memory in the face of the furious Devil who was now staring daggers at him. For the first time in a long time, Nate also didn't have that tiny voice screaming at him internally, telling him how big of a burden he'd be if he acted out like this. Right now, that voice was actually quiet.

Maybe it shouldn't have been.

Maybe then he would have been smart enough to apologize and run, instead of doing what he did next.

"You're wrong," he stated. "I didn't enjoy a single thing about that night. I don't trade my body and I don't hate myself. Not sure where you got that impression," he'd probably said something at the bar, but that was neither here nor there, "but you're wrong."

"That so?" Kazimir rubbed at his split lip, glancing down at the spec of red he wiped off onto the pad of his thumb.

"Yeah," Nate said.

"If it isn't self-loathing, what is it?" Kazimir tilted his head in thought, eyeing Nate down like he could see beneath his skin at his insides. "You do seem rather confident, not typically a trait in someone who hates themselves, even secretly...But it's something similar because you wouldn't have wallowed so pathetically after drinking.... I can tell that you've been thinking about me, how much you hate that you enjoyed—lie all you want, baby, I know you did. I was there, remember?"

Some sick part of Nate had enjoyed it, but that didn't matter. "Whether I got off in the end or not doesn't change anything."

"Sure it does," he corrected. "It changes how you view the interaction as a whole. Because I made you come, you feel pathetic. Because you feel pathetic, you've been thinking about it."

"The only pathetic one here is you," Nate snapped. "I don't have to force people to sleep with me."

"I don't usually either," Kaz said.

"Then why did you?" he tried to keep the hint of confusion out of his tone but failed.

"It wasn't about sex. It was about control. It was about tearing you down and feeding your self-loathing. Only, now you're saying that you don't actually have that affliction. I'm not usually wrong about these things."

"You don't usually fuck people against their will and can usually read their minds, that it? Sounds like a load of bullshit to me. News flash, I didn't sign up to be your freaky firsts. I'm not some experiment you can get your kicks off to. I'm not interested."

"If I tied you up right now, I bet I could get you interested. Your body, anyway."

"Just leave." A part of Nate was afraid he was telling the truth, not just about his plans, but about the fact that Nate's body might betray him the same way it had that night. He'd been hard and achy, and toward the end there, he'd pushed back to meet each and every thrust of Kazimir's thick length.

Nate didn't hate himself. He hated what his choices could mean for the people around him. That wasn't the same thing, but it did boil down to a similar point.

This conversation had to end.

"You said you needed me to play a part? I'm not going to do that. If you're planning on competing with your cousin, find someone willing to help you. That's your best shot, and I'm not that person. I'm not selling myself to Mit or anyone else. You're right about one thing, I don't have the kind of money you and Madden do. But I'm not desperate enough to be in that kind of business. My brother raised me better than that. You took what didn't belong to you once. I won't let that happen again. I don't owe you anything, Ambrose. And I never will because this is where you and I come to a close."

Kaz eyed him for a moment and then said, "I get the sense that if you did owe me, you would cave."

"But I don't." Although that statement was true and the fact he'd been able to guess as much made Nate infinitely more uncomfortable. "Please. Just go."

Kaz clicked his tongue. "It's too late to plead now. Maybe if you'd led with that a few minutes ago I might have listened, gotten bored, and given up. I figured it out though, during your little speech.

That's the missing piece, isn't it? The part I didn't catch, the thing that changes it from a self-loathing issue to another one altogether."

Nate didn't feel good about this.

"You brought up that I have a complex? What about you, Pretty Boy?"

"I don't know what you're talking about."

"No? Should I spell it out for you?" Kazimir slid his hands into his front pockets and smirked. "You got me. I was wrong. It's not that you don't like to lose, it's that you don't like to disappoint Big Brother."

"Shut up." Nate felt himself go cold. There was no way Kaz had picked up on that from just a few thoughtlessly spoken sentences. Maybe if Nate downplayed it now, he'd at least—

"Does he even know you race, Narek? What about all that time spent with Mit Parker? Does Nuri know about that?"

"Shut up!" Nate swung a second time but Kazimir saw it coming.

He captured Nate's wrist and twisted him, forcing his back to his front so he could contain Nate even through his struggles. "What about that time you spent with me, hmm? Does he know about that?"

Nate froze. "Stop."

"Should I tell him?"

"Kazimir. Stop."

"If you want to get people to do what you want, Pretty Boy," Kaz told him, "you need to get better at reading them." He glanced over toward the back of the building where everyone else was working—thankfully—out of sight. "Here, let me demonstrate."

Nate tripped as he was suddenly shoved out of Kazimir's arms. By the time he spun around, Kaz was back to that casual stance, as if their minor scuffle had never happened.

"I need someone to be my boyfriend, to help me convince Baikal that I'm capable of something like that. But also because I'm curious and want to give it a shot. We had fun that night at the bar."

"That wasn't fun for me," Nate corrected, but Kaz merely shrugged.

"Next time we do this, I suggest you know your place and give in sooner." Kaz's eyes twinkled knowingly. "I wonder what Big Brother would think if he knew you'd been reprimanded by your boss."

"I don't know what fucked up game you're actually playing here," Nate's voice shook slightly, "but I want no part in it. This is my *life*, asshole. You can't just—"

"Everything okay out there, Mr. Ambrose?" Sier suddenly called from her office, leaning out of the doorway with a concerned look painted across her brow.

Shit.

"Actually," Kaz sent Nate a quick glance, "your employee was just explaining to me that there's nothing he can do. Unfortunately, I guess the bike is a lost cause."

"What?!" Sier stormed out and rushed over to them, violently shaking her head. "Surely that's not the case, Mr. Ambrose! We're the best in town! You want it fixed? We can do that for you!"

"According to Nate here, you can't." Kaz motioned toward him with his chin and then shrugged. "It's fine. I suppose I should have known. Wishful thinking on my part. Anyway, since there's no longer any reason for me to hang around…" He winked at Nate. "I'll see you later, Pretty—"

"Wait." This wasn't happening. Nate needed to stop him. He couldn't just say all of that nonsense and then leave!

"No can do," Kaz said, already retreating toward the wide-open doors. "Got the response I was looking for, so now I need to, how did you put it? 'Get out'?"

Sier was fuming. "You did not say that to a client, Narek."

"No way to talk to anyone," Kazimir agreed, digging the hole even deeper for Nate and seemingly enjoying every second of it. "Even if we are friends."

"We are *not* friends," Nate snapped, clamping his mouth shut too late. He could practically feel the fireballs shooting from Sier's eyes as she glared at him.

Kazimir chuckled, winked a second time, and then swiveled on his heels and disappeared into the night.

Like the total nightmare, demonic hell beast he was.

"Narek," Sier snapped. "In my office. Now!"

CHAPTER 6:

"I don't want it," Nate barely recognized the restraint in his own voice as he spoke. He was standing in his garage, staring at the delivery the postman had made the other day, with a sick, twisted feeling in his gut.

After Kazimir's impromptu appearance, Nate had come to the stark realization that if he could stand up against a Devil of Vitality, he should be able to muster the courage to do so with the other psychopath who'd inserted himself into his life.

"It's a gift," the man on the other end of the line replied back cooly. The sound of keys clicking and papers shuffling came through every now and again, cluing Nate into the fact he was in the office. "Didn't your brother ever teach you it's rude to refuse a thoughtful gesture?"

"Don't." He stopped himself from losing his cool and closed his eyes. "Don't bring him into this."

"It isn't my fault you both make it so easy."

"Silver."

His brother-in-law chuckled. "He does that as well, whenever he's cross with me. Says my name in almost that exact tone. You two are very alike, you know? But also, incredibly different. Street racing, Nate?" He made a sound of displeasure. "What would Nuri say about that?"

And there it was. The real reason Silver Rien had sent him a brand new hoverbike. Not just any bike, either. The X-Con Rien 243 was worth more money than Nate could make in a decade.

"Is this a bribe," Nate asked, "or a threat?"

"I used to think you were a slow moron," Silver told him, sounding pleased. "It's nice to know that isn't the case after all."

"I don't want or need this," he tried again. "Just tell me what you want and then have someone come pick it up."

"The bike is yours. If you want to get rid of it, do it on your own dime."

Nate bristled. He could never do that.

"You can't, can you?" Silver said a moment later. "Do you want to hear an interesting theory I came up with the last time we saw one another, Nate?"

"No." No he really did not.

The last time they'd seen one another had been at the wedding. Nate had been the only one in attendance who hadn't been ecstatic at the merger of their two families. Everyone else seemed to think it was inevitable—apparently, most people on the planet Ignite had already assumed Nuri and Silver had been dating for years and years. Even Neve had been happy for them, though she'd been the hardest to sell on the relationship at the start.

Nate accepted that Silver was the person his older brother had chosen, but that didn't mean he had to one hundred percent *like* it. Knowing who Silver was made it impossible. Though it was a well-kept secret.

"I know secrets too," he said, even though that little voice inside that fought for self-preservation begged him not to. "You're a psychopath."

"That could work in your favor," Silver didn't sound even remotely surprised that Nate knew. Ignite wasn't like Vitality, where the rulers unapologetically marched the streets uncaring if anyone knew they had an anti-social personality disorder. On their home planet, Silver had hidden that particular fact from his people, most likely to protect his position as CEO of Rien Inc. more so than the crown atop his head.

"How do you figure?"

"The expensive piece of machinery in front of you is one indication," he replied. "The only attachment I have is toward Nuri. I'm also an emperor. Money means nothing to me. If there's anything you want, I can gift it to you as easily as I did that bike."

"It's not a gift," Nate argued. "Stop calling it that."

"All right."

Nate waited for him to continue, but the silence quickly became too much for him to handle, no doubt exactly what Silver intended. He dropped his head, defeated. "Are you going to tell him?"

"That you're risking your life and reputation by illegally street racing?" He grunted. "That wasn't my intention. Nuri has enough to worry about without adding the things his little brother gets up to on the list."

Nate winced.

"Did that hurt?" Silver asked, a creepy note to his voice that hadn't been there a minute ago.

He went cold. "What?"

"The secret I was referring to before," he said. "That's it. I have a serious question for you, Nate." Silver paused and then asked, "Would you like to see a doctor?"

"There's nothing wrong with me," the lie shot off his tongue.

"I didn't say there was."

"Then—"

"Many people suffer from depression," Silver stated. "There's nothing to be ashamed of."

"I'm not ashamed." He wasn't.

It was tempting to ask how Silver knew though. Over the years, Nate had become a master at keeping those darker feelings of his hidden from the world. Hell, even his sister, who up until six months ago had lived with him, didn't know. He was careful not to—

"You think you're a burden," Silver's words cut through his thoughts like a knife and Nate sucked in a sharp breath. "I knew that was it. You're so opinionated, and yet one look from Nuri can instantly silence you."

"He raised me." After their parents had died suddenly in an accident, Nuri as the oldest had been forced to take on all of the responsibility. Eventually, he'd shipped both Nate and Neve here to Vitality in order to give them their best chance at a good education, but the vast distance didn't change anything.

Every month, the two of them would receive money in their joint accounts to help keep their lives comfortable here. Even when he'd been younger, Nate had recognized the sacrifices Nuri must have been making in order to support not just himself, but his siblings as well.

The sole reason Nate tried so hard to keep his depression under wraps was because he didn't want to add more to his brother's plate. If Nuri found out, he'd worry, maybe even get into a fight with Silver and try to take leave off of work and come visit... The two of them had only been married for a little bit now, and while Nate didn't like the Emperor of Ignite, or think he was anywhere near good enough for his brother, that didn't mean he wanted to be the thing that came between them.

Nuri was happy?

That was all that mattered. That couldn't change, not after all the hardships he'd endured for them.

"Will the bike help?" Silver asked then, and at first Nate didn't understand the sudden change in topic. "Racing seems to make you feel good," he elaborated. "Will the bike help?"

"Are you…trying to fix my depression?" That was…odd. And unexpected.

"Only you can fix that," he said. "But I am trying to make it better. You matter to Nuri, which means you have to matter to me."

"…Thanks?"

"It's both a bribe and a threat, Nate."

Well. The gratitude had lasted longer than three seconds at least.

"Your brother wants to visit sometime after New Year, and I've approved the leave for us both."

"What?" Nate's gaze whipped around the practically empty garage, panic setting in when he thought about the backed-up bills he'd yet to pay. New Year's wasn't for another month and a half, but so much could happen within that type of timeframe.

What if they came over and realized how much he was actually struggling? Since he'd yet to return to the races since the incident with Kaz, he'd been relying on his paychecks from Quartet Air. He could barely make both the electric and water payments. If either was turned off while they were here visiting…That'd be almost as bad as Nuri finding out he hated his life.

The life Nuri had literally shed blood, sweat, and tears to give him.

Nate sucked.

He was a monster.

A selfish, self-centered, ungrateful monster.

Nuri deserved better. So much better. So did Neve.

Hell, everyone who came into Nate's life deserved—

"We'll be staying at the Venture," Silver's comment put a stop to Nate's spiraling. "The hotel is better equipped to deal with my needs. I'm sure you agree."

"Yeah." Of course, he did, but now there was also the fear that Silver knew about Nate's dwindling —empty. It was empty—bank account. If he did, though, surely he would have sent more than the bike? Unless this was a test to see if he'd sell it for the funds?

"I can't sell the bike," he said; the admittance meant more for him, but he spoke out loud before he could think better of it.

"I'm well aware," Silver said. "If you did, you'd feel guilty, wouldn't you? Because even though there are strings attached, it is a gift from me, and since my money is now your brother's money...Well. You could never give away something your brother spent the time and energy choosing just for you, could you? That would make all his efforts a waste."

"They were your efforts," Nate corrected in a poor attempt to deflect, but of course, the emperor saw through him.

"You have a month."

He frowned. "To do what?"

"Fix yourself," Silver ordered. "I don't care how, just do it. There's only so long you can keep this from Nuri, and I don't want him finding out about it any more than you do. Do you want him feeling the same way?"

"No, of course not."

"He will though. You know he will. He'll feel awful and blame himself that you're unhappy. Beat himself up over it and think it's because he wasn't a good enough caretaker."

"He was!"

"Yes, which is why you're going to get your act together. You have a month to do it on your own, Nate, otherwise, contrary to what I implied earlier, I will find a way to do it for you. Whether you like that outcome or not. Are we understood?"

"It's not that easy." If it had been, Nate would have found a way to get over his depression and this feeling of uselessness before, without needing threats from Silver to do so.

"Find a way to make it easy then," Silver said. "One month. The clock is ticking. Until then, your secrets are safe with me."

"Gee," he somehow managed to drawl out sarcastically, "thanks."

"You're welcome."

The line went dead and Nate tugged the earpiece out of his ear and shoved it back into the side of his multi-slate, a flash of annoyance mixing with the sheer panic he was now feeling. There was little doubt in his mind that Silver would follow through on his claims if Nate didn't magically find a way to handle his depression on his own.

The thing was, it wasn't even really depression. Not entirely, in any case. Nate didn't struggle to get out of bed in the morning or want to kill himself or anything like that. He just wished he could vanish. Disappear one day, leaving no trace. Remove himself from the lives of the people he cared about so there was no longer a chance of him disappointing them.

The fact that in and of itself would then cause them greater grief and disappointment was the only reason he didn't act on those wants. Why he didn't simply give into the urge to pack up and run.

Nate had been old enough to remember the pain losing their parents had brought them all, and there was no way he could do that to Nuri a second time. So he stayed and he pushed through and he pretended like everything was fine. Like he didn't spend every waking moment terrified that he was going to make a mistake and become an even bigger burden to his brother.

Street racing was the one thing he allowed himself, and that was mostly because he'd already gotten into it by the time these fucked up feelings had begun. He couldn't pinpoint exactly when it'd started, only knew that one day he'd woken up with the crippling fear that he wasn't good enough and never would be. That his brother had wasted his life making those sacrifices for him.

That Nuri would be better off if he didn't have to worry about Nate and what he was doing.

Fuck.

Nate tried hard not to look at the bike as he twisted on his heels and stormed upstairs, headed straight for the bathroom. The house was tiny compared to most, but had three bedrooms, though two of them hadn't been occupied for some time. The paint on the walls was peeling and the kitchen faucet leaked, but it was the only home he really knew, and even though there was no great attachment he felt toward it personally, it was the place Nuri had purchased for them when he'd first sent them to Vitality to start their new lives.

And here Nate was, allowing the place to go to ruin.

As soon as he was in the bathroom, he flicked the shower on, getting under the spray without bothering to strip out of his clothes first. It'd been months since Neve had moved out, and yet the old habit of secluding himself away whenever he felt a breakdown coming on was too hard to shake.

How had Silver noticed?

He'd been surly at the wedding, sure, but Nate had been sure not to appear sad. He hadn't even been sad, really. Had actually been happy, despite not liking Silver very much, that his brother had found someone and was starting a new chapter in his life. If, for a brief moment, the demonic voices in his head had pointed out Silver's station also meant Nate could cause more damage if he messed up... He'd shut them down. Tucked them away.

Silver Rien, the Emperor of Ignite and CEO of Rien Corp, could protect both himself and Nuri from bad press. If anything, Nate should have felt more freedom, felt like he had more room to breathe, instead of the opposite.

At the wedding, the cold realization that now more eyes would be turned to him, trying to find his flaws whenever he was on Ignite just so they could use it against Nuri, had momentarily gotten to him. But Nate had done what he'd always done.

Gone to the bathroom to wallow alone and breathe through the sense of panic. There hadn't been a shower there, of course, and even if there had been, he certainly wouldn't have dared get his suit wet, but there was no fear of drenching himself now, while in his own home.

Showering was a part of the routine. Part of the ruse. So long as he washed off the mistakes and shortcomings of the day, he could always start tomorrow fresh. Clean slate. No matter what, Nate had to keep going.

He couldn't be a burden.

Recollections of the other day, when Sier had torn him a new one in her office after Kazimir had left returned, and he grimaced. The hotshot's words trickled back through his mind, tickling at his psyche like the monster it was, and Nate grit his teeth against the wave of pathetic self-loathing he momentarily felt.

He should have acted better and kept his cool longer. If he hadn't snapped at the end there, the screaming from his boss wouldn't have been so bad.

And that self-satisfied gleam in Kazimir's eyes

wouldn't have been so damn bright.

Nate had been telling himself since that day that it was over, that the Devil had come to toy with him out of some sick sense of retribution for losing the race all those weeks ago, and now that he had, that was that. It was easier to convince himself when he didn't think about the other comments Kaz had made. The more confusing ones about relationships and wanting him.

Want him? Nate? A guy like Kazimir Ambrose?

He was a total dick, sure, but he was also a Devil with a title and a future brighter than the god's damn sun. He had money and fame and respect. He wasn't like Nate, and therefore, there was no chance in hell he could actually *like* Nate.

It'd been a fucked-up game, a momentary blip that was now over.

Nate had to shake it, shake the cloying feeling of dread and trepidation. Shake the urge to glance over his shoulder whenever he was at work now. Kaz hadn't shown up again, which should be further proof he wouldn't ever.

He inhaled slowly and exhaled, imagining that all of that self-pity and doubt was spilling out of him at the same time.

Because not releasing those feelings, keeping them, and feeding them would be the same as giving up, and if he quit, he'd well and truly become burdensome. Sure, the lights were about to be shut off and he still wasn't sure how he'd pay to keep them on. Yeah, he'd only made it to Mid tier in the races even after all these years.

Big deal that the most romantic attention he'd received since graduation had come from a psycho with control issues and a penchant for gambling.

Nate had a job and a home and siblings who loved him. That was more than many others could say. He needed to be grateful. Needed to remember that even if it didn't feel like it, all of those things still gave him a purpose, murky as it was.

If he mattered, the world kept turning. If he mattered, no one would regret having him in their life.

Nate had to matter. He had to.

So, whether Neve was still living here or not, Nate would wash this sticky feeling down the drain, change into his pajamas, and go to bed with a smile on his face. Because that was the one thing that had ever been asked of him.

Keep it together.

Always keep it together.

Silver thought his threats were enough to get Nate to seek professional help, that much was apparent. But Nate didn't need it.

Nate was fine.

He had to be, and it was going to take a lot more than Silver Rien to get him to admit otherwise.

CHAPTER 7:

Someone was sobbing in the next room, but they all pretended not to hear it as they stood around. Baikal had called this meeting, and they'd assembled at the Bunker, a secret location owned by the Brumal that not even the Imperial family could find. The bottom level, where they were currently, was mostly used for housing prisoners and interrogating, but it was also where the official Butcher conducted most of his experiments.

"Can you shut him up?" Flix acknowledged the crying first, heaving a sigh of annoyance as he set the to-go coffee cup down on the long wooden table he was seated at. He and Baikal were the only two using it, the others standing around the perimeter of the room for one reason or another.

"It is getting rather tiresome to listen to," Saint agreed, holding up both hands when Berga tore his gaze off whatever the fuck he was working on to send him a dark look.

Kazimir crossed his arms and propped a shoulder against the wall, glancing over toward the closed door that led into the side room. He'd just come from campus, and he was hungry, which meant he wanted this over and done with as soon as possible.

"How are you two settling in?" Baikal asked Yuze, who was hanging by the exit.

Both he and Saint had been located on the other side of Vitality for the past two years, sent there by Sullivan Void to oversee part of the business with their parents. Since his death, Baikal had made it his mission to rearrange things as he saw fit, reform the empire in his own image, so to speak.

It'd caused problems amongst the older generation who worked for Void Conglomerate. They lacked the same kind of loyalty the Bruma mafia had, and were giving Kal a hard time over anything and everything. Because of that, he'd ordered Saint's mother back to Valeo to help get them in line. Yuze's father had also been called home for a similar reason.

It sucked that they were still in schooling, that their age affected widespread opinion of them within the business world, but Kazimir also understood it. There was a lot left to learn from those older than them, and they'd been thrust too quickly into these leadership roles. No one had anticipated Sullivan's untimely death, even after he'd been diagnosed with the disease.

Still, the silver lining was having Saint and Yuze back, making the Satellite complete for the first time in years.

Not that Kaz had missed them. He hadn't. He

was simply sick of having to listen to Flix and Berga interact like an old married couple on his own.

"Fine," Yuze replied. "Vail is an interesting place. The curriculum is a lot better than Spring where we were going."

"All of our credits transferred as well," Saint added.

"And the rest?" Baikal was sitting at the end of the table, his back facing the door where the crying was still coming from. He had his legs crossed and a glass cup filled with black coffee he regularly sipped on. "Have you caught up on everything else?"

Everything having to do with Brumal business, he meant.

"I have questions about the Shepherds, actually," Yuze said.

"Talk to Flix then."

"Why me?"

"Because you're the one I'm assigning as an intermediary."

Flix groaned. "What? No, come on, Kal. Pick someone else."

"You're the Runner," he reminded. "Are you really telling me to give someone else your job?"

He sat back and scowled. "I don't want anything to do with them, and you know it."

Kazimir's interest was piqued by that. "Why not?"

The Shepherds had recently had a change in leadership as well. Kaz hadn't bothered with their little gang unless necessary—which wasn't often—

but it was important to keep them in line and establish ground rules before this new boss got any bright ideas. The only reason their operation had been allowed to keep running at all was because they were small fry.

"They don't step on our toes," Baikal said, "and we can continue coexisting in peace. Their last leader was pushing it. If he hadn't been murdered by someone else, I was this close to giving the order myself. Tell the new guy in charge as much."

Flix didn't seem pleased at all.

"No, really," Kaz pushed. "What kind of problem do you have with them?"

"Nothing," Flix muttered, a bald-faced lie if Kazimir had ever heard one, but there was no chance to point out as much.

"I should have this perfected by the end of the week," Berga informed Kal, holding up a glass vial. He swished the golden liquid within it, eyeing it carefully before placing it back within an odd machine that made too many noises.

That, coupled with the crying, pushed Flix over the edge—or maybe he was just being pissy over his orders, who knew—and he shot to his feet dramatically. "If my part here is done, I've got somewhere to be."

"Yeah," Baikal waved him toward the door, "meeting with the Shepherds."

Flix made an annoyed sound but bowed his head and turned, practically shoving his way past Yuze.

"What is that?" Saint asked Berga a moment later.

"A way for us to get those board members under control," Baikal answered for him. "What? You didn't really think I was going to rely solely on your parents, did you?"

Saint chuckled.

"It's a slow-acting poison," Berga explained, the note of excitement building with each sentence. "Tasteless and odorless. As long as the antidote is taken, it'll remain dormant in the body, but if a dose is skipped within the first six months…"

"What happens?" Kaz was morbidly curious. The Butcher always came up with the best stuff.

"Microscopic lab-grown parasites eat their insides," he said. "I've named them glorp. Would you like to see a blown-up image of what they look like?"

"Pass," Yuze made a face of disgust, but Kaz was already crossing the room.

He leaned over the small workstation Berga was at, staring at the computer screen at pictures of weird creatures that appeared to be fuzzy coins more than anything else. "What are those?" He pointed to the things that looked like long hair follicles coming off the circular body.

"Hooks," Berga stated proudly. "Everything is better with hooks. They burrow them into whatever they can and use them to pull things apart."

"It shreds people's insides?" Saint let out a low whistle. "And you're planning on using that on the board members?"

"They won't know until it's too late," Baikal told them. "Then it's a matter of holding the antidote over their heads to get them to comply."

"That's twisted," Kazimir straightened and clapped Berga on the shoulder. "I love it."

For the most part, they always tried to keep Brumal dealings separate from the official business side of things. Running Void Conglomerate was completely legal throughout the entire universe, after all. But when push came to shove, they were mafia at their core, and sometimes the best way to deal with a problem was reminding people of that fact.

Maybe that's the angle Kaz should have used on Nate Narek, instead of showing up at Quartet Air with a used bike he'd purchased for pennies. The excuse had been mostly to test the waters, a way for him to see how open to the concept of becoming his the pretty racer would be. Not very had been the answer, and despite his parting threat, Kazimir intended to leave things where they were.

Nate wasn't interested? Fine. It hit at Kaz's pride, sure, but there were plenty of fish in the sea, and he had enough on his plate to not need to add seducing a man who claimed not to want him to it.

It was Narek's loss.

That shop was a sinking ship, anyone with eyes could see that. Soon, even having patrons such as Mit Parker wouldn't be enough to keep Quartet Air afloat, and then Nate would be out of a job and scrambling to figure his life out at the last minute.

Perhaps he'd turn to Mit.

Kaz wasn't overly pleased with that prospect, but he forced himself to shove all unpleasant thoughts of the racer out of his mind. He wasn't the type to dwell on pointless things.

What Nate Narek did or didn't do was of no concern to him.

"How are things going with Pious Prince?" Baikal asked.

"We've given him access as requested," Kaz said. "But there's no word on whether or not he's been successful in finding what he's looking for."

"What is he looking for?" Saint hummed in thought. "Has to be important for him to come all the way here. Isn't he usually located in another galaxy?"

"The Ancient keep to their own territory," Baikal agreed. "That's why it's so important we handle this with finesse."

"Then why put Kaz on it?" Yuze laughed when Kazimir growled. "That was a joke. Mostly."

"Pious has something I want," Baikal told Yuze. "I need someone with enough skill at playing people to get him to give it to me with little complaint. Unless you've somehow developed that particular skillset…"

"Nope." Yuze ran a hand through his light hair and shrugged. "I still trip over my own words, thanks."

"Sometimes being a narcissist comes in handy," Saint teased Kazimir, elbowing him lightly in the side.

"You'd all crash and burn without me," Kazimir said.

"*And* sometimes being a narcissist turns you into an egomaniac."

"Those two things are more often one and the same," Berga informed them, as though they really weren't aware. "You should pay more attention in Professor Delmar's class, Saint. It will be a riveting learning experience. He's the most knowledgeable on the subject, after all."

"What subject?" Yuze cocked his head.

"Psychopathy, of course."

"Of course."

Berga frowned and glanced up from his work once more. "Weren't we discussing Kazimir just now?"

"Pot calling the kettle black," Kaz drawled.

"Oh, you and I are vastly different in our neuropsychiatric disorders," he disagreed. "For example, I've displayed a complete and total lack of empathy toward others. You, however, have the ability to empathize, at least on the surface level. Though I do suppose we both suffer from poor behavioral controls." He abruptly stopped talking and stared off into the distance for a full five seconds before snapping his fingers. "I forgot to administer the antidote."

"Huh?" Yuze frowned.

"To test subject 5," Berga said. "That's my error."

"Test subject..." He pointed toward the door to the adjoined room. "That guy?"

"Yes." He sighed. "How very disappointing."

"When did he stop crying?" Kazimir hadn't noticed.

Baikal checked the time on his multi-slate. "About four minutes ago."

"Too long ago to correct now, I'm afraid." Berge shook his head and then motioned to Yuze. "Would you order the man in the hall to bring me another test subject, please?"

"Another one?" When all Berga did was stare, Yuze gave in. "All right, hold on."

"Try not to run through bodies like the last time," Baikal ordered. "We're running out of enemies."

"Isn't that a good thing?" Saint asked.

"That depends."

"On what?"

"On whether you're Berga or not," Kazimir laughed and finished for Kal, knowing exactly where his cousin had been taking it.

"It would be unfortunate to have to start using innocents," Berga agreed absently.

Kaz snorted. "Define innocents."

He considered it and then admitted, "I'm unclear of those exact parameters. I'll need Flix to help me if it ever comes to that."

"It will not," Baikal warned.

"What's this thing you want so badly from Pious?" Saint changed the subject.

Kazimir groaned and rolled his eyes. "It's so dumb, man."

Baikal glared. "It is not."

"It is though."

"You wouldn't understand."

"Stop—"

"Oh," Saint cut Kaz off, "So it's something for Rabbit?"

Kazimir turned to him. "How did you know that?"

"Easy." He shrugged. "There's only one thing you suck at, Kaz."

"What's that?"

"Caring about people," Berga filled in. When that earned him a bitter look, he tried soothing the sting by adding, "Don't worry. I don't comprehend it either."

"Oh great," Kaz did nothing to mask his sarcasm, "I feel so much better."

Berga nodded like that made all the sense in the world and he'd just done a good job.

Kazimir had half a mind to bargain for the rare instrument Baikal wanted from Pious and use it to beat the ever-loving daylight out of everyone in this room.

CHAPTER 8:

Nate tapped his foot nervously as the therapist went over the questionnaire he'd just filled out. Part of him still believed this was an epic waste of time, but the other hadn't been able to escape the urge to call and book the appointment.

At least he'd be able to tell Silver he'd tried, even if nothing came of being here. And so long as he did that, this secret would be kept between them, right?

"Have you always been a people pleaser, Nate?" the therapist, a woman in her mid-fifties with curly red hair and a kind smile asked from her seat across the long desk.

He was in a leatherback chair in front of her, the clock hanging on the wall to his right slowly ticking down the time. Their first session was an extensive one meant to last for two whole hours, and he was hating every single minute of it.

"I wouldn't say I am one," he replied.

She hummed and set the tablet down on her desk before meeting his gaze. "No? Then how would you explain your reaction to your boss in the story you told me earlier?"

He'd opened up about Sier screaming at him the other day. It'd gone on for a while and had been loud enough that the rest of the shop had overheard most of it. When Nate had finally been permitted to leave the office, they'd all averted their gazes.

"You mean how I was quiet?" He shrugged. "How else was I meant to react? She's my boss."

"Yes, but you told me you hadn't done anything wrong. If you weren't deserving of being yelled at like that, why did you allow it to happen?"

"Because she's my boss," he reiterated. "I need my job."

"Do you?"

"Yes." What kind of question was that?

She nodded. "And what about this? When asked if you would talk back to a stranger who bumped into you on the street, you said no. Why not?"

"I don't know them," he said. "Maybe they're going through something."

"So you wouldn't want to risk upsetting them."

"Yeah." He realized where she was going with this and adjusted himself in the seat. "Hold on. Isn't that just common decency? How does that mean I'm a people-pleaser?"

"On its own," she told him, "it doesn't. When considered with all of the other signs, however..."

"I know how to stand up for myself when the situation calls for it." His mind wandered to Kaz, the problem that had set Sier off in the first place. He'd managed to stand his ground against him, hadn't he?

"Yes," she scanned the tablet screen, "once you've already decided someone isn't worth the effort of pleasing."

Nate sat back. "That's sort of a messed-up way of putting things, don't you think?"

"Do you?"

"Yeah."

She jotted something down with her stylus. "You'll go out of your way to ensure you don't upset a stranger or someone with a higher social stature or more power than you. Basically, if you know nothing about someone, you bestow them with respect."

"Isn't that normal?"

"If you know more about someone," she ignored him, "you act as though they're up on a pedestal and it's your job to ensure they're happy at that height."

Nate frowned. He didn't like bothering anyone, that was true, but calling him a people-pleaser...He didn't feel like that was an accurate description of who he was, and yet...Wasn't the whole reason he was here because he couldn't deal with his shit on his own?

"Do you know what fawning is, Nate?" Dr. Vera asked then, continuing when he silently shook his head. "It's typically thought of as a trauma response. An individual perceives danger, and tries to abate that danger by appeasing the source of that perceived threat. According to these results, this is something you do often. Your default, response, so to speak."

"I don't have any trauma." Wouldn't he know if he did?

"No? Your parents died when you were young and you came to this planet on your own, with only a sister, younger than you, whom you then needed to raise."

"My brother did his best."

"I'm not attacking your brother, Nate. I'm sure he did. He was also a kid when this tragedy happened to you three. What I am saying is your fear of placing more burden on your brother, and those around you who were there to help, was internalized and has negatively impacted the way you view and handle people you interact with. I know trauma sounds like a very serious word, and it is. But it doesn't only apply to the worst things you can think of. You don't have to have witnessed a murder to be traumatized by something."

Did it really matter that he liked helping people so much? What was the big deal? Who cared if he went out of his way to ensure everyone else was as happy as they could be?

"I see you're struggling with this." She nodded like that was to be expected.

"It's just...I don't want to burden anyone with my mistakes, yes," he said. "But I'm not *afraid* of them, like, hurting me or anything."

"In certain situations, you might be," she disagreed. "Take your boss, for example. You couldn't tell her to stop mistreating you out of fear she would fire you for it. It might not be physical harm, but it's harm nonetheless. Think back. Has anyone ever threatened you physically? What was your instinctual response to that?"

"No," he immediately replied. "No, no one ever has. People typically like me." There was Silver a time or two, but that didn't really count. And then—

Kazimir.

"Actually, there was one occasion," he admitted. "Someone was angry that I'd messed up and demanded I pay them for my mistake."

"How did you react?"

"I was quiet at first, but then they kept pushing. Eventually, I told them off. It wasn't fully my fault, that's why. If it had been, I would have taken responsibility."

"You don't need to convince me of that, Nate. I won't judge you for it."

"Isn't that your job?"

"No," she said. "I'm here to help you understand how your mind functions and potentially figure out why. There's no judgment in that, not from me. This is a safe space. Back to this situation, though. What made you able to talk back to this person specifically? Were they not a stranger?"

"We didn't know each other beforehand, but I was aware of him." It was impossible to live on

Vitality and not be aware of the Devils who ran the place.

"Aware enough to form an opinion of his character?"

"He sucks."

She chortled but caught herself and cleared her throat. "Ah. Well. There we have it. You were able to stand up for yourself because he wasn't on a pedestal in your mind. You didn't care about disappointing him and he posed no real threat to you."

"Oh," he interrupted. "He threatened me later."

She paused. "Is that so? And, how did you react that time?"

Nate dropped his gaze to his folded hands.

"I see." She jotted down more notes.

"I was drunk at the time," Nate said, but he wasn't convincing even to himself. He'd tried not to think of it, but now that he was forced to... There was a good chance he would have given into Kazimir in the bar bathroom even if he hadn't been wasted. Kaz had been too forceful, too persistent. The obvious threat of pain had been there, and he'd made it even more clear when he'd taken the time to open Nate up before giving him his cock.

Having never had anal sex before, Nate had been understandably scared. He'd heard stories about how painful it could be, first time or not, and hadn't wanted that experience for himself. Giving into Kaz, letting him bend him over that sink—

"There's nothing to be ashamed of," Dr. Vera told him. "We're all just doing the best we can."

"Yes, well, clearly I need to do better."

"And we'll get you there. I promise. First, you need to realize that pleasing everyone is impossible and that trying to do so isn't being kind. I've gathered you want to be a good person, Nate, and there's nothing wrong with that, but you are not solely responsible for how everyone else feels."

"Right." He picked at his cuticles.

"Who takes care of you?"

"I'm sorry?"

"If you think it's your job to manage everyone else's emotions, what about you? Who takes care of you when you're upset? Who helps you ease the toll of everyday setbacks?"

"I don't—" At her pointed look, he shut his mouth.

"Has there ever been someone in your life you've felt like you were safe to be your authentic self with? One hundred percent, no holding back. Your brother," she held up a hand when he went to speak, "does not count. If anything, your need to please him specifically is the root cause of why you now subconsciously feel like you have to do it with everyone. No, I mean someone you aren't uncomfortable making boundaries with. Someone you were able to express your wants and needs with, without feeling like you were burdening them with that information."

Nate really wished he could say yes, but not a

single person came to mind, no matter how hard he thought about it.

If *this* wasn't his authentic self though, then who was?

Who was he?

"We'll stop here for the day," she said, possibly noting his distress. She closed the tablet and smiled at him. "My receptionist will schedule your next appointment. In the meantime, I'll start thinking up ways we can work together to break you out of the people-pleasing cycle."

Nate stood awkwardly when she did, but hesitated.

"Thanks for your time, but I don't think—"

"I can help you?" she cut him off knowingly. "You want to tell me not to bother rescheduling because it would be a waste of my efforts, don't you?"

"I—" he gulped, seeing that he'd walked right into that one. "Yes."

"You aren't wasting my time, and you won't be even if this takes us years. This is my job. I want to help you, Nate. You do deserve to be happy. You deserve to not be afraid to make your own choices, even if they may go against what others want for you or consider right."

He grunted. "Sounds like you've been living on Vitality too long."

"Or perhaps," she held his gaze, "you simply haven't been living here long enough."

* * *

When Nate stepped out of the office he felt like shit. He didn't know what he'd expected when he'd arrived, but being told he had a problem with giving in to others hadn't been on the list.

Sure, he always did what Nuri wanted and what he thought would be best for Neve. And, maybe he went out of his way to make sure his friends were always happy with him and around him. Weren't happy people better people though? It sure beat being sad or pissed off.

"Hi," he crossed the reception area and walked up to the desk where a woman who appeared to be only a couple years older than him was seated. "I need to schedule a follow up appointment."

"Of course." She smiled at him and started typing on the keyboard in front of her. "I have an opening for next week, on the eighth?"

"Can we do two weeks from now instead?" He didn't think he was mentally ready to come back in only a few days.

"Sure thing." She looked up a new date. "How about the thirteenth?"

"Great, thanks." It was not great. Not even in the slightest.

"Perfect. You're all set Mr.—"

"Narek?" a familiar voice called from the head of the room and Nate turned to find Kazimir with his hand still on the door. He'd paused beneath the entrance and was staring.

"Did you follow me here?" Nate blurted, unable to hold back the accusation.

The receptionist glanced between the two of them and then broke the silence by greeting Kaz. "Good afternoon, Mr. Ambrose. She'll be with you in a couple of minutes, if you wouldn't mind waiting."

Oh. Nate frowned. "You're a patient here?"

"What about you?" Kazimir moved gracefully toward him. "I don't think I've ever seen you here before. New?"

There was no reason for Nate to answer that, so he stubbornly remained silent.

Kaz rolled his eyes. "Cute. What, now you won't even talk to me?"

"I didn't want to talk to you before."

"Touche. Too bad for you, sounds like I've got time to kill. So," he tossed himself into the nearest chair. The room was filled with three rows of them, but right now it was just them and the receptionist, "What are you in for?"

He scowled. "This isn't prison."

"You sure about that?" Kaz clicked his tongue. "Guess no one's forcing you to be here."

"Someone's making you come?" That sounded strange. "Who has the ability to do that?" And how did Nate get on their good side?

Kazimir's expression soured. "My father."

"Your dad makes you come to therapy?"

"Don't get it twisted," Kaz said, "I can tell you already are. He's not doing it because he gives a shit about me. My father couldn't care less if I dropped dead this very instant. We're the furthest thing from close you could be. Hell, you and I have had more interaction in these past five minutes than he and I have all year."

Nate cocked his head. "Then why make you do it?"

"It's a power play. A reminder that even though I'm part of the Brumal in charge, I'm still beneath him." He snorted. "As if."

"Then why come?"

"Because daddy holds the key to the kingdom, so to speak, and I want it. Ambrose United is a major corporation."

"You're interested in business?"

"Not in the slightest. But I have to inherit my father's company in order to burn it to the ground, right? It's the only thing he's ever cared about. Which means I want it. In order to achieve that goal," he threw out his arms, "I come here once a month and pretend to listen to that crazy old bat's drivel."

"I thought she was nice," Nate said.

"You would, Pretty Boy."

"Your relationship with your dad sounds messed up," he gentled his voice some. "I'm sorry."

Kazimir quirked a brow. "What, that we're not the perfect family?"

"No," he shook his head. "That you have to do something you don't want to. That sucks." And for a guy like Kazimir? It probably drove him half mad.

The look in Kaz's eyes shifted, but Nate

couldn't place whatever emotion he was now feeling. "Sounds like you can relate, Narek."

"I didn't want to come to this planet," he divulged, the words spilling out of him for no comprehensible reason at all. He blamed the therapy session he'd just come from. It'd loosened his tongue and somehow put him in a sharing mood. "I cried in the shower every day for a month leading up to getting on the ship."

"Why the shower?"

Nate shrugged and glanced away. How embarrassing. What was he thinking talking to the Devil about such personal things? Fortunately for him, the door to Dr. Vera's office opened then, and the woman stepped out with that same friendly smile plastered over her face.

She set it on Kazimir. "Hello, Mr. Ambrose. My apologies for keeping you waiting. Please, come in."

Kaz shot to his feet and went to pass by, hanging back at the last second. He stared at Nate until he met his eyes once more. "Remember what we talked about last time we saw one another, Pretty Boy?"

Nate felt his stomach coil with dread but somehow managed to nod his head anyway.

Kazimir grinned. "Good."

Then he turned and walked into the office without another word, leaving Nate feeling even more unnerved than he'd been during his damn session.

CHAPTER 9:

Kaz stared at the swirl of cigarette smoke that drifted up toward the hotel ceiling. The flavor of musk and fruit coated his tongue—one courtesy of the man currently slipping back into his jeans, the other from the umberberry cigarette—and he thought about how badly he wanted a cup of black coffee to help chase both flavors away.

He wondered what kind of coffee Nate Narek liked and then grinned thinking about the shocked look on his face the other day. "Ever have an intrusive thought about someone?"

"Unless it's about murdering them," Zane replied in that smooth tone of his, the one he always slipped into at the end of their sexcapades, "it's not an intrusive thought."

"Bullshit."

"Who are you thinking about?"

"You, baby." Kaz winked and chuckled when Zane rolled his eyes in response.

"Unlikely," Zane said.

"Why?"

"Because you just had me."

Kazimir made a big show of checking the holographic numbers displaying the time in neon red floating above the end table to his right. "Still plenty of time for another round, if you ask me."

"I didn't ask you." Zane finished buttoning up his black dress shirt and then reached down to adjust the circular pin attached to his belt. The Vail crest logo. Their color-coded system helped to immediately identify what grade a student was in, something Kazimir had always appreciated since he'd been brought up to believe in hierarchy and respect. Black was the color seniors wore.

Kaz's shirt in the same color was somewhere on the floor where he'd stripped it off and left it a couple of hours ago. Sex usually did the trick and helped take his mind off of things, and he'd been eager to get over thoughts of Nate Narek by getting Zane under him. Clearly, that hadn't worked.

It'd been a week since he'd showed up at the shitty little hole-in-the-wall shop Nate called his place of business. Quartet Air was a crappy, run-down single-level auto and air shop that was barely staying afloat—even with higher clients like Mit Parker.

Kazimir had done some digging when he'd discovered that's where Nate worked and all that'd done was bolster his idea that Nate was getting something more out of his interactions with the rich geezer than simply bikes or hovercars to work on. There was no reason someone like Mit would bother with a shop like Quartet Air if he wasn't getting flesh out of the deal. Considering how attractive Nate was? Yeah, Kaz could understand the appeal. He'd throw money at a body like that too, and he'd yet to see Narek fully undressed.

"Thoughts on paying for it?" he asked, the question rolling off his tongue, giving his current companion pause.

Zane was a member of the Retinue, not an enemy, since the two groups had been ordered to get along since the beginning when they'd all been children, but not exactly a friend either.

Kazimir had been dicking him down for over three years now. Not something he typically did with his friends.

"Last I checked," Zane clipped a moment later, "neither one of us is hurting for coin."

"I'm not saying we pay off each other," he snorted.

"Why? You interested in a sex worker all of a sudden?" There wasn't so much as a hint of hurt in Zane's tone. Nothing to indicate the thought of Kaz wanting to stick his dick into another person was upsetting.

That was why this twisted thing worked between them. Because, at the end of the day, it wasn't twisted at all. They contacted one another whenever the other had an itch that needed scratching, did the deed, and went their separate ways. They never interfered or even showed an interest in one another's personal lives, and when they were with the rest of the Satellite or Retinue, they acted the same as everyone else.

Close enough to make jokes.

Distanced enough to draw blood in the ring.

"Calling him a sex worker is...hasty." Kaz may have had his suspicions, but according to Nate, nothing had happened between him and Mit. Yet. It was so obvious that's why the old guy kept coming around, that he was hoping he could eventually convince Nate to give him a try.

Training with the Brumal had taught him never to make rash decisions based on what he supposed the truth to be, to instead always seek out the real answer beforehand. He wasn't the best at following that line of advice, admittedly, but he was getting better. Had to, now that he'd been upgraded to the important role of underboss. Especially when he thought back on the harsh words Baikal had tossed his way the other night.

Knowing his cousin, Kal had most likely just been irritated because Kazimir had brought up Rabbit. He was overprotective on a good day and a total dragon-hoarding-gold-nightmare on a bad one where his Possessio was concerned.

"But you think you can sway him with money?" Zane hummed. "Why bother? Your looks and prestige aren't enough?"

Kaz thought about the way Nate had been at the therapists yesterday. He'd been surprised when he'd walked in and found the pretty racer there, but even more so when Nate had apologized to him and sounded like he'd meant it. Most people told Kaz to suck it up when he told him about his daddy issues —he was rich and protected because of the Ambrose name, they'd say. Who cared if it came with strings?

But Nate? Nate hadn't pointed out that he was a spoiled prick for feeling the way he did toward his dad. Hadn't told him to get over it, or appeared disgusted when Kazimir had mentioned wanting to destroy his dad's business.

Narek had tried to comfort him.

Him.

How absolutely absurd.

So why had Kazimir kind of liked it?

"We weren't all given flowery titles like Prince of Medicine, Your Highness," Kaz drawled, making himself focus on the conversation. "Some of us got stuck with Devil of Vitality and never moved into any other category."

Zane had never cared about what the other students at Vail called him—to his face or behind his back. Appearances mattered to him, but only because they mattered on a professional level. If it wouldn't affect his future as the head of medical staff for the Imperial family, Zane wouldn't give it the time of day.

Kazimir was the one strange exception, and that was simply because everyone, even someone as perfect and untouchable as Zane, needed an outlet once in a while.

"We both know you like being a Devil, Kaz," Zane said.

He sighed. "This guy, he doesn't like me."

"Most people don't, not once they get to know you, anyway."

"Someone's asking for a spanking."

"Take your darker proclivities out on this new target of yours. I've got to go."

"At least help me beforehand," Kazimir argued.

"I just did that." He glanced down pointedly at the spot between Kaz's thighs, currently soft and hidden beneath the thin white sheet.

"Come on, Z. You're the only one I can ask."

Zane cocked his head. "This have something to do with the other Satellite?"

"They think I can't commit."

"You can't."

"Sure I can. I just haven't found the right one, that's all."

"And this new guy, he's the right one?"

"No." Kaz stopped and considered it more seriously. "Probably not. He's poor as dirt yet arrogant as all hell. Hot, but in that boy next door kind of way. Not sexy, not like you, baby." He left out he part about how Nate was actually more his style, at least in the looks department.

"Focus. I'm only giving you another two minutes of my time."

"Fine." He rolled his eyes and slumped back against the mahogany headboard. "He isn't the type of person I imagined myself spending the rest of my life with, let's leave it at that."

"You haven't imagined that ever, Kazimir.

What's brought this on now? Is it just because the others goaded you? Or," a knowing look entered his inky-colored eyes, "are you envious? Because Baikal has Rabbit?"

Kaz looked away, scowling.

"You always had a serious competitive streak when it came to him," Zane continued. "I shouldn't be surprised. Was that really all it took? Kal had to find someone to make you finally want to get serious and settle down?"

"It's not like that," he insisted. "It wouldn't be real. Hence why I'd be paying the guy. I just want something believable enough to show Baikal and Flix that I can do anything Kal can."

"If it's fake, it'd be a lie."

"Thanks, Saint Zane. I wasn't aware."

He shrugged. "If you're going to sin anyway, may as well go all in."

Kazimir frowned in silent question.

"Sounds like you're not sure offering him money will get this guy to accept you and play along."

Even though they'd only had a couple of interactions, it was obvious that Nate was too stubborn and prideful to jump into Kaz's palm. He could offer more money than Mit Parker could even dream of, but there was still no guarantee Nate would take the deal.

"Like I mentioned," Kazimir said. "He doesn't like me very much."

"How'd you get involved in the first place?"

"He owed me. Sort of."

"You aren't exactly one to overlook a debt."

"Exactly."

Zane dropped to the edge of the bed and started to put his shoes on. "You're making this more complicated than it needs to be."

"How so?"

"The solution you're looking for has already been spoken of in this room."

"Cryptic bullshit is not really my forte. If you're leading me on—"

"Only one of us is good at that game," Zane cut him off. "And it isn't me." He stood and smoothed down the minor wrinkles of his shirt before turning to Kaz. "This guy owes you? You want him? And there's a good chance he can't be bought. Correct?"

"Yeah, that's the gist of it."

Zane reached back and removed a weapon from where it'd been hidden on his person. Not even Kazimir knew where he kept them, not for lack of trying to find out. The knife was part of a set, double-edged and shaped like a long raindrop with a tip sharp enough to draw blood at just a prick. The handle was intricate and carved out of clear star crystal, one of the hardest materials on the planet.

He handed it over to Kazimir, ignoring the surprised look he received in return. These weapons had been a gift from Kelevra Diar, and it was unheard of for Zane to go anywhere without them, let alone loan them out.

"I expect it returned," Zane said before Kaz

could get any bright ideas about absconding with it. "The consequences otherwise would be severe."

"And," Kazimir twisted the weapon, watching the way it glinted in the dull motel room lighting, "what exactly are you suggesting I do with this?"

"You're a Devil of Vitality, Kaz. This shouldn't be so hard for you to piece together on your own. Laws are for the rest of the world to follow, not us. Whoever this guy is, he's nothing. He has no rights but the ones we allow him."

Sometimes, it was very easy for Kazimir to forget that Zane Solarice was fucking crazy.

And other times he made it strikingly obvious.

There was a reason Zane had been chosen as Kelevra's second-highest-ranking member. They both suffered from ungodly amounts of arrogance and entitlement.

Not that Zane was entirely wrong here...

"What should you do?" the medical student clucked his tongue chidingly. "Do what you do best. Don't make offers. Don't waste time on compromises. You want something from him? *Take it.* Manipulation has always been your mode of attack, true, but let's be honest here. Brute force is your specialty." Something flashed behind his eyes, there and gone. "I should know."

There was the slight issue of Nate being on good terms with Flix, Berga, and Madden but...None of them held a higher station than he did. None of them would get in his way if he made a claim on

Nate. The only way they could is if one of them tried to do it first, and as far as Kaz was aware, that wasn't going to happen.

Still...

"I want it to look like we're together, remember?" He ran a hand through his dark hair. "Won't it be obvious if I'm always holding a knife to his throat?"

Zane tossed his coat on and started for the door. "Not if you're sure to keep the blade shrouded in shadows. Threats are meant for the dark of night, Kaz. Not the light of day. When the sun is out, that's when performances take place, but as soon as the curtains close...You know exactly what I'm talking about."

"Do I?"

He stopped with his hand on the door handle and glared. "Owning people through threats and extortion isn't a new concept for you. It's how you got me, remember?"

Kazimir had been curious about what Zane would be like in bed without all the prim and properness. Mostly though, he'd hated the way the other man always looked down his nose at the rest of them. He'd never tell Zane that, of course, but that'd been the root of it all, and yes, Kaz had resorted to physical assault and threats to get the other man into his bed that first time.

"You keep coming back on your own," he reminded.

"My point exactly. If you could do it to me..."

He could do it to Nate Narek.

"Force him," Zane reiterated. "It doesn't have to be for long. Trick your friends and then break up with him. That's the plan, right?"

"Right." He spun the dagger in his hand. "This is confidential. If you spoil things by telling on me—"

"When have I ever cared what takes place between your little Satellite?"

Kazimir's gaze hardened. "I can't believe after all of this time I still haven't fucked the insolence out of you. Come back here, let me try again. We can pull out the chains this round."

Zane flipped him the middle finger in response. "I'll talk to Kelevra about giving you access to the imprinting system, but no promises." He didn't give him a chance to respond to that, slipping out into the hall and slamming the hotel door shut behind him.

Alone, Kazimir clicked the button on the side of the cigarette, the clear plastic going dark a moment after. He tossed it carelessly onto the end table and sighed, wondering what he was supposed to do with the rest of his night now that his source of entertainment had ditched him to no doubt study for a midterm or something equally boring.

Zane was hot and a badass in the ring, but that was pretty much where the excitement with him ended. He was studious and stuffy, with his head constantly elsewhere—aka, either on medical terminology or thinking about the Imperial

Princess. Bleck. It was obvious to Kaz that Zane only used him whenever Lyra and he fought, but that didn't bother him in the slightest.

Considering Kaz was using him in return, why should it. He'd gotten tired of the options on campus. Maybe it was because he was close to graduation, or maybe because since Baikal's ascension to the throne, he'd had his hands full learning how to properly fill his new role as underboss. Either way, chasing Vail tail was no longer as appealing as it once was.

Everyone there was there for a reason. They had a purpose and a plan. Even though most of them gushed over him when he passed, whispering adoration for the Devils of Vitality, Kaz knew better. They were attracted to the idea of him. The idea of hooking up with a Devil, getting bragging rights. No one would ever want him for longer than that single romp between the sheets. For more than a story they could tell to their friends.

Kazimir Ambrose wasn't just a member of the Brumal. He was cousin to the Dominus and the underboss who handled all the underlings that Baikal didn't have time for. He was the line between them and their leader. Not only did that keep him busy, it also implied he was dangerous. It wasn't an inaccurate implication.

Why would anyone want to throw their fate into the ring and get serious with a mafia member when they had bright and shiny futures ahead of them? A degree from Vail pretty much-guaranteed success anywhere within the Dual galaxy, let alone on the planet itself.

Sure, he liked to play the big and bad role, but at the end of the day, Kazimir was a bit...lonely. He'd never admit it to the guys, but he could be honest with himself, right? Seeing Baikal and his Possessio together had sparked something within him he hadn't known existed before. The way Rabbit looked at Kal...The way the two of them pushed and pulled at one another...Kazimir wanted that.

It wasn't just about proving a point, but he could never say that to anyone, not even Zane.

Nate Narek may not be the all-around cure he needed, but adding him to the mix certainly couldn't hurt any. If nothing else, it would help shut his cousin and Flix up, and that was more than enough reason in Kaz's book to proceed. The fact that it'd also help ease his loneliness for a bit? Bonus. That particular ailment was new anyway. With any luck, after some time steady time with another person, Kazimir would find himself reset and could return to the way he'd been before.

He had his multi-slate out and a number dialed in a matter of seconds, twirling the knife in his hand some more as he waited for the person he'd called to pick up.

"Hey," he grinned a moment later, "I'm looking to get into business owning, and I've got just the place in mind."

CHAPTER 10:

"Maybe you should slow down," Annya suggested, glancing between Nate and Sier, who was seated in the booth across from them.

Their boss kept sliding drinks Nate's way, watching until he downed them and then clapping like an excited kid.

Or a psychopath. Take your pick.

"It's fine." It wasn't anywhere near the amount he'd had a couple of weeks ago at the bar, and while he was starting to feel it, it wasn't intense enough to cause him any real worry. "At least she's talking to me again."

After Kazimir's visit, Sier had torn Nate a new one and then given him the cold shoulder.

She'd also taken him off most of his shifts, which absolutely sucked. He'd just barely managed to squeeze in his full payment to keep his damn lights on at home even. So, if she wanted to ply him with drinks now? Fine. He'd take it, so long as it meant come Monday morning, she'd go back to giving him his usual hours.

It's not like it mattered if he got wasted

anyway. What was the worst that could happen?

Oh right. He'd already experienced that.

"I can't even remember the last time I wasn't tense," he sighed.

"Yeah, well that's not going to help you," she rested a hand on his thigh under the table and gave a friendly squeeze. "I promise. We never have one of these things without a reason, you know that."

He did. Sier was too cheap to pay for dinner on the company's dime without needing a damn good excuse. Typically, that was her showing off in front of their few higher-class clients.

Like Mit.

Nate's stomach sank. He'd been so distracted with his self-wallowing that he hadn't even considered that Mit might be showing. Every other time they'd done this, the older man either arrived before them, or came with. He placed the beer down on the table and scowled. There was no way he wanted to deal with that creep's advances while buzzed, let alone actually drunk.

But it wasn't like he could actively tell Sier no...

"Why don't you try sneaking out back?" Annya said. "I can cover for you."

He considered it.

"You shouldn't have to put up with this just because of that guy." Word had quickly spread once Kaz had left what'd supposedly happened—that Nate had lost a big client. Annya wasn't the only one on Nate's side, but she was the only one who'd dared voice as much out loud. "Everyone knows losing that client was in our best interest. Catering to a Devil of Vitality? Not worth the hassle."

Nate snorted. "You say that like you have experience with them." No one else would dare make a comment like that, that was for sure. Everyone in the workforce was too busy trying to suck up to people like Kazimir Ambrose, or at the very least, trying to avoid him due to his standing within the Brumal.

"My sister does," Annya confessed, not meeting Nate's gaze.

"You have a sister?"

"Not all of us are as lucky as you are," she told him. "She and I don't really talk much. She's currently attending Guest, the fine arts academy?"

Nate knew of it. It was a pretty ritzy school, but then, pretty much all of them on Vitality were. The planet was known for its riches and wealth. Very few people worried about surviving paycheck to paycheck like Nate did.

"She was always dad's favorite, especially when she chose to go into music after him. She hangs around with some of the Devils sometimes," Annya continued. "I've seen it on her social media page. Anyway, enough about her. All I'm saying is we dodged a bullet, and if Sier can't see that then—"

"Did someone say my name?" Sier popped her head up and took in all of the workers around the table. When no one stepped forward, she clucked her tongue and then got to her feet. "Since I have all of your attention now anyway, I would like to make an announcement."

Annya sent Nate a look that screamed, 'I told you so.'

"We've sold the business!" Sier's wide grin turned to a frown when out of the twelve employees there, only two remained quiet at the news, the others instantly voicing their complaints.

Nate didn't say anything because why bother, and Annya was too busy shaking her head in disbelief. They'd only just sold the company a year ago, and now it was changing hands again? He wasn't a fan of Sier, but she'd only held onto the place for a bit. And how the hell had she managed to find someone willing to buy her out when they were doing so poorly?

"What does that mean for us?" Foh, one of the older workers demanded.

"Yeah," Greta, a woman who'd been working for a couple of years there, asked. "Are we losing our jobs?"

"As far as I know, the new owner has no intentions of making any cuts," Sier reassured. "Honestly, there's no reason for any of you to be this upset. This is a good thing!"

"For you maybe," another worker, this one seated on Nate's left, muttered under his breath.

"Who's the new owner?" Annya finally piped in, crossing her arms. None of them liked the uncertainty this news brought.

"He'll be here in a moment to greet you all,"

Sier promised. "Please calm down. We don't want to make a terrible first impression, now do we?" It seemed lost on her that she was speaking to them like they were children and not her employees, or that this was probably the single worst way to deliver this news—in public during what had been pitched as a company dinner to thank them for all their hard work.

Nate set the glass he'd been forced to drink from down and rubbed his hands together nervously. There weren't many people out there who'd bother buying a little shop like theirs, especially when it hadn't been placed on the market. The last time, Quartet Air had been actively trying to sell for almost a year before it'd been purchased.

His gaze drifted toward the drink Sier had poured him, the fifth one in the past ten minutes, and Annya's earlier concern came back to him.

"It's not Mit Parker," he asked, voice low and somewhat shaky, "is it?"

Everyone grew quiet and turned to stare at Sier expectantly. Not a single one said anything about that being a wild suggestion. They all must be thinking the same as him. Mit Parker had been the only one who'd shown even a slight interest in the shop these past few months.

Interest in Nate, really.

But…enough to buy the place? Nate had done a decent enough job of rejecting the older man's advances. He'd hoped Mit had taken the hint since it'd been weeks since he'd come around the shop.

Could the reason for that be because he'd been getting the paperwork in order? Planning to buy?

Mit Parker was known for being disgusting, but this would be extreme.

Nate internally shook his head at himself and the direction his thoughts had taken. He was self-aware enough to admit he was an attractive person, sure, but he was nowhere near hot enough to justify buying a whole business. He was being ridiculous, his paranoia getting the best of him. No one in their right mind would ever—

"Ah, here he is now," Sier said, turning to clap as someone slipped into the private corner of the restaurant their group occupied.

Because she hadn't answered the question, Nate half expected Mit Parker, so when he glanced up and found a tall, young man in place of the withered old dude he'd anticipated, it took his brain a little longer to process his identity.

"Let's all give a hand to Kazimir Ambrose," Sier announced as the Devil came to a stop at her side. "The new owner of Quartet Air!"

The mutual hesitation only lasted a moment before everyone seated at the circular booth started to clap, though the confusion lingered. It was obvious in the way everyone was glancing at each other and then over at Nate, their gazes remaining on him a little longer than he would have been comfortable with if he'd been paying them much attention.

Which he was not, because he was far too

distracted by the smug expression Kaz had aimed his way.

He'd clearly just come from campus, still dressed in his black button-up silk shirt, the school's official crest pinned to the belt he wore secured around his matching jeans. In the dim lighting of the restaurant, dressed in all black, he looked like a demon straight from hell come to collect his due.

Only, Nate stood by what he'd said. He didn't owe the guy anything, and this...this was too much.

He was on his feet before he even processed what he intended, ignoring Annya when she grabbed onto his wrist and tried to tug him back down onto the crimson leather seat. Pulling away from her, he tore his eyes off Kazimir and pushed past the two coworkers who were blocking the exit to the booth. Once out, he turned on his heels and headed toward the back of the restaurant, recalling that there was a door there that would lead to the employee parking lot.

He had enough of a mind not to make a scene here in front of everyone, but there was no way he was staying. No way he was going to sit there and listen to whatever bullshit Kazimir was about to spout.

He'd bought the shop?
Him?
To what end?

Nate ran a hand through his hair, tugging roughly at the dark strands as panic threatened to consume him. This couldn't be real. All these years, he'd been able to keep his shit together and make it through, and now this? Why? Because he'd lost one race? That couldn't actually be it...That couldn't be the reason his entire life fell apart.

Someone called his name but he ignored it, traveling through the back of the restaurant, down the narrow hallway that led to the employee break room and the bathrooms. There was a green door set between where the hall branched off and Nate shoved it open, stepping out into the cold night air.

He'd driven there and parked in the front, so started making his way around the exterior of the brick building, head tipped down as his thoughts continued to gnaw at him. If he made it to his car within the next three minutes, he could be back home and in his shower in under—

"Hey." A strong hand grabbed at the collar of his jacket and yanked him back, tossing him hard against the brick. Kazimir crowded him in a second later, his boots crunching in the thin layer of ice and snow on the ground. "What the hell do you think you're doing?"

Nate didn't respond, pressing against Kaz's solid chest in a poor attempt to get him to move. That darkness was still threatening to weigh in on him, and if he didn't get out of there fast, he might find himself spacing out in a last-ditch attempt to keep his mind from completely drowning in negative thoughts.

Like how he hadn't been good enough to take Bay's place during that race and he'd known it.

How that should have been enough for him to tell Madden no, but he'd foolishly been excited to give his skills a test of sorts and see how he'd come out.

How he'd been the one who'd drank so much at the bar, and that's why Kazimir had been able to get the upper hand.

How Silver knew about his racing and was coming for a visit, and his threat that Nate had to get his shit together…

Get his shit together?

He couldn't even breathe! Forget—

"Hey," the word held less bite than when he'd spoken it a second ago, and Kazimir's angry look shifted, morphing into one more akin to concern. "Hey, take a breath, Pretty Boy, I don't like the way you're looking."

Nate already had both hands on Kaz's chest and he tried to shove him away a second time.

The younger guy retaliated by settling a palm against Nate's throat. He didn't apply any pressure, but the silent threat was there, and it snapped Nate out of it enough he could lift his head and meet that garnet gaze.

Kazimir's eyes were so pretty. Nate would be lying if he claimed he hadn't noticed that before. They were an odd deep red color that leaned toward black in certain lighting, intense and calculating. Like the rest of him, there was nothing soft about those eyes, and yet Nate found himself staring up into them, that tight restricting sensation in his chest slowly loosening with each passing second.

"There you go," Kaz noticed and praised softly. "Keeping breathing just like that. Focus on me, baby."

"Do not call me that," Nate sneered.

"All right. At least you're talking now." He cocked his head. "Care to explain what that was, Pretty Boy?"

"No." He dropped his hands since attempting force was a lost cause. "Move."

"Not until we clarify a few things."

"There's nothing to discuss between us at all."

"I'm your boss now," Kazimir reminded, "and I disagree."

"Why the hell is a college kid buying a shitty shop like ours anyway?"

"Don't be like that. You know the reason. Playing dumb doesn't suit you. At least when you were drunk and clueless there was an excuse. But I can tell Sier didn't pour enough drinks down your throat. I'll have to consider that when I go over everyone's employee profile and decide who to keep and who to cut, crazy bitch actually wants to stay on as manager."

"You're going to fire people?" More than half of the people in that restaurant were living paycheck to paycheck just like Nate. They needed this job. They didn't have any other options.

At least Nate had Silver to fall back on if he absolutely had to. It would suck, and he'd probably end up wishing for death, but it was still something. What about the others? He doubted they had that same chance. Emperor brothers-in-laws weren't exactly a dime a dozen.

"Because of me?" Nate made himself ask, even though Kaz was right. He did know the reason. It was so obvious; how could he not? "This is all so you can get back at me. Just because I told you no? That's insane, Kazimir. Even for you."

Kaz stared at him for a moment. "That's the first time you've said my name, did you know that?"

He frowned. Nate was pretty sure he'd said it before, but then again...Whatever. "Is that really important right now?"

"It is if I say it is," Kaz told him.

"Of course." Why did he even bother? "Remove your arm at least."

"Am I making you uncomfortable, Pretty Boy?"

"Always."

Kazimir hummed and dropped his arm, but he didn't step away, making sure to stay close so that the sheer size of him was warning enough for Nate to stay put with his back against the wall. "Did you really think running was going to work?"

"I wasn't." Nate had merely needed to get away in that moment. Recoup and figure out his next move. He wouldn't call it running, since he hadn't fully intended on never coming back. "What did you expect me to do? How did you think this was going to play out?"

He needed to get a grasp on what Kazimir actually wanted from him, because Nate wasn't entirely convinced he knew anymore. Things had gotten way more complicated since the night of the race, and even though that had been weeks ago, it felt like it was all progressing far too quickly. He couldn't keep up.

"Why can't you just leave me alone?" he added.

"I thought, being the desperate employee that you are," Kazimir began, "that you would see me and sit there and listen to my plans for you."

"The company," he corrected. "You mean your plans for the company."

"You should learn now, Narek, that I'm not the type to misspeak. Every word that comes out of my mouth is carefully selected to deliver the exact intention I mean for it to. To confirm, yes, I bought this shitty business because of you. For you. It isn't Quartet Air that I'm interested in owning."

"That's not how this works," Nate said. "You can't buy me the same way you can a building."

"No?"

"No."

Kazimir sighed. "Well, it was a valiant effort on my part. One last ditch attempt to give you a more palatable way to me."

Nate instinctually braced, and not a moment after, Kazimir reached back and slipped something from beneath his belt.

The clear blade of the dagger in his hold sparkled under the parking lot lights as he brought it between them and pressed the tip just above

Nate's navel. It was sharp enough that it nicked right through the thin material of his t-shirt.

"Breathe, Pretty Boy," Kazimir ordered, smirking when Nate inhaled slowly, careful with his movements. "Good, now, eyes on me."

It took a lot for him to tear his gaze off the shiny weapon and tip it back up to Kaz, but he did it. He didn't even think about hiding the fear he was now feeling, or the way his confusion had only grown with this new threat.

"I had a feeling bodily harm wouldn't work on you," Kazimir said a minute later, after he'd kept Nate waiting in the silence. "Was I wrong? You seem scared enough."

"A psycho is holding a knife against my gut," Nate stated. "I don't have a death wish."

"Psycho, huh?"

"Are you going to deny it?" That wasn't entirely fair since there weren't any real rumors about Kazimir being a psychopath out there. Still. "I've spent enough time with Bay Delmar to recognize the signs when I see them. You're not normal."

"And you are? That tongue of yours doesn't seem to know when to quit, does it? Name calling at a time like this? Really?"

"Would you prefer I beg?" Nate asked. "Is that what you want?" Is that what he should have done from the start? Gotten down on his knees and apologized for losing the race? It seemed ridiculous to him to have to take responsibility for something like that, but then, this felt ridiculous as well. "You bought the company I work for because you're that desperate for me to—"

"Yield?" Kaz cut him off. "Yes. And let's leave out words like desperate from now on, or else I might lose my cool and really dig this thing through your insides. Neither of us want that."

"No?" Nate wasn't entirely convinced.

"No," Kazimir insisted. "I think I'd like to see you beg. Down on your knees. With those pretty pink lips of yours wrapped around my cock. But this is hardly the place, or the weather, for that."

Right, Kaz wasn't wearing a jacket.

"If you're cold, go inside," Nate latched onto that one comment.

"Not without you."

"Okay." He'd wait until the younger guy turned his back and then—Nate sucked in a breath when the knife was angled so the edge of the blade was now resting against his shirt. Unlike before, Kaz didn't push it against him enough to cut anything, but the possibility was there.

"I don't like being lied to, Narek."

"Prefer to reserve that for yourself?" he countered.

"You really don't know when to quit."

"I have an older brother, remember?" Nate shook his head. "I'm used to being picked on." That wasn't entirely true either. Nuri would never treat him like this. Nuri was kind, the type of person Nate could only ever dream of being. His one and only flaw was that he'd fallen for a guy like Silver, but Nate digressed.

"Say you'll go out with me," Kaz said, and this time Nate caught himself from outright complying.

"No."

"Why not?"

"Because I don't want to, hotshot. You're not my type."

"You mean I'm not *safe*," Kaz drawled. "I don't fit into the cooker cutter ideal you've mapped in your head of what your life should be. Judging by the way your body always responds so quickly to my presence, you're wrong though, Pretty Boy. I'm exactly your type."

"Well, I'm not yours," Nate blurted.

He quirked a brow. "I'm the one doing the chasing here, remember? Why would I go through all this trouble if I wasn't being serious? I want you. I want you to be my boyfriend."

"You want to use me to help you prove a false point to your cousin," he corrected bluntly. "Sounds like any warm body would suffice."

"I don't just want to fool the others," he said. "I want the experience, or, at least as close to it as I can get. So far, you're the only bed partner I've had that I've thought of after the fact. The sex with you was phenomenal, but I'm starting to think it was a lot more than that. Something about you draws me in, Narek. I don't like unanswered questions. I want to know what this thing is. Want to know why it felt so nice to have you try to comfort me at therapy the other day."

What? He wasn't seriously telling him that Nate was going through all of this now because he'd attempted to be *kind*, was he?!

"You—" The back door to the restaurant suddenly shot open, distracting them both and cutting off whatever Nate had been about to say. Not even he knew really. This whole thing had gone from nightmarish to baffling in under three seconds flat.

That seemed to be a relative theme whenever Kaz was involved.

Nothing ever made logical sense.

Sier popped her head out and shivered, frowning over at them. "What are you two doing?"

Kazimir discreetly lowered the blade and turned, hiding it at his side before he gave her a wide smile. "Just discussing a few things. We'll be there in a minute, you should go back to the others."

"I quit," Nate announced, shifting out from between Kaz and the wall while he had the chance. He retreated a few steps, making sure to keep the Devil in his line of sight, even as he risked a glance at Sier to make sure she'd heard him. "I quit. No two weeks' notice. It's effective immediately."

"Narek," Kazimir dropped his voice and growled, but Nate was still backing away.

"Nate," Sier shook her head. "Where is this coming from? You can't just—"

"Yes," he said. "I can, and I am. I quit." He gave Kazimir one last look. "Enjoy owning Quartet Air, Mr. Ambrose."

He, however, was not for sale.

CHAPTER 11:

"Just wipe down the tables at the end of your shift and that should be it," Jones said as he removed the brown apron and hung it on one of the hooks by the end of the counter. "Thanks for doing this on such short notice, man. I really appreciate it."

"Are you kidding," Nate finished learning the ins and outs of the computer and shook his head, "You're doing me a favor."

He'd been without work for only a few days and it was almost enough to send him over the deep end. Despite his thoughts about relying on Silver, Nate hadn't been able to get himself to actually give his brother-in-law a call.

He could handle being unemployed for a little while. There was enough in his savings he could get by on groceries for a couple of weeks since he'd just paid the electricity off, and since he could withstand cooler temperatures if the heat went out at his place, it wouldn't be the end of the world. Really, the issue would come at the end of the month when electricity was due again, but Nate would cross that bridge when he came to it.

Besides, this could work.

Jones was a friend from college that Nate had kept in touch with. The other day, he'd posted on Inspire, the social media app, asking if anyone was interested in becoming a barista at his coffee shop. He'd opened it just after graduation, and sales had been good; even Nate came often, but apparently, a couple of employees had quit on him at the last minute, and he'd been desperate to fill their spots.

Nate had needed a job and had barista training, so...it'd been kind of a no-brainer. The pay was less than he'd been making at Quartet Air, of course, but this gave him the chance to make something while he prepared his resume. Quitting on the spot would cost him the good recommendation he may have otherwise received from Sier, but that wasn't enough to make him regret his choice.

Getting away from Kazimir Ambrose had to be the top priority, even if it meant giving up on the job he'd so desperately clung to all this time.

It was fine. Nate could start fresh.

And his siblings never had to know.

He hadn't even given Annya a decent explanation when she'd called after the incident at the restaurant. If he'd complained about Kaz, there was a chance she'd get roped into his mess. He'd even warned her not to mention to anyone that the two of them were on friendly terms, citing the reason as not wanting Sier to take out her frustrations on her.

The reality was, he didn't trust Kazimir not to.

He was probably pissed. All that money he'd spent on buying Quartet Air in order to get to Nate, wasted.

"All of the red envelopes are set out randomly. We should be fully stocked for the rest of the evening shift, but if you run out, there's more in the back storage closet," Jones explained.

The month before New Year's, everyone began celebrating by giving out red envelopes. Each envelope contained an animal native to the planet. There were meanings behind each, and when you gifted one to someone, it was supposed to symbolize either something you experienced this year and needed to let go or something they wished for you for the new year.

It was bad luck to open any envelope before the clock struck midnight, so you never knew who gave what. Whichever animal you ended the night with the most was supposed to be the real New Year wish and what you had to look forward to in the coming months. It was really different from how they celebrated on Ignite, and when they'd first arrived, it'd taken both he and Neve days to fully grasp the concept and memorize the various meanings behind the animals, even though there were only five of them.

Businesses often took part as well, leaving out a basket or two filled with sealed envelopes. Customers were encouraged to take one with them once they'd paid.

"Don't worry," Nate reassured. "I've got this."

"I know. I remember how hard you worked whenever I grabbed a coffee while we were in school. I know the shop is in good hands. I'll leave you to it," Jones said, gathering his things. "If you have any questions, Arlet here can help you out."

Arlet, the other worker, waved at Nate from where she stood on the opposite end of the counter. She was in the process of helping a customer and had been busy with it since Nate's arrival an hour ago, so the two hadn't really had a chance to speak much yet. She seemed nice though.

The uniforms for Velvet Brew Café were pressed cream-colored shirts beneath a chocolate brown apron and charcoal pants. Pretty standard stuff, and all items—minus the apron, of course—that Nate had in his closet, which was great since it'd meant he hadn't needed to waste money on new clothes.

At the center of the apron and on all of the cups was the mascot of the chain coffee shop, a jackalope with a sleepy expression in front of the orb of a sun. It was cute in that kitschy kind of way, and Nate smoothed his hands over its design on his chest. It could be worse. A job was a job, and at least at this one, he'd be able to keep busy. Plus, Jones was a good guy, and as a bonus, Nate got to help him out by becoming his employee. It was a win-win all around.

Until the door across the room rang, and Nate lifted his head and saw who was walking in.

He'd specifically agreed to work with Jones because his Velvet Brew was located the furthest from the Vail University campus. Nate had just assumed he'd be in the clear because of that, but now that he was forced to stand there as Kazimir approached the counter, he was realizing how stupid that assumption had been.

Kaz wasn't alone either. Two members of the Retinue were with him, an odd combination to see out and about, but not unheard of.

Nate recognized them only because they were also students at Vail, though he'd never spoken to either of them.

Ledger Undergrove had a leather jacket over his school uniform and wore a couple of thick silver chains around his neck. His dark brown hair hung just past his chin, and he ran a hand through it absently as he approached the glass case in front of where Arlet stood that held the baked goods.

"Want a muffin?" he casually asked the man standing just over his shoulder.

Pavel Hart shook his head, and though Ledger had his back to him and therefore couldn't have seen, that seemed to be enough to get his point across.

With a hum of understanding, Ledger pointed to one of the berry muffins in the middle and said to Arlet, "One. Thanks, doll."

The two of them were brothers, though the word was Pavel had been adopted as a child by the Undergroves. It was rare to see them separately, so whether there was a connection by blood or not between them, it was obvious they were close.

Ledger was the louder and more boisterous of the pair, while Pavel...Well. Pavel gave Nate the straight-up creeps. And this afternoon was no different.

He was staring at Nate, for one. Those dark eyes of his unblinking as he stood there, still as a statue, and just looked at him. Like he was waiting for something. He was the same height as Ledger, though a little broader in the shoulders, and dressed a lot less flashy. The single black chain he wore around his neck was the only piece of noticeable jewelry on him, and his plain black pea coat was a pretty common item amongst the rich kids who attended schools on Vitality.

Even Nate had one, a gift from his brother one birthday after Nuri had visited and noted what everyone else had been dressed in at his and Neve's school. Nate only wore it for special occasions, though, too afraid of ruining it and having to explain to Nuri he'd wasted his money.

Kazimir tapped the glass countertop in front of Nate, jolting him out of his staring contest with Pavel, and Nate actually gulped.

"Eyes on me, Pretty Boy," Kaz said darkly.

"How did you know I was here?" Nate asked.

Ledger snorted. "Presumptuous."

"Arlet told me," Kazimir confirmed before Nate could feel too embarrassed by his friend's comment. "Thanks," he called to her.

She shrugged at Nate and mouthed the word sorry before handing over a paper bag to Ledger with a big smile. "Enjoy your muffin!"

"Thanks," Ledger winked, "I will."

Pavel tapped his shoulder with a single finger.

"What?" Ledger turned to him. "It's called a break. We're allowed to take them, and damn it, I'm hungry."

"This is not a break," Pavel disagreed in that cool tone of his. He tipped his head toward Kaz. "Paying your boy toy a visit in the middle of important business isn't a break, it's negligence."

"He's not my boy toy," Kazimir replied snidely. "Nate and I are dating."

Nate blinked at him, waiting for a punch line that didn't come. "What—"

Kaz hushed him. "There's no need to hide it, baby. They'll find out eventually."

"You two are together?" Arlet pouted. "Why are all the good ones always taken?"

She thought Kazimir Ambrose was good? In what way? Where?

"Are you blind?" it was out of his mouth before he could help it, and Nate froze up the second it was.

Ledger burst out laughing.

Pavel stared.

Kazimir grinned, but there was little humor in the look.

Nate needed to salvage this before it got ugly, so he cleared his throat and did the first thing that came to mind. "I told you not to call me baby."

The corner of Kaz's mouth twitched. "That's right. Sorry, Pretty Boy. Forgive me?"

"You have to order something," he said. Yeah, get them to order so they could be on their way. "It's my first day of work. I can't just stand around."

"Put you to work?" This time the devilish smirk seemed genuine. "Don't mind if I do."

"Wait," Ledger wagged a finger between them, "You two really dating? No. You?"

"What about me?" Kazimir asked tightly.

"Enough, brother," Pavel warned and Ledger rolled his eyes.

"Fine, who cares." He headed toward the door. "We'll be in the car doing our jobs before Pavel here has a stroke. Hurry it up, Ambrose."

"Not a problem," Kaz called back. "Nate never lets me near him for too long."

"Still in the flirting stage?" Ledger grunted. "That makes more sense."

Kazimir waited until his friends were gone before he propped his elbows on the edge of the counter and leaned in. "Hear that? We've got more convincing to do."

"I never agreed to that," Nate replied tightly, keeping his voice down in an attempt to keep their conversation from being overheard by Arlet, who was still watching closely from less than ten feet away. He was a bit miffed that she'd given out his location without asking, but then, against one of the Devils of Vitality, could he really blame her? "Why won't you just let up already?"

"When I want something, I've got to have it." He lifted a single shoulder. "Speaking of. Make me a bulletproof coffee. It's looking like it'll be a long night."

"Size?" Nate pulled up the item on the computer screen in front of him, grateful to at least be doing the job he was there for. Was it because of Arlet? With an audience around, would Kazimir behave?

"Large."

"That'll be—"

"Buy it for me."

So much for behaving. Nate huffed. "No."

"Come on," Kazimir smiled at him. "Buy me a coffee, Narek. We'll count it as a date."

"No."

"I'll buy it for you, Kaz." Arlet strolled over and twisted her wrist, aiming her multi-slate against the pay window before either of them could tell her not to.

Not that Nate had half a mind to stop her. He didn't. If she wanted to get herself involved with a guy like Kazimir? That was her prerogative. Actually...He took a deliberate step back and waved at the computer. "Would you like to take over?"

"Don't tell me I need to purchase this place as well?" Kazimir didn't seem pleased that he'd gotten his coffee for free.

"Jones isn't selling," Nate replied, selecting one of the paper cups from the bunch, opting to just make the damn thing himself after all and get it over with.

"You're on a first-name basis with the owner?"

Nate didn't bother replying, giving him his back so he could start work on the coffee order. Back in high school, he'd worked part-time at a different Velvet Brew after school and over the summers. Though the machinery had improved and there were different specials on the menu, it'd come back to him fairly quickly during his brief training with Jones earlier that day.

Arlet laughed uncomfortably. "They're just friends. Tell him, Nate." She moved up to his side and bumped her shoulder against his, turning so she could speak to him from the corner of her mouth. "Seriously, you aren't this obtuse, are you? He's a Devil of Vitality. You want to get Jones in trouble because of your little lover's spat?"

Nate sucked in a breath, his hands stilling. Nothing had happened to any of his coworkers at Quartet Air—he'd heard as much from Annya—so it hadn't even occurred to him to worry for Jones' safety.

Which was practically unheard of for him.

All he ever did was overthink how he could become a burden to those around him, and yet here he was, spouting off Jones' name like it was nothing. Since when was he that careless? That selfish?

He finished the coffee quickly and brought it back over, nervously smoothing his palms down the front of the apron. "Can we please not do this here?"

Kazimir took the drink and sipped, watching him over the plastic top. "You sound apprehensive, Pretty Boy."

"I just don't want anyone else getting hurt because of me."

"Who's been hurt? I haven't touched a soul. Just you, Nate. I'll be satisfied with just you, you're the one making things difficult."

"I don't want to do this," he reiterated, glancing at Arlet, who was pretending not to be paying them any mind and failing at it.

"Give me a good reason."

"Because I don't like you."

Arlet gasped and then spun in a circle, catching sight of the door that led into the back where they baked the goods. "I'll be back there. Doing work. Work stuff. Back there. Behind that thick door no one can hear through. Yeah."

"You scared her," Kazimir said the moment the door slammed shut behind Arlet. There were two customers still in the shop, but the space was large enough that they were spread out and paying neither of them any attention.

"*I* did?" Nate asked incredulously. "She left because she was afraid you're going to do something."

"I am," he countered. "But the only reason for it is because you've pushed me."

"That's bullshit." Nate slammed his hands down on the counter between them, his irritation returning. It seemed his usual state of being, the one that bent over backward to do damage control and protect those around him was also in hiding whenever Kazimir was around. "Can you just take responsibility for your own actions for once?"

"Can you?"

Nate let out a frustrated sound and then opened his mouth to argue further when his multi-slate dinged, stopping him from most likely making a mistake. He swore and then turned it to check the screen, pausing when he read the name flashing over it in yellow neon letters. "I have to take this."

Kazimir was silent, and when Nate glanced back up it was to find he was also looking at the device. He only snapped out of it once Nate pulled it away, then he took his coffee and shrugged. "You do that, Narek."

He hesitated.

"I'll see you later." Kaz left, just like that.

For a moment, Nate stared after him, completely baffled by his sudden shift in mood, but then the device stopped and started up again and he snapped out of it and answered the call. "Hey, Port, where have you been?"

His friend had been missing for a while now, though he'd apparently called in to quit his job. When Annya had gone by his place a couple of weeks ago, no one had been there. It'd looked a lot like their coworker had just vanished into the void.

"Nate," he sounded out of breath on the other end of the line, "are you home?"

"No. What's wrong?"

Port cursed. "It's freezing out here."

"Out…Are you at my place right now?"

"Yes. When are you coming?"

"I," he checked the clock hanging on the far-right wall, "have an hour left. It's my first day. I can't leave early."

"It's cool," Arlet poked her head out from behind the swinging door leading to the back. "Go on, I'll cover the rest of your shift. If Jones finds out I'll just say you had an emergency."

Nate wished he wasn't automatically suspicious of her but… "Why would you do that?"

"You're dating a Devil," she said, as if that was all the answer that was required and it should be obvious. "Where are you from? It's not Vitality, clearly. We're raised knowing in order to survive, we need to be careful around them. You seem nice. If I do a favor for Kazimir's boyfriend, I'm sure you'll help me out in the future if I ever take a wrong step."

What she was describing was literally everything Nate hated. He didn't want to take advantage of anyone, not even Kaz. When you did that, you inadvertently became partially that person's responsibility, and Nate didn't want anyone to be responsible for his actions aside from himself.

And yet…

Instead of correcting her and telling her to forget about it, Nate found himself nodding like an idiot, his fingers already making quick work of the knot tying the apron around his waist. "Thanks."

He told himself it was because there was

something up with Port and his friend needed him, but a tiny voice in his head laughed at that and called it an excuse. A part of him liked the idea of getting something in return for all the crap Kazimir had put him through. Liked the idea of using him.

"Port? Hey, I'm on my way now. I can be there in ten. Just wait for me, okay?" he said, heading out of the coffee shop and into the parking lot. There were only four cars there, the empty spaces already blanketed in a fine layer of snow. It drifted down around him and a strong gust of wind kicked up, shoving some into his face as he made his way toward his car.

The forecast hadn't called for a storm, but then, this was winter on Vitality, so it wasn't completely unheard of for there to be a random blizzard. He could handle the cold temperatures, but if Port was waiting for him outside...

"Stay on the line with me," Nate demanded. "Tell me where you've been."

"I can't," Port said. "It's not worth it. I shouldn't even be here right now, talking to you."

Nate started the car and pulled out onto the road. He wouldn't make the other guy tell him what was going on if he wasn't comfortable with that, but he still needed to keep him talking, just so he'd know he was all right. "Stay on the line," he repeated.

"Yeah," Port sighed. "Sure."

"Are you dressed for the weather?"

He snorted. "You're so funny. This is why I risked calling you, Nate. I knew you'd care even though we've only known each other a short while and we're more work friends than anything else."

"Of course I care." Only a monster wouldn't. "It's freezing outside and the temperatures are dropping."

"I won't freeze to death."

"You don't know that."

"I do, actually, but again. Thanks. I've met a lot of people in my lifetime, and you're one of the few good ones."

Was he though? It was tempting to blurt out that Nate mostly didn't want to have to figure out how to deal with a dead body on his front porch, or the personal guilt that would bring. Yes, he cared about Port because he was a living thing and deserved that much, but Nate wasn't as altruistic as everyone seemed convinced he was.

Just look at what had happened at the Velvet Brew. He'd needed Arlet to tell him he shouldn't have named Jones. The second he let his guard down, his true persona came out, and that guy? That guy clearly only looked out for himself—

He was doing it again.

Letting those intrusive thoughts creep up on him and paint him in a negative light.

Nate forced himself to stop thinking and focus on the matter at hand.

Port believed in him and was asking for help.

No matter what, Nate was going to come through, because that was the kind of person he wanted to be.

Burdenism be damned.

CHAPTER 12:

"Are you feeling any better?" The two of them were standing in his kitchen with Port seated at the small island while Nate stood next to the stove. He'd heated up some water and made his guest hot cocoa to help warm him.

They'd already been inside for over fifteen minutes, but Port's shoulders still noticeably quaked. His color was returning to normal, however, so that was a good sign.

"Yes, thank you." Port kept his hands wrapped tightly around the white mug he'd been given. "I'm sorry about this."

"Don't be," Nate said. "You can stay for as long as you want. I keep my sister's room made just in case she ever needs to pop by for a night, so the bed's made and the bathroom is stocked. If you're missing anything, just let me know. I try to keep extras of the important stuff in the hallway closet."

"Thanks," he repeated. "I'll leave immediately if Neve ends up coming home."

"She won't. She hasn't stayed here for a while. She and her boyfriend are pretty happy together."

Since Nuri and Silver would be staying at a hotel, there wouldn't be any reason for her to come back either. Thinking about it reminded him that he was running out of time before then. He cleared his throat, and Port must have taken that as a cue that he wasn't as comfortable with this as he was claiming.

"I'm sorry I can't give you an explanation," Port dropped his gaze. "I don't want to involve you any more than necessary."

"It's cool," Nate reassured. "I get that, really."

"Yeah," the corner of his mouth turned up, "You're the same way. You're always looking out for others."

He winced. "It's not really as deep as you're making it sound."

"I suppose it wouldn't be when being kind comes second nature to you." Port smiled sadly. "I don't know very much about kindness, honestly. We didn't really have that when I was growing up. Your family though...They sound nice."

"They are." Before he'd sent them to live here, Nuri had done his best to pick up where their parents had left off. He'd wanted Nate and Neve to grow up into respectable adults. Whether or not he'd succeeded, at least where Nate was concerned, was yet to be decided, but at least Neve had surpassed both of their expectations. "My sister works at the hospital. She's working on her residency now."

"And your brother," Port said. "He works for CEO Rein on Ignite, right?"

"Yeah."

"Did I hear they're also married?"

Nate bristled a bit. "Yes, but they've only recently gotten together. Nuri wasn't hired because—"

"I'm not accusing him of anything," Port stopped him. "Promise. Is he good to him?"

Nate frowned. "What?"

"Silver Rein. Does he treat your brother right? You said your sister is happy. What about Nuri? Is he happy too?"

"I...Yeah. He says he's happy."

"Why don't you sound pleased about that?"

"No," he shook his head, "I am." He was. He just didn't fully trust Silver. But then, he supposed he didn't really have to. It wasn't his life, as much as he wanted to protect his brother. Nuri was his own person who made his own choices. "He's the oldest, so he can do what he wants."

"You can do what you want too, Nate," Port replied.

"Why are we talking about me?" Nate clapped his hands together awkwardly and then moved toward the entrance to the hallway, located between the kitchen and living areas. "Let me just double-check you've got everything you need in the bathroom. You look exhausted. You should get some sleep."

It seemed like there was something else that Port wanted to say, but in the end, he merely sighed and gave a silent nod.

The house had been purchased by Nuri when they'd first moved here, and they'd stayed in it ever since. The title was in Nate's name since Neve had been a kid at the time, and she'd shown no interest in changing things since. He kept things running smoothly in the communal areas and made repairs throughout the years as they became necessary, but ultimately left the majority of things the way they'd been when Nuri had bought the place.

It was his home, and yet, at the same time...It didn't entirely feel like it. It was hard to explain. Nuri had picked and paid for it, and because of that Nate still felt a little bit like he was relying on his brother to get by, despite the fact that he'd taken over all of the utility payments as soon as he'd graduated from college. Nuri had fought him on it for a bit, but eventually, he'd worn him down. At the time, Nate had hoped putting that line between them would help with the intensifying feeling of not being good enough and being a leech.

It hadn't, not really.

Nate still felt like he wasn't good enough for the people in his life to rely on. To want to keep. Like, if he made one wrong move, he'd not only destroy his own world, but theirs all in one fell swoop. Oddly enough, the episodes he'd experience whenever it got really bad had seemed to lessen over the past couple of weeks, however...

The only change he could think of was losing his job. Maybe leaving Quartet Air was for the best. He was certainly happier not having to always have his guard up around clients like Mit and shitty bosses like Sier.

The stress he'd undergone on the daily had certainly exacerbated his poor mental health. He'd been afraid to, but perhaps he should have quit sooner. So far, the walls hadn't come crumbling down around him—neither of his siblings had called to chew him a new one or ask how work was going, so that was something—and he was managing to keep the lights on. Now that he'd gotten the job at the Velvet Brew, that was going to be a lot easier.

It would give him time to find a better job, too, at a company he actually wanted to work at. There was no shortage in the need for mechanics like him, ones who were trained in both land and air vehicles. Nate could fix a hovercar as easily as he could find the problem with a malfunctioning hovership. Quartet Air only worked on personal vehicles, nothing public, which was why his skills had been going to waste. At the time, he'd been fresh out of school and in desperate need of a job, so he'd taken the first offer made to him. Afterward, he was too worried about being unable to find another to leave.

Kazimir had done him a favor, hadn't he?
Damn.

Nate so didn't want to be indebted to that guy for real, and scowled as he entered the attached bathroom in Neve's room and made a quick check that there were clean toothbrushes and toothpaste in the overhead cabinet.

Why hadn't the guy given up already? Did he seriously intend to drive Nate insane before—

A loud crash from the front of the house startled him, and he dropped the bottle of shampoo he'd been checking. It hit the floor of the bathtub and burst open, sending the scent of strawberries into the air.

"Port?" Nate called and rushed out to check on him. It'd sounded a lot like the back door. Sure enough, by the time he'd made it to the kitchen, the door was wide open, letting in strong gusts of icy wind. "Port?!"

He grabbed onto the handle and popped his head out into the dark night, staring across his empty backyard. It was too dark to make much out, and he certainly didn't see any signs of his friend. "Port?!"

"Stop screaming and turn around," a deep voice said, cutting through Nate's panic.

With no other option but to comply, his hand slipped off the door and he shifted, eyes widening when they landed on a strange man three times his size. "Who are you?"

Whoever he was, he currently had a blaster aimed directly at Nate's chest. The gun was scary enough on its own without needing to be held by someone so massive. Even if Nate had any sort of combat training, which he did not, he wouldn't stand a chance against an opponent like this. Vaguely, he wondered if the crash he'd heard had actually been this guy breaking in and not the back door being tossed open like he'd assumed.

"I ask the questions here, kid." The large man glanced over his shoulder toward the backyard. "The Jump, where is he?"

Nate didn't know how to respond since he had no clue what he was talking about.

"Port," the man snapped, impatient. "Where the fuck did he go?"

He was after Port? What for? Port had always been the quiet type that stuck to himself. What could he have possibly done to piss off someone like this?

"Start talking right now or else I'll—" the man stopped abruptly, and for a moment, Nate couldn't figure out what. Then suddenly, his body toppled forward, slamming to the ground with enough force to rattle the dining room table and the rest of the furniture.

Kazimir stood at the man's feet, that crystal blade of his smeared in blood that rolled down the handle and coated his fingers. He spat down on the body and then lifted his dark gaze, eyes locking onto Nate with enough intensity that it actually caused him to shiver.

"Kaz," Nate whispered, unsure where he was going with that. Fortunately for him, the hotshot wasn't in the mood to let him figure it out.

"Listen carefully, Narek. In less than a minute, the others are going to show up. You do as I say, understood? Play along. None of that bullshit resisting you're so fond of."

"I don't—"

"You don't need to understand," he growled. "Just tell me you'll do as I say."

Nate licked his lips. There was a dead man bleeding all over his floors and a pissed-off Brumal member still holding a dangerous weapon glaring him down. He needed a minute to think.

"You don't have that much time," Kaz snarled.

Nate hadn't even realized he'd spoken out loud. Before he could say anything else, his front door clattered open, and one of the Retinue, Pavel, entered with Flix hot on his heels.

"Where is the target?" Pavel asked, absently taking in the body like it was no big deal.

"Not here," Kazimir said.

"Is that so? Then," he tipped his head and directed his next question at Nate, "Where is he?"

"He doesn't know." Kaz wiped the bloodied blade off on his thigh and exhaled, filling the sound with frustration. "Wherever this asshole got his intel," he kicked at the dead man's foot, "he should ask for his money back."

Flix was staring at Nate with an unreadable expression.

"That's a lie," Pavel stated cooly. "You're the one who directed us here, Kazimir. You knew this was where he was coming."

Nate didn't know what was going on, but it was obvious from the tense way everyone was standing that it wasn't anything good. If they were also here looking for Port, that meant his friend had gotten mixed up with both the Brumal and the Imperial family, and that...There was nothing Nate could do to protect him from something like that.

But Kaz could...

"I told him," Nate exclaimed, ignoring the way Kazimir's shoulders stiffened slightly, hoping that no one else in the room noticed.

"You did?" Pavel didn't sound convinced.

"Yeah." He licked his lips. "You're here for Port Grier, right?"

Kaz pinched the bridge of his nose, potentially guessing where Nate was taking this.

"This guy asked me the same thing. Port isn't here. I haven't seen him in weeks," Nate said. It was too late to turn back now, and this was the only thing he could think of, the only way to throw them off Port's scent and help explain why Kazimir had arrived.

"That so?"

"He called me earlier," Nate added, just in case they checked his phone records—that was more than something people in their positions were capable of doing. "But he wasn't here when I arrived. Maybe he caught wind this guy was around and took off."

"He hasn't called you since?" Flix asked, finally speaking up.

"No."

"Have you tried calling him?" Pavel said, and then before Nate could come up with a reason why he wouldn't have, Flix snapped his fingers at him.

"Try now," he ordered.

Nate's hands shook slightly as he lifted his multi-slate, but any hesitancy shown would tip them off, and he knew better than to do that. If he did, it wouldn't just be him on the line, it would be Port as well. They couldn't know he'd only just left; otherwise, they'd give chase. If they found him, who knew what their plans were.

He'd already decided to help his friend out however he could. Nate wasn't going to go back on his word, no matter what that might cost him personally.

"Put it on speaker," Pavel told him once he'd dialed the number, and they all waited as Nate complied, listening to the sound of it ringing on the other end over and over with no answer. With a grunt, he walked around the body and past Kazimir, who straightened even more, eyeing him suspiciously as he headed toward Nate.

Nate froze up as well, but instead of touching him, Pavel merely slipped by him, stepping out onto the back porch. "Call him again."

As the communicator rang a second time, Pavel tipped his head, clearly trying to hear any sounds outside. After a moment, he seemed satisfied and reentered the house, shutting the door carefully at his back. "No one is out there."

"My boyfriend wouldn't lie to us," Kazimir said. "Would you, Pretty Boy?"

Nate tried to avoid meeting Flix's questioning gaze as he shook his head and forced himself to say,

"No, of course not. What is this about?"

"None of your concern." Pavel headed back over to where Flix was standing in the middle of the living room, closer to the entrance to the house.

"There's a dead body in my home," Nate pointed out. "Kind of my concern now."

"I'll call the cleaners and have it removed," Pavel said, already lifting his multi-slate.

"No," Flix disagreed. "This is Brumal business, you and your brother are just on loan to help with the job, remember?"

The corner of his mouth tipped up coldly as he stared Flix down. "If this is how the Brumal does work, I'm shocked you've managed to stay in power for so long."

"Relax," Kaz held up both hands, though the move also meant he was waving the blood-stained blade in the air as well. "We weren't on retrieval duty. This was a trade deal and we upheld our end of the bargain. Baikal just wanted to know what was up, that's all. You know the drill. Kelevra no doubt put you on this for the same reason."

Pavel's jaw tightened. "None of us trust Pious Prince." He motioned toward the body. "How are you going to explain that to him? Rumor is he's protective of the Ancient, and you've just slain one."

What?

Nate turned to Kazimir, but the annoying younger guy didn't seem as worried. Or worried at all, for that matter.

He actually shrugged like it was no big deal.

"We'll toss his body by the cove. Pious will simply assume his target got to him."

"How do you figure?" Flix asked.

"Remember what he told us at the meeting?" Kaz smirked. "He said Port could take care of himself. This shouldn't be that big of a shock if that was true."

"You're relying a lot on assumption," Pavel drawled.

"Keeps things interesting." Kazimir winked at him, and Pavel made a face of disgust.

Apparently, Nate wasn't the only one immune to his charms.

"You two get out of here," Kaz ordered next. "I'll take care of the body on my own. It'll be less suspicious that way."

"No," Flix moved forward, "I'll do it. You and Pavel can go, report back."

Kaz stepped in front of him before he could reach the body. "You forgetting who's in charge here, Firebug?"

Flix didn't back down.

"Have your little standoff," Pavel said. "I'll be on my way." He took one last lingering look at Nate before leaving.

"You should go too," Kazimir told Flix once they heard a car engine rev to life outside.

"I'm not leaving you alone with Nate," Flix replied.

"Did you not get the memo just now? He's fine. Aren't you, Pretty Boy?"

Nate glanced between the two of them. On the one hand, he could come clean now that the terrifying Retinue member was gone, but on the other...Whatever Port was involved with, Flix and Kaz were both a part of it. If Nate wanted to ensure his friend stayed safe, he had to play his cards right, which meant he was going to have to do the thing he hated and rely on Kazimir.

Because Kaz was right, Flix might be his actual friend here, but Kaz was the one in charge. If he chose to call Pavel back in and confess that Port had, in fact, been here a moment ago, there was nothing either Nate or Flix would be able to do to stop him.

"It's okay, Flix," he forced himself to say, giving his friend a shaky smile. "He won't hurt me."

"Nate, you don't have to be afraid. If he's making you—"

Kazimir planted one hand on Flix's chest and shoved him. "You're starting to piss me off, Flix."

"Stop." Nate was stepping over the body and grabbing onto Kaz's arm faster than he could process his feet were even moving. He tugged on him, getting him to put a little more distance between him and Flix. "Don't start fighting."

"Why not?" Kaz snarled. "He—"

"Because you literally just murdered someone in my kitchen and I'm freaking out here!" Nate said. He felt their eyes on him, but kept his gaze locked on the third button of Kaz's dress shirt, not trusting himself because that hadn't been a lie.

He was, in fact, freaking out.

"This isn't my normal," he added when neither of them spoke. "I get that it is for you two, that you're used to killing and seeing bodies and being covered in blood. But I'm not. The most illegal I get is racing at the docks."

One of Kazimir's hands settled over his wrists, and Nate realized he was shaking and clinging to the Brumal member now, instead of holding him back like he'd initially been.

"Get this body out of here, Flix," Kaz said in a clipped tone, leaving no room for argument.

Though he hesitated, Flix did as he was told without further complaint. "You'll have to take care of the blood on your own."

"Yeah." Kaz eased Nate closer to him so that Flix could have easier access to the dead man's ankles. When the sound of him being dragged away came a moment later, and Nate squeezed his eyes shut, Kaz lifted a hand and ran it lightly through the hairs at the back of his skull. "It's okay, Pretty Boy. There's nothing to be afraid of. I won't let anything happen to you."

"*You* have happened to me, Kaz," he shot back.

Kazimir's hand stilled, and some of the tenderness was gone when Nate risked a glance up at him. But his voice remained steady when he replied, "Remember our revelation before? When I figured out you'd pay up if you felt like you were truly in my debt."

Nate's hands fell away from Kaz's arm, and he stared up at him.

"I just killed a man for you, Pretty Boy," Kazimir's voice lowered silkily, one of his arms wrapping around Nate's waist to pull him in close until their chests were flush together. "If Pious Prince, the man we're currently in a partnership with, finds out, he'll try for revenge. And if he finds out I also helped your little friend get away?" He clicked his tongue. "It'll be an all-out war between our group and his. People will die horrible deaths."

"It's not my fault," Nate said.

"Narek," Kaz let out a low whistle, "you don't believe that for a second."

"You're trying to manipulate me." Why had Nate thought this was a good idea again? He should have sided with Flix. At least he knew his friend could be trusted.

"It's working," Kaz sounded so pleased with himself.

Yes, though. Yes, it was.

"Should I call Pavel back in and tell him to go hunt for Port?" Kazimir asked. "He's a great tracker. Even with the head start, he'll find him."

"Then you'll be in trouble too, for lying," Nate pointed out, only to have the Devil laugh in his face.

"True," he agreed. "You won't be safe either. You might even have to leave the planet. Your sister too, since she shares the same last name."

Nate grabbed onto Kazimir's collar. "Are you threatening my sister?"

Kaz grinned at him. "Wouldn't dream of it."

Nate wanted to beat the shit out of him for

even daring to bring Neve into this, but logic held him back. He'd never win against a Brumal member.

He'd never win against Kaz.

If only he'd come to that conclusion sooner, maybe all of this could have been avoided.

His grip loosened and he let go. "Tell me what to do."

"What's that?"

"What do you want me to do, Kazimir?" He clenched his hands into fists at his sides. "Tell me what to do to make you stop."

"Stop?" He grunted. "Babe, I haven't even started yet."

Nate glared at him. "You can't be serious?"

"Of course I am. You want to thank me for saving your friend? Repay me for risking my life—and taking one—for you? That's a substantial debt you've accumulated, Narek. Much bigger than the mere coin you'd cost me before. Tell you what to do? How about this, Pretty Boy, we'll start off slow. For now, all you have to do," he captured Nate's chin and tipped his head up, "is kiss me."

Nate's brow furrowed, certain he'd misheard.

"What?" Kazimir smirked. "Don't want to? All right. Pav—"

Even though they'd both heard the sound of car engines leaving his driveway and knew both Pavel and Flix were long gone, the threat was still there, and Nate reacted to it the way Kazimir no doubt had hoped.

Before the Brumal member could finish that

sentence, Nate lifted onto his toes and planted his mouth against Kaz's.

The first thing he noted was the lingering taste of coffee on Kazimir's lips.

The second was the bulge suddenly pressing insistently against his lower abs as Kaz hardened from just a single stroke of Nate's tongue against his own.

And, finally, the third thing was how Nate's traitorous body responded in turn.

Despite the threats and the murder he'd just committed, Kazimir was turning Nate on.

Kaz chuckled, clearly aware of the change in Nate as well. "There you go, Pretty Boy. It's about time. We're going to have so much fun, you and I."

Nate opened his mouth to disagree, but anything he was about to say was swallowed up by that wicked mouth and dashed away by Kaz's twisted tongue.

In the middle of his blood-stained kitchen, Nate found himself being consumed by the Devil with nowhere left to run.

Any lingering hope of escape drifted away as he was lifted into Kazimir's arms and wordlessly carried down the hall.

CHAPTER 13:

Kazimir stripped him down and then shoved him face-first onto the bed, but it wasn't until he tugged Nate's arms back and he felt something silky cinch across his wrists that he bothered to struggle.

"What are you doing?" he demanded, trying to rise onto his knees, only for his neck to be captured in a vicelike grip that forced him back into position.

"He speaks," Kaz drawled, tightening the material he was using to bind Nate. "I was starting to think you were disassociating on me."

"What?" How could he know about that?

"Don't sound so shocked. I read your file, Narek. It was easy enough to get my hands on."

"That's illegal!" He'd only gone to one session. How much could the doctor have written about him, really?

"It's not like I learned anything I didn't already know about you," Kaz said.

It was impossible to know if that was true or not because Nate doubted the Brumal member would admit it if he had read something new. He prided himself on being able to see through people, had boasted about it enough times in the past that Nate would be an idiot not to have caught on.

"Considering everything that just happened, it wouldn't be too wild to guess that you'd start freaking out," Kaz continued.

"Is that why you're tying my wrists?" Nate tilted his head on the dark gray pillow and tried to view him over his shoulder. "Just, give me a minute. I need a minute."

"So that you can what? Think?" He clucked his tongue. "No can do, Pretty Boy. Nothing good ever comes of you overthinking. All you have to do is lay here and take it." Kaz gave one sharp slap to Nate's right ass cheek and then rubbed some of the sting away with a caress. "This is mine. Get used to it."

Nate hated how hopeless he felt, but more than that, he hated how Kaz was right about the thinking part. What good would that do him here, while at Kazimir's mercy? "You said we'd start small."

"I only did that so you'd let your guard down, and wouldn't you know it? It worked."

"Bastard."

"Let's see if you'll still be calling me that when I'm balls deep and wrecking your insides."

That picture didn't exactly help calm his nerves any, and Nate tried again to rise up onto his knees, only to be shoved forward and held down. This time Kaz was less forgiving, digging his nails into the side of Nate's neck as he waited for his struggles to subside on their own. Feeling like there was no other option but to give in, Nate stilled, focusing on his breathing instead.

"Angry, Pretty Boy?" Kaz taunted, slowly removing his hand only to lightly stroke it down the curve of Nate's spine. "Want to punch me again?"

"Yes." Lying didn't seem worth it. Besides, the Brumal member had shown him time and time again that words were the only defense Nate had against him. Maybe if he kept talking, he could make Kaz feel even half as shitty as he did now.

Because he did feel shitty...right?

He was face down on his own bed, tied, and on his knees with his ass up in the air, and the only reason was because Kazimir had used the safety of his friend against him. If not for Port, Nate would have fought back in the living room. He would never have—

"Trying to talk yourself down?" Kaz interrupted his thoughts. "You angry because you want it, babe," his fingers slipped between Nate's crack, "or because you don't?"

"I don't," he snapped.

"That so?" When his hand wrapped around Nate's member and squeezed, he was far from easy, laughing when Nate let out a pained cry. "Should have consulted with your dick first. You aren't very good at this, are you?"

"Good at what?" Nate asked through clenched teeth.

"Picking and choosing your lies," he

explained. "That's going to be an important skill to have as my boyfriend."

"I am not—" He stopped on another strangled cry when Kazimir squeezed again and slapped him on the left ass cheek at the same time.

"You held out for an impressively long while, but let's not beat a dead horse. You were always going to end up in this position, prostrating for me."

"You aren't giving me a choice," Nate pointed out. "If you were, I wouldn't be kneeling like this for you, ever."

"*Ever* is a long time, Pretty Boy,"

"I said what I meant."

Kazimir was quiet for a moment, and then he pulled away, the sound of him climbing off the bed emboldening Nate.

He rolled onto his side, careful not to crush his arm since they were still bound uncomfortably, eyes tracking Kaz as he wandered around the perimeter of the room, clearly on the hunt for something. "What are you looking for?"

"Everyone keeps telling me how nice you are," he said, tapping his fingers over the organized surface of Nate's desk. The room had two doors, one to the hallway on the right of the bed and one across that led to the bathroom. Both were currently open, but Kazimir passed by the bathroom with little more than a glance. "But even nice guys like to fuck, isn't that right?"

Nate wasn't following. Since he hadn't been scolded for moving, he took it a step further and pushed up onto his knees so he was kneeling in the center of the bed.

Kazimir was still fully clothed, not even his fly undone like it'd been their first time at the bar. He appeared put together and relaxed as he searched, like they had all the time in the world for him to find what he was after.

Nate hated admitting it, but Kaz was hot. He had the perfect body—not too muscular, not too lean—with wide shoulders and long legs. His hair was always styled neatly, and even though he was dressed in the same bland uniform as everyone else who attended Vail, he somehow oozed sex appeal and danger. Neither of those things should be of any interest to Nate, especially not the latter, and yet...

His eyes drifted down to the spot between his thighs. He wasn't at full mast, but it didn't take a genius to note that he was turned on. It didn't make any sense to him, though. In the past, he'd been gentle with all of his sexual partners. Rough sex wasn't even something on his radar, not something that had ever crossed his mind as a possibility. Nate liked taking care of people.

"The nightstand is too obvious," Kaz said then. "And you're not fourteen, so I doubt you hid it under the mattress..." He grabbed onto the door handle to the closet and peered inside before reaching in to shift a few clothing items around. "That's more like it."

There was no way...

Kazimir pulled a large black tumbler out and

tossed it in the air, catching it with a smug look on his face. "Sneaky, Narek. I like it."

"Put that back."

"Why? Going to spin some tale about how it was a gift from your brother?" He snorted at his own joke. "I've gathered you two are close, but if he's gifting you sex toys, he and I are going to have a problem."

Nate blanched as Kaz twisted the top off the cup and tossed it over his shoulder. The plastic landed in the bathroom and clattered loudly on the tile floor. Then he tipped it so the opening was facing Nate, as though he didn't already know exactly what it was the Brumal member was trying to show him.

"Pretty discrete fleshlight, babe," Kazimir said. "How often do you use it?"

There wasn't anything he could say to that since he had no intention of answering, so Nate remained silent.

"What about this?" Kazimir reached back into the closet and pulled out another toy. "A glass butt plug? Sleek. What about this one? Play with it often? You said you hadn't had sex with a man before, but this explains why you opened up for me so easily the other night. I thought it was just the alcohol. I even came prepared this time."

"What?" Nate must be losing it, because the tiny voice in his head commented on how they should just turn it into a drinking game. Take a shot every time he asks why in that dumb, clueless tone of his.

Kaz slipped two small tubes out of his back pocket and waved them in the air. "Before and aftercare. I anticipated things to get...messy."

As funny as it was to picture Kazimir walking around with those things in his pockets just in case he ever needed them, there were no coincidences where Kaz was concerned. When he said he'd come prepared, he meant it. Meant that he'd specifically selected those items with the intention of using them on Nate tonight.

The conversation from before with Pavol and Flix came back to him then, and he felt a sinking feeling mingle with the lingering trepidation.

"How did you know Port was here?" Nate had lied for him saying he'd called, but they both knew that wasn't the case. He stared at the two tubes still being held up. "How did you know we'd end up having sex again tonight?"

"One question at a time, Pretty Boy. First, I saw your multi-slate at the coffee shop, remember? You should really be more careful with who you let close enough to read that thing. For future reference, if they can, they're too close to you. I don't like anyone getting near my things, that clear, babe?"

Nate's mouth dropped open in surprise when Kazimir tossed the butt plug over his shoulder just as carelessly as he had the top to the fleshlight.

"You won't need it anymore," Kaz explained. "From here on out, the only thing allowed near that sweet ass of yours is me. You want to be filled? You'll get my fingers, my tongue, or my cock. Nothing else goes in there. If I find out you disobeyed, I'll make you sleep, eat, and breathe with my cock shoved so deep you'll be begging me to pull out after the first hour. Understood?"

"This is crazy." Add that to the drinking game.

Nate really wished that sardonic voice would shut the hell up so he could focus on what mattered. Like talking Kazimir down before he did...whatever he planned on doing.

"Since I don't have a vag, and there's no way I'm letting you stick it to me," he shook the fleshlight, "we'll hold on to this one. If you're bad, though, I'll take it away like I did your other toy."

"I am not a child." Nate straightened his shoulders, trying to ignore how ridiculous he must look, naked on his bed, bound. "I'm your senior, Kazimir. You can't just—"

"We aren't on campus," he said. "And I don't see you as my senior, Nate Narek." He made his way back over toward the end of the bed, voice dropping, "You're my little bitch."

Nate winced and felt tears well in the corner of his eyes. He sniffled and looked away, not wanting Kaz to catch on. He'd never cried in front of anyone before, not since he'd been a kid and his parents had died. Honestly, he wasn't even sure why he was doing so now. Did this situation totally blow? Yes. But was it worth losing his shit over?

Actually...probably.

Getting involved with a Devil was bad enough. But being claimed by one like property?

What would his brother think?

If Nuri ever heard any of this, he'd be so ashamed of how Nate had turned out. Would he blame himself for it, too? He'd been the one who'd picked Vitality, so of course he would. Nuri was always taking responsibility for things out of his control, things that didn't have anything to do with him. That's why Silver had liked keeping him around so much, even before they'd gotten together. Why Nate tried so hard not to add to the workload by becoming a burden.

"Hey." Kazimir placed the items in his hands down on the bed and then crawled onto it, moving so that he was now the one kneeling in front of Nate. When he cupped Nate's cheek, his touch was gentle, and he turned his face up so their eyes were meeting. "Not a fan of that phrase?"

Nate swallowed and considered staying quiet, but he'd never been the silent type, and he wasn't going to get anywhere with the Brumal member if he didn't at least try to voice his opinions. "I'm a person, Kaz. I'm not a thing. Not," he scowled at the fleshlight, "a sex toy. You can't just use me and treat me like plastic. I have feelings, you know."

"I know," he said, "I've been manipulating them all this time. Of course, I know."

Nate wasn't even surprised by that, sighing disappointedly. This wasn't going to work. Kazimir didn't care what Nate wanted, only what—

"I didn't tell you to be my sex toy," Kazimir told him. "I want you to be my boyfriend. We're going to fuck—hard and often—but that's not the only thing I want you for. Tell you what, I'll give you a chance to have things your way. How does that sound?"

He searched Kaz's gaze, trying to find the trap. What he was thinking, however, must have been obvious because that only earned him a clicking of the Devil's tongue.

"You can't get out of this, Narek. I've chosen you. That's final. But," his free hand trailed over to Nate's right leg, his heated touch suggestively traveling up his calf, past his knee, and over his thigh, "you want it to feel more legit? Say yes, Pretty Boy. That's all you have to do. Submit to me, and I promise I'll play the role."

"What does that mean?" And why was Nate even considering it for a moment?

He really must be out of his mind. Or maybe just desperate for this to finally end. He was tired of looking over his shoulder, fearing the Brumal member would show up out of the blue again. He'd already lost his job at Quartet Air, and there was the looming threat Kaz had made toward Jones to consider.

Maybe this really was the best option for him.

"I wouldn't call my boyfriend a little bitch, for one," Kaz said. "The rest of the evening will go as I planned, but we can drop the crude name-calling if you're really against that. I want you hot for me, Nate. I could fuck you against your will again, sure, but that's not a long-term solution."

"You really care this much about proving to your cousin you could also be in a relationship?" Nate shook his head. "Blackmailing someone into being your boyfriend isn't real, Kazimir."

"I don't need it to be real," his voice darkened some, "I just need it to be you."

"Why?"

"I'm honestly not sure anymore. Maybe it's because you resisted so beautifully? I've got this inescapable urge to claim you and bend you to my will. If I get to stick it to Baikal in the process? Fantastic. But that's no longer what this is about."

"Then," even knowing he should heed the warning, Nate asked, "Why bother with the relationship at all? We can just have sex because I owe you for letting Port go," he had to pause and swallow the bile that threatened to rise, "and killing that guy. I can do that. We can do it right now, and then—"

"You think once would be enough payment?" Kaz's eyes flashed and the hand on Nate's face shifted to grab onto his chin roughly.

"A few more times than!" Nate rushed to say. "How many times would be enough? Tell me. I'll do it. If you want to tie me up or whatever, okay."

"Just so long as you don't have to be my boyfriend, is that it?" Kazimir said coldly, and Nate realized his mistake too late.

"That's—"

"Exactly what you're trying to get out of," he cut him off. "Here I was trying to do something nice for you, Pretty Boy, and how do you repay me?" Kaz shoved him onto his back and then blindly reached behind him until he grabbed the two small tubes. One was tossed to the side again, but the other was uncapped, and it was impossible not to note how careful he was not to get any of the cream on him as he pinned Nate down with a hand on his stomach and brought it to his flaccid dick.

During their talk, Nate had gone soft, and he let out a hiss when the cold cream first landed on his tip.

"Rub it in," Kazimir ordered, and when Nate hesitated, he growled. "Don't make me pull out my knife. Considering the mood I'm now in, I might actually cut you just for the fun of it."

"My hands are bound," Nate reminded shakily. "Kaz, please."

"You think saying my name will get you out of this?" He shook his head. "Just because I like the sound of it coming from you, doesn't mean shit after the stunt you just pulled."

"Untie me and I'll—"

"Punch me again," Kaz said, and it was clear he was certain of that fact. "You'll take a swing, maybe make it to the hallway, and I'll be forced to drag you back here by the hair. You'll end up on all fours with me fucking you raw."

He shuddered, knowing there was nothing untrue about that statement. If Kazimir was telling him that's what would happen, that's what would happen.

"I can't do anything with my hands tied," Nate desperately told him.

"Use your thighs." He grabbed his legs and pushed them together, yanking so that Nate fell onto his back, arms squished beneath him. After he'd settled the backs on his knees over his right shoulder, Kaz motioned down at him. "You're soft right now. Rub your thighs together. Hurry up, the cream's already drying and I want it coating your cock."

It was awkward and embarrassing, but Nate's arms were already hurt from lying on top of them, and he didn't see a way out of this other than doing what he was told. It was difficult to trap his dick enough, and he wasn't entirely sure he was doing anything other than squeezing himself uncomfortably, but Nate kept at it until Kazimir grunted in satisfaction.

The Devil squirted another glob of the cream onto Nate's base, but instead of ordering him to rub again, he dropped Nate's legs and got off the bed a second time. He maintained eye contact with Nate as he slipped the button of his jeans open and pulled down his fly. Unlike in the bar, he didn't just pull himself free and leave it at that, stepping out of his clothes until he was just as naked as Nate was.

"Good boys get rewarded," Kaz said cryptically, stroking himself with a hand until he was long and hard, his flushed cock causing Nate's mouth to go dry.

How the hell had all of that fit in him at

the bar?! Up until then, he'd only ever played with the butt plug Kazimir had already discarded. It was small, less than three inches, just enough he'd felt like there was something back there when he'd masturbated and that was all. It certainly hadn't ever provided the stretch and burn that Kaz's cock had that night.

His dick twitched, and he felt himself swell a moment before a strange sensation tingled all over his shaft. With a frown, Nate pulled his gaze off of Kazimir and glanced down at himself.

"Bad boys," Kaz continued, "get punished."

Nate sat up and spread his thighs a little, too freaked out to be embarrassed. "What's going on? It feels...weird."

"Desensitizing cream," he explained as he continued to work himself with measured pumps, the tip of his cock dripping precome the only sign he was into it. His voice was steady, and his expression was enigmatic as he watched Nate. "Originally, I brought it to use on your ass. I didn't trust I would be able to hold back enough not to overly hurt you, and I figured you wouldn't be drunk this time to help ease the sting so...As soon as I found this, though," he nodded toward the fleshlight before picking it up, "the plan changed."

Nate didn't like it. He was hard, but at the same time those pangs of pleasure he'd typically be feeling were dull.

"If you want to know why I numbed your dick instead, you can just ask, babe."

"Why?"

"Because we're going to fuck until dawn, and you're not going to be allowed to come until I say so. That's what you get for turning me down. By the end of this, you'll be begging me to be my boyfriend, Nate Narek. Begging me to take care of you."

Nate watched with wide eyes as Kazimir suddenly came, aiming his cock into the fleshlight. He filled the toy with his come, the corner of his mouth tipping up wickedly at Nate's shocked expression, clearly getting off on the fact he'd shocked him again. "Lube is something I didn't bring," he explained. "This should do the trick, though."

When he planted a knee onto the edge of the mattress, Nate instinctively crawled back, trying to get away. Kaz was faster though.

He threw himself on top of Nate, pinning him down as he sheathed Nate's dick in the fleshlight. The button on the top flashed purple as it was turned on, and then the toy started moving over him, sucking and compressing with just the right amount of pressure to have him fully erect in no time at all.

Kazimir laughed and planted a kiss on Nate's jawline before he nipped him hard enough to startle him all over again. "How's that, Pretty Boy?"

Nate shook his head against the pillow and stared sightlessly up at the ceiling. He could feel the toy sucking on him, knew he was turned on, but the sensations were there yet just out of reach.

"I don't like it," he admitted, lifting his hips off the bed in a poor attempt to gain more friction. He slipped deeper into the toy, but Kaz held him steady and didn't turn the settings up any higher, so there was no stronger wave of pleasure gained from his efforts. A whine slipped past his lips and Kazimir kissed him again.

"Don't cry yet," he said. "I'm only getting started on you."

CHAPTER 14:

Nate sobbed into the pillow as Kazimir thrust into him, pounding his hole past the point of pleasure and into that mixture of bliss with a dash of pain. He'd lost track of how many times they'd done this, but the pool of sticky fluids coating his entire body, turning to adhesive beneath his knees as he was bent over the ruined comforter on his bed, was an indicator it'd been a lot.

The fleshlight continued to suck on his dick, milking him for the third or fourth time despite the desensitizing cream. The first orgasm had taken over an hour for Nate to achieve, and the relief he'd felt after he'd blown his load had been the most intense part. In that moment, he'd foolishly believed Kaz would end things after.

He'd realized the truth since.

Kazimir was a Devil in and out of the bedroom. He'd fuck Nate into oblivion, come, and then start the whole process up again in under three minutes. It should have been impossible, but Nate had felt him harden while still inside of him mere moments after he'd pumped him full.

Forget never having had rough sex before. Nate had never had sex anything *like this*. It'd never gone hours, for one, and certainly hadn't crossed that line of comfort and pleasure. His entire being was buzzing with a strange sensation he couldn't quite place and his mind was a jumbled mess. Thoughts came and went before he could latch onto them, and he was switching between moans and sobbing without even really processing he was doing as much.

Kaz plugged him up and draped his body over Nate's back, flattening him against the mattress so he could run his lips up the back of his neck and across his shoulders. When Nate sniffled, Kaz undulated, causing him to gasp instead.

It wasn't just physical things; if Kazimir Ambrose wanted a specific reaction from someone, he got it. He'd wrung so many out of Nate already, had worked him so thoroughly his sense of time was gone. They could have been doing this for days instead of hours and Nate wouldn't be surprised to learn as much.

He felt disgusting, covered in dried, drying, and still wet come, and his legs ached from being shoved apart. The position had altered; sometimes, he was on his back, other times on his side or bent over like he was now, but the fleshlight never came off, and Kazimir only pulled out for a handful of minutes at most. He'd been well and truly used, and he wasn't sure how much more he could take before he physically hit his limit. Hell, maybe that wouldn't be a bad thing.

Maybe that was how he'd finally put an end to this. Passing out.

Or maybe Kaz would simply continue fucking his unconscious body.

Probably that one.

Kazimir took Nate's chin and tilted his head on the pillow so that his face was exposed to the air scented with sex and sweat. "What do you say, Nate?" he asked, only slightly out of breath, despite the full-on marathon he'd enacted on this bed. "Still feel like a person? Think carefully before you answer."

Be prepared to tell him what he wanted to hear, was what Kaz meant. Nate could read between the lines, though barely, with how desperate he felt to take a rest.

That's what all of this had really been about. Kazimir wasn't sexually torturing him simply because he was horny, he was doing it to teach a lesson. For the first time ever, Nate wished he'd paid more attention to Bay's ramblings whenever he entered professor mode and started spouting statistics and facts about psychopaths. He knew a little—enough to decide without a shadow of a doubt that Kaz fit the bill—but not nearly enough to feel like he could properly defend himself.

He was pretty sure Kaz was trying to condition him, and using sex to do it. What he wasn't clear on was how they'd gotten to this point or why.

"Do you feel good, Pretty Boy?" Kaz said when he didn't get an answer to his first question fast enough. "Feel," he pushed in as deep as he could go, grinning when Nate whined, "full?"

His sheathed dick was pressed against the mattress, crushed like the rest of him, and if nothing else, Nate really just wanted that piece of the puzzle gone. He'd been pushed so far past the point of over-sensitivity that it was safe to say this was more akin to sexual sadism than it was regular sex. At least... he hoped so...

"Is this," his voice was scratchy and raw when he used it and he had to pause for a second before finishing his sentence, "how it usually is with you?"

"How many bed partners do you think would let me fuck them non-stop for six hours?" Kazimir replied, reaching out to run his fingers idly through Nate's damp hair.

Six hours? His eyes drifted shut of their own accord. "Is that all it's been?"

"Why? Need to go for another six? We can. I'm good for it."

Nate had the sense to shake his head, and Kaz hummed in understanding.

"Ready to answer me now, then, babe? Now that you've had a taste of what being my sex object is like, you still willing to pay off your debt that way?"

If it was going to be like this each and every time? Of course not.

"You won't be walking tomorrow," Kaz noted.

"At least, not without my help anyway. Don't worry, though, I do have something that could fix that problem for you. I know how important it is for you to get to work. Can't miss your second day at the coffee shop, can you? What would Jones do without you?"

He shuddered at the veiled threat and the way that comment licked at his guilt.

"I don't have anywhere to be," Kaz continued. "No plans. Nothing that could take me away from this warm bed and your tight hole. I could stay here the rest of the weekend, in fact, using you to my heart's content."

Nate snickered before he could help it, a bit too dehydrated and delirious now. "You don't have a heart, Kazimir."

"Sure I do," he disagreed, lowering his lips to the curve of Nate's ear. "It just doesn't empathize with yours. I always get what I want, Narek. Even if I have to fuck you senseless, I'll have you begging for me. Forget about the rest of the world. From now on, you don't have to worry about pleasing them. I'm the only person you have to care about disappointing. Focus on me, Pretty Boy. Just me."

It hadn't even been half a day and yet Kazimir had done exactly what he'd claimed he would. He'd reduced Nate to a thing because, no, no, he did not currently feel like a person. A person had their own autonomy. They had the right and ability to say they didn't like something. No matter how many times Nate had said it at the start, however, his objections had fallen on deaf ears. Kaz had practically looked through him this whole time, rearranging his body however he liked, all while ignoring Nate's pleas to stop or pull out.

Even if he tried to argue that he didn't owe Kaz a damn thing after this, he knew he didn't have enough power to actually make that so. If the Devil thought you had a debt, you had a debt, plain and simple.

That was another thing Nate wished he'd figured out sooner.

"I don't want to pay you back with sex," he murmured, hating himself a little for being so weak. But if he didn't give in now, what then? He couldn't see a way around this, a way around giving Kaz exactly what he'd wanted from the start.

There was still Jones to consider, and his new job at the coffee shop. Kaz had already wrecked his place at Quartet Air. Nate's bank account couldn't handle losing more work. He needed that time to get his resume in order and send it to potential shops. Right now, to achieve that, the most important goal at this moment would be to get Kaz off his back—both literally and figuratively.

"Oh, fucking is going to be a part of the deal no matter what," Kazimir corrected. "I like it too much. Like the feel of you under and around me. The broken sounds you make and the way your insides tense and grip me despite the way you keep saying you don't want it. You want it. You're just confused why."

Did he want it? Nate couldn't think straight. Maybe he did. He was still hard, after all. His dick still responded, and Kaz was also right about the rest of him. His hole cinched around that thick cock with every outward stroke, as if he was trying to keep him buried deep.

Since this was his first experience with it, maybe rough sex was actually enjoyable for him. Maybe this was something he would have been into if given the chance to explore it with someone else...

Or maybe the Devil was getting to him and putting bullshit in his head.

Nate didn't *feel* good right now, so didn't that mean he felt bad? Could a person both love and hate something at the same time?

"You want me to explain it for you, Pretty Boy? Why you actually like it even when you consciously think you don't?" Kazimir tucked his chin against the curve of Nate's shoulder. "It's because this is simple. There's nothing you have to do, no reason for you to overthink or worry. You can't do anything wrong here because I'm the one in control. There's no chance of you burdening me because you're doing exactly what I want you to do exactly when I want you to do it."

"That's..." That made him sound like a hot mess in every other aspect of his life but...The more he considered the truth of that matter, the clearer it seemed to be. Nate did overthink *every little thing*. If he didn't, he could end up making a mistake that bothered someone else. Everyone in the universe was dealing with their own crap. They didn't need Nate's garbage piled on top of theirs.

"It's not that you're a nice guy," Kaz said. "It's that you hate the idea of letting anyone down. Being the cause of their negative feelings."

"What? No, I *am* a nice guy." Nate was sure of it. Even if the rest of that couldn't be disproven.

"Then why won't you help me out?" he asked. "I needed you to be my boyfriend, but you said no. You were really mean about it, too. Rejection isn't nice, Nate."

Okay, that definitely was straight-up manipulation. The sex part of the equation was confusing, but Nate knew who he was at his core, and it would take a lot more than a dozen forced orgasms and a single hot—even if it was as hot as Kaz—body to shake him in that department.

"You're twisting it. Turning someone down has nothing to do with being a good person or not. Sometimes, they're just not interested in you. Stop trying to villainize me. Stop trying to convince me I did something wrong." He hadn't.

Work hard, treat people right, and good things will come to you. That's what his brother had taught them growing up, and Nate had done his hardest to follow those guidelines.

If this was the good, however, he could have done without.

Kaz sighed. "True, we both know who the real villain is here. I guess I haven't worn you down enough. Okay. We'll keep going and—"

"No, wait!" Nate tried to wiggle his hands, but they were trapped between the two of them.

"That tickles," Kaz said lightly, relaxed. He started to flick his hips in shallow motions, just enough to jostle the mattress beneath them.

"Kazimir." Nate flinched as his prostate was tapped against over and over again for the millionth time. If he had to guess, he'd say he'd made up for his lack of sexual experience with men enough to last a lifetime. "Please."

"I gave you a breather," he pointed out. "What you did with it was your choice. Don't blame me."

"You are literally the only one who can be blamed here!" Nate snapped back, frustrated. He growled and twisted his head to bury it against the soft material of the pillow, finding it soaked with his sweat and tears.

Kaz had talked him into circles on purpose, distracted him and tested him all at the same time. He'd wanted to see how close to the edge Nate was, whether or not he'd give in.

Vaguely, Nate wondered if the Brumal had taught him this kind of torture method, but the idea of Kazimir doing this to anyone else oddly didn't sit right with him and he cut the thought short before it could ruminate any further. He didn't want to overanalyze his feelings, not unless they were ones of desperation.

Which he was. Nate was desperate to get this to stop. To be able to breathe and not feel so much stimulation all over.

"Boyfriend," he mumbled the word into the material of the pillow, but somehow Kaz heard him, his movements slowing before coming to a stop. The silence at his back was clue enough that he was waiting, so Nate forced himself to turn his head again, glazed-over eyes staring across the room at the open bedroom door.

Thank Light Neve no longer lived here and there was no fear of her walking in, witnessing this, and being scarred for life.

"I want to be your boyfriend," Nate gave in with an edge of resignation.

Nothing was ever that simple with Kazimir though.

"Why should I agree to that, Pretty Boy?" He pulled out and rolled Nate onto his back, spreading his legs and tugging him so the backs of Nate's thighs were resting on top of his own. His expression was dark as he sat there and stared down at him, a wicked glint in that garnet gaze, his mouth upturned ever so slightly. "I could just keep fucking you like this and go find someone else to play the part. That's what you suggested, wasn't it? There's always Zane. I'm sure he'd play along with the right…motivation."

Who the hell was Zane? Nate almost asked, catching himself at the last second.

Kaz's hand dropped down to the fleshlight and he switched it off but didn't remove it yet, keeping his hold lightly on it instead. "Besides, remember how you said it wouldn't matter? Even if you were my boyfriend, I'd never be able to rival Baikal."

"I never said that."

"Sure."

"I didn't." He hadn't, he knew that for a fact. "Kazimir, don't put words in my mouth. Sexual deviancy and physical coercion are one thing, but don't you dare try and gaslight me."

Kaz blinked at him, momentarily caught off guard before he'd gathered himself. "Is that really where you draw the line, Narek?"

"I'm only worth as much as my word," he said, realizing how stupid that sounded but unable to backpedal now.

His eyes narrowed. "Let me guess, another gem you picked up from Big Brother?"

"Leave Nuri out of this."

"I took a photo at the bar. Did you know that?"

Nate sighed in frustration. "You don't have to do that."

"Do what?"

"It worked, okay? This," he motioned down at their naked bodies, "worked. So did buying Quartet Air and stalking me to the Velvet Brew. I get it. You can overpower me in the bedroom and outside of it." Hadn't Kaz proven that time and time again? "There's no use fighting a Brumal member. You don't have to bring my brother or the threat of leaking a lewd photo into the mix."

"It's always sex with people like you," Kaz drawled. "I fuck your brains out, and then you're scrambling to give me what I want. Either to make it stop, or make it continue. You like my cock, Nate, and what's more, you like it when it's inside of you."

"I also like to feel my insides and breathing," he said. "Two things I haven't been able to do for the past few hours."

"Touche."

Nate hesitated and then blurted, "How many people have you done this with, exactly?"

He'd made it sound like there had been many, and while he did want this to end, he also wasn't too keen on becoming another statistic to the Brumal member. There was no good reason for it, but that was how Nate felt. For him, sex had always been about connection, and even though he'd had no say in this particular link, it was seeming harder than he'd hoped to switch that part of his brain off.

Kaz had seen him in ways no one else had ever seen him. Had stripped him bare in more ways than one.

Nate couldn't stand the thought that this was just another day ending in Y for him when it was life-altering for Nate. Whether or not they went their separate ways come morning, there was no denying this event would affect him for years, if not forever.

"Gotta be more specific," Kazimir said. "Do you mean how many people have I fucked well into the night?" He shrugged. "Couldn't tell you, though typically I do the deed, get off, and leave. Going multiple rounds is only something I bother with when I'm really into it. Lucky you."

"Lucky me," he repeated dully.

"If you're asking how many people I've made be my boyfriend, the answer to that question is a lot simpler." Kaz eased the toy off of Nate's dick and let out a low whistle at the sight of it. "You're bright red, babe." He flicked it with a finger and quirked a brow when Nate cursed. "Sensitive?"

"Bastard."

"What did I say about calling me that?"

"How about you consider it a term of endearment and let it slide?" Nate took a stuttered breath and held Kaz's gaze. "If you want me to be your boyfriend, Kazimir," he stated boldly, acting confident even though he wasn't feeling that way. "Treat me like it."

"Treat you like my boyfriend?"

Nate licked his dry lips and forced himself to nod once, shivering when Kaz grinned at him viciously. The triumphant look on his face twisted his expression into something wicked and sinful. Something terrifying that almost had him second-guessing his choice.

That was until Kaz reached underneath him and untied his wrists, pulling his arms to his front so he could gently massage the feeling back into them. Then he lowered himself over Nate and lined himself up with his abused hole, shushing him when he went to complain.

"Don't worry, *boyfriend*," Kaz reassured as he slowly eased his cockhead inside. "Last time for the night, I promise." He grabbed the second tube of cream he'd brought and leaned back just enough to bring it down between them.

Nate lifted his exhausted head to glance there, watching as Kaz smeared the white stuff on his own cock before he reentered Nate's body fully.

"Sun cream," he explained once he'd settled over him again, careful not to crush Nate beneath his weight this time. His movements were slow but deep enough to hit all those parts within him that made his nerve endings sing. "The deeper we can get it, the better. You'll heal overnight and be fine come morning."

"*Come* doesn't seem like the correct word choice," Nate pointed out. His arms hurt, but it was awkward leaving them on the bed, so he risked lifting them, hesitating before giving in and settling his hands over Kaz's hips.

"If that's your subtle way of asking if I plan on cleaning you out before I put you to bed," Kazimir smirked, "then no. No, I do not. You'll sleep full of my come like the good boy you are, won't you, boyfriend?"

"No," his face scrunched up. "That's gross."

"Want to rethink that?" Kaz's next thrust came with more force than the last. "You're already so over-stimulated, Pretty Boy. You really want to keep fighting me on the details?"

"I don't like being dirty," Nate tried, but merely received a snort in response.

"You're no Berga Obsidian. Nowhere in your file was there any mention of being even slightly germophobic."

"Those two things are not necessarily—" He stopped himself. "Forget it."

"Nice choice." Kazimir slipped a hand between them and carefully wrapped his fingers around the head of Nate's dick, circling his thumb around his flushed crown before pressing against his slit. When Nate's back bowed off the bed, he chuckled. "There's my good boy. So sensitive."

"Kaz." Anxiety crashed through Nate with the sudden spike of arousal. That mixture of euphoria and fear that it would never end had tears prickling at the corner of his eyes all over again.

"Don't worry," Kazimir said, "We're winding down to the finish line. Promise." He leaned in and captured Nate's mouth, the kiss this time light and clearly meant to comfort. His lips coaxed Nate to open for him so his tongue could slip in and casually explore, like they had all the time in the world for him to map Nate's insides despite his reassurance.

Just as Nate was about to lose it and turn his head away, Kaz changed his grip on his dick, delivering steady strokes of his fist with every pump of his cock, the motions mirroring one another and causing the bed to quake beneath them.

The sounds of the springs going and the feel of Kazimir all around him had Nate's breath catching in his throat, the small gasp instantly swallowed by Kaz's still-seeking mouth.

When the orgasm hit him this time, Nate felt the world wink in and out around him, stars bursting behind his closed eyes as his entire body shook as if electrocuted. He spasmed, and his dick wept, covering them both in more come a second before he felt Kaz give one final deep push and hit his own peak.

Kazimir grunted and shuddered through his own release, keeping himself buried so that Nate could feel the entire surge he let off inside of him.

That added stretch and sensation ended up being too much, and Nate met his breaking point after all. He only just managed to tighten his hold on Kazimir's hips a second before dizziness warned him what was about to happen.

He'd never been so happy to pass out before in his life.

CHAPTER 15:

Something was...off. Kazimir came awake and instantly felt it, though it took him a while to figure out exactly what the cause was.

The room he was lying in was smallish compared to the sprawling penthouse suite he kept in the city, and lacked the bustling sounds of hovercars zipping through the air. The smell was different too, less mountain flowers, more dark chocolate and coffee. His nose twitched as he lifted himself into a seated position and glanced around.

He'd walked the small perimeter of the room last night during his search for Nate's stash of sex toys, but he'd barely taken anything in. The lights had been kept dim then as well, and now, with sunlight pooling in through the open window to his left, everything was lit up in bright clarity.

The place looked lived in. Knickknacks cluttered every surface area, some piled high with old-school paper books, the kind typically found only in libraries and Baikal Void's bedroom.

Kaz gracefully lifted himself off the bed and

ambled over to the desk, picking through the books to read the titles off the spines. There was a mixture of fiction and nonfiction, some of them textbooks purchased for classes at Vail and kept for some unknown reason. It felt a lot like Nate simply kept all of his belongings confined to this single space, despite the fact he now lived in the house alone.

He replaced the items and then turned, seeking out his pants. He'd left them in the center of the room and made quick work of getting back into them before reaching into his back pocket to pull out the small green notebook he never left home without.

The mini red fountain pen that was attached made a satisfying snicking sound as he pressed it to the page, scrawling in messy cursive, "Likes paper too," under the bold "Nate" that had been written already at the top. Taking notes was a habit he'd formed as a child that he'd never been able to shake, and he had closets filled to the brim with used notebooks just like this one, all filled with a mixture of the mundane and the important.

The process gave his hands something to do and kept him from lashing out with violence at every waking moment. He could collect his thoughts better this way and sort through his feelings at an easier pace—because despite what Narek probably believed, he did, in fact, experience emotion.

Like irritation.

If he wasn't careful, Kazimir was the type

who'd allow emotion to rule him, and often found his actions dictated by his mood before realizing. That was partially how he'd ended up here in the first place, standing in a tiny home in the middle of the poor part of town.

Alone.

There was no point in searching, he could already tell Nate was no longer in the house with him. With his other hand, he picked up his multi-slate and adjusted the strap so it was back on his forearm before sending off a message.

Kaz: Better not have run far, Pretty Boy. I'm in no mood for a chase.

The opposite, in fact. Kazimir found himself wishing Nate had stuck around so he could have rolled on top of him and fucked him again, nice and agonizingly slow this time. He was curious what the sexy racer looked like taking it in the light of day. Would he pout like he had last night? Blush and turn that hot pink shade that had only served to spur Kaz's dick on further?

That wasn't even getting into the sounds... Good Light. The shortness of breath as Nate had struggled to contain himself and hide that he was enjoying it had been so hot. And later, once he'd lost his mind and come completely undone for Kaz, the tiny mewling noises...It'd been pitiful and filled with vulnerability, and Kazimir was ninety-nine percent certain he'd never heard anything as beautiful in his entire life.

And he wanted to hear it again.

Right the fuck now.

As he waited for Nate to reply, he continued to snoop, fiddling with things he found interesting as he made his way around. When he roamed into the bathroom and still hadn't gotten a message back, he shook his head at himself in the mirror and sent off another as he plucked Nate's toothbrush from the lone cup on the eggshell-colored countertop.

Kaz: I'm not someone who can be ignored, especially not by you. Or did you already forget? Last night, I became your literal everything. So, unless you want your new god razing everything to the ground, respond, Narek.

The toothpaste tasted like frosting, and Kazimir wasn't sure how he felt about it as he brushed his teeth and idly tapped his fingers against the leather cover of his notebook. Admittedly, he hadn't given much thought to the type of person Nate was outside of stubborn and attractive, and these little discoveries were making him excited in all the right ways.

He put the toothbrush back and then reentered the bedroom, sighing when he doublechecked to find there still wasn't a response.

The room was set up with a bed, dresser, desk, and two end tables, filled with clutter but nothing substantial. The windowsill was the cleanest spot, with only a single item placed on it. Taking a wild guess, Kaz selected the small item, giving it a quick inspection before he activated camera mode on his multi-slate and snapped a pic of him holding the stuffed toy up by his face.

The small red dragon plush looked stupid as hell next to his fine-ass self, but if it would get the point across, he could live with having it in existence.

Kaz: Should I start by lighting this on fire?

He attached the image and then dropped down onto the edge of the bed, whistling an old tune he hadn't thought of in years as the seconds ticked by.

There weren't many of them before his multi-slate dinged.

Finally.

He snorted. Typical. That had almost been too easy.

Pretty Boy: How did you even get this number? I'm at work. I can't check my phone whenever I please.

Kazimir knew exactly where he was, he'd had Arlet send him Nate's full schedule, but that was neither here nor there. He wouldn't come second to anything, not even a job. In fact, he'd been contemplating whether or not to make good on his comment and offer that Jones guy a large sum of money in exchange for the coffee shop.

Last night had worked in getting Nate to finally submit, but something told him his sexy racer was still going to cause him trouble. If he took away his source of income and cornered him into only having Kaz to rely on...That could be the ideal situation. The best way for him to take full control and ensure Nate could never step out of line.

His things were *his.* Which meant putting him first and giving him what he wanted when he wanted it.

Kaz: Who gave you the stuffed animal, Narek?

Something in his gut soured, and Kazimir chucked the dragon at the window, watching it hit the pane of glass and drop to the floor.

Pretty Boy: My brother. It was a New Year's gift. Put it back.

Nuri? That was kind of cute, then. Big Brother clearly cared for Nate the same way Nate cared for him. Considering the two lived on different planets, Kazimir wondered how they managed to keep that bond so strong. It didn't take a genius to figure out that Nate would do literally anything for the oldest Narek. Even the therapist had noted that he may idolize his brother too much, to the point it was affecting his mental health by always making him feel inadequate in comparison.

Nate felt like he was somehow less important than his brother and everyone else around him. Like he needed to shoulder everything in order to keep them and keep them happy.

Kaz was the one who'd been diagnosed as certifiably insane, but what kind of crazy put that much pressure on themselves without even being asked?

He'd needed a boyfriend and Nate had seemed like an easy target that night he'd spotted him with Mit Parker. Since, Kazimir had come to the realization he'd been mistaken—not a thing that happened often—but...he sort of got off on that?

The racer's push and pull was hot in its own way. Typically, Kaz would have slit the throat of anyone who dared talk back to him, but with Nate, he found himself wanting to push those buttons on purpose. Wanted to get a rise out of him just to hear the things he'd say and watch the worry flash over his face as soon as he realized who he was saying them to.

Pretty Boy: I have to get back to work. Leave my stuff alone.

Kaz: Don't think you won't be punished for slipping out this morning before I could take that ass at least one more time.

Pretty Boy: You really need to do some research. Boyfriends don't punish each other when they do something the other doesn't like. They discuss it like adults. You promised you'd treat me like your boyfriend. I expect you to keep your word.

Was he...scolding him right now? Kazimir blinked incredulously down at the screen, rereading the words for good measure. Was a repeat of last night already in order?

At the mere prospect, his dick twitched in his pants and he shifted to adjust himself on the bed.

Kaz: Keep yours. Classes end at three. Then I'll come for you. Be ready, Nate Narek. We've got a new score to settle.

Insubordination would not be tolerated.

His confusion only grew, however, when there

came no response, and after about ten minutes of waiting he finally gave up and called the one person he could think of that wouldn't make fun of him for asking questions.

"What?" Zane's voice came through the line, strong and partially uninterested. "I'm busy."

"Not a booty call," Kazimir said, leaning forward to prop his elbow on his knee as his frown deepened. "I'm confused about something and would like clarification."

"Proceed."

"Is it not standard form to punish bad behavior?"

"In what kind of context?"

"Relationships."

There was a pause and then, "Are you asking if it's normal for you to beat your lover?"

"No," he scrunched up his nose. "Of course not. I would never beat him. Not, like, with my fists or anything like that."

"So," Zane drawled, "with your cock then. That's what you're thinking?"

"How'd you know?"

"If you've considered punishing someone for bad behavior, that means you've also thought of rewarding them for good behavior. There are only two ways you would do that, Kaz. Either by using your hands to harm, or soothe them or by using your dick. Fair warning, using sex as a punishment/reward system can get tricky. But also, to answer your question, no. Normal people do not discipline their significant others."

"No?"

"No."

"Then how do they train them?"

He sighed. "They don't."

"That seems stupid." If Kaz didn't teach Nate what he did and didn't like him doing, how would he be able to ensure Nate behaved in an agreeable way?

"For someone like you," Zane said, "it would. For most people? Not so much. Is that all? I have a medical report that needs to be finished within the hour."

"Hold on."

"It's simple, really. People typically date because they like one another. Relationships are all about acceptance and compromise, two concepts you've never been able to grasp."

"Yeah," Kaz agreed, "because they're pointless. Why should I have to make sacrifices for someone else? I know what's best. Period."

"Correction, Baikal does, that's why he's the Dominus."

Kazimir scowled. "Low blow. That was cheap of you."

"I'm hanging up now."

"Fine—" He glanced down at his device to see that Zane had already ended the call. "Prick." Before he could think too hard about what he'd just heard, however, his multi-slate chimed again.

When his cousin's name was on the screen instead of Nate's, he scowled and reluctantly read the message.

Baikal: Where are you?
Kaz: 37 Grand Street.
Baikal: Where the hell is that?
Kaz: What do you need?

Because Kazimir needed for this conversation to get to the damn point. He wanted to ignore the messages altogether, but there was a chain of command, and as much as Kaz liked being in charge of things, he also liked structure too damn much to mess with stuff like that. It was also why he was fine treating his seniors with a little more respect when he'd been in lower grades at Vail.

Now, he was the senior, and he was the one gaining from that rule. Full circle.

Was that maybe what Zane meant about dating? Would Kazimir benefit more from following these bullshit rules? He didn't see how that was possible no matter which way he turned the problem in his head.

Nate was a handful. Look what Kaz had needed to do just to get the guy to agree to date him. Nothing was going to come easy with him, and now Zane was agreeing that punishment wasn't the right way to go?

Or, actually. He'd merely stated it wasn't the typical way. Sure, Kaz liked to stick to certain rules, like filial piety, but that was because he'd been brought up in such a way that he would have been whipped if he'd been rude to an older person. Behaving the way his father wanted had been beaten into him and he'd turned out all right, and it wasn't like he was planning on laying hands on Nate—not like that in any case.

He had no intentions of hitting his pretty racer. Abuse like that didn't do it for him.

Baikal: Rabbit is sick, so I won't be going to class. Take notes for me.

Kazimir cocked his head.

Kaz: What does your boyfriend not feeling well have to do with you skipping class? You feel fine, don't you?

Had they possibly caught something together? Food poisoning? A cold? Would Kazimir have to take over even more of the responsibilities amongst the Brumal until Kal recovered? He didn't have time for that, and what's more, he couldn't risk it. If he let the leash loose so soon after tying it around Nate's neck, it would set the wrong precedent. Hell, he was already sitting here struggling over how to proceed after his talk with Zane. He didn't need his cousin making things any harder on him.

Baikal: I'm fine, but I don't want to leave him alone when he isn't.

Kaz: Why not? Aren't you risking catching whatever he has? You should put some distance between the two of you before it's too late. There's that important meeting coming up with the new leader of the Shepherds that you have to be present for.

Baikal: You wouldn't understand.

Okay, he was getting real tired of people telling him that.

Baikal: You know what being sick is like, how much it sucks.

Kaz: Yeah, which is why I'm telling you to give him a wide berth. So that you don't get sick and feel like shit too.

Baikal: He feels shitty, so I feel shitty. If you cared about anyone besides yourself, you'd get that. Whatever. Just take the damn notes and send them to me. Oh, and check in with Whim before you head to campus.

It was tempting to press the issue and make Kal explain the whole sick thing in more detail, but truthfully, Kaz actually understood what he was trying to say. Kazimir was able to empathize with people in the sense that he could grasp what they were feeling and understood those feelings because he had, in fact, experienced them himself. However, it didn't make him relate.

For him, it was more cut and dry.

Being sick sucked.

Fact.

Rabbit was currently sick.

Fact.

Rabbit felt bad.

Fact.

Kazimir currently was not sick.

Fact.

Kazimir did not feel bad.

Fact.

Simple. Replace Kaz with Baikal, and the concept should have been the same, and yet his cousin wasn't built the same way he was.

Not for the first time, a small part of Kaz felt a little envious of that. They'd been raised in a similar fashion with one major difference. Baikal Void's father had loved him.

Kazimir's dad could barely look him in the eye.

He hated being that pathetic dude who cried that his parents didn't love him, blah, blah, blah, but even the doctors had explained that was a large reason behind the way his mind had formulated.

Baikal was an arrogant, spoiled, rich, mafia leader. He didn't like losing because he'd been raised knowing he was above everyone else. Kazimir, on the other hand, was an arrogant, spoiled, rich, high-standing mafia member who didn't like losing because his brain *told him* he was above everyone else.

When he'd been forced into therapy as a young teen, the hope had been to teach him various tools and tricks to help normalize him, but Kaz hadn't been interested in that then, and he wasn't interested in it now. He was fine with who he was.

The fact that his dad hated having a son who fit within the parameters of the dark triad?

Even fucking better.

Kaz: Something happen?

He wasn't due for his meeting with the old underboss for another day.

Baikal: Apparently Pious Prince found what

he was looking for. Whim is escorting him off planet as we speak. Afterward, he'll need to give you a briefing so you're caught up on all the details.

Right, because Kazimir was the new underboss and therefore needed to know everything there was to know about Brumal business. That was well and good, but he found himself stuck on the first part of that message.

Looked like Nate's friend hadn't managed to escape in the end. Oh well. Kaz had given him a phenomenal head start last night. Wasn't his fault if the guy hadn't been able to avoid capture.

Kaz: Will do.

He stood up and stretched his arms before his eyes dropped to the fallen plushie. When he picked it up and replaced it on the windowsill, he was careful to make sure it was in the exact position he'd found it in, staring at it for a long moment before shaking his head.

Screw this. Maybe other people didn't discipline their boyfriends, but Kazimir wasn't like other people. He only deserved the best, and he was going to ensure that Nate was it. Still, the punishment had to fit the crime, so he needed something that wasn't too over the top. Something that would make his point without risking pushing Nate too far…

The idea formulated in his head quickly and he got to work executing it. In less than fifteen minutes he was finished and calling Whim to find out his location.

Kaz locked Nate's front door on his way out and drove off with a smile on his face.

CHAPTER 16:

The last time Nate had visited campus had been a little under a year ago, when his sister had needed to pick up some paperwork after graduation. When she'd still been attending, he'd also visit on occasion and eat lunch with her in the cafeteria. Even though the two of them had lived together then, they were close.

Which was the reminder he needed that he should give her a call. He'd been avoiding her all week after losing his job at Quartet Air, but any longer and she'd start to get suspicious.

He parked his car outside the business lecture hall, taking the space closest to the front entrance, and then got out and rounded his vehicle to perch on the edge of the hood. The clock on his multi-slate said there were still ten minutes to go before three, so he had time.

"Where the hell have you been, brother?" Neve picked up on the third ring and greeted with a sharp tongue.

Nate chuckled and crossed his ankles, propping a hand back on the warm hood. The sun was out today, hanging bright in a cloudless sky, and if it weren't for the blanket of snow and the chill, he'd call it a perfect day.

Well, technically, he did still think it was one, but others might not. Proof was in the fact that most of the students who were walking around campus were bundled up and huddled together if they were with friends.

"I've already got one sibling who's constantly MIA, I don't need another," she added.

"Never." He'd never abandon her. Knew how hard it'd been for her at such a young age to be told she was being shipped off to a new planet and the only parental figure she had left was staying behind. Nate had done his best since that day to fill in the role, but he could never measure up to Nuri. "How about dinner this weekend?"

"Yeah, I can do eight. Our place?"

"Sure." It'd been a couple of months since they'd last eaten out together. "Or, why not go out? Movies beforehand?"

"Sounds way better." Neve's voice got distant as she turned away and spoke to someone else. "Verga says hi."

"Hi back." Nate liked his sister's boyfriend. The two had dated for a while before making the decision to move in with one another. "Invite him if you want."

"You sure?" Neve hesitated. "You won't feel like a third wheel?"

"Not at all." He would a little, but that didn't

matter. He could handle a bit of discomfort if it meant making his sister happy, and he knew she'd be pleased with the offer. It was important to her that the two of them get along, which meant Nate went out of his way to subtly reassure her they did. Peace of mind was priceless, and Neve deserved nothing less.

"I'll ask him then," she said, her excitement obvious. "He was just telling me how much he wants to get to know you better."

"Was he?" Nate doubted that.

"Of course. I talk about you all the time. Why wouldn't he?"

"Nate Be'tessi?" a light voice called out to him from the sidewalk, and Nate turned his head to find a girl walking toward him. She was in a thick winter coat in white with a matching hat and set of gloves, but her shirt was black, indicating she was a senior.

"Did someone just call you brother in the old tongue?" Neve let out a low whistle. "Someone has a crush."

Be'tessi was used between someone and a male older than them by a few years. It roughly translated to "older brother", but wasn't used on those who shared a blood relation. When he'd first arrived on this planet, there'd been a whole book of terminology Nate had needed to memorize in order to properly fit in. Though most of the younger generation no longer used traditional terms like that one, many of the elderly did.

"Shut up," Nate hissed and then waved at the

girl who was still approaching. "I'll call you back later."

"Sure, big brother," Neve laughed. "Have fun flirting!"

He really wished she hadn't called him that; all it did was remind him of Kazimir and why he was here. Pulling out the earpiece, he inserted it into the side of his multi-slate just as the girl reached him, sure to keep the casual smile on all the while.

"Hey, Odette. What's up?" He'd been a senior when she'd first started school, and they'd spoken a bit through the mentorship program he'd been a part of to help younger classmates deal with the transition from high school to college. They'd gotten close enough that when she'd asked if it would be all right to refer to him as Be'tessi, he hadn't found reason not to agree.

Since she was in the same grade as Kaz, he wondered if the two had any classes together.

"Prepping for finals." She waved the tablet she held. "What about you? How have you been?"

"Good," he lied. "How's your grandfather?"

She glanced down at her boots. "He passed away last month."

"Oh, I'm so sorry."

"No, it's okay. He'd been sick for a while. I like to focus on the fact he's no longer in pain, you know?"

"Yeah," he nodded solemnly. "I get that."

The sound of laughter reached them, and Nate glanced over to the front of the building, watching as students began to pour out. It didn't take long for Kazimir to appear with them, two Brumal members Nate didn't know the names of with him.

He hated to admit it, but it was easy to see why everyone on campus swooned for the new underboss, even knowing he was in the mafia. It wasn't just the impressive height or the sexy strands of dark hair the wind blew over Kaz's forehead that made him attractive. The intensity in his gaze as he set his sights on Nate, how he seemed to take all of him in through a single glance…

Kazimir could make a person feel like they were the only one on the entire planet. That was part of his charm.

And where the true danger lay.

Nate understood Kaz's game now a little better than most. How he used tricks and manipulation tactics to get what he wanted. Making you feel seen and important? Just another strategy meant to maneuver a person right where Kaz wanted them.

Screwing him when he'd been wasted that night at the bar had been meant to humiliate Nate. It'd been retribution for losing the race. Things should have ended there, and Nate honestly didn't understand why they hadn't, but it was clear Kazimir's visit to his place of work had been more about him testing the waters than any actual belief he'd had Nate would agree to date him.

Buying Quartet Air had been a statement. An "I have the money and the power you never will."

If Nate had to guess, he bet he'd surprised Kaz when he'd quit. The Brumal member had no doubt thought buying the business meant he had the means of controlling him, and after he'd lost that? He'd stalked him to the Velvet Brew to make the threat again, only he'd spotted Port's name on Nate's multi-slate and had switched gears.

That was the other dangerous thing about Kazimir. He could adapt on the fly. Reassess a situation and come up with a new plan.

Like how he'd done last night when he'd come to Nate's house and used his friend's safety against him. Kazimir had figured out that outward force wasn't going to work on Nate. It never had. Bringing things home, however? Yeah. That would do the trick.

He'd grown up with middle-class parents who'd done their best in raising their three children, but there were everyday struggles that came along with that. And then they'd died, and Nuri had been put in charge at too young of an age, meaning Nate had also had to give up the rest of his childhood to help keep things together. Since the age of thirteen, Nate's life had constantly changed and altered at the flip of a coin.

Kaz wasn't the only one who'd learned how to adjust.

"Anyway, what are you doing on campus?" Odette asked, and Nate tore his gaze off Kazimir to give her his attention once more. "If you haven't had lunch yet, we could grab something to eat at the cafeteria. Catch up."

Nate gave her another friendly smile, pretending not to be aware of the Devil who approached with his two friends hot on his heels. "Sorry, I already have plans. Maybe some other time."

"Oh, really?"

"Yeah, I'm here to pick up my boyfriend," Nate said, motioning with his chin toward Kaz as he finally straightened off the hood of his car.

"Your—" She turned her head and gasped at the same moment Kaz stepped up to them. "—Boyfriend."

"You two are dating?" one of the Brumal members with Kazimir sounded just as surprised as Ledger had the other day at the café. He was dressed in a dark gray button-up, showing he was a junior, and had pale pink hair with darker highlights. The hair gave away that he was a born Vital.

"Hi," he held out a hand toward them. "I'm Nate."

"Take that," Kazimir interrupted, "and I'll slice yours off, Saint."

The other member, also dressed in dark gray, leaned toward the pink-haired guy—Saint—and said not so quietly, "He doesn't mean your hand, man."

"I got that." Saint slipped both of his into the pockets of his jeans.

"What's going on here?" Kaz turned that irritation on Nate and Odette, glancing pointedly between them.

"I came to pick you up and ran into an old friend," Nate said nonchalantly, reaching out to slip his pointer finger into the empty belt loop at the front of Kaz's pants. He tugged him closer, smirking at the momentary look of befuddlement on the other man's face a second before he kissed the expression away.

He'd meant for it to be a peck, just a quick meeting of lips to get the point across to their audience, but Nate found himself lingering there at the first touch of warmth from Kaz's mouth. When he pressed in a little closer, Kazimir opened for him, allowing Nate's tongue to slip inside and tangle with his in a slow, sultry exploration.

Last night, things had gone according to Kaz's schedule, with Nate half out of his mind the entire time. Now, in the light of day, without overstimulation to distract him, he was able to note the slight hint of sweetness Kaz's mouth offered and breathe in the scent of something floral and earthy coming off of him.

It was pleasing to the senses, and Nate shifted in even closer, his free arm banding around Kaz's narrow waist to urge him to stay close.

Until Odette cleared her throat and he recalled the purpose of kissing Kaz in the first place.

Nate pulled away, carefully keeping that one finger in the Devil's belt loop as he turned to Odette. "Sorry. Things are still new and exciting. You know how that is."

She nodded and took a tentative step back. "Of

course. Hey, I should get going."

"Right, you said you were hungry. Here." Nate tapped at his multi-slate. "Let me buy you lunch, at least."

"No, no!" She waved her hands in the air and almost dropped her tablet in the process. "That won't be necessary."

"Come on," Nate pushed. "I insist. You're my junior. I should take care of you."

The Brumal member standing next to Priest made a choking sound and smartly hid his face behind his friend.

Nate pretended not to notice, hitting the button that would transfer twenty coin over to Odette instantly.

The white device on her wrist dinged a second later and she turned beet red.

"What about you two?" Nate turned to the Brumal. "Are you eating? I can—"

"They have their own damn money," Kazimir stated.

"Of course they do," he agreed. "That's not the point, Kaz. They're your friends. I need to make a good impression."

Kazimir blinked at him.

"Are you seriously dating him?" the other Brumal asked, taking a risk, though he kept a wide berth by staying on Saint's other side. "I'm Yuze, by the way."

"He doesn't need to know your name, Yuze." Kazimir grabbed Nate's hand, tugging it loose from his pants before he linked their fingers and pulled him over toward the side of the car. "Enough. Get in."

"Are you guys' Satellite too?" Nate asked, unable to contain his laughter as Kaz yanked the driver's side door open and practically shoved him inside. He poked his head out before the door could be slammed shut on him. "See you around!"

Kazimir stormed around the front of the car and practically tossed himself into the passenger seat. "Drive."

"Seat belt," Nate countered.

"You're seriously—"

"Not starting this car until you're buckled in, princess."

Kazimir stilled and slowly swiveled his head toward him. "What did you just call me?"

He made a big show of sighing before leaning over to reach for the belt himself. Once he was close enough, he pressed his mouth to Kaz's ear and whispered, "They're all still watching. Wipe that scowl off your face and pretend you like me. This was your game, remember?"

The buckle clicked into place and Nate sat back and smiled at him, winking for good measure before he started the hovercar. Giving a wave out the window to the three still standing there staring, he pulled out and headed toward the exit of the parking lot.

"Explain yourself, Narek," Kazimir growled as he took the first turn away from the school, and Nate instantly dropped the smile and happy-go-lucky attitude now that they were in the clear.

"I'm playing the part," he stated. "This is about proving to your friends you're not the type of dick who can't commit, right? Your boyfriend would need to be the kind of person who's optimistic and playful in order to put up with your crap. Trust me. I totally sold it just now. Next time you hear from your cousin, he'll be asking you about it. Saint and Yuze seem like the gossiping type."

"They are," Kaz agreed, going quiet for a moment before he propped a shoulder against the window and shifted in the seat to better face him. "Okay, let's say that's why I buy you being overly friendly with *them*. What about Odette?"

"What about her?"

"You two seemed awfully chummy before I showed up."

"Chummy?" He snorted. "What are you, fifty-seven years old? We weren't *chummy*, Kaz. We're friends from when I went to Vail. I haven't spoken to her in years aside from the occasional comment on Inspire." The social media app he barely used now that he was no longer in school and it wasn't as necessary to have visual proof he was fine for his brother to use to check in on him.

Nuri would never have admitted it, but Nate knew he looked at both his and Neve's pages frequently to make sure they were all right and living good lives on Vitality.

"Don't talk to her again," Kaz ordered.

"You sure about that?" He glanced at him then

back at the road. "You think your Brumal members will spread the news, they're nothing in comparison to Odette. I bet you five coin she's got us both tagged in some obscure photo neither of us is even in with a comment about how happy she is for our relationship before the night is through. Girl loves being the first in the know. The only thing she loves more is when other people know she's the first in the know."

"You're trying to tell me you planned it?"

"I'm not trying anything, that's what happened. Didn't know she'd be there, but it was a happy coincidence if you ask me."

"Have you fucked her?"

"Dude, what the hell is wrong with you?" Nate started to turn left, but Kazimir stopped him, directing him in the other direction with a finger point. Whatever. Didn't matter to him where they went. They needed to iron out a few details about this arrangement, for lack of a better term. He'd agreed to be Kazimir's boyfriend, but there'd been no mention of a timeframe or how deep into the role he was expected to get.

"What are you so upset for?" he risked asking. "I was only doing what you wanted. There's no way anyone wouldn't believe we're together now."

"Yeah," Kaz said, "that's true. I'm curious, though, how you seem so good at reading everyone around you *but* me?"

The direction Kazimir had taken them turned out to be a wide wooded area with no other traffic.

The hovercar passed a foot over the paved road as Nate drove, keeping it lower to the ground than he would if they'd been on one of the main ones.

"What—" He let out a startled sound when suddenly Kaz's hand was on the steering wheel, jerking to the right with all his strength.

They twisted off the path, the car spinning once before coming to a stop when the side of it slammed into a large oak tree. The hit was hard enough to jostle them, but not enough to cause any real damage—To their bodies, in any case. Nate's car was going to be messed up for sure.

"What the fuck is wrong with you?!" he screamed, snapping off his belt before reaching for the door handle. He only got it open an inch before Kaz was there, hauling him back by his collar and slamming the door once more.

His hand came down on the lock, then he tapped the button on Nate's multi-slate that would control the car and unhooked the device from his wrist before tossing it into the back.

Nate stared at him incredulously as Kaz went for his own shirt, stripping out of it faster than Nate could blink. "What—"

The knife came out next, that damn crystal blade that had been used to threaten him one too many times now. Instead of aiming it his way this time, however, Kaz silently sheared off the sleeves of his dress shirt.

One of them was already tied around Nate's right wrist before he had the good sense to resist, not that he was very capable of that. He found himself bound with both of them attached by the cloth to the sides of his headrest in under a minute, gaping as Kaz resituated the seat so it was in the resting position a moment before he straddled him.

"Stop!" Nate struggled to free himself, grimacing when Kazimir's heavy thighs pinned his beneath him. "Get off! What are you doing?! We're out in the open!"

"Perfect," Kaz said. "We're close enough to campus still that any students driving by will recognize us both and paint their own conclusions for what they're seeing."

"You can't be serious?" Nate tried to twist away when Kazimir's fingers dropped to his fly. "Don't! Let's go back to my place, huh? We can do it there! I promise! Kaz, please, stop!"

His protests turned into a moan when Kaz freed his dick and started immediately jerking him off, making him hard in no time at all. The sound of another zipper going a minute later had him glancing down to find Kaz's cock also exposed.

Kazimir shifted as close as he could get, his legs spread wide over Nate's lap. His thick cock bumped up against Nate's smaller member, and they both sucked in a breath, the sounds turning into harried grunts when he started rubbing them against one another.

"What's wrong, Narek?" Kaz huffed, waiting until Nate lifted his gaze to meet his. "I'm your junior, too. What? I'm not good enough for you to take care of?" He captured Nate's jaw in a tight grip and brought his face directly in front of his, the flash of manic violence in his eyes impossible to miss. "Seems like you're only giving toward people who aren't me."

He picked his backpack off the floor and opened it up to reveal a mess of leather and chains that had Nate's confusion prickling with fear.

"Let's modify that behavior, shall we, Pretty Boy?"

Nate did everything he could to resist, but with Kazimir's stronger form over the top of him, it wasn't long before he found himself strung up. A leather collar had been latched around his neck, golden chains attaching it to the straps that had been locked around his ankles. His pants had been shucked off, so now he was forced into an awkward position, with his hands tied to the headrest and the short chains keeping his legs high in the air and spread for the demonic hellspawn who was putting him through this.

"If you're really that worried someone might drive by and see," Kaz told him as he leaned back to take in the view, stroking himself a couple of times while he did, "you should beg me to make this quick, Pretty Boy. I have half a mind to keep you here like this until it gets dark."

"Kazimir," Nate firmed his voice, but it still shook a bit at the end, giving him away. "I'm not into any of this."

"Your dick softening clued me into that fact,"

he replied, pulling something else from his bag, "Yeah."

"Then stop."

"No, because I'm into it."

"That's not how—"

"If you say that's not how boyfriends work, Narek, I'm going to gag you."

"Is this the punishment you spoke of earlier?" He hated that there was a twist of excitement racing through him despite everything. His legs weren't used to being forced into this position, and true, he wasn't hard anymore, not since Kazimir had stopped stroking him. Yet, even though he didn't show it on the outside—thank Light—Nate wasn't disliking this as much as he claimed.

Which made him hate it all the more, because what the actual hell?

"Not at all," Kaz said. "This isn't a punishment."

"Pretty sure it is."

"I assure you," he grinned, "it isn't. You did a good job back there, babe. Too good of a job, actually."

Nate frowned. "You're angry."

"I'm confused about my own emotions, and I don't like that," Kaz clarified before snapping something around the base of Nate's dick, chuckling when that had him jerking. "Ever use a cock cage? No, you wouldn't have had. I picked this one out, especially for you."

"When?" He ground his teeth together as

his dick was pressed into the toy, feeling confined and uncomfortable in an instant. "Last night, you promised if I agreed, you wouldn't do this anymore."

"This won't be like last night." Kaz pushed a hand against the back of Nate's thigh, bending him forward even more, tipping his ass in the process. "You can come in some of these, but not this one. The cream wasn't enough to keep you from orgasming over and over again. We'll try something different this go at it."

"Kazimir—"

"You want to know something else your therapist wrote in your report?"

He frowned. Why was he bringing that up now?

"He said you were too tightly wound," Kaz told him without waiting for an answer. "That on the outside you may appear happy and well-rounded, but on the inside, you're suppressed and afraid of your own wants and needs. That true, Pretty Boy?"

"What? No. That's crap." Nate was glad he'd only gone to that one session, but also…How much had this therapist managed to psycho-analyze him in those brief two hours they'd been together in that stuffy office? Unless… "You're making this shit up."

"Am I?"

"You'd tell all sorts of lies if it meant getting you the reaction you want."

"And what reaction do you think I'm after from you right now?" Maintaining eye contact, Kazimir stuck two fingers in his mouth and lewdly sucked on them, smirking slightly when that had Nate going quiet with anticipation.

There was no logical reason for Nate to find any of this arousing, and yet, when Kaz suddenly shoved those two digits deep into his hole and curved them against his prostate, he threw his head back and howled.

CHAPTER 17:

Kaz didn't know what he was doing.

All he knew was there'd been this inescapable urge to secure Nate, tie him down, and ensure he couldn't go anywhere or do anything Kazimir didn't like.

That he couldn't slip a text message to Odette when Kaz wasn't looking, or have time to ask him any personal questions about either Saint or Yuze. If he had, there was no guarantee this vicious sensation in his gut wouldn't take control and take it out on the other Brumal members. He'd always been possessive of his things, so this shouldn't have come completely out of left field the way it had. However, he'd been unprepared for it.

After weeks of trying to trap him and one night of success, was he seriously that attached?

"What is it about you that I even like?" he asked out loud, digging those fingers in deeper into Nate's hole.

A strangled sound slipped past Nate's lips and his skin glistened in a sheen of sweat despite the cold temperature outside the car. He was still in his long-sleeved shirt to help abate the chill, but it was starting to seem unnecessary for Kaz to have allowed him to keep it.

He ran his palm up from Nate's navel, pushing the material of his black sweater out of the way as he did to expose his pale skin. "Don't get enough sun?"

The sounds of the car rocking with the movements of his fingers pumping in and out of Nate was the only reply. The pretty racer had closed his eyes and was clenching his jaw, no doubt fighting against the off-putting sensation of the cock cage keeping his dick from lengthening. "What's it feel like, babe?"

"Stop," Nate inhaled and then glared directly at him, "talking to me."

"Trying to focus?" Kazimir tilted his head. "Or trying to pretend like you're not enjoying this? What happened to not being into it?"

"We both know what happened," he snapped. "Your damn conditioning last night took, okay? Good Light, could you either hurry it up or *do something* other than blab all day long?"

"Did you really just tell me to shut up?"

"There's no one else here," Nate said, tugging on his bound wrists again with obvious frustration.

"Give a guy the dicking down of a lifetime, and suddenly he's brazen." If anyone else had taken that attitude with him, Kaz would have taken the knife and gutted them. But there was something interesting about the way Nate's skin flushed with hints of red whenever he got angry. He wondered if he was even aware his muscles were clenching down around Kaz's fingers.

"Six hours was really all it took to turn you into my needy bitch?" He grunted. "Aren't you ashamed of yourself?"

Nate shook his head. "Why would I be?"

That…was not the response he'd been expecting. Kaz's fingers stilled inside of him, and Nate protested by groaning.

"You were upset by it last night," Kaz pointed out.

"Sure, because last night I was just a thing to you. Today is different. I made sure of it, remember?" The chains attached to the collar around Nate's neck jangled. "You can string me up like this and try to humiliate me all you want, Kazimir. If it does get out, all I have to do is remind everyone that I'm your boyfriend. Having sex—even rough and kinky sex—when you're in a relationship with someone is pretty par for the course."

Coming from anyone else, Kaz would consider it pride, but coming from Nate it was obvious that wasn't it at all. Everything, no matter what the context, always circled back to one thing for him.

Not wanting to disappoint or burden others.

"So what, being fucked by a Devil on the side is embarrassing for Big Brother, but taking it from your man in an official capacity is somehow different?" he snorted derisively, but Nate didn't rise to the bait.

"You wanted this to stick it to your family member," he said matter-of-factly. "I agreed to protect mine. You were fairly straightforward that sex was going to be a part of it no matter what I chose."

The pieces clicked into place. "You didn't come to Vail for my benefit. That act you just put on, that was for you."

"Another thing you taught me last night?" Nate quirked a challenging brow. "I have to protect myself. Any way I can."

"You mean *Big Brother*," Kaz sneered. "You don't actually give a shit about yourself, Narek. Tell me, is there anyone you actually do care about other than Nuri?" It bothered him. Even knowing they were brothers by blood, it irked him to think about the lengths Nate was willing to go to for someone other than him.

Sure, Kazimir had forced him into this, but the goal had been to fuck him into giving into him. Not fuck him to the point he realized if he didn't, he was risking Nuri's reputation. Which reminded him—

"Big Brother wouldn't approve of you sleeping around with a Devil, is that what you said? Why?" Some of them were princes, for fucks sake. It wasn't like they were lowlifes. "This is Vitality. We're gods here. More than half the population would beg for me to use these straps on them."

"Should have bought all of this for one of them instead of me then." Even though he had to be getting uncomfortable in the stuck position, Nate wasn't cowering before him like he wanted. "And to answer your other question, yes of course Nuri isn't the only one I care about." He held his gaze. "I have a sister, too."

With a growl, he pulled his hand free and lined himself up to Nate's entrance, that coil of anger within him spurring him on. Later, when he was in his right mind, he might look back on this and wonder how the hell he'd allowed Nate to gain the upper hand the way he had, but for now, all he could think of was punishing him.

Making him *feel* Kaz in all the ways he could.

He notched his crown against Nate's rim and hissed at the heat as he pushed inside. Even after the insane pounding he'd given that hole last night, it gripped him tightly as he entered, his cock sinking inside of him inch by delectable inch.

"You should see the view," he teased as he was swallowed whole, circling his hips the way he remembered Nate liked.

Sure enough, his pretty racer tossed his head back against the seat, the cock cage shaking as his dick tried to lengthen again. He might protest all of this, but Nate's body was still so responsive. It'd been the same when they'd been in his bed. He'd cried and begged and said no and stop more times than Kaz could count, and yet every single time Kazimir had wanted him to, he'd come.

Kaz didn't want him to come now.

He was angry, and even knowing that it was childish of him, he wanted to take it out on Nate for making him this way. He'd fucked a lot of people in the past, so why had Nate's fake kindness toward his friends aggravated him so much? Why did knowing that had come from a place where Nate's goal had been pleasing Nuri and not him infuriate him?

He started thrusting with no warning, putting all of his frustration behind each and every spearing of his cock. "Remember what I said, babe? Pretty sure I told you that from now on, you only have to worry about pleasing me. So then why the fuck were you asking Saint and Yule if they wanted lunch money? Why are you only thinking about your brother, even now, when I'm claiming this sweet ass of yours?"

"Kazimir!"

He adjusted his legs so he could penetrate at a different angle, one hand dropping onto the cage when Nate cried out.

"There's literally no way of pleasing you!" Nate growled. "I did exactly what you asked! Yet you're still—"

"Fucking you senseless?" He shook his head. "You didn't do anything for me. Talking to them, spreading the rumor we're dating, that was all for you and *Nuri*."

Something came over Nate then, and he stopped resisting all at once. "You're jealous."

"Shut up." Kazimir didn't get jealous over a person. Especially not someone he'd literally picked up off the streets. "You aren't important enough for me to do that."

"Yeah?" Nate wasn't even remotely buying it. "So it won't bother you that I think Saint's pink hair is sexy? It looks fantastic on him. Makes his tanned skin really stand out."

Kaz made quick work of the cock cage and tossed it into the back before he gripped Nate himself with a warning growl.

Which only had Nate moaning and then laughing.

The absolute audacity.

He opened his mouth to threaten him, but Nate beat him to it.

"It's okay, *hahzi*." Nate smiled at him, not one of those fake smiles he'd given the others either, but one of the real ones, the one Kazimir had only ever caught a glimpse of aimed at someone else before. "This is the most human I've seen you since we met. I like it. Can I be honest? It wasn't just about protecting my reputation. I took things too far on purpose."

"What?" And what on Vitality did *hahzi* mean?

"I wasn't sure it would work and I was curious. We don't really know each other that well—or at all. Mostly, I know what your cock feels like and that you're sort of a domineering asshole. It didn't make sense to me that you'd want a boyfriend, or that you'd pick me."

"And...," he was struggling to keep up with this conversation, and not because he was still balls deep inside of Nate either. "Now it does?"

"Not exactly," he said. "But at least now I know."

"Know what?"

"That you legitimately like me." When Kaz's brow furrowed even more Nate chuckled. "Relax. I meant my body. You like having sex with me."

That wasn't untrue. He thought back to the good mood he'd been in after fucking Nate in the bar that first time, and how long that mood had lasted. Maybe that was it. When he'd spotted Nate with Mit Parker, maybe he'd instantly and subconsciously hated the idea of anyone else getting a taste of him before Kaz had had his fill.

"That...puts things into perspective," Kaz admitted.

"Didn't realize it either?" Nate nodded. "Figures. Guys like you are too hyper-fixated on how best to throw your weight around and get other people to dance to your tune to notice when there's an inner change."

Kazimir's eyes narrowed as a dash of that anger from earlier returned. "Know a lot of guys like me, is that it?"

"Kaz," Nate gave him a pointed stare, "there are no guys like you, *hahzi*. I'm not above acknowledging that, and it isn't because I'm currently beneath you, either. If I promise to tell you something you'll like hearing, will you promise to finish this quick and let me drive us somewhere more discrete? I meant it when I said I wasn't into this whole exhibitionism thing."

"Because if it gets back to your siblings, it could affect them?" Kaz took a shot in the dark and guessed.

"Mostly," Nate said. "You knew that bit about me even before you read my file, though. I'm not that hard to figure out."

"That's a lie," he stated before he could stop himself, shocking them both.

"Oh. Well then." Nate went silent.

It took Kaz longer than it should have to realize that it was because he was waiting for an answer to his proposal.

Something he'd like to hear? He liked hearing Nate moan for him but...

"Okay. Deal."

"Swear?"

"Yes," Kaz rolled his eyes. "I swear. Tell me."

Nate shifted his hips, moving on Kaz's cock. "I like sleeping with you, too."

There was no reason for that to spark anything within Kazimir, and yet he felt it like a bang. Draping himself over Nate's folded body, he went wild, that tight control he always had snapping in the blink of an eye.

He fucked him like a madman, like it was their last time, and if he didn't do it right, he'd burst into flames or some other such nonsense. When the pretty racer went crazy beneath him, howling and shaking the chains, he went harder, spearing into him with thrusts that shook the vehicle so roughly it was a wonder it didn't roll down the road.

The orgasm took him by surprise, creeping up on him and yanking him under a sea of intense pleasure. He moaned but didn't stop, continuing to pound into Nate's heat through it, filling him with every drop he could spend.

Nate came soon after, spasming and twitching, his eyes rolling back in his head. His pretty dick painted their chests in white, seemingly never-ending.

There was something sexy about the fact Kaz wasn't the only one totally lost to these sensations, and with a growl, he captured Nate's mouth, nipping at his bottom lip to force him to open so he could plunge his tongue inside and taste him all over.

It wasn't until Kazimir went to pull away that he registered that Nate was responding, kissing him back with just as much fervor. He grunted and slipped a finger beneath the leather strap of the collar and held Narek still as he disengaged, taking in his flushed face and blown pupils.

He had the unexplainable urge to tell Nate that he was his. To verbally claim him the way his cock had just claimed his hole, but he caught himself.

"Who has sexy hair again?" he asked instead, the warning note clear in his smoky voice.

Nate actually cracked a smile, taking Kaz's breath away, but if he noticed, he didn't let on. "You do," he replied, lifting his head to plant a soft kiss to Kazimir's mouth. "You do."

Something awoke inside of Kaz.

Something foreign and jagged.

Something potentially more dangerous than anything he'd ever experienced before.

CHAPTER 18:

Kaz set dinner on the table just as the sound of the shower turning off came from down the hall. He grinned at himself, thinking about what he'd done earlier before leaving, then circled around the small living area as he waited.

He'd already snooped through the kitchen while he'd plated the takeout he'd ordered. Originally, he'd figured he'd cook them something, but the fridge had been barren. His little green notebook already had a reminder in it to schedule a grocery delivery for tomorrow. Considering the pretty racer had only just lost his job at Quartet Air, and how driven he was to take care of those around him, Kaz had expected him to be better at looking after himself. The empty fridge and the overdue bill he found on the small table by the front door proved otherwise.

For a split second, he felt a bit bad that he'd ousted Nate from Quartet Air, but he got over it quickly. It wasn't like that'd been his intention, after all. Nate had been the one to make that foolish decision. Kaz would have kept him on and merely made his life harder to manage until the older guy had agreed to date him.

He paused in front of a framed photo of the Narek siblings and poked a finger against Nate's smiling face in the middle. "Why do you always have to overcomplicate everything?"

It should have been fairly easy to win him over, either through money or his good looks, but no, Nate had made things difficult for them both. On the outside, he looked neat and tidy—aka, simple and easy—but it was a farce. He put up a front just like everyone else, hiding his true nature away.

And if what he'd confessed in the car was real, his true nature liked being tied up and taken advantage of. For all his protests about not wanting to be treated like an object, Nate sure enjoyed it when Kaz had him bound and trapped and at his mercy.

He listened to Nate puttering away in his room, figuring he was most likely realizing what Kaz had done, and swept his gaze around him. The small house was modest, with signs of life in bursts of mismatched colored throw pillows on the faded couch, and a gaming system set on the floor. Even though it was filled, every item seemed to have a place.

Bedroom aside, Nate kept his house tidy just like he did his outward appearance.

Still, Kaz could see through it the same way he was starting to really see through the pretty racer.

"He's lonely," he mumbled to himself, picking up a red egg-shaped stone and tossing it absently back and forth between his hands. Lived in, but untouched. That was the actual vibe when one peered a little closer. How often did Nate flit through these rooms, barely seeing any of it as he moved from one to the other?

Kazimir had his multi-slate lifted and his fingers flying over the keypad before he knew it, shooting off a message to the assistant he'd placed in charge of Quartet Air—since he had no actual interest in running the place.

Kaz: Look into past employee records for Nate Narek. I want to know how many hours he averaged a week since he started working there.

Hyn: Right away, sir.

"Put that down," Nate's irritated voice cut through Kaz's thoughts, and he turned to find the older man entering from the hallway, drying the back of his damp head with a white towel.

Wearing clothes.

Kazimir scowled. "Where did you find those?"

This morning, he'd been sure to remove every single item of clothing he could. That'd been his intended punishment, forcing Nate to parade around naked for him.

"You mean how did you miss them when you were raiding my closet?" Nate made a beeline for the fridge and grabbed a bottle of water. "Tell me you're an only child without telling me you're an only child."

He still didn't get it and waited for Nate to take a drink.

"I have a younger sister, remember?" he clarified once it became clear Kaz wouldn't speak until he did. "She used to steal my clothes all the time. Something about them being bigger and comfier."

Kazimir swept his gaze down the loosely fitting white t-shirt and the gray sweatpants that hung low on Nate's hips. He wasn't wearing socks and his bare feet padding against the tiled floor of the kitchen was the most domestic thing he'd ever seen in his life.

It felt odd suddenly, that he was here. That he was part of this moment.

Clearly Nate didn't have the same problem. "Hey." He snapped his fingers. "Seriously. Put that down. My—"

"Brother bought it for you," Kaz sneered. "Yeah, yeah, yeah." Nuri had purchased every damn thing in this place, he was willing to bet. "It's a wonder you let me touch anything at all."

"I didn't let you do anything if you recall." Nate seemed to notice the set table for the first time. "What's that?"

"Food," he ambled back over and pulled out one of the chairs, motioning down at it with his chin, "I know it's probably been a while since you've last seen some. You need to stock your fridge, Narek. I won't have you starving to death on me."

He rolled his eyes but came over and took the

offered seat. "Just freezing to death, that it? I want all of my clothes back, by the way."

"If you're good." Kaz grinned when that earned him a scowl. "What's wrong, Pretty Boy?" He moved to stand behind him and leaned over, trapping Nate between his arms. "Thinking about being bad, so I bend you over the table and eat you instead?"

"No." His cheeks turned pink, and it was clear he was imagining it.

"Too bad," Kaz straightened and rounded the table. "Blow jobs are a reward, not a punishment."

"You really need to stop with this whole punishment bullshit."

"No can do." He sat down and picked up his fork. "You and Zane both need to adjust the way you see relationships. Why should I have to?"

"Zane?" Nate repeated.

"Yeah." Kaz speared one of the greens and popped it into his mouth. "He also scolded me when I suggested punishment."

Nate's shoulders stiffened and he fiddled with his utensils.

"Do you not like ress?" Kaz had automatically ordered his usual dish from his favorite restaurant, and it was just now occurring to him he probably should have asked Nate what he felt like eating.

"No," he shook his head and took a small bite, "it's fine."

"Fine? This costs eighty coin a plate."

"I'll pay you back tomorrow."

"That's not what I meant, Narek."

"I didn't ask you to order dinner," he stated. "Or come home with me, for that matter."

"Then next time you'll come home with me."

"That's—"

"We're only here because I thought you'd be more comfortable in your own space while you adjusted," Kazimir told him. "I'd certainly prefer to be in my warm house with the fully stocked kitchen and the king-sized bed."

Nate waved over his shoulder. "There's the door."

"Why are you angry with me all of a sudden?"

"Is it sudden?"

He nodded. "You were sweet in the car on the drive here."

Sweet was maybe taking it a bit far, but he hadn't sworn or glared at Kaz, at least, and that was an improvement in his book. He'd also driven them straight home and agreed to go take a shower while Kazimir waited.

"Just," Nate set his fork down, "tell me how long you want this to go on for."

"What?" He took in the set table. "Dinner typically lasts until the food is gone or the people eating it are full."

"No, not—" Nate pinched his brow. "I meant this whole dating thing, Kaz. How long do you want us to date? Give me a timeline."

He frowned. "I don't think relationships usually work that way. Do you usually plan out the finish line with the people you're going out with?"

And his friends thought he was the one with commitment issues. Yikes.

"We aren't really dating, though," Nate argued. "We're doing this to convince your friends, remember? That's what you told me."

"We fuck like the real thing," Kazimir stated, not liking the turn this conversation was taking. "That means we are the real thing." He must not have made that clear enough. He'd correct that.

"Okay, but until when?"

"Until I say otherwise," he snapped.

"Why are *you* getting so angry?"

"You're trying to break up with me."

"What?" Nate gave him an incredulous look. "No, I'm not."

"Explain why you'd bring this topic up then?"

"Kaz, you're the one who—"

"Enough." He held up a hand. "Change the subject, or I really will bend you over the table and fuck you hard enough the only sounds you're capable of making are moans and sobs."

Nate gave him a dirty look. "Why does everything have to come back to sex with you? Can't we just have a normal conversation? We're dating, fine. You can dump me whenever you want, but I can't do the same. Understood. Anything else?"

"Yeah," he was pleased he was asking, "No more flirting with other people, whether it's in front of me or not. If I find out you were hitting on someone behind my back, I'll make you watch while

I seduce and fuck them before—"

This time Nate was the one to hold up a hand. "I'm good."

"I'm not," he said darkly. "—Before I cut out their tongue and make you eat it."

He went to put his fork down and Kaz stopped him.

"Don't even think about it."

"I'm hardly hungry now that you've put that image in my head," Nate argued.

"Not my problem," Kaz replied. "Eat. You'll need your strength for round two."

Nate stiffened.

"What? You asked for us to come back here so I could fuck you somewhere private," Kaz reminded. "Don't think for a second you're getting out of it."

"Can we please at least talk first?" Nate huffed.

"Sure, let's talk about you coming back to work."

"No, I meant—"

"If you'd rather not, you don't have to," Kaz talked over him. "That place is a dump. But still, it's better than telling everyone my boyfriend is a barista."

"What's wrong with being a barista?"

"Nothing. Unless you're a Vail University graduate. Your brother also bought your degree, didn't he? Now who isn't treating his things carefully."

"That's totally uncalled for, Kaz."

"Is it?"

"Yes! There's no reason for you to be mean. I haven't done anything!"

"Except try to break up with me."

Nate dropped his head into his hands and let out a sound of frustration. Then he inhaled deeply, and when he lifted his face, he seemed miraculously calmer. "This is getting us nowhere. Let's try it this way instead. You're going to give me back my clothes. In return, I'm going to eat the rest of the food you bought me. We'll take it a step at a time, okay?"

Kazimir had no clue what he was talking about but...He did want Nate to eat so... "Okay. Deal."

"Fantastic." Nate slammed his fork down into a part of the meat and picked up his knife, slicing it with more force than necessary. "You are an overgrown child, though, you do realize, right? Who steals someone's clothes?"

"I like it better when you're naked anyway."

"You were throwing a tantrum. Why?"

"I don't like the sound of that, Narek."

"I'm not going to understand what I did to upset you unless you spell it out for me, *Ambrose*."

"That is a sound argument." He smirked. "You aren't allowed to disappear in the morning."

"I'm not going to ask permission to leave my own house," Nate countered.

"Did I say I wanted you to do that?"

Nate frowned. "Then...what do you want?"

"At least wake me up and tell me goodbye. It

sucks being left behind with no warning."

For a moment, the pretty racer merely stared at him, and just as it was starting to become uncomfortable, he broke the silence. "Okay. I can do that. Sorry."

"Good. I'll do the same." Not that Nate had asked that of him.

"Is it abandonment issues?"

"Wow, really going straight for the jugular." Kaz would have been impressed if he hadn't been the target.

"Just trying to get to know my boyfriend better," he shrugged.

"For the record, it's not fear of abandonment per se," he found himself confessing, not even sure why he was bothering to explain himself. This was a subject he never spoke of, let alone shared, and yet Kaz wanted to tell Nate. Wanted him to understand. "My mom left and my dad never listens to me. I like closure, so to speak. Knowing when you're coming and going? Knowing that you're taking the time to inform me and—"

"Let you know I'll be coming back?" Nate hummed. "I'll trade you. No more sex out in the open. Private places are all right, but nowhere we can be walked in on or photographed. You do that, and I'll do my best to listen. I won't make you wake up alone in the morning with no goodbye."

This must be that compromise Zane had mentioned. Kazimir had been against it before, but hearing Nate's proposal now made sense. He tugged out his notebook and made a note to himself. "All right, Pretty Boy."

In less than ten minutes, he'd somehow managed to get Kaz to agree to his terms not once, but twice.

Impressive was an understatement.

"What is that?" Nate pointed to the notebook.

"I like to jot random shit down," Kaz said. He moved the small book close enough and flipped through the pages so Nate could see. "It's just a hobby."

"You journal?" He seemed surprised. "Why is it written in red?"

"It's blood. I use a fountain pen."

Nate laughed. "Very funny."

"I'm serious." Why would he joke about something like that?

The pretty racer blinked at him.

"Berga saves me some whenever he—" Kaz stopped when Nate held up his hand, looking a little paler than usual.

"Nope. You can spare me the gritty details, thanks."

"Sure. Subject change. What is this?" He held up one of the paper coasters that were piled neatly in the center of the table.

"What's it look like?" Nate took a bite and chewed. "It's so drinks don't make rings on the table."

"Yes, I know the purpose of a coaster, thank you. I mean why do they all have the Vail crest on them?"

"Because I stole them from the Velvet Brew I used to work at," he explained. "The one on the same street as campus? They had a bunch and I managed to take the extra home. Saved some money that way."

"Have you always been this...poor?"

"I'm not poor." He snatched the coaster out of his hand but discarded it back onto the table. "There's just no reason to toss out items that are perfectly useful, or waste money on things I don't need."

"You're mindful of your spending," Kaz said. "So...poor. What if I offered you a raise?"

"What?"

"Would you come back to work then? I have no use for Quartet Air, Narek. I only purchased it to get close to you. Kind of doesn't play out the way I'd hoped if you're not there, don't you agree?"

"That isn't my problem." He took a sip of the soda Kaz had ordered for him, seemingly liking the flavor.

Kazimir had taken a guess since he didn't know what was and wasn't to Nate's tastes. Now that he was considering things, there was actually a lot he didn't know about the pretty racer. Being in the dark irritated him, but he contained his emotions so as not to cause another argument. As much as he enjoyed their banter and the wild way Nate fought him, he was starting to see he also liked when he was amicable.

"Let's talk about this later," Narek ended up saying.

Was there a chance he also liked it when they got along?

Kaz set his elbows on the edge of the table and watched him, and when Nate didn't glare or tell him to stop, he felt something odd bloom in the center of his chest.

Something a lot like contentment.

People were kept around as entertainment or out of duty and convenience. He couldn't recall the last time being in someone's presence had actually put him at ease. Couldn't recall the last time someone had made him feel comfortable.

Made him feel like…he was home.

"Things just got serious," he mumbled to himself, shaking his head with a smile when Nate sent him a questioning look, having clearly not heard him.

That was for the best. It was too soon for his pretty racer to come to the conclusion Kaz just had.

How long did he want them to date?

For-fucking-ever with a dash of eternity.

He'd pick apart the reasoning and how it'd happened later, but for now, it was easier to accept the truth when it was right in front of his face. This may have started off with a random selection, a means to prove himself to his cousin—a childish means, *his boyfriend* would say—but it was so much more than that now.

Nate Narek wasn't a means to an end like Kaz

had originally believed.

    Nate Narek was *his*.
    And he was going to stay that way.
    Whether he agreed to it or not.

CHAPTER 19:

Nate arrived at the movie theater a bit late and with a stained shirt. A customer had spilled their entire red velvet latte over the counter when he'd been handing it to them, and the contents had splashed over his pressed white shirt, despite the apron over it. Part of him wanted to blame Kaz, since the whole reason he'd had to wear white in the first place was because the guy was a total liar.

Even though it'd been two days since their agreement, Kazimir had yet to return all of Nate's clothes. Instead, he'd lay out an outfit for the next day—complete with socks and underwear.

Like Nate was a three-year-old child.

Every time he attempted to bring it up, Kaz would kiss him until his toes curled and he was rock-hard. How the guy had managed to program his body to be so damn responsive to him already was beyond him, but that was the case. He even found himself wondering when he'd see the Devil next, since they'd both had busy schedules between school, work, and whatever the hell the Brumal was getting themselves up to.

That last part should have been enough to knock some sense into Nate, and yet...When he thought back to Kaz's reaction in the car, everything came together with more clarity.

Kazimir Ambrose, the big bad Brumal mafia underboss, was nothing more than a giant kid, right down to the temper tantrums whenever he didn't get his way. That's what the sex in the car had really been about, and that's why he'd made off with Nate's clothing after waking alone.

When she'd been younger, Neve had done similar things. If she was mad at him, she'd hide the holo-vision remote, or leave the microwave counter on so it would go off at random intervals in the middle of the night. Once, she'd even soaked his shoes in water and covered them with glitter.

A Devil of Vitality might be too much for Nate to handle. But a full-grown adult acting like a pre-teen? Been there, done that.

"Hey!" Neve spotted him the second he entered the theater, standing over by the concession stand next to a tall man with lilac hair and chunky gold glasses. She beamed at Nate as he headed over and handed the popcorn tub she was holding to the guy at her side. "You made it!"

"Sorry, I'm late." Nate engulfed her in a hug, taking momentary refuge in the familiarity of it. Ever since she'd moved out, it felt like his life had taken a nose dive, and he hadn't realized just how bad things had gotten until now.

Still, he couldn't hug her forever, so forced himself to pull back, patting the top of her head the way he knew annoyed her. Sure enough, she scowled and he laughed, stepping over to the guy with lilac hair.

"Hi, Verga." They didn't hug or shake hands or anything, but things had always been comfortable between them.

Verga Faw was the perfect partner. He had a steady job, a good reputation, and was close with his immediate and extended family. The latter was especially important to both Nate and Neve because that was something they'd lacked and something Neve had always longed for. The Faw family had accepted her with open arms, and the two had moved into a nice apartment together and were already looking at a more permanent residence. He treated Nate's sister like an equal and the two made decisions as a team.

Basically, he was everything Kazimir Ambrose was not.

Nate inwardly cursed himself.

Why the hell was he thinking about the Devil right now?

"It's good to see you," Verga replied back in a calm and steady voice. He smiled and there was nothing intense or dangerous in the look.

No spark.

He really was losing his mind, wasn't he?

"The movie doesn't start for another ten minutes," Neve linked her arm through his and motioned toward the concessions behind her. "Do you want anything?"

It occurred to him he hadn't eaten since that morning, but a glance at the long line had him shaking his head. He'd already made them wait for him, he wasn't about to also leave them standing around while the clock ticked down to the start. What if they missed something?

"I'm fine. Let me just buy a ticket and—" A hand settled over the nape of his neck, possessive and hot to the touch. Nate didn't have to turn to know who it was, stilling a second before the newcomer at his back spoke.

"I got you." Kaz stepped forward to his side but didn't drop the hand. Instead, he eyed down Verga and Neve, not bothering to hide the fact he was clearly assessing them.

"What are you doing here?" Snapping out of it, Nate brushed his arm away. He hadn't mentioned his plans for the day... "Did you follow me?"

"Not exactly," he replied cryptically.

"Kazimir Ambrose?" A look of worry and doubt came over Neve as she glanced between the two of them before her gaze settled on Nate questioningly. "You two know each other? Since when?"

"Wow," Kaz drawled lightly, the sarcasm the only thing saving him from Nate's wrath for talking back to his sister, "Girl graduates and forgets all about us underclassmen, huh? I see how it is." He quirked a brow at Verga, a little less friendly when he added, "You forget who I am, too?"

"Not at all," Verga shook his head and forced an uncomfortable smile, blindly reaching for Neve's hand. "I think we're just surprised to see the two of you together. It's definitely...an unexpected pairing."

"Oh? You know a lot about the type of people Nate likes to get with?"

"No, I—"

"He's messing with you," Nate put this little dance to an end and sent Kaz a warning glare. "He's done now."

Kaz lifted a single shoulder. "Whatever you say, boyfriend."

Neve let out a startled sound. "You two are dating? Like, each other?"

"Seriously though," Kazimir leaned into Nate and practically growled, "Why does everyone keep saying that?"

"Because I'm a straight-A student and all-around good guy," Nate stated, "and you're you."

"Is it weird I'm starting to find it cute when you insult me?"

His brow furrowed. "Yeah. Yeah, it is."

Neve clapped her hands loudly and cleared her throat for good measure. "Okay, well, I guess since you're here, the four of us should head in and find our seats." It seemed to occur to her that since Nate hadn't selected tickets with them, they wouldn't be together and she pouted.

"Don't worry about it," Nate ruffled her hair

again, grinning when she cursed at him. "It just means we'll have plenty to talk about over dinner after, right?"

"Did I miss something?" Kaz asked.

"You get used to it," Verga replied with another smile, this one seeming a bit more genuine. "The two of them sometimes read each other's minds."

"Not actually," Nate corrected, in case he got the wrong idea since there were, in fact, people in the universe who could read minds. "We get just each other, that's all."

"Years of living with a person will do that," Neve laughed, then stuck her tongue out. "Anyway, I was bummed that we won't be sitting together, that's all. Since you bought both of your tickets without checking where we were first."

Kaz cocked his head. "Was I meant to do that?"

"You weren't meant to be here at all," Nate reminded, then sighed. There was no point in being mad at him for something small like that. They'd have to talk about how the younger guy had located him, but now that he was here, Neve's approach made the best sense.

To just roll with it.

"How about I buy more snacks," Kaz surprised him by suggesting to the group, "To make up for it." He motioned toward the popcorn tub in Verga's free hand. "You're almost out already."

Neve grew sheepish when Nate turned to her. "We really weren't waiting for you that long. I was just super hungry."

"Let's skip the movie," he said. "We can go eat now instead."

"No way," she objected. "I've been looking forward to seeing this for months. We're staying. Besides, your boyfriend just offered to feed us." She turned to Kaz. "I hear you're loaded."

"Neve." Nate set his hands on his hips.

"It was a joke." She rolled her eyes. "Relax, big brother. It's not like I'm going to ask him to buy me one of everything."

"Would you like one of everything?" Kaz took a single step back toward the concessions, stopping only when Nate grabbed a fistful of the material of his shirt around his waist.

"Don't even think about it," he warned him, then to his sister, "She'll have one large popcorn and one drink. That's all."

"What about candy?" Kazimir grinned when that earned him another scowl. "Come on. Movies aren't the same without candy. I'm going to buy some." He walked off before Nate had the chance to stop him again.

"I'll go with him," he muttered to his sister before following. The line was still fairly long, with them seven people behind, and Nate checked the time on his multi-slate again. "The movie starts soon."

"You don't have to do that," Kaz said lightly.

"Do what?"

"Your sister is standing too far away to

overhear. You don't have to act like everything's cool. Talk about what you really want to talk about, Pretty Boy. We've got time."

"First of all," he stated, not liking the odd rush those words brought him or how easy it was for the tension to slip out of his shoulders as he turned to give Kaz a piece of his mind, "No, we do not. The movie is going to start soon, and if I miss any of it, I'm going to be pissed. Neve likes talking about the previews. Second of all, what the hell are you actually doing here, and how did you even know where I was?"

"Do you like it?" A couple grabbed their items, and the line moved forward. Kaz casually slipped his hands into his pockets while they waited, his eyes scanning the large holographic menu hovering behind the workstation.

"Being stalked? No."

"Not that," he corrected. "You said your sister likes to discuss the previews. Do you?"

He frowned. "Sure, I guess."

"Doesn't sound very convincing."

"Why does that matter?"

"Wasn't the whole point of going to therapy so you could start working on yourself?" Kaz challenged. "People pleasing comes in all shapes and forms."

He bristled. "I don't think I should be taking advice from someone like you."

Kazimir finally tore his gaze off the board to look at him. "What's that supposed to mean?"

"Come on," he drawled. "Are you seriously going to try telling me that you take therapy to heart? You're not there to change. You're there because your dad makes you go."

His expression darkened. "Don't ruin the mood, Narek."

"Why? Does just mentioning your dad piss you off?"

"What do you want?" Kaz changed the subject and jutted his chin toward the menu.

"I'm not hungry." Dropping the conversation seemed wise, so he let it go. There were lines that you should never cross with people, and messing with family was one of them.

"Liar. You just came from work."

"So?"

"You get a half-hour break, and I know you don't use it to feed yourself."

He'd been searching on his multi-slate for job listings.

"How...? You're not actually stalking me, right?" That seemed stupid, all things considered.

"No, it's just obvious. You're shit at taking care of yourself."

"That's not true." Nate's stomach chose that exact moment to rumble in protest. He covered it, but it was too late. When Kaz grinned at him smugly, he crossed his arms. "Fine, whatever. I'll have..." His eyes scanned the menu, but the hotshot clicked his tongue at him before he could choose something.

"Don't go for the cheapest item," Kaz said. "We're dating. It's customary for boyfriends to buy each other food."

"Doesn't mean I have to take advantage of your bank account."

"Why not?" he sounded sincere when he asked. "I take advantage of you plenty."

"You're comfortable doing that, I'm not." Another two people left the line, and he let out a relieved sound. It wouldn't be too much longer now. Nate took a look over his shoulder and smiled when he found Neve watching him.

"You don't have to force yourself to do and say things you don't like when you're with me," Kazimir said then, and Nate gave him a pointed stare until it seemed to hit him what he'd actually just uttered. "Fuck. You know what I mean."

"I don't," he corrected. "I have no idea what you mean or why you're even here, Kazimir."

"I'm here because I thought you might be meeting up with someone behind my back," he replied. "Odette seemed way too comfortable with you the other day. And not just her. Now that you know how much you like cock, there's no way of knowing if you'd sneak off and try to give Saint a try."

Nate scrunched up his nose. "What the hell?"

"I had a weird feeling and I acted on it," he continued.

"Next time, don't."

Kaz's eyes narrowed. "Why?"

"Because this is weird. And I'm not going to cheat on you. I can't even cheat on you because we're not really—"

"Finish that sentence." He was up in Nate's face in a heartbeat, the threat apparent.

A couple of the people around them even noticed the sudden tension and started whispering.

Nate pressed his palms to his chest and tried to get him to back up, taking in all of the curious looks they were getting. It made him uncomfortable to think of them all watching and making their own presumptuous theories about what was going on. Not to mention, there was the fact Neve was also here...

"We really are dating," Kaz's voice was sharp enough to cut through glass, but at least he had the good sense to talk quietly so the words remained just between the two of them. "Don't make me repeat myself about that again."

"You said you just wanted to prove Baikal wrong," Nate reminded, keeping his gaze downcast. If he made things worse, his sister would react and butt in and potentially get hurt in the process. "Since when did that change?"

"Since the morning I woke up to a cold bed and you gone," he admitted, and it seemed to catch them both momentarily off guard because he was silent for a few seconds after that before adding, "I don't like that you left me, Nate. I like the idea of you leaving me again even less. Isn't that what a real relationship looks like?"

"This isn't what we agreed on, Kaz." And he honestly didn't know how to feel about it. Trapped? Scared? A little bit thrilled?

Thrilled?

What the hell was he thinking?

Only an idiot would be thrilled that a Devil of Vitality wanted them.

"I get possessive very quickly," Kaz told him. "It's one of the things we frequently talk about in therapy. That's just how I'm wired. I can pass by the same object every day without taking notice, and all it'll take is one time for me to really see it for obsession to bloom. You're that new object, Narek, whether either of us likes that fact or not."

Was he saying he didn't like that he wanted to date him?

"Why is everything with you so complicated?" Nate ran a hand through his hair, but before Kaz could reply, he glanced over and realized with a start it was their turn in line. He pushed at his arm and pointed. "Table this for later."

"You're always saying that," Kazimir snorted but listened, stepping up to the counter. He smiled brightly at the woman standing across from them, and when she blushed, he leaned into the attention. "Hi, can I get four large ferd sodas, two large popcorns, and one of each candy option, please. Oh," he snapped his fingers, almost making it believable that he'd actually forgotten the next item, "And one yurdog lunch box. Thanks."

During dinner the other night, Kaz had

bugged Nate until he'd caved and agreed to answer questions. He'd expected them to be intrusive and vulgar but had been surprised when they'd geared more toward everyday things like his favorite foods and hobbies. Hell, the guy had even wanted to know his favorite color which...

Nate blinked when he noticed the brown socks peeking out from Kazimir's black sneakers. After all the fuss over how dumb of a favorite color brown was...He couldn't actually have worn those for Nate, right? Was it just a coincidence?

He was certain if he asked, the younger guy wouldn't hesitate to tell him the truth. Kaz couldn't be trusted not to use manipulation tactics against people, and of course, dishonesty was one of them, but it'd become apparent during their past interactions that Kazimir preferred to be blunt over anything else.

In fact, had he ever outright lied to him before?

Would Nate have even been able to catch him in the act if he had?

"Hey." Kaz gave him a questioning look and pressed the back of his hand against Nate's forehead. "Are you feeling all right? You turned pale all of a sudden. You don't even lose your color like that when we're hours into—"

Nate brushed his hand away and clicked his tongue in warning. "Stop talking. Some things are meant to stay private."

"Like how I'd prefer you let me keep you

naked?" He sighed when that earned him another glare. "You'll be happy to know that I've returned all of your clothing."

"About time."

The girl behind the counter set two trays before them and then started to ask, "Are you two—"

"Yes," Kazimir swiftly cut her off, picking up one tray to hand over to Nate before taking the other. "Yes, we're dating." He turned away without another word, shaking his head as they returned to Neve and Verga. "Seriously. Why does *everyone* ask that?"

"Your reputation proceeds you," Nate guessed with a shrug. He held the tray out to Neve when she reached for it.

"Thank you for this," she directed the comment to Kaz. "I'll buy dinner in return."

"That's not necessary," Kazimir told her.

"No, I insist. I plan on grilling you all about how you managed to convince my brother to actually date someone. We'll call it compensation for the interrogation to come." She laughed and then bumped Verga with her elbow excitedly. "It's about to start! We should hurry."

The two of them started to the right, but Kazimir noticeably stepped to the left, giving them all pause.

"Where are you going?" Nate had a sinking feeling.

The Seaside Cinema was one of the most popular theaters in the city because of its dual offerings. The building had been sectioned off, with everything on the right open to the general public. They played all sorts of films from PG to R-rated, but they were just regularly airing movies.

The left side, however...

"Please tell me you didn't." Nate felt his cheeks heat as his sister and Verga shifted uncomfortably next to him.

Kazimir, to his credit, looked just as perplexed as they were. "We're all over the age of adulthood, so I naturally assumed..." He turned to Neve. "You're not here to see the new Bind installment?"

Nate didn't even know what that was. "Of course not! We're seeing—"

"We figured we'd leave that to when we come just the two of us," Neve interrupted with a laugh. "I've been waiting for months though. Wasn't the last one the best?"

"But aren't you curious who's behind the mask?" Verga jumped in. "It drives me nuts sometimes wondering."

"He fixates," she said.

"What are you guys talking about?" More importantly, did Nate want to know?

"You haven't seen one yet?" She tilted her head at him, then told Kaz, "Hate to break it to you, new guy, but that's not really something I can see my brother getting into."

Kazimir's mouth quirked up in a knowing grin. "Oh, you'd be surprised."

"Hey!" Yup. Nate didn't like this. At all.

"Really?" She gave him an appreciative look that had Nate bristling. "Good for you, big brother."

"Please just stop talking." He covered his face and wished the ground would open up and swallow him whole.

Until it hit him…

"Wait." He stared at her. "You…?"

"Am a full-grown adult who gets up with adult things with my adult partner?" she filled in. "Yeah. Kinbaku is fun."

"Kin—" Right. It was called Bind. Question—unfortunately—answered.

"You guys should see it," Verga not-so-helpfully suggested, taking Neve's hand and stepping toward the right side of the theater. "We'll meet up after and do dinner still, how does that sound? Nate?"

"Like an actual nightmare," he stated. "I came to watch a movie with my sister, not—"

Neve pulled him to the side suddenly and huddled in. "Don't be an idiot and ruin this. He's hot, like, *super* hot, and he's into you. Those tickets cost a small fortune too, by the way. We've been saving for weeks so we can go see it."

They were expensive? It wouldn't be cool of him to waste—

Wait. No.

"He's the one who bought the wrong tickets," Nate pointed out. "How is that my problem?" It was easy to say, but on the inside the guilt was starting to gnaw at him. Except, it was tearing him in two different directions. "What about you? I promised we'd watch Get Friends together."

"It's not like I'm alone," she reminded. "Besides, I'm guessing the two of you haven't been together that long?"

He hesitated but then nodded.

"This is a date, then," she seemed more excited about it than he did. "Unless you don't like him?"

Nate couldn't exactly explain to her how things had started between them. He also couldn't bring himself to tell her he didn't like Kazimir at all because, well, that wouldn't be entirely true. It was unclear when he'd started hating Kaz less—maybe it was just a sex thing—but the fact that he felt bad over potentially wasting the guy's money was proof that was the case.

"Go," Neve insisted. "You deserve to have some fun, and I can't remember the last time you liked someone enough to agree to date them! This is great. I'd feel awful if I stood in the way of that."

Nate winced, but she didn't notice, already turning back toward the others.

"It's settled then!" She looped her arm through Verga's and quickly pulled him away. "We'll see you in the lobby after!"

Nate watched her go incredulously.

"Looks like Little Sister approves," Kazimir grinned and reached out to link their pinky fingers together.

With a sneer, Nate slapped him away and

turned toward the left side of the theater. His bravado fled a second later when it really hit him what they were about to do.

"Nervous?" Kaz asked challengingly.

Nate glared. "Lead the way."

He chuckled. "To the pits of hell, it is."

CHAPTER 20:

Admittedly, Nate had always been more than a bit curious about the private viewing rooms at the Seaside Cinema. But that didn't mean he'd ever intended to actually see one for himself.

There were different offerings for this section of the theater. Some films were preplanned and screened in a similar fashion to the regular movies, only these were adult movies meant for a specific purpose. Patrons could also opt to choose their own films from a wide selection if they didn't want to purchase tickets for a specific one, like Kaz had.

It was obvious he knew exactly where he was going, leading Nate up the steps and down a long hallway decorated in shades of red and gold. He checked the digital tickets on his multi-slate once and then stopped them at a room with a numbered plaque next to it.

The ticket scanned on the lock pad next to the handle and then there was a click. Kazimir entered first, holding the door open wide for Nate. He watched him silently as Nate hesitated, not saying anything to try and force him to enter.

It almost felt like Nate actually had a choice in the matter.

If only he hadn't already known better.

With a sigh of resignation, he stepped in, the door locking at his back, sealing him in a small room with only two pieces of furniture. A black leather couch with a plastic film over it was set in the center, closer to the screen that took up the entire wall in front of it than it was to the exit. To the left of that there was a counter, and Kazimir went and placed the tray with their food on it.

"Sit down," he instructed. "I'll get the movie going."

"Did you do this on purpose?" Nate blurted. He'd seemed sincere out there, talking with Neve, but if this were some sort of setup... "Today was important to me. I don't appreciate you stepping in and ruining it."

"Is it ruined?" Kaz tilted his head and leaned back against the counter. The move stretched the thin material of his shirt across his taught chest. "It was an honest mistake, really. It never even occurred to me you'd be seeing a kids' movie."

Nate opened his mouth to argue but ended up clamping it shut instead. Get Friends was an animated film, yes, and it was true the preview had made it seem kid-friendly. "Neve is a big fan of the animator."

"You'll be a big fan of this, promise," he winked, and when it was clear Nate wasn't amused, rolled his eyes. "Come on, Pretty Boy. You're already here. Give it a shot."

"Pornography isn't really my thing."

"This is so much more than that. It's an experience." He moved closer, quirking a brow when Nate gave him a suspicious look before pressing his palm to the control panel on the right wall only a foot away from where Nate was standing. "Relax. It's not like I brought you in here to kill you."

"Just torture me some more."

"Is that how you've been thinking of it?"

Nate crossed his arms. "Are we really just going to watch a movie?"

"A sex film," Kaz corrected, easing in closer until he'd forced Nate to retreat back against the closed door. He lifted a hand and planted it at the side of his head, the other reaching down so he could slip a finger through Nate's belt loop. "And no. You're going to watch the movie. I'm going to be watching you. Now," he stepped back all at once, "go sit down like a good boy so we can get started."

"If I say I don't want to?"

Kaz sighed. "What are you so afraid of, Narek?"

"You." He shouldn't have said it, but the word popped out of his mouth before he could stop it.

"Why?" Kazimir seemed to genuinely be asking. "There are so many people on this planet who have reason to fear me, but you're not one of them."

"You literally followed me here," he reminded.

"Stalking isn't cute. It's off-putting."

"Is that all?"

"That's more than enough reason for me to be uncomfortable."

"We weren't talking about your comfort level, babe." He sidled in closer, slipping a knee between Nate's thighs. "But I can think of a few things that can take care of both problems for you."

Nate opened his mouth to protest, but Kaz was quicker, sealing their mouths together in a heated kiss. The temperature in the room seemed to rise exponentially, and he found himself panting, rubbing himself against Kazimir's knee before realizing what he was even doing.

The kiss was rough and claiming, enticing Nate to let go of all the reasons holding him back. Most of them boiled down to basic insecurities, like being embarrassed his sister knew where they were and what they were about to do.

People didn't book one of these private rooms just to watch porn on a big screen.

She'd been really chill about it, but no one could be comfortable picturing their sibling engaging in sexual acts, right? What if she couldn't concentrate on her movie? She'd been so excited about it. What if Nate had ruined—

"Just me," Kaz breathed, waiting for Nate to peel his eyes open. "You only have to please me, remember, Pretty Boy?" He brushed his thumb tenderly over Nate's bottom lip. "You're going to forget about everyone outside of this room and focus on us, going to be so good for me, aren't you?"

It was a leading question, an attempt to pull Nate out of his tumbling thoughts, and knowing that, being able to see it for what it was, it shouldn't have worked.

And yet...

Nate found himself leaning into that touch, relishing the warmth that drifted off of Kazimir's large form. The smell of him was familiar and oddly comforting—hell, even the hint of arousal in the air helped to ease some of the tension he'd been feeling.

"Kaz," it came out pleading, but even he wasn't sure what he was pleading for. Did he want him to stop or keep going?

"I've got you, Pretty Boy," Kaz reassured, clearly understanding even if Nate himself didn't. He reached for something out of Nate's line of sight and then attached it to one of his wrists.

Nate frowned and glanced down, staring at the black strap circling his wrist. When Kazimir started to walk backward, tugging Nate after him, he went willingly, curious to see where this was going. He even lowered onto the couch once they'd reached it, not even needing Kaz to tell him to this time around.

"I'm going to take your clothes off, babe," Kazimir said, dropping to his knees to start on Nate's shoes. He had the rest of him undressed in a matter of minutes, working the shirt off over the black strap and the attached pieces with ease.

The screen suddenly came alive behind Kaz,

drawing Nate's attention.

"I turned it on when we entered," Kaz explained, moving to secure another black strap around Nate's other wrist.

The movie began, but the Devil didn't seem like he was in a rush to view it himself, taking his time even as the camera traveled down an empty white hallway and turned into a large open living room. Sunlight filled the space, making the white walls shine brightly. It seemed warm and inviting, and for a moment, Nate was confused over what they were about to see.

Then the camera panned to a couple sitting on the leather sofa, and it all made sense.

Nate gasped, unable to tear his gaze away from the redheaded man positioned at the center of the screen. He was blindfolded and had a ball gag in, but that wasn't what had Nate staring.

An intricate set of block ropes had been secured all over the man's fit body, starting at his neck, trailing down his chest, and over his thighs. Knots were placed intricately throughout, the spacing adding to the visual appeal, and he found himself tracking them, searching for reasons they'd been placed where they had been.

Another man stepped into the frame and eased the redhead onto his side, and Nate realized that his arms were tied behind his back.

Suddenly, Nate found himself repositioned, his eyes momentarily forced off the screen as Kaz lifted him beneath the knees. The straps at his wrists were pulled and then the extended part was wrapped around Nate's lower thigh and snapped into place. He sucked in a breath, watching wide-eyed as Kaz did the same to his other side.

Kazimir made sure he was leaning back against the couch and steady before he stood and stepped back to admire his handy work. He let out a low, appreciative whistle that had something jumping in Nate's chest. "Looking hot, Pretty Boy."

"What is this?" He licked his lips but didn't struggle against the bindings. It was similar to the position Kaz had forced him into back in the car the other day, only then he'd been attached to a collar with his arms up by his head. This time, he had less movement, the straps connecting his forearms to his thighs, so that the most he could do was rest his palms on his knees.

"Nothing as extreme as what you're seeing on TV," Kaz reassured him. "I like to watch, but I don't have the patience for all of that myself. This is more than enough for me. What about you?"

"I..." He swallowed and shook his head. "I don't know."

"You'll like it," he promised, and then, before Nate could say anything to that, he wandered around the couch and over to the counter where he'd placed the tray of food earlier. When he returned, he was carrying it, smiling when Nate frowned. "What? Did you think it was for show? You need to eat, Narek. Then we'll play."

"You can't be serious?" He wiggled a bit

pointedly. "This position isn't exactly comfortable." His legs were forced to hover in the air, after all. "Plus, how do you expect me to eat without the use of my hands?"

"That should be fairly obvious," Kaz stated, picking up the yurdog. He brought it up to Nate's mouth and chuckled when that earned him a dark look. "Open wide for me, babe. Up here," he tapped the tip of the grilled meat to Nate's lips, then motioned down to Nate's spread thighs, "not down there."

"Kaz."

"Relax, we'll get to opening you up down there too."

"You know that's not at all what I'm annoyed about."

"Don't be a baby. Eat. If you wait much longer, the movie will get to the good parts and then you'll be too horny to focus on chewing."

Nate opened his mouth to argue, but Kaz seized the opportunity to shove the food in. At the same time, one of the two men on screen let out a loud moan, that had Nate's eyes pinging back to them.

The other man, a blond wearing a half-mask, currently had the redhead bent over one of the couch arms, his ass high in the air. His face was buried between his cheeks, one of his hands fondling the redhead's balls as he ate him out.

"Curious?" Kaz asked, grinning knowingly when Nate bit down on the yurdog and chewed.

"Tell you what, finish this off and then I'll let you experience it for yourself."

"You just want me to enjoy this so you have an excuse to keep tying me up in the future," Nate guessed, not that it was hard. He already knew all about Kazimir's proclivities in the bedroom. Though, it was different, having him take things slow.

"So?"

"So?" Nate parroted.

"Does it matter?" Kaz shrugged and brought the yurdog back to his mouth, pressing it against his lips a second time. "Open."

Nate debated whether or not it'd be worth it to fight, but the sounds from the surround sound were picking up, the breathy inhales turning to moans and gasps that had Nate's dick twitching to life. There was little doubt in his mind Kaz would leave him aching and wanting if he didn't comply and just eat the damn food, so with a sigh of irritation, he took another bite.

The couple on screen seemed to be taking their sweet time with things as well, the blond teasing the redhead by pulling back now and again, laughing as he made the other man squirm and wait to be touched.

"If he wasn't blindfolded," Kaz said as Nate continued to eat, "he'd be wearing a mask similar to his partner's. That role changes, the actor always someone new in each of these films, but the redheaded guy, Puck, he's always the star."

"Who is he?"

"Not sure," Kaz replied. "No one knows his real identity. Probably so that he can keep making movies like this, don't you think?"

Nod nodded and swallowed the last bite, surprised when he realized he'd finished off the yurdog.

Kaz crumpled up the wrapper and then dropped it onto the tray he'd left on the floor. Then he stood and tugged his shirt up over his head, discarding that with a little more care. He grinned when Nate noticeably gulped when he took a step between his spread thighs.

"Relax, Pretty Boy," he cooed as he lowered back to his knees. "I promised you a good time, remember? Now, eyes on the screen. Let me show you what it's like."

"What what's like—" He sucked in a sharp breath when Kaz's face lowered and his tongue suddenly lapped out, licking a wet stripe from his taint to his balls.

He didn't allow him the chance to recover, dipping his tongue lower so he could prod against Nate's tight entrance. Skillfully, he worked it in, wiggling it around to help loosen the passage.

Nate clenched his jaw tightly and shook his head, unable to do much of anything with the way he was stuck in position. When Kaz pushed him further back against the couch and drove his tongue in quicker, he gasped. He never went too far in, but the sparks of sensation that skittered over his body were pleasurable without deep penetration.

On screen, the blond finally finished teasing the redhead and pulled away, leaning back on his heels so he could squirt a bottle of lube over his erect cock. He stroked himself a couple of times, then when he was nice and glistening, resituated so that he could aim it at the redhead's fluttering hole.

"Like what you're seeing?" Kaz pulled back enough to ask breathlessly. He pressed his face against the tender flesh of Nate's inner thigh, watching him in a way that, coming from anyone else, Nate would have labeled as endearing.

He considered how he was feeling about the situation and ended up nodding his head once. "Yours is bigger, though."

Kaz seemed pleasantly surprised by that comment. "Into big dicks, that it, Pretty Boy?"

"I don't know about that," he said. "But I'm definitely into yours."

"Look at you being all flirty. Hoping that'll make me speed this process up?"

"Will it?"

"Yes." Kazimir dropped back down between his thighs and started eating at him more vigorously until he had Nate's dick hard and dripping. He switched tactics without warning, licking his way up until he was lightly sucking at Nate's balls, and then taking his heavy member down his throat.

Nate came embarrassingly easily, tossing his head back as he screamed and emptied into Kazimir's mouth. He'd had blowjobs before and had never orgasmed just from the feel of a hot mouth.

"Guess you were worried about whether or not I'd eat as well," Kaz teased, running his tongue around his lips to collect every last drop, laughing when that had Nate turning bright red.

"Good Light." If he'd been capable of using his hands, he would have hidden his face behind them.

"Don't try to run," Kaz said. "Not from me, babe. There's nothing to be ashamed of. I set out to make you feel good and I did. Now," he stood and rolled Nate over on the couch onto his back and crawled onto the cushion between his legs, "it's your turn to return the favor."

He freed his cock, his crown already flushed and glistening with precome. Unlike the blond on screen, he didn't bother with lube, leaning into work himself in past Nate's defenses, shushing him when he made a sound of protest. "You'll adjust quickly."

"I don't want to," Nate argued, and Kaz actually paused. "Some species on this planet don't need lube to enjoy it," he continued, "but mine is not one of them."

"That right?" He tilted his head and considered it, then pulled back enough to reach down, feeling under the couch. A second later he came back with a tube of lube, squirting it over himself generously.

"It was right there this whole time?" Nate frowned. "Then why not use it to begin with?"

Kazimir shrugged and chucked the bottle over his shoulder, getting back to business without further preamble. He slipped himself inside of Nate and then drove forward with one harsh thrust, fully seating himself in less time than it took to blink.

They both moaned, and he started rocking, fucking into Nate with sharp measured pumps.

On the screen, the redhead was getting pounded over the chair arm, his cries growing in volume with each passing minute. The camera kept zooming in on his battered ass, and every now and again, the blond would pull out all the way and give the audience a look at the gaping hole he'd created.

"You tried to make it sound like you were too prim and proper for this," Kaz chuckled, dropping over him to spread open-mouth kisses across Nate's jawline. "Who's the one who can't tear their eyes off the screen?"

"It's..." Nate moaned when Kazimir hit that sweet spot inside of him, then finished, "Hot."

"Yeah it is," Kaz agreed, but he got the impression they were talking about two different things.

"Eventually," he began, tentatively, "I wouldn't be opposed to trying it."

"What?" Kazimir quirked a brow and motioned to the screen with his chin. "That?"

He nodded.

"Do you mean the rope part, or—"

"Bend me over the couch," Nate stated. The redhead seemed to really be enjoying it, like immensely so, and he wanted to experience that as well. That position would no doubt leave him slightly lightheaded, which might add to it all.

Kazimir didn't need to be told twice, flipping Nate over and lifting him until his head dangled over the side of the armrest, his forehead practically touching the thin black carpeted ground.

His dick was pinched between him and the leather and he made a sound of protest before Kaz reached beneath him and readjusted him. Then that massive cock was back at his entrance, thrusting in hard enough to shake the couch beneath them.

Incredibly, Nate came again, spasming and jerking as Kaz kept fucking into him.

"We've still got an hour and twenty-three minutes, Pretty Boy," Kazimir said. "Let's see how many more positions we can fit in in that timeframe, yeah?"

Nate moved his head, too lost to the feeling of Kaz's cock pumping in and out of him to process if he was nodding or shaking it no.

Not that it mattered either way. Just like every other time the two of them did this, the Devil didn't stop until he had Nate a weeping pile of goo beneath him.

The way, apparently, the both of them liked it.

CHAPTER 21:

Kaz's hand rested heavily over Nate's thigh, right where the straps had been only an hour or so prior. They'd reconvened with the others and walked across the street to one of the nicer restaurants in the area at Neve's behest.

She was still adamant she'd be paying for their party, which was the only reason Nate didn't argue—much—when the choice was made. It'd be different if she'd picked such an expensive place knowing Kazimir had offered to foot the bill instead.

That thought had bothered him the entire way here, and still did even though they were seated and going over the menu.

Yes, he'd already tried hard to ensure his sister didn't take advantage of anyone's generosity since he held himself to those standards, but this was *Kaz*. If Kazimir Ambrose got used for his money? He deserved it.

Didn't he?

Since when did he even care?

He'd hesitated at the side of the bed this

morning for a good five minutes before giving in and leaning over to plant a soft kiss against Kaz's plush lips. The younger guy had come alive beneath him, nipping and kissing him back almost immediately.

It'd actually been tempting to shuck off his clothes and crawl back into bed. With the devil.

Nate had sat there on that couch and allowed Kaz to tie him up, to pose him just the way he liked and touch him however he pleased. When had the resistance fallen away? When had this started to feel less like coercion and more like voluntary play? When had he started to, not only like, but crave the twisted type of pleasure Kazimir could coax out of him?

What did all of this say about him? That he liked the care he was getting? That he enjoyed being wanted? Kaz didn't just demand attention, he commanded it, and when they were together, it was as though everything else in the entire universe fell away.

He couldn't even recall the last time his mind was devoid of those nagging voices, trying to remind him not to become a burden, not to complain, or cry. The ones that constantly kept an eye out for others and all the ways Nate could make their lives run smoother.

When they'd gotten to his place the other night, just before he'd gone off to take a shower, Nate had caught Kaz opening the fridge. His expression when he'd seen that it was practically empty had seared itself onto Nate's brain.

There hadn't been any judgment or disgust. Only puzzlement. As if Kaz had struggled to process what he was seeing.

Nate could afford to feed himself.

So why didn't he?

How many days had he gone since graduation, surviving off of one rushed meal? He didn't know, and more importantly, thinking back on it now, he couldn't quite put his finger on why he'd done that in the first place.

"—Brother?" Neve's voice trickled through some of Nate's thoughts, too late for him to grasp anything she'd said at the beginning of the sentence.

Under the table, Kaz's hand squeezed around his thigh, and when he glanced over, that same perplexed look was on the hotshot's face.

Nate cleared his throat and smiled at his sister. "Sorry, what?"

"Are you that hungry?" Neve asked, her brow furrowed slightly. "Order whatever you want."

They'd grabbed a booth in the corner of the room, her and Verga on one side, he and Kaz on the other. The restaurant was decorated in warm tones, and the dark mustard shade of the leather seats only somewhat crinkled beneath them whenever someone shifted. A touchpad in the shape of a square smaller than a coaster was set in the very center of the polished table, and they'd scanned the code to pull up the menu on their multi-slates.

Nate closed his now, the smile still carefully kept in place. "No, I'm fine. I had a lunch box at the theater." Images of how he'd eaten it flashed in his mind, and he felt his cheeks heat. "I'll just get something small."

"Want to split an appetizer?" Kaz removed his hand to flick through the menu on his device.

"You should get something more than that," Nate said. "You didn't eat."

The corner of his mouth tipped upward. "Sure I did."

Verga, who'd been sipping at his water, coughed at that, some of it spilling onto his shirt. He turned toward Neve when she grabbed napkins and started to help dry him off, but it was obvious it was mostly so he could avoid looking at either of them.

Nate reached out and pinched Kazimir's side just above his hip bone, that smile still plastered on his face, all the while, even when the Devil at his side winced.

"My brother has a tendency to put other people's needs above his own," Neve said, glancing between the two of them. "It's fairly typical behavior from him. I hope that's not something you plan on taking advantage of, Kaz."

"Neve." The smile dropped away all at once.

"What?" She tossed the wadded napkins off to the side and cocked her head. "I'm older than him, too, and even if I wasn't, I'm well within my rights as your sibling to speak up for you."

"I don't need you to do that," he disagreed. "I can take care of myself."

"Can you?" Kazimir cut in, propping an arm

up on the table and angling his body more toward Nate. He rested his cheek on his knuckles casually, his other arm stretching out to drape over the top of the booth behind Nate's shoulders. "Does she know about the empty fridge?"

"What empty fridge?" Neve frowned.

"Stop," Nate hissed.

"What about the fact the showerhead in your bathroom needs replacing?" Kaz continued, ignoring him. "Or the cracked mirror hanging over your lime-stained sink? I checked. Even though she hasn't lived with you in months, her bathroom is kept spotless. Wonder why that is?"

He glared silently.

"Why is the house in such disarray?" Neve asked.

"It's not the house," Kaz corrected. "It's only the spaces he knows you won't see. He manages the upkeep to the rest in the off chance you come and visit. He doesn't want to worry you."

"Is that true?" She reached across the table and rested a hand over Nate's. "Is everything okay with work? It's not like you to let things fall behind."

Later, Nate was going to find a way to make Kazimir pay for this, and he was sure that was clear in his eyes as he stared him down a moment longer before finally tearing his gaze away and placing it back on his sister.

"I quit," he admitted, because it was obvious if he didn't, the asshole sitting next to him would. Had he just been thinking about potentially falling for him? What a joke. "I work at a coffee shop now. The one Jones owns?"

She pursed her lips. "Why?"

He shrugged like it was no big deal. "The boss and pay sucked at Quartet Air. It wasn't worth sticking around for." He angled his chin toward Kaz pointedly. "Some things aren't."

A strong hand cupped the back of his nape in warning, but Kazimir was careful not to let the wordless threat show on his face. He couldn't hide the fact he hadn't liked that from Nate, though. Even without the physical contact telling him as much.

Kaz wasn't the only one who'd figured some things out, Nate had a better understanding of what made him tick now as well. It was so obvious he was deflecting Neve's comment because, yes, of course, he fully intended to take advantage of Nate. He'd never attempted to hide that fact from him, but letting his sister know?

He paused, wondering if that was actually more for his benefit than Kaz's before he shook the thoughts loose. It didn't matter. Right now, he just had to focus on damage control before Neve got well and truly worried.

"I'm sorry to hear that, Nate," Verga joined the conversation, but before Nate could reply, Kaz spoke up again.

"The new boss is much nicer," he said. "Nate should be returning to work soon if all goes as expected."

"New boss?" Neve ran a hand through her dark

brown hair, the shade very similar to Nate's. Most of her features were, in fact. They shared the same eye color and pale skin as well. "How do you know?"

"Because it's me," Kaz supplied. "I bought the place after I heard how the employees were treated."

Nate almost grunted, because what a fucking liar, but he caught himself.

"It's undergoing some changes, so for now Nate is planning on staying at the Velvet Brew, but once I've ironed out a few details and am sure everything has been perfected, he'll come back. Isn't that right, Narek?"

He was torn here. Either he joined Kaz in this lie or he caused a scene by rejecting him. The first would suck because he didn't like the idea of stringing his sister on, but the second…A pissed-off Devil of Vitality was dangerous. The palm still at the back of his neck reminded him as much.

"If I'm happy with the changes made," he ended up saying, licking his suddenly dry lips, "yeah."

"That's great!" Neve clapped her hands. "What kind of changes are you implementing, Kaz?"

"Better benefits, more time off, and a name change," he swiftly replied. "I'm also thinking about expanding and moving it to a more lucrative location. It's a fairly big project, so it's taking some time, but I have a team on it to help iron out any kinks."

Why hadn't he mentioned any of that to Nate? How much of it was true and how much was just him bullshitting to convince Neve to like him?

"All of that while you're still in school?" Verga sounded impressed.

"Not to mention the mafia," Nate muttered, downing the rest of his water. "How ever do you make time for it all?"

Neve blinked at him. "Sarcasm? Really?" She let out a low whistle. "Seems like you have the ability to get under my brother's skin. That's impressive."

"Don't praise him," Nate scowled only to have her laugh.

"I'll share a secret," Neve said.

"Please don't."

"He's only like this with people he cares about. It may seem like he's open to a lot of people, but that's not true. Everyone in my family is a bit more selective than that when it comes to trusting others." Their waitress arrived and Neve broke off to place her order.

Nate gave an internal sigh of relief as the rest of them did the same, choosing something random without much thought for himself just to go with the flow. He could tell the moment the waitress turned to leave, however, that the conversation wasn't truly over, and wanting to put an end to it, he sprung up.

"Bathroom," he explained when that received frowns from the table, then he patted Kaz's shoulder. "Let me out."

Kazimir hesitated but eventually slid down the booth, stopping him just before he could move away from them by resting a hand on his hip. "Are you all right?"

"Yeah." He gave what had to be the millionth fake smile in the last half hour alone. "I'm fine."

CHAPTER 22:

He was going to the bathroom to freak out on his own. Kazimir knew this with perfect clarity. It was the reason why that was eluding him.

Things seemed to be going well with his sister, so why was Nate turning that sallow shade he did whenever he got trapped in his head?

Kazimir watched Neve closely, but there were no signs that she'd picked up on her brother's distress. It sounded like she'd known more about him and his affliction, what with all that talk about him putting others' needs above his own, but she sat there chatting happily with her boyfriend now, completely unaware of the obvious.

Was it the fact he was in the mafia? Was Nate still worried over how that would affect his sibling's reputation?

"Thoughts about your brother dating a mafia member?" Kaz asked bluntly, some of the fake pleasant niceties he'd been laying on thick all evening slipping away. There was no reason to maintain that type of act as far as he was concerned, not when she'd proven to be as clueless as this.

She'd grown up with Nate and yet didn't realize he was depressed and too hard on himself? How was that even possible?

"Kaz, if we're going to do this, we may as well be one hundred percent honest," she surprised him by saying. "You're hardly just any mafia member."

So she wasn't as slow as he'd presumed.

"Even if we hadn't gone to school together, everyone on the planet knows who you are."

"Rich," he ticked off the fingers on his left hand, "sexy, and influential."

"Dangerous," she leaned forward and mirrored his motions, "arrogant, and a playboy."

It wasn't just the Brumal that talked about how he couldn't commit? That was…annoying. Kaz had never paid attention to those types of rumors in the past, but now he was wondering if he maybe should have. Could that be one of the reasons Nate had been so against dating him in the beginning?

"My brother might not want for anything tangible," she continued. "Your money could most likely buy a vacation moon for him if you wanted to."

Kaz could afford several, actually, but he didn't correct her.

"And considering how happy he looked when we met up again after the…movie, you two watched together, sure, I'll give you sexy. He obviously finds you attractive. It's that last part that makes me nervous."

His brow furrowed. "What's wrong with being influential?"

"People with power come with strings," she said. "They come with enemies. You aren't a government official or a Royal, Kazimir. You're the wealthy heir of the third richest man on the planet, and the new second in command of the Brumal mafia. Even a nobody like me knows that. I don't want my brother mixed up in anything bad."

"I'll protect him." Even the thought of someone trying to harm Nate sent a wave of pure fury scorching through Kaz's insides. He felt hot and pissed off in less time than it took to blink but kept tight control on his outward appearance to prevent her or Verga, who'd remained silent all this while, from noticing.

"Can you guarantee that?" She shook her head. "You can't. My brother is the most important person to me in the entire universe." Her boyfriend didn't so much as flinch at this revelation.

"You have two of them," Kaz reminded.

"Nuri doesn't count."

"Why not?"

"Because he isn't Nate," she clipped. "I love him, but he didn't raise me. He wasn't the one sitting by my bedside all through the night whenever I got sick. Or the one who attended my parent-teacher conferences. He didn't come to my music recitals or celebrate my accomplishments—both big and small—with surprise trips to my favorite restaurant or my favorite candy. That was all Nate. Nate is more than just my brother, he's like my parent."

"But he isn't," Kazimir pointed out. "He isn't your parent. He's only a year and a half older than you. Tell me, Neve, when he got sick, did you stay by his bedside as well? When he got good grades, did you buy him the snacks he likes and take him out? Who attended his conferences at school?"

It wouldn't have been her, because this was Vitality, and age mattered. Even if it was only by a year and a handful of months, her being younger would have disqualified her from being able to act as his guardian in any official capacity. But that was the extent of it. Everything else he'd just mentioned? She was more than within her rights to do. The question was, had she?

"Let me guess," he drawled. "He was never sick and whenever you did offer to celebrate any of his accomplishments, he told you it wasn't necessary, am I right?"

Neve dropped her gaze.

"He lied to you," Kaz rose to his feet. "Whenever he was ill, he'd pretend that he wasn't so you wouldn't worry. Aren't you the one who said he puts other people before himself? Didn't you realize that also includes you? Hell, you and Nuri are at the top of the list. He never wants to burden you, so he turns down any kind gestures and makes it seem like he's not interested. I don't blame you, it's not your fault you didn't notice since he's such a good actor. But that doesn't mean I'll let you continue living in that bubble where you believe receiving all of him and giving nothing back is a fair tradeoff. It isn't and it never was."

"Oh? And you're going to give him all of you, is that right?" She was clearly angered by his words, but she kept her composure, proving through that one act alone that Nate really had influenced her upbringing. There was a fierceness to her gaze, her challenging look so similar to her brothers; it actually softened a part of Kaz.

Somewhat, in any case.

If nothing else, it served to remind him how important this person was to his pretty racer. And how, no matter how right he currently was in his scolding, Nate wouldn't be pleased to discover he'd spoken to his sister this harshly.

The big kicker was Kaz didn't care about that, for appearance's sake. He didn't want to keep a good standing in Neve's eyes simply so he could use her to make Nate like him. He actually wanted to please her brother. Didn't want to pack on and make things harder for him when they didn't need to be.

Was that…selfless of him?

Or was there some other hidden goal even he was yet aware of?

Either way, it was out of character enough that Kaz was forced to pause and take a moment to evaluate his own emotions and thoughts.

Something that Neve took as hesitation.

"If you're not serious about him—" she began, only to be swiftly shut down.

"Yes," he stated, the truth of that washing

through him, almost like it was always there. Like he just hadn't seen it until now. "Yes, actually, I do intend to give him all of me." He was going to give Nate everything. Everything he could. And not just to ensure that meant he could keep his pretty racer until the end of time, no. He was going to do it because it also meant making Nate happy.

He pictured that smile Nate had given him the other night, the real one. Kaz wanted more of that in the world.

"How can I believe you?" Neve asked.

"Just wait and see," he told her, stepping out from the booth. "I'm going to prove it."

"Where are you going?"

"To check on your brother," he replied. "You didn't notice just now, but he's having a mild panic attack."

She shot to her feet. "What? He doesn't—"

"He does," he corrected. "And unless you plan on barging into the men's bathroom and embarrassing him, you'll sit back down."

"There's no need to get rude," Verga said, but then rested a hand on Neve's elbow.

She eased back down into her seat, eyes trailing over Kaz's shoulder toward the hallway that led to the bathroom before shooting back to his. "Make sure he's all right."

"I don't need you to tell me that." He didn't need anyone to.

Kazimir Ambrose took care of what was his.
And Nate Narek?

Nate had somehow become the most important thing in his life.

"However." There was something she could tell him, though. "What does *hahzi* mean?"

Her eyes widened. "Did Nate call you that?"

"Is it bad?" Was he cursing at him?

"No," she quickly corrected. "No, not at all. There's no exact translation, but it's something similar to darling or sweetheart in old Igna."

Darling or sweetheart?

Kaz tried to contain his grin as he turned and headed to find his *hahzi*.

* * *

As expected, he found Nate hunched over the middle sink in the bathroom. His breathing was uneven and his eyes were squeezed shut. There was water dripping from his chin, a sign he'd washed his face, probably in an attempt to clear his head. An attempt that had failed miserably, if the sight before Kaz was any indicator.

He didn't hear Kaz enter, flick the lock, or approach, startling the second he felt one of Kaz's hands settled around the back of his neck. His eyes flashed open and met his in the mirror a second before a small sigh of relief slipped past his full lips.

"Breathe, Pretty Boy," Kaz instructed, his thumb running through the short hairs at the base of his skull in that way he knew Nate liked.

"Kaz."

"One step at a time," he said. "Let's get your

breathing back to normal first, hmm?"

Nate exhaled shakily and then gave a small nod.

"Good boy." Kazimir wasn't used to taking care of things, let alone other people, but it occurred to him that he'd slipped into that role with Nate subconsciously. From the start, he'd known exactly what to say and do to calm his pretty racer down. Sure, he'd used that knowledge as a means to manipulate him, but that didn't change the outcome any.

He was the only one who could get through to Nate whenever he was in this state of mind.

He was the only one who'd ever even tried.

He thought back to when they'd bumped into one another at therapy, what Nate had said to him when he'd mentioned his father. In some ways, Nate was the only person who'd tried with Kazimir too.

"You're special." The corner of Kaz's mouth lifted when Nate's eyes sought out his reflection in the mirror a second time. "What? Don't believe me?" If that were the case, he'd prove it to him the same way he intended to prove it to his sister.

His sister, who'd apparently helped with Nate's parentification their entire lives without realizing. Kazimir had placed the blame up until this point solely on Nuri, because from all the stories he'd been told, that seemed like the case. But now... Listening to her, seeing that even as a full-grown adult she still didn't recognize what Nate had gone through...

Kaz snuffed out the anger that threatened to rise again, knowing it wouldn't be useful here. He needed to remain relaxed, that way he could coax Nate into calming as well.

Which meant leaving out the revelation he'd just had back at the table.

Eventually, they were going to have to talk about it, because there was no way Kaz could execute his plans without Nate's cooperation, but that could wait for now. Something told him his pretty racer wasn't quite ready to hear it yet anyway. He no longer fought Kaz whenever he was near, but there were still moments of hesitation, moments that made it clear he was waiting for the other shoe to drop, either so he could make his great escape or so Kaz could.

"Should I tell you why I like you?" he asked, only for Nate to snort.

"I'm not in the mood to listen to how much you like my ass, Kazimir."

He chuckled. "That's not at all what I was going to say—although, for the record, yes, I do." It was tempting to grab a handful of that spectacular ass, but he refrained. "Your humor is up there though. Dry and sarcastic. Bet all of your friends think your sense of humor is more the charming, friendly style, don't they?"

"Only the ones who don't really know me," Nate admitted.

"Is that what your sister meant?"

"You already know it is. You've pointed out

how different I am in front of people already. And, unlike her, you know the reason."

He was referring to his file from the therapist. It'd been loaded even though it'd only been his first visit, and there'd been no past records to transfer over. From the outside, Nate appeared to be a well-rounded boy next door.

"I like that you're good at hiding," Kaz said, smiling when Nate quirked a brow. "It means you've got strong survival instincts. But you don't have to hide with me, Pretty Boy."

"More like I can't." He straightened, the move causing Kazimir's hand to fall away. "I didn't have a choice in all of this, remember?"

"I did pursue you relentlessly," he agreed, shifting so that he could cage Nate in between his arms, planting a hand on the sinks at either side of his hips. It brought their faces closer, and Kaz debated whether or not it would be appropriate to kiss him now or if Nate needed a bit more time to shake off the remainder of the attack he'd just had. "I like that you gave in fairly quickly."

"Shut up." Nate glanced away but didn't try and free himself.

Progress.

And proof that Kaz wasn't the only one feeling things here.

"What do you like about me?" he asked suddenly, pouting when Nate grunted.

"Who says I like you at all?"

"Don't be like that, babe." He moved in closer,

so they were chest to chest. "Should I keep listing all the reasons I like you?"

"Do you?" Nate questioned. "Do you like me?"

"I more than like you, Pretty Boy."

He shook his head, not accepting that answer. "You picked me off the street on a whim because you were pissed off at something Baikal said to you."

"I admit," he drawled, "it was childish and rash of me, but I don't regret it. And that's not why I'm still here. On some level, you're aware of that, too." Did it make Nate afraid? "You showed up at my school one time and I haven't asked you to do it again. I haven't even introduced you to Kal. If this was really about sticking it to him and proving some stupid point, wouldn't I have done that by now?"

It'd been weeks since they'd started this and he'd had plenty of opportunity to do so. Honestly though, it hadn't even crossed Kazimir's mind to bring Nate around the rest of the Brumal since the first couple of days.

"I like how you respond to me," he said, seeing that he was going to have to continue explaining in order to make his pretty racer understand. "I liked it that first night at your place. We fucked for hours and even though you were exhausted and spent, your body kept reacting to my touch. Chemistry like that is hard to come by."

"*Sexual* chemistry," he stated. "There needs to be more than that for a relationship to work. A real relationship, Kaz."

"This is—"

"We haven't even been on a date," he cut him off. "This doesn't count. I had no idea you were crashing the movies and you even bought the wrong tickets."

"You enjoyed yourself anyway."

"Yes," Nate surprised him by saying. "I did. But so what? It's like you just said. We've got amazing chemistry when it comes to the bedroom. How long before one or both of us gets sick of relying on sex to connect?"

"I don't do that," Kazimir argued.

"You use sex as a weapon," he corrected. "Sex as a manipulation tactic. You think I don't know what's been up? That night you just so fondly spoke of? We didn't do anything for hours. You fucked me until you'd worn me down and I was half out of my mind. I would have agreed to anything you wanted and you well know it. That was your end goal, after all."

Kaz dropped his arms and stepped back. "You sound bitter."

"I am." He paused and ran a hand through his hair in frustration. "I was. I should still be. That's the problem, I don't know anymore and that's driving me half mad. You forced this on me. No sane person would want to be with you after that and yet…"

"And yet?" He held his breath, shocked to find there was a dark swirling foreign sensation in the center of his chest. Was he…apprehensive? Why? No matter what Nate was about to say, it wouldn't change anything. Kaz was in control.

Right?

"I don't know, Kaz," Nate sighed. "I just...I don't know."

That's it? He'd racked up the anticipation and made him nervous—which was a feeling Kazimir decidedly was not a fan of—all for that?

No.

"You're going to have to give me more than that, Pretty Boy. We aren't leaving this bathroom until you do." It was on the tip of his tongue to threaten a repeat of their very first time together, when he'd taken him in that seedy bar bathroom, but Nate's earlier words stopped him.

If Nate really didn't like it...

"I don't have to use sex as a control tactic," he offered, figuring if he extended an olive branch first, maybe that would get him somewhere. He was used to interacting with people in the mafia, or at least those who were a part of that world. Nate wasn't and never had been. Sure, he participated in the underground race scene, but from what Kazimir had observed, he mostly got in and got out.

Even Madden had mentioned the other day how Nate hadn't been around as much since having to change careers so suddenly. Kaz still didn't know if that was his friend's attempt to guilt trip him or what, but even if it hadn't been, on some level, it'd worked. That was part of the reason Kaz had made that statement to Neve.

It didn't seem right to have taken away the one thing Nate really seemed to care about.

Security.

If Kaz could provide that for him...

"I can take care of you," he said. "You just have to stop trying to please everyone around you. Why are you in here right now? Because of what your sister and I were talking about?"

"I don't like you lying to her." Nate crossed his arms.

"Who says I was?"

"All that stuff about Quartet Air—"

"All of that was true." Kaz frowned. "Why would I have lied about any of that?"

"To make yourself look good in her eyes?" Nate said it, but he didn't sound as certain. "To get her on your side?"

"I don't need her on my side," he replied, stepping back in to bridge the gap between them. "It'd be nice if she liked me because, yeah, that would make things easier, since I know her opinion matters to you. But I don't *need* her to like me, Nate."

"Of course you do," he disagreed. "You're a narcissist."

"I'm also a lot of other things if you recall. Some of those cancel the others out. I don't like being looked down on, fact, but I can live with not being everyone's favorite person. Maybe that's the psychopath in me, who knows. I typically talk about everything but myself during those sessions with Dr. Vera."

"That's not how that's supposed to work."

"Oh? Coming from the guy who hasn't been

back since his first session?" He'd even skipped out on his scheduled appointment and hadn't returned the office's call about it.

"You literally stole all of the doctor's notes," Nate reminded. "Why would I go back?"

"You'd tell me anything you told her anyway," he said confidently.

"What makes you think that? I don't trust you at all."

Something sharp pierced through the center of his chest, and Kaz actually winced.

"What's wrong?" In a blink, Nate was cupping his cheek with one hand and testing his temperature with his other placed against Kaz's forehead. When he found that he wasn't hot to the touch, his gaze dropped down the length of him, lips pursing in concentration as he did a thorough visual search for any signs of injury.

He should let him know that it'd been nothing and he was fine, but Kaz enjoyed the attention too much, so he merely stood there and allowed it for as long as he could before Nate finished on his own.

"Are you hurt anywhere?" Nate finally asked. "Is it a Brumal injury?"

He laughed before he could help it. "What does that even mean?"

"Don't laugh," he scolded. "I know some of the stuff you get up to. Flix talks, you know?"

"Don't I ever." Flix had the biggest mouth of the lot of them. That was why he and Madden got on so well when they were in the same room together.

Kazimir had often thought that the two of them would have been best friends if not for the fact they were loyal to separate princes.

Well. Baikal Void was no longer a prince now, he was a king, but Kelevra Diar, as only the third in line for the throne, would never reach those types of heights.

For the first time, Kaz wondered how Kelevra felt about that. Here he was, currently locked in yet another bathroom with Nate all because of a shitty inferiority complex and he was just Baikal's cousin. How did Kelevra, the legitimate Imperial Prince of Vitality, not lose his ever-loving mind with rage whenever he thought about their stations and titles?

"If you were a prince and someone illegitimate became a king, how would you feel?" Kaz threw the question out there, just expecting Nate to follow along even though it was unlikely—

"Don't be ridiculous," Nate dropped his hands from Kaz, apparently concluding he was fine after all, and rolled those gorgeous brown eyes of his. "Not everyone is as full of themselves as you are, Kazimir. Kelevra Diar and your cousin are on opposite sides. There's no need for them to be jealous of each other. Kelevra runs the planet. Baikal runs the Brumal, who keeps the planet running. Symbiotic."

"Symbiotic?" He scrunched up his nose. "Isn't that a term used for plants and animals?"

"How have you made it to senior year?" Nate griped. "It means there's a mutually beneficial relationship between two people or groups. Like, for instance, the Brumal and the Imperial family.

"Or us." Kaz nodded his head.

"How so?"

"Now who's the dumb one?" he teased. "I push you to focus on only me and help you come out of your shell. You help me understand concepts and ideas I've otherwise never even attempted to, let alone thought I'd get to experience myself."

Nate tilted his head, clearly finding that curious. "Such as?"

The fact that he wasn't arguing Kaz's other point, that he was helping him to cope with his people-pleasing and feelings of burdenism, was pleasing. Nate had supposedly been suffering from depression, but in the few weeks they'd spent together since that last therapy session he'd seemed…lighter. At least to Kaz anyway.

He supposed that wasn't really saying much when taking into account Kaz hadn't known him for long. But he was good at reading people, and whenever he was around Nate, that skill only seemed to amplify.

Which was why it was so easy to figure out exactly what it was Nate was hoping to hear from him now. It was tempting to lie or tease him further, make him work for it, so to speak, but Kaz felt weirdly warm standing this close to his pretty racer. He felt accepted in an odd sort of way that he couldn't explain and didn't really want to.

So, instead of playing games, he opted to give them both what they wanted most.

The truth.

"I like you, Nate Narek. Physically, intellectually," he grinned, "romantically. I've never wanted a serious relationship before. But I'm glad I have a boyfriend now, and I'm glad that boyfriend is you. I like you," he repeated more firmly. "Which means I'll protect you and keep you safe and content. All you've got to do is—"

"Let me guess," Nate interrupted, "be good for you?"

He shook his head slowly. "No, babe. It's way simpler than that."

Kazimir captured his chin and held him still as he lowered his mouth, pressing their lips together in a gentle kiss. "All you have to do," he held Nate's gaze steady with his own as he finally voiced the message he'd been wanting to deliver for ages now, "is be mine."

CHAPTER 23:

"What are your plans for New Year?" Neve asked over the phone a few days later.

Nate was in the car with Kaz on the way to the younger guy's place for the first time, and his eyes shifted toward the driver while he considered his sister's words. Dinner had been awkward when he'd returned from the bathroom, filled with meaningless small talk and fast eating. They'd parted ways with a hug as usual, but there'd been an invisible distance there Nate hadn't liked.

It'd bugged him all week, but between picking up extra shifts at the Velvet Brew and spending time with Kaz, he hadn't been able to work in calling her himself. Now she was acting like the dinner had never happened and asking about New Year's.

When they'd been younger, they used to celebrate together, but that'd stopped years ago when she'd entered high school and made friends that could stay out past eight o'clock, let alone midnight. In college, they'd sometimes attend the same parties, but that wasn't too frequent, and they mostly avoided each other.

"I'm not sure," he ended up replying. "We haven't talked about it yet. Why?" He purposefully brought Kazimir into it so he could gauge her reaction. The two had seemingly been getting along before he'd gone to the bathroom, but there'd been tension when he'd returned. No matter how many times he pressed him on it, Kaz refused to say what they'd spoken of without him.

Since Neve hadn't called to openly bash the Devil or beg Nate to dump him, he figured it couldn't have been that bad. But...He wasn't sure what he'd do if it turned out Kaz had crossed too many lines.

The Devil wanted Nate to put him first, and Good Light knew all week he'd been trying. There was no rhyme or reason for it, no great revelation that made Nate want to stick with Kazimir despite it all, and yet, something between them had shifted during that speech he'd given. He wasn't sure if he fully believed that Kaz really was invested in this as a real relationship, but Nate was willing to wait and find out.

If Neve didn't like him, that was going to complicate matters. She hadn't seemed bothered by the fact he was Brumal, so at least that was one fear alleviated.

"Haven't talked about what?" Kaz briefly glanced at him before setting his eyes back on the road.

The vibrant neon lights at the heart of the city glittered and glowed as they zipped by in his fancy hovercar, taking turns a bit more sharply than Nate would have liked. A steady rain was falling, making everything sparkle even more, and people with colored umbrellas crowded the streets. This part of Valeo stayed open until the early hours of the morning, packed with entertainment, restaurants, and more. It was a bit higher end, and Nate didn't often make his way there, but Kazimir's apartment complex was located in the thick of it.

The skyrise came into view, a sprawling tower amongst others, though the tallest of the nearby lot. Center Grande was lit up vertically on the side in massive white lettering.

"I picked the most expensive one," Kazimir said as he approached with the car. "It's bigger than Kelevra's even."

"Sure," Nate drawled. "But do you own the entire building?" He laughed when Kaz averted his gaze with a scowl. "Bet the Imperial Prince owns his building."

"Sorry, am I interrupting?" Neve's voice came through the earpiece in Nate's right ear, reminding him she was there.

"No, no, it's fine." He ran his palms over his jeans as they pulled into the parking garage.

"Don't be nervous, Pretty Boy," Kazimir teased. "I've already eaten you up. We both know you like it when I bite."

"Gross," Neve said. "I heard that."

"Sorry!" He glared at Kaz and mouthed, "Shut up". "Anyway, I don't know what I'm doing for New

Year's. Why? Did you want to do something?"

"We have plans," Kaz stated, spinning into an empty parking spot fast enough to give Nate whiplash.

The move stunned him and prevented him from replying, so by the time they came to a stop, he was still in a daze and didn't react when Kaz snatched the other earbud attachment out of his multi-slate and popped it into his own ear.

"The first New Year together is supposed to be a really important milestone for new couples," Kaz explained, keeping his tone light and inviting. "I'm trying to do right by your brother, which means celebrating just the two of us. You understand, don't you, Neve?"

Her laughter filled Nate's right ear. "Yeah, I do. Good for you guys. I'm keeping track, though, for the record. Keep your promise, Kaz. If you do, you and I won't have any issues."

Kazimir chuckled. "Anyone ever tell you you'd make a good Brumal member?"

"Flix once, actually."

"Excuse me?" Nate hadn't heard that story before.

"Relax, big brother," she said, and he could practically hear her eyes rolling. "The second he found out I was related to you he tucked his tail between his legs and scampered off."

Kazimir burst out laughing at that description, but Nate still wasn't in the mood.

"If he bothers you again—"

"He didn't bother me the first time," she corrected. "Besides, this was a couple of years ago."

"Flix is away on vacation at the moment anyway," Kaz cut in. "He's not around to bother anyone. Thank Light."

"I'll leave you two alone," she stated suddenly. "Verga just got home. Have fun! And, brother, I want to hear all about your New Year's after!"

"Maybe not *all* of the details," Kaz winked and both she and Nate made sounds of disgust.

"Ew, bye." The line went dead.

"Stop talking to my little sister about sex," Nate stated.

Kaz opened his mouth to reply—no doubt with something witty and absolutely annoying—only for his multi-slate to interrupt. He frowned when he checked the number and then gave a sigh, handing the earbud that went to Nate's device back before releasing one of his own to place it in his ear.

"Head up without me," he instructed. "It's the penthouse suite. You don't need the code, just use the facial recognition pad."

"What?" Nate frowned.

"I added you to the system," Kaz explained. "I have to take this. It's Brumal shit. Could take a while and it's cold out here. Go ahead, make yourself at home. I'll be up as soon as I'm done with the call."

It made him uncomfortable entering the building on his own. He felt out of place in his Velvet Brew uniform, and he badly needed a shower. But Kaz's pinched brow made it clear that the call really was important, and that Nate probably shouldn't be around for it, so he forced his worry aside and climbed out.

"Just," he hesitated with the door partially open, "don't take too long."

"Missing me already, babe?" Kaz grinned wolfishly. "I'll be right behind you. Give it twenty minutes, and I'll mean that literally." His gaze dropped to the spot between Nate's legs and his grin widened when that made Nate slam the door shut.

Nate crossed the lot toward the glass entrance mumbling curses under his breath. Couldn't Kaz ever take anything seriously?

That wasn't fair. He was about to deal with Brumal business. That was serious.

There were sentries dressed in three-piece suits at either side of the door in the gold and cream-colored lobby. The ceiling stretched high above, and at the center was a massive crystal chandelier that was larger than the hovercar they'd used to get here.

Nate half expected to be stopped at the door, but one of the guards merely gave him a once over and then bowed in greeting, the other following quickly after. He nodded back to be polite and passed through, searching for the elevators. There were several seating areas and a check-in station that took up almost the entire right wall. Guests and residents dressed in outfits worth more than a year of Nate's paychecks put together idled and moved around him, not a single one giving him so much as a glance, even in his uniform.

Had he been overthinking again?

Either they didn't care, too caught up in their own existences, or they assumed someone had placed a delivery—which the Velvet Brew didn't do, but whatever.

He found the elevators across the room and it took him almost five minutes to reach them. There were two others sharing the space on his ride up to the top floor, but one was on her multi-slate the entire time, and the other was an elderly man who didn't seem remotely interested in why someone like Nate would be heading to the penthouse suite.

Literally no one was bothered by him. He wasn't causing any sort of problems. This situation was vastly different from most of the ones he'd been in and worried over, of course, but what if the concept was the same?

What if Kaz was right and Nate's biggest issue was himself?

Maybe he should schedule another appointment with the therapist...

The other two got off before him, leaving him some time alone with his thoughts. This past week, he'd played with the idea of taking Kaz up on his offer about Quartet Air, but part of himself had been holding back. He didn't like handouts, had been taught to work for the things he wanted. Nuri was the hardest worker Nate knew, and he wouldn't dishonor his brother by taking the easy route simply because he could.

But...At the same time, Nuri had been trying

to convince him to accept help from Silver for over a year now, hadn't he? Perhaps getting a leg up on the competition wouldn't be such a bad thing...

There'd have to be stipulations, of course. The fact he was dating Kazimir couldn't be a reason he was able to keep the position. Nate had to prove he was capable of it. That was the only way to ensure he didn't become a burden to anyone, not the other employees, the customers, or Kaz. There was also the fact that he didn't know if they really had a future together to consider.

Kazimir claimed that he wanted Nate now, but would that change? People like Kaz, notorious for turning sex partners into notches on the bedpost, had a tendency to slip back into their old ways, didn't they? Could Nate really trust that this was real? Hell, it'd only been a little over a month since they'd started. Two since they'd had that first interaction.

Was nine weeks long enough for authentic feelings to form?

The elevator came to a stop and dinged a second before the doors eased open. Nate was an idiot. How could he stand here and judge someone like Kazimir Ambrose when he himself knew absolutely nothing about long-term relationships? This was also his first, same as the Devil. They were both just trying to navigate a surprising turn of events. Neither one of them had expected to catch feelings for the other—

He had feelings for Kaz.

It hit him as he stepped out and he came to an abrupt halt in front of the closed door to the suite.

Nate liked Kazimir. Like, enjoyed his company and thought about him when they weren't together and wondered what he was up to, kind of liked. Had the Devil fucked his brains out of his skull?

He groaned and ran a hand through his hair, tugging lightly at the strands in a poor attempt to snap himself out of it. The truth was right under his nose however, inescapable now that he'd finally opened his eyes to it. What other reason could he possibly have for spending this past week trying to work on things with Kaz, if not for the fact that *he wanted* things to work?

All those pretty words and promises Kaz had made him at the restaurant must have done a number on him.

And now he was thinking of the word pretty and how silkily it rolled off Kaz's tongue whenever he—

No.

Nate shook his head and took a step forward. He couldn't afford to have this crisis out here in the hallway. If Kazimir caught up and found him standing here, he'd pick up that something was wrong and pester Nate until he spilled. He wasn't ready to talk about his emotions just yet. Wasn't ready to admit out loud that maybe, *maybe*, he wanted to be the Devil's boyfriend more than he'd let on in the past.

A sharp beeping sound pulled him out of

his thoughts and he lifted his head, a green light shooting out from a panel directly in front of him, set in the center of the black door. It scanned over him and then beeped a second time.

"Facial recognition successful," a computerized female voice echoed through the small speaker at the top a second before the clicking of a lock came and the door swung a few centimeters inward to show it'd opened. "Welcome home, Nate Narek."

His mouth dropped open and he stared dumbly for a moment at those last words.

Home? This was not his home. This was—

What was that sound?

Nate leaned forward, turning his ear toward the crack with a frown. There was the distinct sound of...running water? Had Kaz left the sink on or something? Washer machine? Curious, he pushed open the door the rest of the way and stepped into the apartment, pausing once again to take it all in with a gasp.

The floors were dark gray marble, the walls done in more of the same but a shade lighter. The main area was rectangular with curved corners, windows making up practically the entire wall directly across from the entrance. The velvet blinds had been left open to showcase a view of the city at night. There were two loveseats and two couches, organized so that they all circled around a glass coffee table at the center of the living room. A fireplace set on the right wall was lit, the flames glowing flashes of pale and neon pink.

To the left, was a long bar and a billiards table with an unfinished game, a pool cue tossed casually over its surface as if in a hurry. Nate took a step in further and spotted the kitchen on that side as well, attached to the bar, hidden behind a partial wall that separated the foyer from the rest of the floor. Down the right was a hallway, the lights on, casting a golden glow across the polished surfaces.

The sound of running water was coming from that direction, and curious, Nate headed toward it slowly. There were a few closed doors on the way, but he passed them until he found one slightly ajar. Just as he was about to press his hand against it and force it the rest of the way open, the sound stopped.

He hesitated, unsure if it was safe to proceed. This was his first time here, and despite their efforts to get to know one another better, Nate still didn't know much about the sorts of things Kazimir got up to with the Brumal. He had bits and pieces from his friendships with Flix and Berga, but even those were vague. What if this was dangerous? What if someone had broken in and—

He cut that thought short, realizing how pathetic he was being.

Who broke in to take a shower?

Nate shoved the door open before he could change his mind, coming up short when it swung inward and revealed a tall, fit man currently in the process of wrapping a snow-white towel around his narrow hips.

The man glanced up at him, seemingly unconcerned with having been walked in on, and then went back to securing the cloth. Once he was satisfied with that, he ran a hand through his wet hair and nodded at Nate. "Hey."

"Zane?" Nate seemed to be struggling to process what he was seeing, and he swallowed the lump forming in his throat. "It's Zane, right?"

CHAPTER 24:

How he hadn't put two and two together those couple of times Kaz had let the other man's name slip was beyond him, but now that Nate was here, staring at the famous medical student, he realized who Kaz had been talking about.

Admittedly, Nate had not anticipated finding another Devil here, especially not naked. The large bathroom was filled with steam and the glass shower stall he'd clearly just stepped out from gave off the lingering scent of tulips, subtle yet floral and a bit earthy.

Kaz's scent.

It made no sense why Nate was more bothered by the thought of him using Kazimir's shampoo than he'd been with him using the shower in general, but something tightened in his chest.

"Ah, you must be Narek." Zane nodded again and moved toward one of the small cabinets set in the wall, opening it to pull out a hand towel he proceeded to dry his hair with.

"What are you doing here?" Nate was fairly certain that Kaz lived alone. Not only that, but Zane wasn't a part of the Brumal.

Everyone knew he was currently in school studying to become the next Royal doctor to the Imperial family. The Satellite and the Retinue hung out sometimes and basically kept peace with one another, but he'd been under the impression that it stopped there. Even Madden, for example, never hung out with Flix after the races had ended, and the two seemed chummy enough whenever Flix came around.

"Does Kaz know you're here?" he asked, only to be met with a crooked smirk.

"We have an open-door policy, so to speak," Zane replied coyly, and it was impossible to tell if he meant for it to come off loaded with sexual connotation or if he merely felt like he was stating a fact. Tossing the cloth into a wicker laundry bin by the sink, he stepped forward and then tipped his head when Nate didn't move. "Do you mind?"

It took him a second but he realized the guy was trying to leave and quickly stepped back into the hall, trying to remain calm as he watched Zane move around the place like he owned it.

Zane traveled with purpose down the hall, slipping into the third room on the right, leaving Nate to either hang back or follow after him like a creep.

His feet brought him to the room before he could help it, his eyes trailing after the other man as he moved about a bedroom decorated in the same shades of gray as the rest of the house. A set of clothes had been laid out on the king-sized bed, organized and seeming like they belonged there.

Like Zane had done this a million and one times before and had developed a routine.

"Whatever you're thinking," Zane broke the silence first, his voice clear and concise, making it obvious that Nate was the only one currently experiencing any type of confusion, "you're most likely accurate."

"What?"

"You're wondering if we're fucking, aren't you?" Zane glanced at him then reached down to pick up a pair of pressed black pants. He chuckled when Nate looked away, staring off to the side as he dropped the towel carelessly to the floor and began to dress. "It's been…four years now? Perhaps five."

Meaning they'd been in a sexual relationship since before they'd started college at Vail.

"We attended the same preparatory high school," Zane said, as if reading Nate's mind. "Most of us did, the Satellite and the Retinue? Some of us were even able to pick a side that way."

"A side?"

He hummed. "Whether we wanted to follow Kelevra or Baikal. Some, like Kazimir, were dutybound because of their parents, but the rest of us got to choose this lifestyle."

"And you picked Kelevra?" Even though he'd developed something with Kaz? "Why are you telling me this?"

"To help explain why you've never heard of

the two of us or our…relations before."

Nate grimaced, hands tightening into fists at his side. He wanted to call him a liar, but the proof was literally standing right before him. How else would Zane have known the code to Kaz's suite, or where the hand towels were located in the bathroom? This couldn't be the first time he was visiting this place.

What if he hadn't even needed the code? What if the door had scanned him as well and welcomed *him* home, too?

A week ago, Kaz had been all but begging Nate to give them a real chance and now—

"Are you two having an affair?" Nate blurted.

Zane grunted. "That implies that we're cheating on you, and I just got done explaining that I came first." Before Nate could react, he snorted. "But no. We're not having an affair. We'd have to have been in a romantic relationship for that, and Kazimir doesn't do boyfriends."

"I'm his boyfriend," Nate stated.

"Let me rephrase." Zane slipped his arms through his dress shirt and began to deftly do up the buttons as he looked Nate square in the eye. "He doesn't do long-term. You seem like a nice enough guy, Nate. Save yourself while you can."

He quirked a brow. "You really trying to spin this as you're just attempting to help me?"

"As opposed to?"

"You flaunting the fact that you've slept with my boyfriend and know the layout of his place like the back of your hand," Nate said. It was probably wiser to back down and wait for Kaz, but a thread of anger was blooming amidst the confusion and feelings of hurt, and he decidedly didn't want to twiddle his thumbs.

Zane grew quiet for a moment, and all that time spent in the other Devil's company helped make what he was doing obvious. Accessing the situation. Searching for weakness and another angle.

Which meant Nate had hit the nail on the head.

"Do you like him?" he asked. If they'd been sleeping together for that long, it made sense if Zane had developed some sort of attachment toward Kazimir.

The corner of his mouth twitched but didn't lift. "Like is a strong word. Besides, I'm not sure it's possible for anyone to truly like him. We'd all need to forgive him first, and I don't know about you, but personally? I'm not willing."

"Forgive?" He frowned again. "For what?"

Zane heaved a sigh. "This is just a guess, but was your first time against your will?"

Nate didn't respond.

"Did he force you to submit?" he added. "Make you come for him enough times that by the end, you were begging just for it to stop? Just for some reprieve from the constant torture?"

Torture. That's what Nate had thought of it in the past as well. Sexual torture.

"He uses that thing between his legs as a weapon," Zane latched on, clearly having seen the crack in Nate's façade just now. "Our first time? He caught me alone in one of the private study rooms at school. I fought him, but I wasn't well trained in hand-to-hand combat then, hadn't been raised for battle the same way he had. Kazimir had me bent over the desk, pants down at my ankles within minutes. He made sure it didn't hurt though. As if that was something I should be appreciative of. And you know what?"

Nate wanted to stop him from talking, but couldn't seem to get his own voice to work anymore.

"I was." Zane smoothed down the wrinkles on his shirt. "We screwed like that in secret for about a year before he snuck into my dorm room pretending to be a robber and fucked me in front of an audience."

"What?" Oh, his voice worked, after all.

Zane nodded. "Messed up, right? I was terrified before I realized who it was tying me up, spreading me open…Slipping inside."

"Enough." He so didn't need the details of their sex life. Though, from the sounds of it… "Are you saying it's never been consensual?"

"Why? Would it matter if some of the time it was and some of the time it wasn't?" Zane cocked his head. "Is rape only bad if it occurs more than once?"

"Of course not!"

"No? Since the two of you are dating, I figured that sort of thing didn't matter to you. Wasn't abhorrent enough to scare you away. Typically, normal people run the other direction from the man who sexually assaulted them. What's keeping you around, Nate? Usually, if someone walks into an obviously dangerous situation calm and collected like that, it's because they know they can handle it." He swept his gaze down Nate's body, his judgment apparent. "You look even less capable than I was back then in that study room."

Nate wasn't going to win any fights against a Brumal member, or someone from the Retinue either, sure. But he could hold his own long enough for help to be called. Or, at least, he'd believed that before the event in the bar bathroom with Kaz… Except…

"You're mistaken about something," he clipped, continuing once Zane lifted a thin dark brow at him. "Our first time? I didn't fight." He sort of had, a little, but since he was being forced to face it anyway, might as well finally acknowledge the massive elephant of truth in the room. "I wanted him to pin me down and fuck me. Our second time? We were making out while he carried me to my bedroom."

A tiny part of him was stumped over why he was defending Kaz right now. Sure, everything he was saying was a version of the truth, but it wasn't the whole truth. There'd always been coercion on Kazimir's side. Blackmail and threats. He'd painted Nate into more corners than he could count, all so he could get his way, and yet here Nate was, staring another Devil down, telling him all about how he'd wanted it all along.

Had he?

Truly?

Fact of the matter was, Nate hadn't felt centered in a long time, maybe longer than he could even remember. But being with Kaz? Whenever Kazimir was around, he demanded undivided attention. Nate could only focus on two things, the Devil, and himself.

Prior to that, Nate had only focused on himself when those vicious voices in his head got out of hand and started reminding him how useless and annoying he was.

"And if he brings someone else in without permission, like he did with me?" Zane switched tactics, bringing them back to that part of his story. It was impossible to tell from his enigmatic expression whether or not Nate had hit a nerve though, or if he was just rolling with the proverbial punches. "He trussed me up and took me unapologetically before removing the blindfold to show Lyra sitting on the opposite side of the room, watching the whole show."

"Lyra?" That name... "*Lyra* the Heir Imperial Princess, Lyra?!"

"The one and only."

Nate had kept a wide berth between himself and those in power, however, even he couldn't avoid rumors and gossip. "The one you're currently living with, you mean?" He clicked his tongue when

Zane seemed mildly surprised he knew that detail. "Sounds like it all worked out well for you in the end."

"Looks can be deceiving."

"I figured that out a long time ago. Which is why I'm going to cut this short and just ask for you to get to the point. What's the goal here, Zane? Are you trying to break us up? Do you want me to help you file a report for assault—"

"I said I couldn't forgive him," Zane interrupted. "But I wasn't referring to that."

Nate paused. "We're both kind of messed up, aren't we?"

"Yes," he agreed. "Perhaps that's what Kazimir initially found attractive in us."

Kaz took advantage and manipulated those around him, and yet here the two of them were, toeing off for…what? Dibs? To a monster?

"Do you think you can do better?" Nate said.

"Do you?"

"I've never really thought about it."

"I have," he stated, heading back toward him and the doorway he was blocking. Again. "And yes, I think I can do much better than Kazimir Ambrose. But that doesn't mean I don't feel a little bit possessive of him."

So that was it.

"You're staking your claim," Nate surmised.

"I'm checking out the competition," he corrected. "He and I have a good thing going, and something tells me you wouldn't be down for sharing in the same ways I am."

"No," Nate confirmed. "I won't be."

Zane slipped something from his back pocket and held it out, waiting for Nate to take it.

The red envelope was silky to the touch, made of high-quality material, but the same standard card size as all the others that were being passed out this month.

"What's this for?" Why was he giving Nate a New Year's envelope?

Zane tapped the end of it while Nate was still holding it up, staring at it like it might bite him. "I feel the need to remind you, it's bad luck to open one of these before the big day."

Nate scowled, and Zane winked at him before brushing past.

He turned as soon as he was in the hallway, that same empty expression back on his face. "See you later, Competition. If you can last that long, anyway."

Nate let him go, listening to the sounds of his retreating steps down the long hall followed by the clicking of the front door. He exhaled and dropped down onto the edge of the bed, the envelope still clutched between his fingers. That parting comment had sounded a lot like a threat, and there was already so much about this whole interaction that left a bad taste in his mouth.

Vitals may believe opening an envelope early was bad luck, but Nate wasn't a Vital.

He tore open the envelope carelessly, pulling

the small gold card free to see what it was.

The ucina was printed in black, the derpy looking bird-like creature staring back at him mockingly. It wasn't even a bird, the body with beady eyes and a beak a fake. It had bear like limbs and butternut colored fur with a tuft of green feathers on top of its false head. Behind it, the true creature camouflaged itself as five long, smooth leaves with darker green tips and hidden eyes. A long tail with a Venus fly trap tip was the real mouth and contained toxins that would paralyze its prey.

Out of the five cards, the ucina was the rudest one to give out, symbolizing the person who'd received it had spent the year delusional and unable to see reality for what it was. It was meant as a warning to do better in the coming year, pay closer attention, start fresh, have a revelation, that sort of thing. Depending on who'd given it, it could be gifted with good intentions attached.

Something told Nate that wasn't the case with Zane.

He tossed the card onto the end table with a curse, eyes catching sight of one of those tiny green notebooks Kaz loved to scribble in. Even knowing it was wrong to snoop, Nate found himself snatching up the book, flipping through the pages to scan the words written in red ink.

His heart sinking deeper and deeper with every single one.

CHAPTER 25:

Kaz ended the call and stuffed the earpiece back into his multi-slate before exiting the vehicle and quickly making his way across the lot.

Saint had contacted to warn him that they'd gotten word a few of Pious's people had remained on planet, even after their leader had gone weeks ago. There'd been no word about that, and all attempts to reach Pious for an explanation had gone unanswered. Nothing had come of it, and as far as they knew, there was nothing nefarious behind them staying behind, but Kazimir needed to be read into the situation, given his station.

At the moment, he couldn't care less about a few stragglers. Maybe they were sightseeing? Wouldn't be unheard of. Vitality was one of the richest planets in the Dual galaxy. Lots of people traveled there. He'd ordered a few deeper searches into the matter, but had left it at that.

Even still, it'd taken way longer than he'd hoped, and all he could think about was getting upstairs and making it up to his pretty racer. When he'd invited Nate over, he'd wanted to make it special. Give him a tour of the house, offer to make them dinner.

Show Nate what a fully stocked kitchen should look like and how to utilize it.

He chuckled at his own thoughts, but just as he was about to reach the entrance, Zane stepped out.

"Took your time," Zane said as soon as he spotted him, walking over like his presence here was no big deal.

Kaz's gaze swept over his shoulder toward the lobby.

"He's upstairs already."

That comment caused something to snap within Kaz and without thinking, he shot forward. He had Zane slammed against the side of the building, his hand at his throat and the tip of the crystal blade pressed threateningly to his side in less time than it took to blink.

"Going to stab me with my own knife?" Zane asked, not sounding worried in the least. He didn't try to struggle, his arms remaining still at his sides as he peered back at Kaz with that empty look he more often than not had in his eyes.

That emptiness was what had kept Kazimir from ever developing any kind of feelings for the other man. Why it'd worked so well for them to screw on the side and help each other scratch the itch. It was nothing like the fire and passion that could burn behind Nate's gaze. Zane was empty.

Pretty soon, he'd be emptied of his guts, too, if he didn't start talking. Fast.

"Did you touch him?" Kaz demanded.

"No."

He held his gaze pointedly until Zane sighed in annoyance.

"Using your dick to get people to do what you want is your thing, Kazimir, not mine."

"Right," he drawled, "you just take it where you can get it."

The muscles in Zane's jaw tightened slightly, but that was the only indication that he'd hit a nerve. "Sure, you should be the one saying that? Only one of us picked trash up off the streets and it isn't—"

Kaz released his throat only so he could take a swing at him, his fist connecting hard with Zane's right cheek. Pain radiated throughout his hand and up his arm from the contact, but he barely noticed it.

To his credit, Zane remained on his feet, waiting a moment, most likely for them both to calm down, before turning back to Kaz. "You like him that much?"

"What are you doing here?" He didn't ask how the other guy had known he'd be bringing Nate by. It was obvious by the impromptu visit that's why he'd come, and it didn't really matter who'd ratted them out. Yet.

Later, later Kaz would hunt down whoever was running their damn mouth and sew it shut while they tried screaming through the threads.

He'd also be changing the code. It'd been a detail he'd completely overlooked since it was rare for either of them to meet up anywhere other than at a hotel.

"Did Nate see you?"

"Of course," Zane stated. "All of me, in fact."

"What the fuck does that mean?" Kazimir barely tamped down the urge to stick the knife through a person he'd considered sort of a friend all this time. "If you've done anything to him—"

"We just talked." He adjusted the collar of his shirt like the arrogant asshole that he was, moving onto the cuffs of his sleeves after.

"About?"

The smile Zane gave him was the one he usually reserved for the ring, just before he was about to break the rules and cause his opponent injury. It was one of the very few times the real him ever shown through, and had always elicited both curiosity and unease in Kaz.

"Things you'd rather we not speak about," he replied. "You better run along, Kazimir. If you leave him stewing too long on our conversation, I fear he'll turn on you, and nothing, not even that magic dick of yours, will be able to lure him back."

"What's your problem?" Kaz couldn't think of a single reason for Zane to be doing this. "Why would you go out of your way to try and screw me over?"

"That." Zane finally moved away from the wall, jabbing a finger at the center of Kaz's chest. "It's always about you. You can never separate yourself from your delusions of grandeur long enough to take note of the people around you."

Kazimir frowned, still not sure where all of this was coming from.

"What's my problem?" Zane's voice dipped low. "You always seem to forget that I'm the same as you. We're Devils, Kazimir. And Devils always collect their dues. Why would I go out of my way to screw you over? Tit-for-tat, *baby*."

"I've never—"

"We had a good thing going," Zane cut him off. "A thing *you* initiated. Then you had to go and bring her into the mix."

Her? Who...

"Lyra?" Okay, now he was really confused. "Aren't you like, secretly in love with her?" He was pretty certain that was the case, had been certain when the Heir Imperial had come to him asking for a favor for her birthday.

She and Zane had already hooked up on their own once or twice before, as she'd put it, and she was curious to see how he was with other bedpartners. Both he and Zane had been in the midst of their role-play era and had already agreed their next game would be a rape fantasy, wherein Kazimir initiated whenever and wherever he wanted. The unknown was supposed to help Zane cope with the stress of finals, and he'd been the one to suggest it even. Kaz had merely added another player into the mix.

"You stated clearly that you didn't care about

whether or not we had an audience," he reminded. "Not to mention, you weren't angry after the fact, and that whole thing brought you and Lyra closer. Now you're trying to tell me you've held a secret grudge all this time? Why didn't you just fucking say something?"

"Because whenever I slept with you things got confusing for me," Zane replied. "You're a self-centered, entitled asshole, but you're phenomenal with your dick."

Kaz wasn't sure if he should thank him or not. Instead, he said, "I thought we were friends."

"We are."

"You're a psycho." He'd heard that before, though usually directed at himself.

"How's it feel when the shoe is on the other foot?" Zane asked before checking his multi-slate purposefully. "You've just wasted ten whole minutes. Want to take bets? I know you love that sort of thing. Five thousand coin says he walks out on you just like your mommy did."

Kaz froze. "What did you just say to me?"

"What, you've been sticking it in me for four years and two months," Zane drawled. "Did you really think I wasn't playing around with your insides as well? The Machiavellianism comes straight from your dad—an early part of your inheritance, in a way, no?—but the rest? Developed over time from childhood trauma, most notably, being abandoned by your mom."

Usually, Kaz was too guarded to share details

of his sordid past, or how much he actually loathed his father. There were very few occasions he ever felt relaxed enough to even want to acknowledge that, let alone open up about it with another living being.

After sex was typically one of them, and as the years had passed, Zane had at least felt like a safe enough ear to listen whenever it got too heavy to carry and Kaz had felt the urge to unload.

Mistake, clearly.

"You were the last to see her," Zane continued. "Begged her to stay. What'd you do again? Grabbed onto her legs, right? But you weren't strong enough to keep her and no matter how many words you used, it wasn't enough to get her to change her mind. That's when you learned you can't convince people to do what you want by being kind and honest."

He'd said that last part to Zane, too, verbatim.

"Yeah," he agreed, trying to get a handle on his anger before he did something they'd both regret. "And I stand by it. Look what being *kind and honest* with you got me?"

Zane motioned with his chin down at the weapon still clutched in Kaz's hold. "A knife in the palm of your hand?"

"What about the one in my back?"

"There's still time to take it out," Zane said. "But it's ticking. So, going to take that bet or what?"

"Fuck you, Zane."

He shook his head. "My guess is that's off the table from here on out."

"Damn right!" He wouldn't sleep with that asshole again if it was the last one on the entire planet. Kaz would rather screw his own hand raw. "You really did all of this just because you were mad I invited Lyra into the bedroom that day?"

"It's like I said," Zane shrugged like this was all no big deal. "I was simply paying you back. No matter what happens from here on out, you and I are even."

"Think again." As soon as he was sure there was no serious damage done to his and Nate's relationship, he was going to hunt the future doctor down and give one of those autopsies Zane was always talking about a try of his own. "You're dead."

"And start a war?"

"Worth it."

"I'm not sure Baikal would agree."

"My cousin doesn't have a say in this."

"Your cousin would beg to differ." Zane gave him a look. "You're still doing it, Kazimir. Thinking only of yourself. Staying out here arguing with me to soothe your bruised ego instead of rushing inside to check on the boyfriend you claim to care so much about."

"I do care about him," he snarled.

"You don't care about anything," Zane chuckled. "But that's okay. Neither do I."

"Obviously." Because he sure as hell didn't value his life.

Zane must have seen the murderous intent glistening in his gaze still, and he sighed all over again. "Are you really going to kill me over a little thing like this? What happened to being friends?"

"You're crazier than I am." On some level, he'd always known that. Kaz had simply chosen to overlook it, thinking that it wouldn't matter in the long run. Thinking there was no way anyone could ever get the upper hand on him anyway, so it didn't matter. "None of this is even making sense."

Zane was mad about getting Lyra involved but had since moved into the woman's house and agreed to train for the position of Royal Doctor. What the fuck? Didn't sound like someone who was upset with his lot. The two of them had also never been exclusive. Kaz had been fucking Zane the same time Zane had been fucking the Heir Imperial. Hell, sometimes the three of them did it all at once, together.

They'd all left more than satisfied after the fact so…?

"That's the best part," Zane explained. "The most important part, actually. The fact that it doesn't make sense is what makes it the best payback imaginable. Think about it. I can't even convince *you* that my reasoning is sound. Nate Narek? Nate's not going to believe anything you say." He smiled a second time. "I took that one from your playbook as well, Kaz. You very rarely, if ever, make sense. People who act purely on emotion never do. I'll move my bet up to seven thousand coin. Odds aren't looking in your favor."

Kazimir wanted to get to the bottom of this—

one that was believable—but it hit him like a ton of bricks that Zane was right.

And that he'd been stalling on purpose.

With a curse and one last dirty look, Kaz shoved past him and rushed into the hotel.

CHAPTER 26:

He found Nate in the main bedroom, flipping the pages of one of Kaz's notebooks. The look on his face was forlorn and called to Kaz's newfound protective instincts as he slowly entered.

"Nate?" When he didn't get a reaction, he moved closer, still worried about spooking him. Whenever his pretty racer got caught up in his head, trapped by those negative thoughts, it was best to approach gently. So he tempered down the raging beast within him screaming to set the record straight swiftly and loudly, easing down onto his knees in front of the other guy instead. "Nate?"

"Zane has a mole just above his right ass cheek," Nate stated, his tone hollow yet firm. "Apparently, you find it cute."

"That book is old," he began, only for the page to be flipped.

"You wrote here that he smells nice, and you like the feel of his legs wrapped around your waist."

"He must have gone through my old notebooks and picked that one out specifically to mess with us," he explained. "I wrote that years ago."

"It says here you think he's pretty with a blindfold on."

Kaz snatched the notebook and tossed it across the room, instantly losing that battle with himself to remain calm. Screw being calm if it meant no one listened to a word he said. "Stop. I know what this looks like—"

"That's good," Nate said. "Because that makes one of us. I don't know what this looks like. A jealous ex? A current lover? Are you cheating on me or him? Or both?"

"I'm not cheating on anyone," he placed his hands over Nate's thighs. "I haven't slept with him since—"

"Did you sleep with him after sleeping with me?"

Kaz internally swore. "Yes, but—"

Nate shoved him away and Kazimir landed on his ass. "I need to think."

"It's not like that," he insisted, getting up off the ground to grab onto Nate's arm. "Seriously. It was one time and only after we'd done it at the bar. You and I weren't together then." Sure, he'd been thinking about asking Nate out, making him his, but there'd been no cheating involved.

"Then why was he here just now, taking a shower?" Nate quipped.

The bastard had showered? Hell.

"Who are you going to believe? Me or—"

Nate tossed his free arm out and pointed at

the green notebook. "You?"

Kazimir patted down his pockets, swearing when he realized his current notebook must have fallen out in the car. Or Zane had slipped it from his pocket when they'd been arguing without him realizing.

"Let's go back downstairs and I'll show you my recent one, okay? It's only got stuff about you in there, babe. It's just you. I told you—"

Nate yanked his arm free, brow furrowing. "A lot of things. You've said and done a lot of things. I just...I need to think."

"About what? He's full of shit. He came here to —"

"How'd he get in?" Nate stopped him yet again. "He knew the code, Kaz."

He ran a hand through his hair, desperately scrambling to come up with some way to fix this. "Yes, I gave it to him, but that was Junior year. He needed somewhere quiet to study."

Nate snorted derisively, the first show of emotion since Kaz had entered the room. "You really want me to believe he has the code to your apartment so that he can *study*?"

It sounded really stupid, but it was the truth. Last year Kazimir had been busier than usual with the Brumal and hadn't been home as often anyway. When Zane mentioned he was frustrated with the renovations being done on the Little Palace where he lived with Lyra, Kaz offered him one of the empty rooms here. That had been all.

Had they fucked on some of the occasions Zane had come by? Yes. But had Kaz given him the code for that reason? No.

"Move in with me," Kazimir suggested, only to have Nate stare at him incredulously. "If you live here, you'll see that he doesn't come over. You won't have to just take my word for it."

Nate stared at him. "Because you can't just go fuck him somewhere else or anything like that."

"That's not going to happen." He didn't know what else to do here. "I don't want anyone else, Narek. You have to believe me."

"That's the thing," Nate said. "No, I don't. I don't have to do anything. Look at this from my perspective, Kaz. The two of you have slept together for years, and the guy was naked in your bathroom. There's a whole book filled with notes about little things you find attractive about him, and you've never mentioned anything about your relationship with him to me before. I've heard you bring him up multiple times, but you never elaborated. Now I feel like the idiot who didn't see what was right in front of him."

"We don't have a relationship," he argued. "I've only ever been serious with one person, and that's you."

"I want to believe that," he sighed, "I really do."

"So then do."

"I need time." Nate took a few steps toward the door. "I need to think."

"Think?" Kaz repeated. Only bad things ever

happened when Nate got tangled up in his thoughts.

"Yeah. Let's take a break. I'm going to call a cab and go home for now. Some space might be good."

"No."

"Kaz, I need—"

"You don't need to think, or space, or anything else for that matter," he said darkly. Seeing Nate standing that close to the door, intent on leaving... Knowing Zane was right all along about that fact... Something snapped in Kaz and, this time, he welcomed it with open arms.

At least the devil within him always knew what to do.

That's how he'd fix this.

The same way he'd gotten them to start.

Zane had been right about Nate wanting to abandon him after what he'd heard. That must make him right about everything else, as well.

Kazimir had Nate tossed onto the bed, and the door locked before either of them knew what he was about to do. Then he went rummaging through the nightstand, pulling out two sets of shiny handcuffs, mind flipping through all of the possible ways to do this, searching for the best one.

The second the cuffs came out, Nate made a startled sound and tried to book it a second time, but Kaz caught him around the waist and flung him back, toppling after him to keep him pinned to the mattress as he worked one silver ring around his wrist and then the other.

He snapped them to the posts of the

headboard, forcing Nate's arms to spread right above his head, and then straddled his hips, silently waiting for him to tire himself out as he fought beneath him.

"Let go!" Nate shook his wrists, rattling the metal, but there was no give. He tried a couple of times to knee Kaz's back, but their positioning made that next to impossible, and he was left floundering aimlessly a bit before he huffed and dropped his head against the pillow with a glare. "Unlock these. Seriously. I'm not in the mood for this, Kazimir."

"We'll get you in the mood," he promised, sliding back so he was sitting on Nate's knees instead. Then he flicked open the button on his jeans and slid down his fly.

"Wait, don't!" Nate bucked, but all that did was make it easier for Kaz to slip his pants and boxers down to his thighs. He was soft at the moment, but Kaz knew how and where to touch him, was confident he could turn the tide the best way he knew how.

He'd fucked Nate into submission before.

He'd do it again.

And then, once his pretty racer was well-spent and relaxed, he'd explain it all again. No one ever listened to him the first time. He'd thought Nate was different, but apparently, he'd been wrong in that regard. It should have been enough for him to stop clinging to him, but it didn't. Kaz still wanted him, even if he had to fuck him into oblivion just so he'd see reason.

"It's always sex," Kaz mumbled, wrapping his hand around Nate, giving him a few solid pumps of his fist. People didn't want him for his money. They wanted him for his cock. He used his other hand to free himself from the confines of his own pants, stroking himself to full mast as he watched Nate's dick slowly harden in his hold.

His pretty racer was fighting it more than usual, but the body never lied. It was the only thing that didn't. Nate needed to *think*? His dick said otherwise.

"There's my good boy," he cooed, ignoring how Nate growled at that, quickening his movements. He jacked them off simultaneously, listening as Nate's grunts turned to gasps of pleasure the closer he got to release. "You're always so quick to come the first time," he teased. "If I allow it."

"Kaz." Nate was already breathless, a desperate look in his eyes. "I don't want to do this."

"No?" Abandoning his own cock, Kaz shifted even lower, until his face was hovering over Nate's engorged member. "Wanna bet, Pretty Boy?"

"Stop—"

Kaz swallowed him all the way down, feeling his cockhead bump against the back of his throat. He hummed around it and then slowly slid off, allowing it to pop out of his mouth with a lewd sound so he could trace that thick vein with his tongue. The second Nate bucked beneath him, he took him in again, bobbing his head in quick motions, sucking on him, knowing it wouldn't take long.

Nate cried out a minute later, his hips lifting off the bed, effectively burying himself deeper in Kaz's mouth. He emptied out, the salty taste of his come coating Kazimir's tongue.

He waited for him to finish, then released Nate's dick and flipped him onto his stomach in one swift motion. The move forced his bound arms to cross, and he let out a startled sound that only spurred Kaz on.

Kazimir forced Nate's cheeks apart and leaned in, flicking his tongue out over that tight muscle. The mouthful of come and saliva he'd kept followed soon after, and he forced the fluids in past that barrier, pinning Nate down by the narrow back when he started to struggle yet again. He speared at his insides, pushing the makeshift lubricant in as deep as he could with his tongue alone. Once he was satisfied it wouldn't all immediately spill free, he pulled back enough to check.

"Did you just," the side of Nate's face was pressed against the pillow, but he tried his best to glare back at Kaz, "*spit* in me?"

"Admittedly not how I saw the night going." Kaz arranged them so that his knees were planted beneath Nate's hips; the other guy's legs spread wide at either side of him so he'd have better access to his entrance. The position mirrored the one he'd initially taken Nate in all those weeks ago, and that reminder only served to convince him this was the right play. That had ended in Nate becoming his. "When we're done here, I'll make you dinner, yeah?"

"Stop this," he ordered. "Kazimir, you can't just fuck someone into pretending like nothing happened."

"This isn't pretend," he corrected. "It never was." Kaz took his cock and brought it to Nate's wet hole. "Here. Let me remind you."

He wanted to shove himself all the way in, but held back, easing his cock past that tight barrier inch by torturous inch. The grip was insane even as Nate's body opened up for him, sucking him deep the same way Kaz's mouth had just been gulping down his dick.

Nate made a sound and buried his face into the pillow, giving Kaz pause.

"Does it hurt?" He waited for a response, pinching Nate's right ass cheek when he refused to answer. "Am I hurting you, Pretty Boy?"

"Yes!" Nate growled.

Kaz carefully lifted his hips so he could check beneath him, finding that Nate was already hard again, at least. He hadn't properly opened Nate up. Should have, even though it hadn't been that long since the last time they'd done this. "I'll give you time to adjust."

"It's not your cock that's the problem here, Kaz," Nate turned his head again, and this time the tears glistening over his face were impossible to miss. "It's *you*. You are hurting me, and the worst part is you don't even care that you're doing it."

"What?" He shook his head and leaned forward to run his fingers comfortably through

Nate's damp hair.

Only to have the other guy shake his touch away.

"Pretty Boy—"

"Don't fucking call me that," Nate snapped. "Don't you fucking dare."

Kazimir went cold. He'd never spoken to him like that before. Never looked at him like that either, like he actually hated him. Well and truly.

It was like being possessed, Kaz pulled out and quickly undid the cuffs around Nate's wrists with the thumbprint scanner at the center of each, leaving them attached to the headboard in his haste. He rolled him, cupping a tear-stained cheek, gaze traveling down his chest to his still semi-hard dick. There were no signs of any real injury, but the pain in Nate's voice just now…

"Was it the cuffs? Were they too tight?" He checked his wrists for marks, but even with his struggles, none of the skin had broken. "I—"

Nate pushed him off, scrambling over him. Within seconds, he had Kazimir's wrist clicked into the cuff.

The shock made him slow, and he was being pulled in the direction of the other one before realizing it. He tried to force Nate off, but also didn't want to hurt him by accidentally flinging him off the bed, and that hesitation cost him.

As soon as Nate had him bound in place against the headboard, he shot off the bed, practically tripping in his haste. He pulled his pants back on and zipped them, watching as Kaz tried to break free to no avail.

"Narek." He gave up and glared. "These have biometric locking mechanisms. I'm the only one who can undo them, and now," he wiggled his fingers, "I'm unable to."

"Good."

He frowned. "I'm going to be stuck here unless we get metal cutters and—"

"Let's break up," Nate said, deadpan and emotionless.

It was so out of character that for a second he actually thought he was joking, but when he didn't follow it up with a laugh or even a smile, reality started to set in.

"I'm breaking up with you," Nate stated with more clarity.

"No."

"You don't get a say."

"We aren't breaking up, Narek. We are never breaking up."

"We are," he insisted. "Right now. It's over, Kazimir. We're done."

"No, we—" Kaz sucked in a breath when he turned on his heels and walked out of the room. "Nate? Nate! Nate, come back!" He repeated it over and over, fighting against the cuffs even knowing they wouldn't budge.

No matter how many times he called out, however, Nate never listened.

He never came back.

CHAPTER 27:

He'd lost track of how long he'd been in here, standing beneath the shower spray, still in his work uniform.

Nate had returned from his morning shift, half expecting to find Kazimir waiting on his front steps. He'd been like that at the Velvet Brew too, bracing whenever the bell above the door had jingled. But the Devil had never shown.

Or called.

Or texted.

It was an odd feeling, a mixture of relief and something else, something a lot like loss and heartache. Nate was trying his hardest to ignore the last bit, to drown out the voices in his head that had been whispering he'd overreacted ever since he'd hailed a cab outside of the hotel and sped away.

On the one hand, Nate wasn't convinced Kaz really had cheated on him. When the other guy had insisted that wasn't the case, he'd believed him. The issue was what had taken place after that. He'd only wanted time with his thoughts, to figure out why he was feeling so worried over Kaz's past relationship with Zane—even if it was only a sexual one. He hadn't liked the jealous, envious twist in his gut or how fear had set in shortly after.

Ironic, that he'd subconsciously been afraid Kaz was going to leave him, only for Nate to be the one to walk out.

In the moment, it'd felt like the right thing to do. It still did, and yet...

"You do *not* miss him," he growled to himself, voice muffled by the sound of running water. For a month now, a day hadn't gone by that Nate hadn't at least heard from Kaz through a text or a call. That's all this was. This cloying feeling was the absence of contact and nothing more. He just needed to readjust to being alone.

Last night, Kazimir had crossed an unforgivable line. Yes, they'd started in a similar fashion, but that had been then. After everything they'd been through, all the progress Nate had felt they'd made, to have the younger guy pin him down and disregard what he wanted so fully...

Nate was a people-pleaser, sure, but he didn't *actually* hate himself. He didn't want bad things or feel like he deserved them when they came his way. Why he'd settled for someone like Kaz in the first place was beyond him, but he'd snapped out of it now.

Still, he'd thought the guy would at least *try* and fight for him...

He cursed and slammed a hand on the knob,

shutting the shower off. Why was he so indecisive? Why couldn't he just be content with the choice that he'd made and shake the rest of it off? This was for the best.

"You got off track for a second," he told himself as he stepped from the stall and stripped out of his sopping clothes. He was about to shove them in the laundry basket he had by the door, but hesitated, recalling the way Zane had placed his towel in the one in Kaz's bathroom.

Nate dropped them on the floor in a wet heap instead and turned toward the fogged-over mirror. His misty reflection stared back, his skin flushed from the hot spray, hair limp around his face.

Zane's naked torso flashed in his mind, and he scanned himself, taking longer to track over the rise and fall of his abs. Nate wasn't unattractive. He was a bit smaller than the other man height-wise, but he was every bit as broad-shouldered as Zane, and in good enough shape, there'd be no reason for anyone to look at one longer than the other.

And now he was comparing himself to a Devil of Vitality, who also happened to be called the damn Prince of Medicine.

"Good Light." He rubbed at his face in frustration and left the room quickly.

Whether or not Kaz and Zane had hooked up since he'd gotten with Nate shouldn't even matter. The fact Zane had gone out of his way to antagonize him at all was what was important. He couldn't afford to piss off one of the Devils.

The Retinue weren't much better than the Satellite, even if they didn't have a mafia connection. When he'd first become friendly with Flix and Berga, Nate had been nervous enough, and it was a tentative friendship held together through their mutual relationship with Bay. Case in point, Flix had ignored Nate's calls this morning when he'd tried to contact him and let him know about Kaz.

In a moment of weakness, he'd been concerned the lack of contact from Kaz had been due to him still being locked to the bed. Stupid. After what he'd done to Nate, he didn't deserve any of his worry.

Nate grabbed the first thing he came to in his closet and yanked it on, still lost in thought. Despite how things had begun between them, his unwillingness, this had been his first serious relationship in years. Didn't that make it okay to mourn, if only a little? Shouldn't he allow himself that much?

The sound of his multi-slate dinging caught his attention and he grabbed at his wrist before recalling it was the one thing he'd removed before stepping into the shower. They made submergible versions, but he'd never felt the need to spend that kind of coin, so while his was waterproof on the surface, it couldn't be worn while he stood in the stall for over an hour.

He re-entered and picked up just in time, not bothering with the earpiece and opting for a speaker instead since he was alone anyway.

Again.

"Hey," he tried to sound lively but barely managed to even sound awake, "What's up?"

"Are you ill?" Nuri's concerned tone trickled through the speaker of the rectangular device as Nate carried it out into the kitchen. "Have you seen a doctor?"

"I'm fine," he replied. "Why are you calling?"

"If you're unwell, you should really—"

"I said I'm fine," he snapped, closing his eyes and inwardly scolding himself in the middle of the hallway as soon as he did.

Nuri was quiet.

"Sorry," Nate mumbled.

"Interrupting is a bad habit of yours," his brother began after another few seconds of silence, "but the temper is new."

Was it?

"Sorry," he repeated blandly.

"You don't have to apologize," Nuri said. "Just tell me what's going on. It's okay to confide in me sometimes, you know?"

"When do I not?" He started walking for the kitchen once more, glad that he hadn't upset his brother. "I'm always upfront and honest with you."

"Yes, when it comes to my own life or Neve's. You very rarely ever talk about yourself, Nate."

At the mention of their sister, the call suddenly made sense, and Nate sighed. "She told you, didn't she?"

"That you're seeing someone?" He made a

sound in the affirmative. "I wish you'd told me yourself, but I understand wanting to keep that a secret from your older brother."

"It's not like you were forthcoming when you started dating Silver," Nate pointed out, pulling open the refrigerator door. His mind went blank the second his eyes settled on the contents, and he gulped without meaning to.

When Neve had been living here with him, he'd always been sure to keep their kitchen fully stocked. He'd been worried she'd skip meals otherwise and had even gone out of his way to bulk order the snacks she liked from their home planet. She'd thought it'd been Nuri, and he'd let her keep believing it because it hadn't mattered.

Apparently, the second she'd moved out, keeping up with basic necessities like a semi-filled fridge hadn't mattered either.

Until Kaz saw it and fixed the problem Nate hadn't been aware was there.

"Nate?" Nuri called him, and the note of apprehension clued Nate into the fact he'd probably missed something.

"Spaced out," he said. "What was that?"

"Is it the new boyfriend?" Nuri asked. "Has he done something to upset you?"

"He..." He pursed his lips and shook his head even though his brother couldn't see. How did he go about telling him what had transpired between him and Kaz? Nuri would freak out. "It's fine."

"It's not," he disagreed.

Realizing he was going to keep pushing until Nate said something, he slammed the fridge shut and turned to lean back against the counter. "Has Silver ever done anything to you that you didn't want?"

"Well," Nuri sounded flustered, even going so far as to clear his throat, "our situation is a bit... complex. I wouldn't recommend it to most people."

"So, the answer is yes then." Nate had already known that, if he was being fair. Last year, he'd made a surprise visit to his brother and had walked in on Silver, pinning him down to the mattress. He'd freaked out and reacted without thinking, almost getting himself thrown in prison for assaulting the Emperor of Ignite. Nuri had saved his hide by talking Silver out of it.

Nate had secretly carried that for months afterward. The guilt had kept him up at night for weeks until Neve had subtly brought home a bottle of sleeping pills and left it on his night table.

"Have you two talked about it?" Nate had been the one to bring it up, so he may as well follow through. When he stepped back and really viewed the scene, there were similarities that he'd missed before.

Silver was possessive of Nuri and prone to jealousy in the same way Kaz had been. He also took control of Nuri's time, often using work as an excuse to keep him from making visits to his siblings or taking leave. At least, that'd been the case before the two of them had gotten married. Since they'd become official, the Emperor had actually let up a lot. Nuri had seemed…happier.

"We've discussed boundaries," Nuri said. "Again, I'm not trying to make claims that our relationship is in any way perfect or at all times healthy, for that matter. But it works for us. Is this about your boyfriend, or did Silver—"

"No," he interjected. "No, Silver hasn't done anything." Not since he'd called and threatened him over his mental health, of course. But Nate wasn't going to share that part. Possibly ever.

"There you go again," Nuri sighed. "Interrupting. It's rude not to allow people the time to finish their own sentences, you are aware of that, correct?"

"Yeah," he rolled his eyes. "Of course—" Last night, how many times had he cut Kazimir off? He hadn't noticed, but now that it was being brought to his attention, he was replaying the conversation back and…

He'd barely given Kaz a chance to explain. Hadn't been in the mood to listen. After reading all of the things Kaz had written about Zane, Nate had felt too broken and pathetic to hang around; the only thought on his mind was escaping that hotel so he could come home and climb into the shower stall and wallow.

"He's got abandonment issues." And Nate had been so focused on leaving he hadn't thought of how that might come off to Kaz. "Shit."

"Who does?"

"That doesn't make what he did to me right, though," he added to himself, forgetting for a moment in his confusion not to say it out loud.

"What did he do to you?" Nuri asked.

"He—" Nate stopped himself, nibbling on his bottom lip. How did he put this in a way that wouldn't have his brother on the first ship to Vitality? "He tried to initiate sex when I was upset with him."

"Oh." Nuri cleared his throat a second time. "Did he…force you?"

Nate didn't know how to answer that.

"I won't judge you," Nuri reassured. "Was it not the first time he's done something like that?"

Nate understood what he was trying to ask. He wanted to know if Nate had found himself in an abusive relationship one day and now was struggling to get out. It'd be so easy to throw Kaz under the bus and say yes, but the truth of the matter was…

"No," he admitted, "but I liked it all the other times." He blew out a breath. "This is so not a conversation I want to be having with my brother."

"Would you prefer I call Neve and have her come console you?" Nuri drawled, that snooty, sarcastic tone he was known for at the office finally coming through.

"Screw you," Nate chuckled.

"I like…things in the bedroom too, you know."

Nate grimaced. "Please don't give me any details."

"Ditto. All I mean is, there's nothing wrong with having kinks and abnormal sexual desires. As long as they're legal."

"Define legal?"

"Nate."

"Kidding." Mostly.

Nuri clicked his tongue in thought. "So, if I'm gathering this correctly, the two of you frequently engage in a...rougher style of sexual play—"

"Please don't call it that." It made him feel like a child, and this conversation got five billion times more awkward.

"—but this recent time, you weren't in the mood, and he ignored you when you refused consent. Is that accurate?" Nuri continued as though he hadn't heard.

"Yeah," he nodded. "That's basically it." In a nutshell, anyway.

"And you were upset?"

"I broke up with him."

Nuri considered this new information before asking, "Do you regret it?"

"That's the problem," he admitted. "I don't know."

"There's nothing that says you have to figure it out right this second. It's okay to be confused, Nate. Just come at the problem from a different angle and see if that helps."

"This isn't a math equation given to me by Mrs. Spring, brother." However, the advice Nuri had given him in the eighth grade had been crucial to his finally grasping the formulas and passing. "Besides, shouldn't you be telling me I did a good job dumping a guy who was about to take advantage of me?"

"That would certainly be the right thing to say, yes."

He frowned. "So why does it sound like you want to tell me something else instead?"

There was a strange sound from the other line for a second, followed by the sound of Nuri protesting in the background a moment before Silver's voice came through strong and clear.

"Because your older brother likes to be held down and fucked while he pretends he doesn't want it," Silver explained, as if that was the most normal detail for someone to be sharing. "And from the sounds of it, that runs in the family."

"Silver!" Nuri scolded. "Do not tell him stuff like that!"

"Why not?" Silver asked. "He already knows his brother married a psychopath."

That was true. He'd always had a feeling, but that detail had been confirmed the day before the wedding. Nuri had wanted both he and Neve to understand that their relationship dynamics were different and had attempted to get them to understand why he was marrying the guy who'd all but controlled his life up until that point. That had also been an odd conversation. He hadn't labeled him outright, but they'd gotten the gist.

"Yes, but you are a very specific type of person, and I do not want you promoting or romanticizing abuse to my siblings," Nuri declared. "Regular people don't—"

"Here's the thing," Nate interrupted—for the millionth time, "He's not exactly your average guy." He took a deep breath and bit the bullet. "He's got psychopathic tendencies, too." He'd leave out the rest for now. This was already more than he'd been planning to share with Nuri, literally ever.

"He what?" Nuri gasped. "Is this my fault? I'm a terrible influence. I made it seem okay, and now my little brother is dating someone who—"

"I'm twenty-three," he reminded.

Silver snorted. "Yet you still can't figure out what you like and don't like? Pathetic."

"Do not speak to him that way," Nuri said.

"He needs to learn how to stand up for himself and not worry so much about what other people think," Silver disagreed. "Who cares if I think he's pathetic or if you know he likes to be tied up?"

"How did you…?" Too late, Nate realized it'd been meant more as a blanket statement.

Silver laughed. "Really? My, my. Good for you. The crux of it is then, if you like it, what's the problem?"

"I didn't like it last night," he stated.

"No?"

"No!"

"What part?"

"The part where he wouldn't listen to me and ignored everything I was trying to tell him!" Sort like how Nate had ignored everything Kaz had been trying to say...But that was different in the sense that Nate didn't make things physical. "Assault is never okay."

"That's fair," Silver agreed. "But it seems like you're regretting your decision to end things."

"I don't know."

"At the time, you ended it for your own sake, correct?"

"Yes." Nate stiffened, hoping he wasn't about to out his secret to Nuri. He'd promised not to speak about his people-pleasing issue so long as Nate sought help, and he'd been doing that.

Sort of.

"What's the reason you won't get back together?" Silver asked. "Is that also for your sake, or because you're worried it wouldn't be the right thing in society's eyes?"

"What are you talking about?" Nuri was clearly lost.

Nate needed to end this conversation. He needed—

To run away, like he did every single time something got complicated or too hard for him to handle. That was his thing. He'd subtly or not so subtly shut down a discussion and claim he'd return to it later, only for that to never happen. It was one thing to need space and time to digest something, but another if that meant hurting someone you cared about in the process.

"Holy shit," he exclaimed, "I'm a coward."

There were a billion ways Kazimir could have

handled the situation last night, but Nate could have done better as well. None of that meant he needed to forgive Kaz, or that he was going to, but it opened his eyes to the way he'd been living. How he'd allowed his fears of upsetting or bothering other people to turn him into the type of person who hid from any sort of conflict.

He was good at putting up a front, at smiling through the inner pain, but that was all an act. He'd always known that part, and yet, it'd somehow eluded him just how deeply that went.

The doorbell rang then, pulling him out of his revelation, and he startled. A seed of hope had already taken root in his chest when, a second later, his multi-slate dinged with an alert he was getting another call.

When he saw the name Hotshot across the screen, he started for the door.

"I have to go," he said to Silver and his brother hurriedly. "Thanks!"

He ended the call without giving them a chance to respond and then hit accept for Kaz.

"Nate?" Kaz's voice trickled through. "I didn't think you'd pick up."

"That's you outside, right?" He was already in front of the door by the time he asked, hand reaching for the handle. "Look, I'm not saying I forgive you, but we should talk."

"Yes, we should," Kaz agreed, then added, "But what do you mean? I'm at the hotel still. Yuze literally just cut me out of the cuffs, and I called you right away."

Nate had the door partially opened and paused. "What? If that's not you, who is it?"

A hand slammed on the wooden frame, shoving him back so that he tripped over his own feet and hit the ground hard. His multi-slate dropped and skittered across the floor, sliding beneath the couch far out of reach.

"He doesn't look like he's capable of taking out Fry?" a deep voice stated, and when Nate glanced up, it was to find a giant-like man standing in his doorway.

"The trace wasn't mistaken. This was Fry's last known location," another, more clipped tone, stated over the guy's shoulder. "Just grab him and let's go. We'll get answers soon enough."

"Who are you?" Nate managed to ask, just before he was hauled onto his feet and dragged out of his home.

CHAPTER 28:

Kaz had spent the entire night and most of the day stuck to the bed. He would have still been there, if not for the fact the others had gotten worried by his lack of replies all day and sent Yuze to come find him.

Just in time for him to call Nate and hear him get kidnapped.

"Whoa," Yuze grabbed onto the door handle of the hovercar, "slow down!"

Instead of listening, Kaz sped up. "Tell me again."

"We got news the men who stayed behind are looking for the person responsible for their colleague's death," Yuze said.

"But we don't know where they're hiding?"

"No, but the others are on it as we speak. They'll find out—" His sentence ended with a swear as Kaz took a sharp turn.

The Void mansion was just up ahead, a sprawling black iron and glass building that Kaz had mapped and memorized since he'd been a child. He'd spent more time there than he had his own home; after all, he was often hoisted off onto the Voids whenever his nanny or trainers weren't scheduled to deal with him, and his father had better things to do.

He brought the car to the front entrance and then cut the jets, dropping it the two inches it'd been hovering straight to the ground with little care. Kaz didn't even close the door behind him, leaping out of the driver's side and rounding the car to take the steps two at a time.

The door scanned his thumbprint the second he touched the handle, and he tossed it open, not waiting to see if Yuze was following, searching for signs of his cousin. The mansion itself was massive, but this time of afternoon, if Baikal was home, he was typically in the study or lounge area with his fiancé Rabbit.

Kaz took a guess in the dark and went left, but there was no relief when he entered the room and found his cousin in the process of handing a seated Rabbit a steaming cup of something. They both looked up when he stormed in, but he went straight for his cousin.

"Have they located Pious's people yet?" he demanded to know.

Baikal straightened and propped an arm against the back of the leather chair Rabbit was sitting in. "Not yet."

"They need to find them. Now."

"What's going on?"

"Those bastards took Nate."

Baikal frowned. "Who's Nate?"

"Isn't that your boyfriend?" Rabbit asked, elbowing Kal afterward. "You heard all about this from the others a few weeks ago."

"Right. So that's why you've been slacking lately," Baikal said to Kaz.

"I have not." He'd kept up with his Brumal tasks as per usual.

"I couldn't reach you all day."

"That's because he was handcuffed to his bed," Yuze called. He and Berga came rushing into the room then, but Kaz didn't turn to acknowledge them.

His infuriating cousin quirked a brow. "Excuse me?"

"Lovers spat," Kazimir shrugged like it was no big deal even though, on the inside, he was still raging over it. "We'll get through it."

"Not if he's dead. They're after whoever murdered their comrade," Berga stated. "If they took Nate, that means they either think he's the one responsible, or they think he knows who is. They'll torture him until he confesses to one or the other."

"Or dies in the process," Yuze added bitterly.

"Nate isn't one of us," Baikal reminded them all.

"He's mine," Kaz growled, "which makes him one of us. The same way Rabbit is now one of us."

"That isn't the same," he disagreed. "Rabbit is my Possessio. He has a station and position in the Brumal."

"Nate's my Onus," Kaz retaliated, and for a moment afterward, the silence was actually deafening. "Good Light, *what*?"

"Your...That's a joke, right? *You* named an Onus?" Yuze asked incredulously.

Baikal glanced over Kazimir's shoulder toward Berga. "Did he?"

"I was not made aware," Berga replied, but he didn't sound as shocked as the others.

"Flix knows," Kaz lied.

"Convenient, since he still isn't back from his vacation," Baikal drawled, clearly not believing him.

Kazimir cursed. "Damn it, Nate is going to be! That should mean the same."

"An Onus is a serious deal."

"No fucking shit." This was an epic waste of time. Kaz had been planning on waiting until New Year's to bring it up to Nate. He'd wanted to make it special and take the chance to explain to him exactly what being an Onus meant and how important of a position it was to the Brumal.

The Dominus had a Possessio, while the members of his Satellite were allowed to name an Onus as their significant other. Only someone intended as a life partner was given the honor, especially when it meant they were considered a member of the Brumal from there on out. Typically, an Onus was already another member of the organization; it wasn't often that a stranger was brought in, since most of them were too cautious and paranoid about outsiders.

"You've been together for a month," Baikal said.

"One month and two weeks," he corrected. "And does that matter? You knew Rabbit was the one after one night."

"Hey," Yuze stepped forward, staring down at his multi-slate, "They've got something. Looks like Pious's people got permission from the Imperial family to linger."

"Call Kelevra," Baikal ordered.

"Not him," he shook his head. "The Heir Imperial. She gave the order. They explained they were looking for a murderer and told her that Pious had ordered them to search."

"So, if we interfere, we're risking instigating a war with both the Imperial family and the Ancient," Berga translated.

"We can't do that." Baikal crossed his arms. "Things are already rocky as is with my sudden rise to power. If we piss off the Imperial family enough, they turn on us; we're at a disadvantage. Not to mention the Ancient. No one knows their numbers. They're too secretive even for the best of spies."

"I'm going," Kaz insisted darkly. "Even if I have to go alone."

"And put the entire Brumal at risk?"

"Fuck the Brumal," he jabbed his finger in the air, "and fuck you! Like hell am I going to sit back and let the man that I love get pulled apart for a crime I committed! Either the Brumal is with me, or we can go our separate ways right now—Why the hell are you looking at me like that?!"

Berga coughed. "Did you just say the L-word?"

"What are you," Yuze turned to him, "five? The L-word? Good Light."

"Children." Baikal stared Kaz down for a minute, seemingly sorting through his options. If he decided not to allow Kaz to take the others with him, he really would have to go on his own.

He'd never make it in time if he didn't have their backing. And Nate…

Kaz did the one thing he could think of to show his sincerity and dropped down to his knees.

Everyone except his cousin gasped at the sudden move, but Kaz remained where he was.

"You actually like him that much?" Baikal asked. "Enough to throw everything away for him? Your father—"

"Is nothing more than a sperm donor to me," he stated. "You know that."

"Still," he cocked his head. "You've always tried your best to impress him."

Yeah, Kaz had become a good little soldier in the mafia his daddy was a part of and was even majoring in business so he could take over the company he had absolutely no interest in. But none of that actually mattered. It was as much a smokescreen as everything else about him had been.

Before Nate, Kaz had hidden behind his charm and his intelligence and his money. His position in the Brumal made him untouchable and he'd used that to his advantage. But when you could have everything with the snap of your fingers, did you really have anything at all?

Now that Kazimir had Nate, he felt a fullness in his chest he never had before. A warmth.

Last night he'd done a piss poor job of showing it, but he'd meant it when he'd announced he was in love, at least, as in love as someone like him could manage to be. Nate kept him grounded, and despite how awfully things had ended when he'd walked out, Kaz was still eighty percent certain he helped keep Nate grounded, too.

Maybe Nate had really meant it and they weren't going to get back together, but Kaz at least needed to try. He needed the chance to beg and plead and apologize. If something happened to Nate and he never got that, he would never forgive himself for being so foolish.

His father always put business before everything else, including family, and in some way, Kazimir had conformed to that. He'd respected the hierarchy and played his part. Took what he pleased so long as it didn't affect the company or the Brumal.

"I'm a self-centered prick," he said. "But I would never abandon my family."

Baikal seemed surprised. "He's your family now, is he?"

"Yes."

"I didn't know you had it in you, cousin."

Was he seriously mocking him right now? Kaz opened his mouth to say as much, but Baikal waved him off.

"We still don't know where to find them," he reminded. "Until we have an exact location, there's nothing more we can do. I can call Kelevra and see if he's heard anything. Perhaps he has some information he'd be willing to share."

"I have someone I can call, too." Kazimir got back to his feet and turned to his multi-slate.

"Don't remember telling you to stand," Baikal stated dryly, but went ignored. He grunted. "That didn't last long at all, did it."

"Who are you contacting?" Yuze leaned over Kaz's shoulder to try and get a peek at his device. "Zane?"

"He might be involved," Kazimir admitted. Zane had shown up at his place and caused a huge mess. "He told me last night he was out to get me."

"Get you?" he frowned. "For what?"

"Doesn't matter."

"Would make sense," Berga chimed in. "The Imperial family has always been good with keeping us in the loop. They knew we were involved with Pious and should have informed us when he ordered some of his men to hang back. But we had to make that discovery ourselves."

"Zane might have intercepted the communication requesting permission," Kaz surmised.

"He does live at the Little Palace," Baikal agreed. "It would have been easy for him to. He's also a trusted member of the Retinue."

"Plus, he and Lyra are fucking." Kaz hit call

and switched the device to speaker phone so they'd all be able to hear.

"I'm sorry he's what?!" Yuze stared at him like he'd grown a third head.

Kaz couldn't focus on that. Instead, he listened to the other line ring continuously with no answer.

With each chime, the fear in his gut grew larger and larger until it was practically consuming him.

CHAPTER 29:

"Apparently this is Shepherd territory," a gruff voice said.

"Who cares?" another scoffed. "Our job with the Brumal is done. Boss didn't even get what he was after either."

"Think he's going to kill Brantley?"

Nate listened to the conversation happening around him as he tested the bindings at his wrists and ankles. They'd dragged him out of his house and tossed him into the back of a truck before pulling a blaster gun on him to keep him quiet and still as they drove through the city.

Their final destination was some old apartment building that was currently on the waiting list for redevelopment. It was in a shady part of town, somewhere Nate had never been before.

And it felt cliché as all hell.

They'd tied him to a metal chair situated over a plastic tarp in the center of the room and had left him there for a bit while they conversed amongst themselves in the hallway. It gave the impression they were waiting for someone.

Tape secured his limbs, and no matter how much he struggled and twisted, he couldn't seem to get it to loosen. He'd hoped, given the poor execution of this whole ordeal, that they were low-level thugs who'd simply grabbed the wrong person, but the more they spoke, the more it became apparent they weren't from Vitality.

"Wouldn't you? This mission has been ongoing for over fifty years," the slightly taller one, the one who'd been at the door when Nate had first opened it, replied. He had a bulky shoulder propped against the rusted railing of a stairwell that led up to the other floors.

Nate was in the living area of the third apartment on the right, though the place had been gutted and there were holes in the ceiling and piles of torn papers no doubt left by vermin. No one would even think to look for him here, even if they were coming.

Was anyone coming?

Had Kaz overheard the commotion over the multi-slate?

Would he care?

The other man, with black hair and bright red-dyed bangs, let out a low whistle. "Pious Prince needs to learn when to let go."

"He'd probably say the same about us," the other chuckled darkly. "If he finds out about this—"

"He should be thanking us. Fry deserved better than what he got."

There was a pause and then, "You really think that guy in there did it?"

"It was his house," he said matter-of-factly. "Whether he had a hand in it or not, he knows something. You know what, screw this. Let's get this started."

"We were told to wait," the larger one reminded. "That was the agreement."

"Screw the agreement." The one with the dyed bangs stepped into the apartment and Nate stilled. "That's gya tape. No getting out of that without a pair of sheers, so don't even bother."

"Who are you?" That thread of hope that this was a mistake had died the second they'd mentioned his house being the location of something. It didn't take a genius to figure they were probably after information regarding the man Kazimir had stabbed in Nate's kitchen last month. Still, couldn't hurt to double-check. "Is this about a race? I haven't lost in weeks!"

Mostly because he hadn't been down to the docks in that much time. Between figuring out his job situation, how to handle the attention of a Devil of Vitality, and managing his own feelings, Nate simply hadn't had the time. He'd removed his name from the roster and asked for some time off, much to Madden's chagrin. It left the other racer scrambling for replacements but that was unavoidable.

Nate enjoyed racing, but it was a pastime that had given him something to do and a means to get out of his head. He tried his best to win, yes, but aside from that, there was no pleasing anyone else involved when he rode a hoverbike. It'd been the one thing he'd done for himself.

Then Kaz had come along, and suddenly, there'd been another option. Something else to occupy his time and help him focus on a singular thing instead of getting caught up in all of the possible ways he could screw up and disappoint those around him.

Maybe he'd never fully get over being a people pleaser, but at least with Kaz, Nate had been able to be more himself. He'd been able to recognize that he didn't always have to cater to others' whims.

Including the Devil's.

He'd come to the realization that the emotions he felt toward Kaz were very real. Nate wanted to make things work between them, but in order for that to happen, they had to be on the same page, and if the other night was any indicator…They weren't. At the time, breaking up had seemed like the best solution, but his talk with Silver and his brother had given him a fresh perspective.

What Kaz had tried to do to him was wrong, but Nate wasn't entirely blameless. He'd gone along with everything else all this time, had he not? He'd allowed the coercion knowing full well what it was. Had given in and rolled with the punches fairly easily, not because Kazimir had actually worn him down, but because he'd been sick of struggling in general.

Sick of fighting against himself and his own

hopelessness. At least having Kaz gave him someone else to place the blame on, someone else to turn to when the voices got too much. In the beginning, he'd figured it'd be perfect since he hadn't cared about displeasing Kazimir the same way he did everyone else. So what if he pissed him off or disappointed him? He'd owed the Hotshot nothing.

It was blurry, the moment those lines had crossed and merged. He couldn't pinpoint when exactly it'd happened, but somewhere along the way, he'd started caring after all. When it came to his siblings, everything he said and did was carefully thought out beforehand, but with Kaz, it was different. He cared about causing him trouble, but not with the same urgency.

With Kaz, the world didn't feel like it would end if Nate made a mistake. Maybe that was why he hadn't noticed the change until it was too late.

And now might really be, because if he didn't find a way out of this, it was looking likely he'd die here.

"Racing? What's that got to do with anything?" the man asked then, cutting through Nate's thoughts. He'd been carefully reloading his blaster, most likely hoping to intimidate Nate with the action, completely unaware that he'd spaced out for the whole thing. "Forget it. Doesn't matter. I'm going to ask you some questions, and if you're honest with me, we both get to leave here on our own two feet. If you're not..." He turned and aimed the gun at the spot between Nate's brow.

"If you're intent on starting, just get it over with already, Martyr," the larger man called from the doorway, leaning against it so that he could easily turn his head to view the room and down the hall.

"Someone was at your place last month," the man with the gun, Martyr, said to Nate. "Big guy. You couldn't have missed him. Well, if he'd come to the door, in any case."

That clarified they were definitely looking for the person Kaz had killed. Nate tried his best not to let that show, frowning as he pretended to think it over.

"I had a couple of my friends visit," he tentatively began, "but there were never any strangers."

"He's lying," the one by the door chimed in dully. When Nate gave him a questioning look, he tapped the side of his skull and grinned. "Ever heard of a Mendax?"

"Basically, they're walking lie detectors," Martyr helpfully stated. "Lucky you, Hernan is one of them."

"Yes," Nate drawled, "I'm feeling very fortunate to have met you both."

His eyes narrowed. "You aren't as innocent as you appear, are you, kid?"

"Okay, I did see him, your friend. I think, anyway." If they could tell when he was lying, he was going to need a new strategy. Nate had never heard of the Mendax before, but it wouldn't surprise him that species like that existed in the universe. "But it was only briefly."

Martyr glanced over his shoulder toward Hernan, who gave a single curt nod of his head. "That's more like it. You talk, and we'll get through this just fine. Neither of us wants to deal with a body on a foreign planet, isn't that right, Hernan?"

"Why would you ask me that?" he replied, and Martyr snapped his fingers.

"Oh, that's right. The drawback with being a Mendax is they're also unable to tell any lies of their own." He shrugged like he hadn't just subtly threatened Nate. "So, you saw him? Did the two of you speak?"

How exactly did this lie detection work? Technically, they'd sort of had a conversation—

The blaster went off next to Nate's left ear and he jolted in his chair. The ringing lasted for a long time, rivaling the sound of his speeding heart. Reality crashed in on him hard, and he felt the fear within him grow.

"Don't think," Martyr growled, pressing the tip of the blaster against Nate's thigh. "Just answer."

"Yes," Nate said. "We spoke, sort of. It was only a couple of sentences, though."

"What'd he ask you?"

"Something about a target." Nate licked his lips and shook his head slightly, mind scrambling to sort through the panic.

"What'd you say?"

"I didn't know what he was talking about."

"He's telling the truth," Hernan said.

"Doesn't mean he didn't kill him," Martyr sneered.

"I didn't!" Nate's eyes landed on the Mendax. "I didn't kill him!"

Hernan frowned. "That's also the truth." He cursed and straightened from the doorframe. "Shit, what if we really have the wrong person?"

"That it?" Martyr dug the barrel of the blaster in deeper. "We got the wrong person?"

Fuck.

Nate nodded.

The metal weapon connected with the side of his face in a flash, causing stars to wink in his vision.

"Use your words," Martyr demanded, replacing the blaster to Nate's thigh in warning. "We got the wrong person?"

What should he do? If he said no, would Hernan process that as a lie? It wasn't entirely, because Nate hadn't been the one to murder their friend—or whoever the hell he'd been to them—but on the same token, he was aware of who had…There were two other people involved in this. Kazimir and Port.

He shouldn't give either of them up, especially not just to save his own skin.

Nate just needed to think, but he wasn't going to be given that luxury. Choices. He was terrible at making them on the fly because actions had consequences and he was always too afraid his would burden someone else. If he didn't make one now, however, there was a very real chance he was about to die.

Good Light, Nuri, and Neve would never survive losing him suddenly like this.

"I didn't kill him," Nate repeated, tentatively at first, just to stall for a few extra seconds as his mind scrambled to come up with a feasible plan. "But he was asking about my friend."

"Your friend?"

During their talk amongst each other earlier, they'd mentioned that the target had gotten away. That had to be Port. If it wasn't, if Nate was about to throw his friend under the bus…He stopped himself. No. No, Port had brought these people to his doorstep and was apparently already off planet, if their words were to be believed. Nothing Nate said here could make anything worse for him.

"We worked together," Nate continued. "His name is Port. The man asked me about him and I said I didn't know where he was. Which is the truth. I didn't know then, and I don't know now."

"Our boss is the one concerned about finding that Jump," Hernan said. "We're here to catch a killer and make him pay for murdering Fry."

"It wasn't you?" Martyr hummed. "Fine. You know who did it though. Tell us. Now."

If he said it'd been Port, they'd know he was lying, but there was no way in hell he was going to give them Kaz's name.

"Have you ever received a romantic confession before?" Nate found himself asking, ignoring the confused looks they gave him. "How do you know if the other person is serious or not? Oh." He glanced at Hernan. "I guess you would just know, wouldn't you?"

"What the hell are you going on about, kid?"

"I received one recently," he said. "I've been on the fence over whether or not I think this person is telling the truth. Maybe I'm lucky, after all. I think I'll get an answer soon, one way or the other."

Despite his momentary uncertainty earlier, facts were facts. Kaz had been on the line when they'd taken Nate. He had to have heard what was happening. If he'd really meant it and nothing was going on with him and Zane, and he wanted things to work with Nate, then he'd come for him, right?

And if he didn't, and Nate really did end up dying here today…Well, that was an answer as well. His siblings would be hurt and would grieve, but some things were simply unavoidable.

"Just tell us who killed Fry," Hernan insisted. "That's all you have to do, and we'll let you go. Still breathing."

"There," Martyr joined in. "Since it's coming from him, you know it's the truth. Who murdered Fry?"

If he told on Kaz, they'd let Nate live.

"Have you ever fallen for the devil before?" he asked.

"Enough with the bullshit questions!" Martyr hit him again, harder this time. "What does any of this have to do with anything anyway?"

"I'm dating the Devil."

Hernan quirked a brow. "He's weirdly telling the truth."

"Who killed Fry? Last chance," Martyr warned.

"My boyfriend."

"What's his name?"

Nate tilted his head and caught Hernan's eye. "I'm not going to tell you."

Hernan sighed. "He's telling—"

The sound of the blaster going off a second time was just as deafening as the first, only this time, the pain wasn't just the ringing in Nate's ears. A startled sound slipped past his lips, followed swiftly by a groan as he processed he'd just been shot.

Blood instantly started to pool from the hole in his thigh, seeping through the material of his black jeans around it. The pain was excruciating, shockwaves flashing through Nate as he tried to breathe through it and not give in to the burning sensation or the threat of more to come. Instead, he dug his nails into his palms, trying to focus on that lesser sting and block out the agony his leg was undergoing.

"Going to take this seriously now?" Martyr asked, crouching in front of Nate. He shifted the blaster so it was aimed at his other thigh. "Or we going to keep going until you crack anyway?"

"Wait," Hernan pursed his lips, "Aren't there devils on this planet? Like, not real ones, but that's what they're called. I think we were ordered to steer clear of them. Something about political entanglements. Do you think that's why the boss left without investigating the death?"

His partner rolled his eyes. "What, are you saying you want to quit now? Kind of too late, don't you think?"

"Now that you've blown a hole through him?" He grunted. "I mean, yeah."

Martyr heaved a sound of frustration and slammed the handle of the gun into Nate's face, on the side he'd yet to touch. "Name."

"No." Nate's stomach twisted in knots, and he waited for the all-consuming guilt over what him refusing to give up Kaz meant for his friends and family. Only, while he did feel guilty, he was surprisingly unrepentant.

"Does your boyfriend really deserve this kind of loyalty?" Hernan asked, and since he'd know, Nate told the truth.

"No," he confirmed. "He really doesn't. My boyfriend is an asshole."

"Then why not just give us his name? We'll take care of him for you."

"I said he was an asshole," he reiterated. "I didn't say I wasn't into that sort of thing."

"Well, that's just messed up."

"Yeah," he nodded. "There's something seriously wrong with my psyche, that's for certain."

"What's for certain is I'm about to give you a matching wound," Martyr stated angrily. "What's your boyfriend's name? If you don't tell me this time, I really will shoot you again, and then we'll be moving onto your arms. Did you know you can survive getting shot by a blaster there? At least for a while, until you bleed out. We've got at least an hour, is what I'm saying."

"Come on, kid," Hernan motioned at him with his hand. "What's your boyfriend's name?"

Nate opened his mouth to refuse again, hoping they couldn't tell how scared he actually was, but before he could, another voice echoed through the empty hallway at the Mendax's back.

"You should have waited until I arrived." Zane stepped in when Hernan moved to the side, eyes immediately taking in the scene. His expression was empty, gaze barely lingering on Nate's before he slipped a crystal blade from a hidden sheath at his back and offered the handle to Martyr.

Nate frowned. The blade was the same as the one Kazimir had always carried around. Did they… have matching knives, or had Kaz given it to him?

If not for the pain he was in, he probably would have laughed. How ridiculous of him, to be concerned over something like this while he was currently tied up and bleeding out.

"Here," Zane directed. "Use this instead. It'll slice through flesh without causing too much blood. You could dice him up for hours this way. Using a blaster is just crude."

Nate tried the bindings at his wrist again, momentarily forgetting there was no chance they'd budge when the urge to punch the medical student in the jaw arose. "Are you fucking serious right now? You're *helping* them?"

Martyr, who'd been reaching for the knife, hesitated. "You two know each other?"

"He's a graduate of my university," Zane said blandly with a single-shoulder shrug. "We've spoken less than a handful of times, if even."

He turned to Hernan who nodded that it was the truth, then took the knife and secured the blaster behind his belt at his narrowback before holding the new weapon up to the light. "This is cool, what is it?"

"Star crystal," someone answered from the hallway a second before the sound of a blaster went off.

Zane moved faster than Nate's eyes could follow, grabbing the weapon tucked into Martyr's belt, aiming, and firing it at the man's head before any of them even had a chance to react to the shot from the hallway.

Blood splattered all over Nate, but he was still staring at the doorway where Hernan's body was now dropping, a bullet hole through his forehead, same as his fallen partner.

The body hit the ground with a thud, and Nate felt a rush of deja vu when Kazimir was revealed standing there.

"And my name is Kaz," he said down at the dead body, "by the way."

A feeling of relief rushed through Nate, so strong that the world spun and suddenly his head felt too heavy to hold up. "You," he struggled to get the words out, eyelids already drooping, "are such an asshole."

He managed to catch Kaz rushing across the room toward him, saw him shove Zane out of the way, and then, knowing he was finally safe, he gave in and allowed the darkness to take him.

CHAPTER 30:

Regret was an interesting emotion.

Kazimir wished he'd never learned that.

He stood by the side of the bed, watching the even rise and fall of Nate's chest. The doctor had already come and gone, treated him and given the all-clear, yet Kaz couldn't shake the uneasy feeling.

If he'd been just a minute later, how much more would Nate have had to suffer?

"Kind of creepy, don't you think?" Nate's weak voice pulled Kaz out of it. He was awake and staring up at him. His coloring hadn't returned yet, and the swelling on both sides of his face would take a bit longer, even with medicine, to subside it, but at least he was conscious. "Watching me sleep like that?"

"You passed out," Kaz said. "Due to shock."

"Ah, because I was shot? Yeah. Makes sense."

"You remember everything?"

"Like how Zane was there?" He snorted and winced when that seemed to hurt.

"Don't move," Kaz ordered. "Just try and stay still. I made them give you the best pain meds available, but you woke sooner than anticipated. It'll take a few more minutes for them to really kick in."

"I thought he'd screwed me over," Nate told him. "When he first walked in, I was so sure of it."

"You aren't the only one." Zane appeared in the doorway and entered, holding up his hands when Kaz gave him a steely look. "I'm only here to inform you that we've found the last member of their party. They're currently being shipped off planet as we speak. We were also finally able to get in touch with Pious Prince."

"And?" Kaz asked.

"He claims he had no knowledge that some of his people had stayed behind."

"He's saying they lied to Lyra about having his permission?"

"That's the story."

"Do you believe him?"

Zane thought it over. "It's plausible. There's no reason for him to care enough to risk angering the Brumal. The man who was killed was supposedly a new hire. There were no strong ties between them, and the Ancient have numbers. What's one or two shaved from the ranks to a leader like Pious?"

"Or three," Kaz grunted then nodded and waved him away. "Thanks. Now get out."

Zane turned to Nate. "We've both killed on your behalf."

"Want a cookie?" Nate stared him down.

"So you aren't just with him out of guilt or obligation."

"Did you think I was?"

Kaz couldn't blame Zane for the assumption. It made sense. Nate was the type of person who'd give up a piece of himself to make it up to someone else. Wasn't that the exact thing he'd figured out about him early on and used against him?

"I'm dating him because I like him," Nate stated, and Kaz tried not to let on how surprised that made him. "I can't say the same about you."

"Even after I helped save your life?" Zane persisted.

Kazimir had called him, fully intending to threaten him and risk a war between them and Kelevra, but Zane had been just as surprised when he'd learned about Nate's kidnapping. He had, however, known all about Pious's people.

And where they were located.

With Zane's help, they'd managed to arrive less than two hours after Nate had been taken. To avoid Nate somehow getting caught in the crossfire, or them just outright killing him, they'd decided to send Zane in first to distract them. It'd been risky, and after the stunt he'd pulled, Kaz didn't trust him like he used to, but...There hadn't been any better options.

"I tried to break the two of you up for sport," Zane added. "True. But there's a difference between ending a relationship and ending a life. If you had died, I would have caused a major problem for the Retinue, since Kazimir would have found a way to blame me for it."

"And here I thought you were lingering because you were gearing up to ask if we could share him," Nate drawled. "Clearly not, though, if you're leading with 'I saved you because it was easier than pissing off my leader'."

Zane cocked his head. "Would you share him?"

"No," Nate said firmly. "*My* boyfriend is just that. Mine."

"Does that mean we're together again?" Kaz asked hopefully.

"Shut up." Nate continued to glare at Zane, ignoring him.

Zane sighed and took a deliberate retreating step. "Can't blame a guy for trying. I'll see myself out."

"You do that." Nate waited until they were alone then questioned, "Is there anyone else here?"

"A couple of the Brumal are downstairs," Kaz told him. "I wanted them close in case the last Ancient discovered where we are and tried anything. Now that he's been handled, there's no need for them to stick around. I'll dismiss them." He lifted his multi-slate and sent a message off right away, when he finished, he found Nate staring at his surroundings.

"You brought me back to your place."

Kaz hesitated. "The hospital wasn't safe enough and I didn't want to risk going back to yours. I'm," he licked his lips, "sorry. If this isn't where you want to be, I understand. As soon as the medicine starts to work, we can relocate you wherever you say."

"This is fine."

"Are you sure?"

"Yeah,"

They fell into an uncomfortable silence and Kaz debated whether or not he'd be allowed to sit down on the edge of the bed next to him, or if he should remain standing. "On a scale of one to ten, how mad are you still?"

"That's what you're leading with?"

"I don't know what I'm doing," Kaz explained. "I've never..." He waved between them then ran his fingers through his hair. "I've never tried to make up with anyone before. In any capacity."

"Usually, you start with an apology, Hotshot," Nate suggested, slowly, like he was talking to a small child.

Or an idiot.

Kazimir chuckled indignantly but then got a hold of himself. He didn't have a right to his pride here. If he wanted this to work, if he didn't want Nate to up and leave him all over again the second his leg healed and he was able to, he needed to convince him to stay. But how? Would saying he was sorry really work?

"I was an ass," he began, figuring it couldn't hurt to try. "I—"

"You were panicking," Nate said.

Kaz paused. "Yes. Yes, I was."

"And I kept interrupting you," he added. "I'm sorry about that."

It was delivered simply but sincerely, and Kaz felt a prickle of something pleasant creep up on him at hearing it.

Maybe there really was something to saying that word after all.

"It's my fault, I should never have treated you like that," Kaz began. "Not after promising that I would treat you like my boyfriend. You deserved better. You deserve better. I'm sorry."

"Okay."

Kaz blinked. "Okay? Okay as in you forgive me?"

"That depends."

"On?"

"I like the rough kind of sex we have, Kazimir. I like when you take control of the situation and I don't have to worry about anything. But you can't keep weaponizing it like that. Sex isn't a means to control *me*. It's something I want us to share. Can you understand that?"

"Honestly?" A part of him whispered he should just go with the flow and worry about the rest later, but if this was a real chance, it could be his last, and he didn't want to blow it. "Only a little. My instincts are telling me to order you to stay here, with me, in my bed, forever. To tell you that you can never leave me, no matter what. I want to own you, Narek. But…I'm trying to be better. I'm trying to readjust my thinking. It's going to take time, and I might not ever be fully successful. Just, please give me a chance, hmm? I don't want to live without you."

"Why?" Nate asked.

"Because you're the only person on the entire planet who might actually believe change is even possible for someone like me." Nate was the only one who'd ever called Kaz out on his shit, spoken to him like he was a regular person and not a feared Brumal member or a spoiled corporate heir. "I forced you to come to me. But I don't want to force you to stay."

He wanted Nate to make that decision all on his own.

For once in his life, Kaz wanted to be chosen.

He wanted someone to pick *him*. He didn't want them staying or leaving based on his last name or threats.

"All right," Nate replied calmly, so calmly, in fact, that for a moment Kaz was certain he'd misheard him.

"What?"

The corner of his mouth turned up, his split lip reopening from the move, though he didn't seem to notice. "I said, all right. Let's give this another try. I'll be your boyfriend. I want to be."

"You do?"

"What happened to all that confidence you've always carried around in spades?" he teased.

Kazimir had lost that the second Nate had walked out the door and left him chained to the bed. He'd shattered and come apart right then and there, and even though Nate was back, in front of him and smiling, the reminder of that pain lingered still.

He never wanted to experience that type of loss again.

His gaze swept over Nate's battered face and he leaned in, gently running the pad of his thumb over his brow, one of the few places that wasn't bruised. "I should have done worse than merely shot them in the head. They deserved to be tortured for this."

Nate slipped an arm out from beneath the blanket Kaz had tucked him under once the doctor had finished and grabbed his wrist lightly. "It's fine. It wasn't that bad."

"They shot you," he reminded with a growl.

"Right, about that. What's the damage?"

"Are you asking if you'll ever be able to walk again?"

"For the most part," Nate nodded. "Yeah. So?"

He blew out a breath. "You'll be fine. They missed anything major. It'll take a couple of weeks and a few visits from the doctor for extensive treatments, but there won't be any lasting damage. Not even a scar."

"Nice to have money. I can barely afford a visit to the regular doctor, let alone fancy treatments."

"If you're about to refuse—"

"I'm not," Nate said. "You owe me one. This is how I'm choosing to collect."

"That so?" Kaz lowered down to the edge of the bed, and when that didn't earn him any protests, took it a step further by draping an arm around Nate's waist. "Anything else you'd like to demand,

Pretty Boy?"

"Yeah, no more stalking me places. If you want to know where I'll be, ask."

His controlling nature wasn't a fan of that one, but he forced himself to nod his head anyway. "Okay."

Nate's smile widened. "I promise I'll work on the interrupting thing. But it'll be hard for me to accomplish too. Apparently, that's just how I get when I'm comfortable with someone."

"Are you comfortable with me, Narek?"

"I'm getting there," he said. "Yeah."

"You're safe with me," Kaz reassured.

"I know."

"Is this a bad time to ask you to consider becoming my Onus?" He'd meant to hold back, but old habits died hard and after being given an inch, Kaz found he wanted the whole damn mile.

Nate frowned. "What's that?"

"It's a Brumal thing. It's similar to marriage, but isn't. I guessed it was too soon to ask about that, since we've only been together a short amount of time, but an Onus isn't recognized by the government, only within the Brumal."

Nate seemed caught off guard, but collected himself. "When…would you say is enough time before someone asks about marriage?"

"I don't know," he confessed. "I've never considered marrying anyone before. I always assumed my dad would one day try and betroth me to someone for a business merger and I'd just go along with it."

"What? Why?"

He shrugged. "Why not? I'll inherit his company one day. What's good for the company can only be good for me in the long run."

"Is that going to be a problem in the future?" Nate asked. "What if he tries to get you to marry someone else later down the line? I meant what I said to Zane. I'm not sharing you with anyone. If we're going to be together, then I want everyone to know it, including your shitty dad. If that means I have to become this Onus or whatever, then I'll do it."

"You will?" Kaz hadn't really expected an answer right away. He'd thought for sure Nate would make him wait for it, need to time to think things through. "It's a big commitment."

"How big?"

"I can only ever give out the title once in my lifetime."

"Oh, like how the Imperials can only ever name one Royal Consort?"

"Yes, exactly like that."

"Perfect."

"I'm not sure you're fully grasping—"

"I'm going to interrupt you again," Nate cut him off. "Sorry." He freed his other hand and grabbed a fistful of Kaz's shirt, keeping him close. "Can we hold off on the official announcement until after I've fully healed? Give me that much time. Let us both make sure that it's real, this thing between us. A couple of weeks should do it." He grinned. "We move fast, after all."

Kazimir didn't need a couple of weeks. He didn't even need a couple of hours. But he nodded his head anyway and took Nate's hand in his own, bringing it up so he could plant a soft kiss to the backs of his knuckles.

"Should we bet on it?" Nate threw him a curveball, laughing when Kaz didn't reply. "I bet I'll gather enough courage to talk to my siblings about it before time is up. I'm going to leave out the part about being kidnapped and almost murdered though, cool? I'm willing to displease them a little by saying I'm choosing a Brumal member as a life partner, but there are still lines."

"Speaking of which," Kaz quirked a brow. "Kind of chose the worst time to stop caring about disappointing Big Brother, Narek. You could have been killed for real. All you had to do was give them my name."

"I would never do that to you," Nate stated.

"I'm Brumal," he pointed out. "You just said as much yourself. I can handle a couple of rouge losers."

"What if they'd snuck up on you?"

"The only person who's ever been able to sneak up on me is you." Kaz hadn't seen this coming, not even when he'd been the one going after his pretty racer in the first place. "How's it feel to tame a devil, babe?"

Nate pretended to think it over. "Pretty good, actually."

"Keep in mind what that entails. When you tame something, that person is yours to do with as you please. The devil dies for you, Narek, not the other way around. Don't ever put yourself in danger like that again. Not for anyone, not even me. Agreed?"

Nate clicked his tongue at him. "First you don't understand the basic concepts of boyfriends, and now this. Listen up, Kazimir, I'll only explain this once. If we're going to eventually get married, you have to know what that means. It's a partnership. You protect me," he tapped him on the chest, "and I protect you. That's how that goes."

"Pretty Boy—"

"It's non-negotiable."

"What was all that talk about how you'll stop interrupting me?" Kazimir asked pointedly, only for Nate to smirk suggestively.

"You could always make me. There's something better I'd prefer doing with my mouth anyway."

"Oh, hell no." He shook his head and tried to pull back, but Nate grabbed at his shirt a second time and tightened. "The doctor said you had to take it easy, and sex between us is many things, but that is not one of them."

"I'll be fine."

"You were literally just shot!"

"Since when did you do what you were told?" Nate challenged, staring him down with that infuriatingly adorable look on his face. "Come on,

Kaz. I want it."

They really shouldn't…Yet Kazimir wanted to touch him too. Felt the urge to feel him writhing, hear his moans, to prove once and for all that he was all right and here with him. That Nate Narek was alive and *his.*

"You can have my hand, Pretty Boy," Kaz offered. "That's it. Take it or leave."

"I'd rather have your mouth."

He huffed and gently eased the comforter down Nate's body. "Always have to be so difficult."

"Regretting selecting me already?" Nate teased, and even though it was clearly a joke, Kaz paused.

"No," he replied seriously. "I will never regret that."

Nate held his gaze. "Wanna bet?"

"Yeah." His fingers slipped beneath the waistband of Nate's boxers, cupping him. "Yeah, that's a bet I'll take."

And it was one Kazimir had no intentions of ever losing.

CHAPTER 31:

"Let me help you." Kazimir followed Nate into his house and tried to walk with him toward the hall, but he shook his head at him with a smile.

"I can move on my own," he reminded. The doctor had told them as much, though it was still difficult at times and hurt if he put too much pressure on his leg. It'd only been a week since the kidnapping, but the wound had mostly sealed, and the bruising on his face was long gone. Aside from a slight limp, no one would be able to tell there was anything wrong with him at all.

He closed the front door behind him and hesitated, clearly wanting to argue.

"I'm just grabbing a few things," Nate said. It was the first time he was returning home since. "I want a minute to sort through my stuff."

"And your thoughts." Kaz nodded in understanding, though it sounded like he still wasn't a fan. He was trying though, like he'd promised he would, and that was more than enough at the moment. "Okay, Pretty Boy. I'll check on the kitchen. The stuff in your fridge is most likely rotten now."

Nate chuckled. "Is the big bad Brumal underboss about to clean out my refrigerator? What's next? Want to fix my leaky faucet, too?"

"No," he replied. "Because that would give you a reason to move back here, and I'd prefer you stay with me."

He'd agreed to remain at the penthouse until he was fully healed. After that, they'd discuss it again and see where they both stood on the matter. In the beginning, Nate had figured it was smart in the off chance they ended up being terrible roommates. Kaz had stayed many nights here with him after they'd started dating, but it wasn't the same as officially moving in together.

But things had actually gone really well. They'd synced their schedules almost seamlessly in the past week.

"I have to go back to work eventually, Kaz," Nate told him, stopping at the entrance to the hall. "I won't be comfortable living off of you forever. That's just not in my nature."

Jones had understood when Nate had needed to take sick leave, but he'd also managed to find a replacement in that timeframe. He'd called to tell him the other day, letting him know that he wouldn't fire him if he still wanted the job, but that his help was also no longer necessary.

Basically, that meant he was back at square one.

"Come back to Quartet Air," Kazimir suggested, and it was obvious by the way he said it that it'd been on his mind for a while. "Just, hear me out before you say no. Please?"

Nate nibbled on his bottom lip but ended up nodding.

"I know you don't want to feel like you're taking advantage, but that's not what this would be. I've looked through your records, Narek. You're a top-notch employee. You never missed a day of work and you always stayed extra hours to get the job done. You're also one of the few who never had a complaint filed against them. That type of thing is rare, trust me, I've been interning at my dad's company since I was sixteen. I know a thing or two."

Nate understood his worth, at least when it came to work. He'd never slack off at something like that and had taken pride in his skills and abilities. And he did miss it, working at a shop. Getting his hands dirty and covered in grease. Joking around with Annya on their breaks.

"I just want something stable," he admitted.

"I know, babe. I can provide that. Not because we're dating, but because you deserve it." Kaz took a step closer and linked his pointer finger with Nate's. "I've already fired Sier. Not only was she a shit boss, she was also skimming off the top."

"Really?" He hadn't guessed that.

"She's going to have a great time explaining that to the authorities," Kaz stated. "I've also purchased a new location and plan on having the business rebranded and moved."

"What about the rest of the employees?"

"They've been given the choice to stay on or take their leave. If they choose the latter, they'll be given letters of recommendation to help them find new jobs. Unless you tell me now that there was someone else who treated you poorly there."

"So much for not doing any of this because we're dating, huh?" He snickered. "No, no one else was bothering me. Just Sier."

"Good. So you'll come back?"

"I didn't say that."

"Nate."

"Let me think about it, okay?" He laughed when Kaz made a face. "I swear I'm not going anywhere either way. I just want to be sure this is the right career move for me, that's all. My life has already changed so much in the past two months. It's a lot. I need to digest it all, preferably without pain meds still coursing through my system."

"All right." He let him go and then motioned toward the hall. "Hurry up and pack. You refused breakfast, but there's no way I'm allowing you to skip out on lunch. Speaking of those meds, they aren't meant to be taken on an empty stomach."

"I'm the one who took care of my sister whenever she was ill, remember?" Nate headed to his bedroom.

"Yes, and now I'm the one who's going to take care of you," Kazimir called after him.

Nate didn't respond, not sure what he'd say.

He was still getting used to this, the softer side of Kazimir that touched him delicately and looked at him like he was afraid he'd up and vanish in a puff of smoke. The kidnapping hadn't just affected Nate, it'd done something to Kaz as well.

He'd skipped out on classes all week, ignoring Nate when he'd told him to go and he'd be fine on his own. Even the Brumal had been rejected, Kaz shutting his multi-slate off more often than not. It seemed like they were both trying to relearn the other, testing if they could be more than sharp tongues and biting words. So far, it was looking like they could.

Which meant Nate really had to speak to his siblings, sooner rather than later. After he'd fully healed, then he'd—

He reached his room and came to an abrupt stop in the doorway, momentarily wondering if he was hallucinating from the drugs. It wasn't meant to be a side effect, but still.

Then the figure by his desk turned and caught sight of him, smiling in that familiar way that proved he was really there and Nate wasn't just imagining it.

"Nuri?" He blinked when his brother walked over and gave him a strong hug. "What are you doing here?"

"We moved up our visit," Nuri informed him. "After the way our call ended last week, I felt uncomfortable. It wasn't sitting right with me so I decided to come check on you." He frowned. "Are you okay? You're moving funny."

"Oh." Nate instinctually placed a hand over his thigh, though there was no sign of the wound with his pants on. "It's nothing. I'm good."

"Did something happen?" his brow furrowed deeper. "Was it your new boyfriend? Did he hurt you?"

Nate had contacted Nuri through message since that day, but he'd kept things vague on purpose. Now that he was physically here, however, that didn't seem possible. "Something did happen, but it wasn't his fault. And I really am okay. I've gotten the best medical aid available thanks to Kaz."

"Kaz?" He tipped his head. "Kazimir Ambrose? That's who you're dating?"

Nate tried to read between the lines, but for the life of him, he couldn't tell how Nuri felt about that. "Yeah. Wait, did you say we just now? As in...?"

"Silver is here, too," he nodded. "Didn't you see him? He was parking the car in the garage when I came inside."

Nate had not, and that also explained why he hadn't seen their car either.

A crash from the front of the house cut their conversation short, and they both rushed from the room, Nate momentarily forgetting all about his injury as the adrenaline kicked in. When they entered the kitchen, it was to find Kazimir and Silver toeing off.

Kaz had the CEO pinned to the refrigerator, the tip of his crystal dagger pressed to the side of his jugular.

Meanwhile, Silver had the end of a blaster up against Kaz's side.

"Stop!" Nate scrambled over, coming to a halt when neither of them so much as budged. "Damn it, I'm serious! Both of you, cut the shit."

"Do you know him?" Kaz asked, voice dark and filled with threat. He didn't tear his gaze off of Silver, but he did cock his head in Nate's direction.

"Uh, hello," Nuri approached, coming up to Nate's side. He waved awkwardly. "I would appreciate it if you would release my husband, Mr. Ambrose."

"Ambrose?" Silver lifted a dark brow. "Ersa Ambrose's son?"

"What of it?" Kaz kept the knife firmly in place.

"If we want to diffuse this situation," Nate said, "don't bring his dad into this."

"Daddy issues?" Silver chuckled. "Cute."

"Unless you want me to let him stab you," he switched tactics, not liking how Silver was so brazenly looking down on Kazimir, "you'll shut the hell up."

"Did you just…" Nuri sputtered. "Nate! How could you say that to the Emperor?"

"Emperor, huh?" It seemed to finally click for Kaz and his shoulders relaxed some. "You must be Big Brother then."

"Yes, that's right," Nuri cleared his throat. "Hello."

"Hey."

"Okay, Hotshot," Nate clapped his hands. "Point made. You're both big and bad and blah, blah, blah. Put down the weapons."

"Him first," Kaz lifted his chin toward Silver.

"And simply trust you to keep your word and follow suit?" Silver snorted. "I don't think so."

Nuri started to rub at his temples, a clear indicator he had a migraine coming on. He was prone to them and they could last for hours if they weren't dealt with right away.

"Kaz," Nate switched tactics. "I'm hungry."

"I'll make you something as soon as your brother-in-law concedes," he replied.

Fucking child.

He rolled his eyes and took it up a notch, swaying slightly on his feet for good measure to help sell it.

"I ran here just now. My leg—"

"You what?!" Kazimir shoved away from Silver, completely forgetting all about the standoff as he moved to Nate. He slipped the knife into its sheath at his side and took Nate settled his hands on Nate's waist, easily lifting him up off the ground to set him on the kitchen counter at his back.

He dropped to his knees before Nate could get another word out, gently touching his thigh around the area where he'd been shot. "How does this feel? Do you think you pulled any of the stitches?"

"Stitches?" Nuri's eyes went wide. "Why do you have stitches?"

"Because he was shot," Kaz replied absently, still focused on checking Nate. It was clear he wanted to remove his pants so he could get a good look, but smartly refrained.

"He what?!" Nuri was at his side a second later, grabbing onto his arm. "You were shot?!"

"By who?" Silver asked.

"They're dead now," Kazimir said. "I dealt with them."

There was a moment of silence before Silver hummed. "I approve of the new man, Nate."

"Yes," Nuri adjusted his wirerimmed glasses and nodded slightly, "yes, he does seem rather fond of you. I'm glad to see you're being taken care of here. But don't think this lets you off the hook. I want to know the whole story about this shooting and how you got involved in the first place."

"If this is Ersa Ambrose's kid," Silver stated, "that means you're Kazimir, correct? He's the underboss of the Brumal mafia, Nuri."

"Oh." He blinked but didn't seem as opposed as Nate had feared he would be. "That helps put things in perspective then."

Nate narrowed his eyes and thought it over. This mild reaction to news that big could only mean one thing. "Neve blabbed about that already too, didn't she."

"She was concerned you wouldn't want to tell me," Nuri admitted.

"Wouldn't want to disappoint your family," Silver added, a note of taunting in his tone that didn't go unnoticed.

"What did you just say to him?" Kaz rose to his feet, but Nate caught onto his elbow.

"Don't, it's not worth it." He sighed and leaned back against the cupboard. "Do you mind giving Nuri and me a moment alone?"

"I don't," Silver said, giving Kazimir a challenging look.

The two stared each other down for a lengthy moment before the Hotshot rolled his eyes.

"Whatever. But call if you need me, and don't try to get down on your own." Kaz turned and placed a soft kiss on the center of Nate's forehead, lingering for a second longer before he gave in and moved off to the living room. He paused on his way and motioned to Silver. "Coming or what, Royal Asshole?"

"Family get-togethers are going to be a lot more fun now, aren't they?" Silver grinned, but before Nate could feel nervous about that, he left with Kaz, not even sparing them a backward glance as he turned the corner out of sight.

"Is everything really all right, Nate?" Nuri asked softly. "If he's making you do anything you don't like—"

"I have depression," he blurted. Once it was out there, it seemed stupid not to elaborate, and he found the confession spilling past his lips in a rush. "It isn't technically clinical yet, but it could easily have turned into that if not dealt with. I do have other issues, however. My therapist says its people pleasing and burdenism."

"You've been seeing a therapist?" Nuri sounded surprised.

"Sort of," he said. "My point is, it's stupid, and I'm working on it, but I really need you to be okay with this. With Kazimir and my relationship. Don't get me wrong, I won't end things with him even if you aren't, but it will really suck." Like, a lot.

"Nate," Nuri waited until he lifted his face and met his gaze, "I don't have any right to judge you or who you choose to be with. Did you judge me when I told you I was dating Silver?"

"I mean," he shrugged, "yeah, a little, remember?"

"Okay," he sighed. "So I do think it's risky being with someone who is in the mafia, but that doesn't change the fact that it's your life and your decision to make. I don't get to look down on you for living however you see fit. Neither does Neve, or anyone else, for that matter."

It was spoken so simply, but Nate struggled to comprehend what he was hearing anyway. A closer look at his brother told him that everything Nuri had just said was the truth, that he meant it, but those negative voices in his head started whispering like they usually did.

"Really?" He licked his lips. "Aren't you disappointed? You raised me and made all these sacrifices, and now I'm unemployed and dating a Devil of Vitality."

"You're unemployed?"

He let out an awkward, humorless laugh. "Whoops. Don't worry though! I've got that figured out already." He left out how he was seriously considering Kaz's offer to go back to Quartet Air and help him run the place. It was probably best to take one step at a time here. His brother seemed like he was okay with it, but... "This is a big deal."

"I didn't say it wasn't," Nuri replied. "You dating anyone is a big deal."

"Are you...Really okay with it?"

"Brother," he took hold of his face and squished his cheeks like he used to when they were kids, ignoring Nate's squirms, "Yes."

Nate got free and pushed his hands away.

"You're your own person, Nate," Nuri said once he was done laughing. "And for the record, I didn't really do all that much for you. If anything, I should be the one turning to you asking if you're disappointed in me."

"What?" Nate frowned. "Why? Why would I ever be?"

"I shipped you off to a foreign planet and made you raise our sister alone," he pointed out. "Anyone would be bitter in that position."

He shook his head. "I've never once been bitter, I know you only did that because it's what you thought was best for us. I know if you'd had the chance, you would have moved here with us. It just wasn't possible. I've never blamed you for how we've lived, Nuri. Not ever."

"No?" he didn't sound convinced, and for the

first time, Nate realized maybe he wasn't the only one who'd felt like he couldn't live up to his family's expectations.

"Hey," he clapped a hand on Nuri's shoulder, "I love you. You've been the best big brother anyone could ever ask for. Don't doubt that for a second."

"Ditto," Nuri said. "You raised Neve all on your own. The way you look up to me? That's how she looks at you, Nate. You could never disappoint us. As long as you're happy, that's all we've ever cared about."

He felt tears threaten and forced them back. There was no way Nate was going to embarrass himself by crying.

"Kaz makes me happy," he said instead. "Surprisingly so."

"That's great." Nuri smiled at him, and it was easy to tell this time that it was genuine, none of those negative voices clamoring for attention in Nate's mind now.

Later, he'd ponder over that and where they'd gone, but his focus was on making sure they both got the closure they so clearly needed. If he'd known his brother also felt a similar way, that he'd been carrying that same weight, wondering if Nate resented him for his choices, he would have sucked it up and broached the subject sooner.

"Just remember," Nuri added. "If he ever does anything you don't want, you have me and Silver in your corner. Even if you don't like him very much, Silver view's you as his brother now. He'll protect you."

"I know." Weirdly, he did, despite the threats made against him before. On some level, Nate had always understood Silver was only trying to protect Nuri, and that he'd do anything to ensure that.

Kind of like how Kazimir would do anything to keep Nate safe as well.

He'd risked starting a war for him—twice.

"We should go then," Nuri said then, smiling when that caught Nate off guard. "What? It seems like the two of you were in the middle of something. It was rude of us to show up unannounced. We've got our hotel room booked already and it's almost check-in time anyway."

"Are you sure?" Nate asked. "You can stay."

"No, it's fine." He waved him off. "We'll see each other soon. How about lunch tomorrow? With Neve?"

"Yeah, that sounds great."

"What sounds great?" Silver and Kaz entered from the doorway to the garage. "You were taking a really long time. I got worried."

"He got bored," Kaz corrected, moving over to Nate to help him down from the counter. "All good, Pretty Boy?"

He nodded at him.

"Perfect." Kaz turned to Nuri and bowed his head. "It's nice to meet you, Nuri. I'm Kazimir."

"My brother's boyfriend," Nuri smiled. "Yes. It's nice to meet you too. We were just talking about grabbing lunch tomorrow. Will you join us? I'd love to get to know you better, and I'm sure Neve will say the same. She spoke highly of you the last time you dinned together."

"She did?" Nate's eyes widened.

"Why so shocked?" Kaz grunted. "I'm awesome. And yes, thank you, I'd love to come."

"He can suggest the restaurant," Silver stated, wrapping an arm around Nuri's waist. "He knows this planet better than most. He helps run the damn thing, after all."

"Fantastic," Kaz agreed, holding his gaze challengingly.

"We'll see you tomorrow then." Nuri waved and took Silver's hand, pulling him back toward the entrance to the garage, his voice dropping, though they were still able to pick up on his words. "You better have been nice to him while you were alone together. If I find out you were rude to my brother's boyfriend, I'll—"

Silver slammed the door shut behind them, cutting off the rest of that sentence.

"Hey," Kazimir pulled Nate in, "you really okay?"

"Yeah, you?"

"Your brother-in-law is…interesting, to say the least."

"Isn't he though?"

He snorted. "I'm way better than he is."

"Of course."

"I hope that wasn't sarcasm, Pretty Boy."

"And if it was?" he teased. "What are you

going to do about it?" Nate wiggled his brow suggestively.

"You're still healing," Kaz reminded.

"Come on."

"I don't want to hurt you."

"A little pain never killed anybody."

"Pretty Boy. That's not funny."

"So tie me up and teach me a lesson, Hotshot." Nate pushed him away and took a step back toward the hall. "Or should I go find my glass toy and take what I need from that instead?"

Kaz tipped his head. "I threw that in the trash weeks ago. The fact you didn't notice proves you know only I can give it to you the way you really want."

"Give it to me then," he insisted. "Please, Kaz." His hand slipped down his front, stopping at the button of his jeans. "It's been so long, I really need a reminder."

"Reminder?" Kaz took a step closer.

"Yeah," he nodded and smirked. "Of what it feels like to be stretched by your cock."

Kazimir exhaled sharply. "Okay, Pretty Boy. Just remember, you asked for this. I'm going to make you scream and beg for me."

"Wanna bet?"

Kaz lifted him into his arms, careful not to jostle his bad leg as he carried him to the bedroom with fire in his eyes. "We both know I always win at those, babe."

Nate kissed him, nipping at his bottom lip.

"I'm counting on it."

There was nothing to be ashamed of when it came to giving in to Kazimir.

Who stood a chance against the Devil anyway?

EPILOGUE:
Five Months Later

"I didn't buy this so we could play with it here," Nate whisper-yelled as he was yanked back and forced further onto that persistent cock. He was bent over his desk in his private office, the glass fogged over so no one could peer inside at what was taking place there.

During working hours.

To their boss.

He tried to be quiet as he was drilled into, but the burst of sensations as he was stretched by Kazimir made it difficult. There was also the delicious sting of the leather straps secured around both arms. They crossed between his shoulder blades and then had another strap that connected to handcuffs.

Kaz had entered the office under the guise of needing to speak with Nate about a potential new client. The second he'd ensured their privacy, however, he'd pounced, getting Nate into the harness before he could stop him. There were thigh sling attachments as well, but he must have left them at home because he'd stopped there.

Nate's pants were down by his ankles with his front pressed to the surface of his desk. Kaz was between his spread legs, using the spot where the leather crossed at his back for purchase as his thrusts increased in tempo.

"Don't lie, Pretty Boy," he drawled a moment later once he seemed to catch his breath enough. "You knew exactly what you were suggesting when you left the box for me to find on the kitchen counter this morning."

The two of them were still living in Kaz's penthouse suite, though there were talks of finding their own place soon. Living together had worked out really well long-term and, if anything, had helped bring the two of them closer.

Which was part of the reason why Nate had finally caved and taken him up on the job offer. He'd had stipulations, of course, and had insisted that he undergo regular evaluations just like everyone else every year to ensure he was always the right fit for the job, but he'd accepted, and now here they were.

Fucking in his office.

So professional.

"How about a deal?" Kaz reached around him and found his dick, giving it a quick stroke that had Nate gasping and grinding back onto him. "You tell me something I'll like to hear, and I make this quick for you. Not sure if you noticed the time, Pretty Boy, but you're due for that meeting with Annya in less than fifteen minutes. We both know I can keep this up for fifteen *hours* if I want."

"Kaz," Nate moaned as he dragged the crown of his cock against his prostate. "*Hahzi,* please."

"Think I'll go easy on you just because I like it when you call me that?" Kaz clicked his tongue.

They both knew it had the opposite effect, actually, making him want to pound in harder, deeper, force his way inside until he was sure Nate felt all of him and knew without a shadow of a doubt who he belonged to.

"You're so hot, babe," Kaz growled the words behind him as he fucked in with more frenzy. "So sexy. The way you're clenching around me right now. Want to milk me, babe? Want me to fill this pretty ass up with my come?"

He slapped him and the sound echoed in the room, causing Nate to suck in a breath and shake his head against the desk.

"Keep it down," Nate ordered, biting on his tongue when that only earned him another pump of his dick in time with Kaz's thrusts. He was so close. Any second now, he'd unload...The problem was that Kazimir had long since learned his tells. If he wanted to deny him the orgasm and draw this out like he'd threatened... "Deal."

"What was that?" Kaz leaned in, a teasing note to his voice proving he'd heard him just fine. "Gotta speak up, Pretty Boy."

"I'll tell you something you'll like hearing," Nate promised. "But I have to get to this meeting in time. That means we finish, *and* you clean me up after, Kaz."

"Demanding," he said with a chuckle. "Deal."

"Turn me around."

Kaz pulled out and flipped Nate, lifting him onto the desk. He helped lean him back so he was partially balanced on his bound hands, and then pulled him to the edge and drove back into him hard enough to have him mewling.

One of his hands drifted to the end of his shirt and then slipped underneath it, making its way up Nate's chest to tweak at his right nipple. When he got the reaction he wanted and Nate jerked in his hold, he did it again before moving on to the next bud. "I'm waiting, babe."

Nate struggled to keep focused, but it was hard to do with Kaz so skillfully playing his body. His moans grew in volume, but he was too far gone to notice or care about being overheard by any of the workers who may or may not be passing by the office.

"Focus on me," Kaz suggested in a silky tone, laughing again when Nate made a frustrated noise. "Less than ten minutes before the meeting now."

To buy himself another moment, Nate rocked forward and captured Kaz's mouth with his own. The kiss was frenzied, and he poured all of his longing into it as he widened his thighs to better accommodate Kaz's thrusting cock.

A few months ago, if anyone had told him he'd be here, bound while he was fucked senseless by a guy like Kazimir Ambrose, he would have laughed in their face. Now he was practically begging for it, wishing they were back home where they could make good on Kaz's threats and allow this to last for hours. After, Nate would shower while his Hotshot made them dinner, and they'd end up cuddling on the couch watching one of the true crime shows they were both obsessed with.

It sounded good enough it was tempting to call off the meeting with Annya and head home early. But Nate had never been one to shirk his responsibilities, and besides.

Not giving in now meant there was something for him to look forward to later.

"I love you," he pulled back enough to whisper the words against Kaz's lips, smirking triumphantly when Kaz's hips slowed and came to a stop. "What? Not good enough for you?"

"Say that again," he ordered, only to have Nate shake his head stubbornly.

"The deal—" Nate yelped, not quiet at all, as Kazimir lifted him and dropped him down on his cock, driving in deep enough he saw stars.

"Say that again, Pretty Boy," Kazimir urged, swiveling so he could press Nate back against the wall, pinning him between two hard surfaces as he started to move again. The framed photographs rattled as he pounded into him, clearly uncaring if they were overheard either. "I love you so much." He started stroking Nate's dick in time with his thrusts. "I've been waiting so long for you to feel the same.

Say it back, babe. Say it again."

The clock on the wall mocked Nate, reminding him that there wasn't any time left for him to keep teasing. He grabbed Kaz's face and kissed him again, just as desperately as before, grinding down on him for good measure.

"I love you, Kaz," he said, gasping when he felt Kazimir's cock explode deep inside of him. He grunted as he was filled, the sensation causing him to tip over the edge himself. His dick spurted between them, and Kaz kept pumping his fist, ringing him dry, completely uncaring of the mess he was making of their shirts.

Nate went boneless as soon as he was finished, slumping over Kazimir, their mingled pants the only sound filling the room for a long while as they both came down from their highs.

"I've got to put you down, babe," Kaz broke the silence first, clicking his tongue when Nate made a sound of protest. "I have to clean you up. You're going to be late."

"Screw that. We're the boss."

He snorted. "It's cute of you to say, but we both know you don't mean that."

Nate had been working hard on his people-pleasing, but there were still things he found difficult. Making people wait on him was one of them. Although, he was still of a mind that was simply common decency. Still, call it whatever, Kaz was right.

He groaned and lifted his head from Kazimir's

shoulder. "I don't want to move."

"You don't have to yet," he reassured, shifting to plop Nate back down on the desk. He undid the leather straps binding him and dropped the harness under the desk out of view of the door in case they forgot about it after. Then he planted a palm on the center of Nate's chest and eased him back down until he was lying over the smooth surface.

He pursed his lips. "Kaz?"

"You wanted me to clean you off, remember?" Kaz eased Nate's thighs wide and lowered with a mischievous grin. "I'm only doing what you asked."

"Kaz." Nate's eyes drifted closed despite his protests when he felt the first swipe of that tongue against his abused hole.

"Just be a good boy and take it." Kazimir licked and sucked at him, seemingly pleased with himself when he had Nate writhing all over again in less than two minutes. "Boyfriend, or Onus?"

"What?" Nate frowned, barely keeping up as he struggled to keep himself from getting hard all over again.

"Boyfriend," Kaz repeated, "or Onus? Which will it be?"

Nate cried out when he worked a finger past his entrance and curled it against his prostate. "You promised."

"I said I'd let you come quick and clean you off after," Kaz agreed. "That's what I'm doing, Pretty Boy. Don't worry. We'll be done in time for your meeting. I'll get you off quick. Just need you to give me an answer first." He slipped in another finger.

Nate had originally asked him to hold off until after he'd healed from the blaster shot to his thigh. But then they'd gotten distracted with moving him in and reforming the business—which was no longer called Quartet Air—and...They'd sort of just never brought it up again. Honestly, he was impressed that Kaz had held back this long. There was little doubt that he'd wanted to ask about it sooner but hadn't for Nate's sake since he'd already been adjusting to so much.

That was...kind of sweet.

When it came to the little things, that's how Kaz always was with him. He had breakfast ready and on the table most mornings and always let Nate pick the movie or the restaurant when they went out. If Nate wasn't careful, soon he'd become spoiled.

He didn't hate the sound of that. The old him would have freaked out and been wrought with guilt, but now?

Nate wiggled on those fingers, pushing them in further, and then let out another shameless moan. As his boyfriend, Kaz treated him pretty damn good. How much better would it be if he moved up a notch? If they took their relationship to the next level?

One step closer to marriage and true forever.

"Onus," he panted, opening his eyes to meet Kaz's garnet gaze. "I want to be your Onus."

His Devil grinned widely and removed his

fingers, lining his erect cock up and slamming into him with one solid push that had Nate screaming and coming all over again.

"See?" Kaz teased as he fucked him through the orgasm. "Told you I'd get you there quick."

Nate would be embarrassed by how shortly he'd lasted if not for the fact it wasn't the first time. Kaz knew where and how to touch him to get him to respond the way he liked, and that was something they both actually enjoyed.

He wrapped his legs around Kaz's waist and dug his heels into his ass. "Should I tell you who you really are, Kazimir Ambrose?"

The Devil blinked at him, then seemed to recall he'd spoken those very words once before and nodded for him to continue.

"You're mine, Kaz," Nate said. "All mine."

"That's right, Pretty Boy," he drove in deep and nipped at his chin. "I'm yours. And I'm going to be so good for you."

Nate pulled him in close and showed him that he already was.

That together, no matter what anyone else said or thought, they were perfect.

CHARACTER LIST:

Most of the main characters mentioned in the books so far!

The Satellite:

Baikal Void
Kazimir Ambrose
Flix Fulmini
Berga Obsidian
Saint
Yuze

The Retinue:

Kelevra Diar
Madden Odell
Zane Solace
Lake Zyair
Pavel Hart
Ledger Undergrove

Vail University Students:

Rabbit Trace
Sila Varun
Bay Delmar (teacher)

Nate Narek (graduate)
Baikal Void
Kazimir Ambrose
Flix Fulmini
Berga Obsidian
Zane Solace
Pavel Hart
Ledger Undergrove
Saint
Yuze

Academy Cadets:

Rin Varun
Kelevra Diar
Madden Odell
Lake Zyair

The Shepherds:

Aneski Kendricks

Guest Fine Arts Academy:

Arlet Zamir
Aneski Kendricks

HIS DARK PARADOX EXCERPT:

Curious about Silver and Nuri? Their story is told in *His Dark Paradox*, a book I wrote under the penname Avery Tu, with my friend Kota Quinn! Keep reading for a look at the book! Please keep in mind this is also a Dark Romance, with its own set of trigger warnings!

Prologue:

There was a psychopath on the throne.

Nuri kept his hands folded in front of him, his expression docile to help hide his swirling thoughts as the ceremony progressed to the speech portion. He stood on the large stage, at the far back in a row with other people on the royal staff, looking out over a massive crowd.

Reporters flooded the front, cameras flashing, lighting up the otherwise dimly lit throne room. The middle and back of the crowd were made up of important people in the government, such as the generals and the high council, as well as the upper-level employees of Rien Inc., the largest technologies corporation in the Dual Galaxy.

The CEO and newly crowned emperor stood at the front of the stage, currently in the midst of his speech about how he planned on following in his father's footsteps to ensure Ignite remained the universe's top technologically advanced planet. His smile was charming as he spoke, his inflection upbeat and confident. When Nuri glanced back at the giant screen displayed behind them, showing the blown-up live footage of the new emperor, even he was almost convinced they'd gotten a caring and devoted ruler.

But he knew better.

The speech may flow perfectly and genuinely from Silver Rien's perfectly sculpted lips, but Nuri had been the one who'd written each and every word of it. Silver smiled like he was honored to be there, humbled even, but he'd been complaining to Nuri all morning about how ridiculous and irrelevant having an official ceremony was.

As the only child of the late Emperor Sij, there weren't exactly any other candidates around to take the throne. The crown was always going to be his, whether they broadcast him accepting or not.

Silver had always been like that. If it wasn't work-related he didn't care, and it was rare to get him to partake in anything he didn't care about. The only reason he was even here now and hadn't gone through with trying to cancel the entire thing was because Nuri had reminded him how important this all was to his late father.

Nuri hadn't been certain it would work when he had, was actually a bit surprised that it'd changed Silver's mind, but he wasn't going to overthink it. What mattered was they were here, on stage, in front of the entire planet—and much of the galaxy, since it was being broadcast throughout—and Silver was now officially the Emperor of Ignite.

Which meant Nuri had fulfilled his promise to Sij Rien.

His resignation letter burned in his jacket pocket, almost as if he could feel the thin paper searing over his heart. It was rare to write things on physical paper now, but he'd wanted to be sure there was proof that couldn't be deleted. Something tangible he could place down on Silver's desk later.

Nuri Narek was quitting.

Silver wrapped up his speech and Nuri clapped along with the rest of the crowd on autopilot. He'd been planning this day out for months, ever since they'd been told that Emperor Sij's health was deteriorating and he didn't have much longer to live.

When Nuri had been a desperate youth, he'd made a deal with Sij for the betterment of his family. Now that they'd all moved off planet and it was just him remaining, there was no reason for him to stick around other than his job. He'd been unable to quit beforehand but now that his promise had been met there was nothing left to hold him back.

As soon as the ceremony was over and the two of them were back at the office, he'd hand in his resignation letter and that would be that. Most of his belongings had already been packed, his desk left neat and tidy for the next person who was assigned his position. He'd carefully organized all information about how to do his job in a digital information packet that he would send directly to the main office once he'd left. Since he'd been the secretary to an Imperial Crown Prince, and now Silver was an emperor, he assumed duties would alter, and the best thing to do was leave before that happened and made things even more complicated to go later.

Because he would be leaving. Nuri had already decided. No matter how secretly scared he was about starting a new life elsewhere, or how his heart clenched whenever he thought about not seeing Silver every day, he was going.

He had to.

Security went to escort Silver off the stage, Nuri and the others there falling into line to exit with him. Before they'd taken more than three steps, however, the lights in the room flickered, followed swiftly by a piercing sound through the loudspeakers.

He slapped his hands over his ears and cringed. The images on the screen behind him changed, going from them on the stage to footage of a hospital room.

The room was three times the size of a regular

hospital room, spacious and filled with sunlight that lit up the pale blue walls. The soft humming of machines came through the speakers, but aside from that there were no other sounds. It was clear this wasn't a recording meant to expose something anyone had said. It was meant to expose someone in another way.

The late emperor was lying unconscious in the bed, hooked up to machines. Even with their advancements in the medical field, his doctors had exhausted all possible solutions to his illness and he was succumbing to it quickly. His skin was sallow and his hair, which was usually a thick, deep brown, had gone completely white on his head. Sticking out, two shiny dark blue horns protruded.

As a Swift, snow-white hair and horns were normal. But not during the day. It was the biggest sign of them all that Sij was dying, and it was being broadcast to the entire galaxy right now. His final moments laid bare.

Nuri felt sick.

The reason this video was being shown became apparent, however, and it wasn't to expose how weak the once proud and strong ruler of Ignite had become in the end.

Silver was in the room as well, standing next to the bed, arms lax at his side. The camera had captured his expression perfectly, all of his features clear to those viewing the video.

He was staring down at his dying father, his last surviving family member completely blank-faced. There was nothing in his eyes, no sadness, no worry or grief. He could have been staring at a wall for all the emotion he was showing.

Nuri took in the navy suit Silver was wearing, the one with the thin golden pinstripes, and gasped, recalling the last time he'd worn that particular outfit.

"Get that down now!" he ordered, tearing his gaze away from the screen as he shot into motion. He rushed toward the steps on the side of the stage, intent on making his way to the operations room to put an end to it himself, but was stopped.

Silver grabbed his arm, holding him still when he tried to pull free.

"We need to stop the video," Nuri told him, voice dropping into a frantic whisper. "It's—"

"Too late," Silver cut him off, motioning toward the screen with his chin.

Turning back, Nuri sucked in a breath, seeing that he was right.

A second after his eyes made contact, the machines went wild, blaring and beeping with flashing lights. A medical team appeared, racing over toward his bed even though they all had to know there was nothing that could be done at this point. One of the nurses urged Silver to step away and give them room and after a brief hesitation, he complied.

The sound of the late emperor flat-lining came next, an eerie, steady noise that seemed to fill up the throne room they were standing in. This was footage of the day Sij had died, an event that had taken place two weeks ago.

Because it was footage taken from the security cameras, there was no way for whoever was airing this to zoom in, but they didn't have to. Even with all the frantic motions of the doctor and nurses, the second Silver's expression changed it stood out.

Silver Rien, the Imperial Crown Prince of Ignite, stared at his dying father…and grinned.

The room erupted, the reporters who'd only just been nodding their praises for Silver's speech now turning their microphones and cameras on him demanding answers. Voices carried over voices, drowning out any discernible words as the footage on the screen froze in that spot, as if whoever was illegally showing it wanted to be extra sure everyone got a glimpse of Silver's expression.

Someone wanted the world to know that their new emperor wasn't as charming and altruistic as he'd led them all to believe.

Nuri swallowed the sudden lump in his throat and turned his head to meet Silver's gaze, pausing when he found that the new emperor was already looking back at him.

"Well?" Silver asked coolly. "Aren't you going to do something about this, Royal Secretary Narek?"

In his pocket, his carefully crafted resignation letter seemed to laugh at him.

Chani Lynn Feener has wanted to be a writer since the age of ten during fifth grade story time. She majored in Creative Writing at Johnson State College in Vermont. To pay her bills, she has worked many odd jobs, including, but not limited to, telemarketing, order picking in a warehouse, and filling ink cartridges. When she isn't writing, she's binging TV shows, drawing, or frequenting zoos/aquariums. Chani is also the author of teen paranormal series, *The Underworld Saga*, originally written under the penname Tempest C. Avery. She currently resides in Connecticut, but lives on

Goodreads.com.

Chani Lynn Feener can be found on Goodreads.com, as well as on Twitter and Instagram @TempestChani.

For more information on upcoming and past works, please visit her website: **HOME | ChaniLynnFeener (wixsite.com)**.

Printed in Great Britain
by Amazon